E. J. Swift is the author of *Osiri* [...]
Project trilogy. Her short fiction h[...]
Publishing, NewCon Press and Jurassi[...]

She was shortlisted for a 2013 BSFA Award for her story 'Saga's Children'.

Praise for E. J. Swift

'Dystopia is back . . . fascinating . . . [a] promising debut novel' *SFX*

'An assured and accomplished debut novel . . . an absolute gem'
Interzone

'A fantastic blend of worldbuilding, excellent storytelling and complex characters' *SF Signal*

'Swift's first novel, with its brilliant near-future vision of an ecologically and socially devastated world and characters who resonate with life and passion, marks her as an author to watch'
Library Journal

'Marvelously well done. A glittering first novel: a flooded Gormenghast treated with the alienated polish of DeLillo's *Cosmopolis*. The result is a gripping novel, readable, beautiful, politically engaged and wholly accomplished. Swift is a ridiculously talented writer' Adam Roberts

'*Cataveiro* has a soulful, lonely quality as Taeo and Ramona embark on their missions, haunted by memories of the past and visions of what lies ahead . . . an intriguing world to get lost in' *SciFi Now*

Also by E. J. Swift:

Osiris
Cataveiro

TAMARUQ

BOOK THREE OF THE OSIRIS PROJECT

E. J. SWIFT

DEL REY

1 3 5 7 9 10 8 6 4 2

Del Rey, an imprint of Ebury Publishing
20 Vauxhall Bridge Road,
London SW1V 2SA

Del Rey is part of the Penguin Random House group of companies whose addresses
can be found at global.penguinrandomhouse.com

Copyright © E. J. Swift, 2015

This edition published in 2015 by Del Rey

www.eburypublishing.co.uk

A CIP catalogue record for this book is available from the British Library

ISBN 9780091953102

Typeset by Palimpsest Book Production Ltd, Falkirk, Stirlingshire

Printed and bound in Great Britain by Clays Ltd, St Ives plc

Penguin Random House is committed to a sustainable future for our business, our readers
and our planet. This book is made from Forest Stewardship Council® certified paper.

MIX
Paper from
responsible sources
FSC® C018179

For M–P, my old friend

March 2412

After seven days of tornados it's safe to go outside. Smoked a cigarette in the yard, watched the sunset — red and cloudless, almost peaceful. I saw a sandstorm swirling on the horizon but it was moving south, away from here.

I was glad of a few moments alone. The latest reports have frightened me, more than I like to admit, enough to break my hiatus from here. There's been a spate of outbreaks across the Boreal States, and worse, it's infiltrating south. Thousands in the Patagonian capital, one of the Indian enclaves entirely wiped out. We're told to keep our spirits up, the work is valued, but when I ask for more funding, there is none. Are the banks losing confidence in the project? Are we hearing the full truth, or do they pacify us, like children? Has it reached an epidemic, a pandemic? Only Antarctica and the Solar Corporation remain unaffected since inception; up in the Arctic Circle our borders are too porous, the virus slips through like a devil in the night.

Remote as we are it's easy to feel that we're indestructible, that nothing can touch us here. The deliveries keep coming. We continue the work. We occupy our minds. Some of us pray, some of us drink. But on days like this it's all too easy to imagine an alternate scenario: one in which we send our weekly report, and nothing comes back. We wait. We tell ourselves some other crisis has delayed the response – an airship crash, an assassination, the Africans squeezing the energy line, it could be anything – we tell ourselves we'll hear back soon. Days slip by. Weeks. We wait. Eventually we can't ignore it any longer, the absence of contact, the diminishing supplies, and we have to admit to ourselves what none of us wish to admit. No one's coming.

There's one explanation. The redfleur took them, every one; there's no one *left* to come.

Just us, and the desert sky.

And them.

There would be a certain irony to that.

PART ONE
NOT DEAD YET

OSIRIS

They pulled her out of the water and took her away from the place where he died. She was half drowned, saltwater swilling in her lungs, howling and delirious. One of them gripped her beneath the ribcage and pushed upwards until she vomited all the liquid and could only retch, twitching in the stern of the boat like some strange sea creature they had dredged up from the deeps. All around them the derelict west was on fire. The ocean gleamed red with the reflection of flames and the pitted towers were outlined in stark relief against the night. Skadi boats weaved ribbons across the surface. One of the two could hear sirens and human screams, tormented sounds issuing from the water and from behind the fire, and the other watched the flames and sensed the burn of heat on skin.

They took her home, a run-down apartment where the electricity was touch-and-go and several but not all of the appliances worked. It was not the worst they had lived in but not the best either. Broken objects stood where they had last been used with a vaguely helpless air, as though there might one day be the means to fix them, and they hoped, while not entirely believing, that this might be the case. The rescued woman from the sea became a fixture like these other things.

They put blankets and pillows together and tried to get her to sleep, but she lay catatonic, her body racked with tremors, and no matter how many covers they pressed on top of her she remained cold. She stared upwards, appearing to see nothing. Nothing physical, anyway. When she did sleep it was never for long. She woke screaming and so she became afraid of sleep; they could see the fear spark beneath her lids even as they drooped, the terror of what sleep might bring. Ole Larsson, who was deaf, saw only the open mouth of the girl, muted, a hole stretching in her face. Mikaela Larsson heard the cries, and made soft, pacifying noises. They tried to quiet her, although there were others who screamed too in this tower. She was not out of place. She was not the only one with demons.

When she screamed too loudly they put a hand over her mouth and tried to calm her until she shook with dry sobs. They patted her shoulders, which were thin and bruised. They put salve on her skin. Both of her wrists were hurt; they chose not to think about why that might be. What might have caused those marks to be there.

They were not sure what to do with her. Through the first night they murmured. *There, there. There, there.* They stroked her forehead, her hair. It was long and russet and rough with saltwater. They remembered a bird they had once nursed back to health. They had found it tangled in a cluster of junk on the surface, plastic wires twined around its feet, flapping helplessly, without the tools or knowledge to free itself. It was like that. They guessed the girl was a resident of the unremembered quarters. If so, she had no family. They were not sure what had brought them out on the night when their city burned and the old haunted tower collapsed, releasing all of its ghosts into the open air like spores, where they must be drifting now, without sense or direction. A bad thing, to set those ghosts free – they felt it with a sense of unease. If asked, Mikaela Larsson, a kind-faced woman who believed in providence, would struggle to explain their motives. They were part of no movements. They had no political agenda. But they had found they could not stay inside. Something was happening. A need to aid propelled them. With their habitual, unspoken symbiosis, they fetched their boat and rowed the short distance from the tower where they lived to the unremembered quarters and there in the water they found the woman, half-drowned.

And now they had her and did not know what to do.

The woman was someone, but they did not recognize her. Even if she had told them her name, it would have meant little to them. Nothing the City had done had ever made much difference to their lives. On the other side of the border, laws were passed and acts declared. Ole and Mikaela took shifts at the plant and sat together in the evenings, one listening to scratchy music on the o'dio channels, and the other reading, salvaged books and papers, or they played cards or bones, or went to watch the gliders practise, stood arm in arm, with a flask of warm spiced raqua if money was better. They kept to themselves. The City was another country.

The morning after the tower collapsed they coaxed her into clean clothes, noting the abrasions on her body, and tried to make her eat. They gave her coral tea. When her hands shook and she spilled the steaming liquid, they wiped it up and pressed cold cloths to the scalds. *There, there.* They had a son, but he visited rarely. She was like the daughter that had never been. *There, there.* When she managed to eat a few mouthfuls they watched with pleasure. Good, Mikaela encouraged her. And another. Ole smiled and nodded. They spoke little. The woman did not speak at all, except in dreams. What she said in her dreams was incomprehensible. They did not try to understand; they only wanted her to be well again.

The woman did not know it yet, but being found by these two was her first piece of luck for some time. For now, she was in the fog. There were senses here, premonitions and paranoias, sudden horrors that sneaked up with moist hands at her back, but there was nothing that could be grasped. Here, everything slipped. Mostly it felt as though she had never come up for air. She was still underwater, suspended somewhere between life and death, turning over and over in a watery limbo without name.

* * *

'Ata,' says Mikaela Larsson.

Ata. Ole mouths the syllables, testing them silently first.

Ata.

This is what the woman who used to be known as Adelaide Rechnov writes for them on a piece of paper, a week, or maybe a fortnight, after. She is no longer sure about time, about anything that once could be counted and now cannot.

The paper is spotted with grease from the work surface. The word sits upon it. Ata. A-ta. A part of her must be working, still functioning, because she chose the name. It sounds not unlike the old one, so she will not be caught out when someone calls an unfamiliar word. She will not be caught again. She cannot be caught.

Ole and Mikaela Larsson take turns to go to their shifts at the plant and to look after the woman, until they feel they can leave her alone. One day they come home and find a tail of matted hair lying in the sink. She has taken a pair of scissors to her head. She sits on the floor snipping away at what is left. They watch silently. Eventually Ole removes the tail of hair and washes it out in a bucket and sets it out to dry, separating the strands. The woman is angry when she sees it but Mikaela takes her arm and says they can use it. Hair is good for pillows, or some other insulation, they can sew it into her clothes, she says. It will keep her warm in the winter. Gently, she takes the scissors from the younger woman, prying them out of her hand. *Let me.* The woman falls abruptly still and obedient and Mikaela takes the ends of her hair, clipping at them neatly, leaving the fringe long when the woman insists.

The woman sweeps up the cuttings of hair and that evening she helps them clean the apartment, awkwardly, trailing them from one side of the room to the other, copying what they do. If they think her behaviour strange they do not say so. She is grieving, they have decided, but she will not – or cannot – say what she has lost.

Later she writes:

I need to change my hair.

They look at the note, confused. Mikaela thinks of those women on the boats whose hair is always sheer and black and she worries. You want a different colour? Is that it?

Ata nods. She hesitates. They watch her pick up the pen again.

She writes:

It isn't safe.

They look at the three words for a long time. Without having to exchange a glance they realize that they have always known this. *It isn't safe.* They do not know who she is but it is not safe for her.

They remember the damage to her wrists when she arrived. The bruising. The skin there is still new, pink and shiny. They find they cannot bear the idea of her being harmed.

Ole and Mikaela circle her in their arms and hold her in a hug. They can feel her trembling. Mikaela says, we will look after you. We will keep you safe. She leans into them, shaking, absorbing their kind, open-hearted warmth, wanting to believe that it is true. That it could even be possible.

Mikaela procures the dye for her. Something plain and brown, innocuous. If she were in the City she could get lenses to change the colour of her eyes, but she is not in the City now, and has no intention of going back. In the trash banks of the tower she finds a pair of discarded glasses and the couple help her to change the glass in the frames to something that does not blur her vision. After a while she gets used to the rub of plastic against the bridge of her nose.

On the o'dio, she is reported as missing. There are patrols out there, searching the western waterways. Then she is pronounced dead. It is a relief, to be dead.

She makes herself useful to the Larssons. She can see the pleasure in their faces with each small achievement, preparing a meal, or taking her first steps outside the apartment. She lets Ole show her how to drive their boat, a small motor with blue and white stripes, pretending she has never driven before. It gives her a reason to keep going. For them, she will do this. For them, she will clean her teeth, do the shopping run and scrub the windows, polishing in round, persistent motions until the glass sparkles like sunlight on the waves of the ocean that rush by, below, below, below.

She does not allow herself to think about him. Not even his name. His name is a whirlpool waiting to open up and engulf her. It could appear at her feet at any moment, through any matter: on the interlocking decking around a tower, or the fibreglass floor of a waterbus. Where there was ground underfoot, suddenly there is an abyss.

But sometimes it happens by accident and the pain is so acute she wants to cry out. She pushes her fist against her mouth, biting into the skin of her knuckles. Mikaela wraps tape around her fingers and tells her not to touch them. She remembers being told not to bite her nails as a child. Who told her that? Her mother, probably, but to think of *them* is another trip-up, another entry to the whirlpool below; it is because of *them* that all this has happened, that a man has died, that many more than one man have died.

The last words they exchanged were not happy ones. She was angry. She felt betrayed. He told her the truth and in that moment she hated him for it.

Had she known there was no more time, it might have been different.

There were other things she would have said. There are things she would say now, but will never have the chance.

At night she dreams of all the dead in conference and sees herself as reported on the o'dio among them, slowly decomposing beneath the surface. The dye comes off her hair, and then the skin comes off her face, and she rots. A strange relief in seeing the pieces of herself come adrift, the molecules of blood and tissue flying apart in a slow-motion explosion. What is left is a stillness of water, gently reddened, translucent. An after, as if there were never a before.

One night they sit together at the table, eating a stew she has prepared from a recipe of Ole's, chewing slowly. The occasional nod: it's good. If she needs to communicate something, she gestures, or writes it. At first she tried to talk, and found her throat was blocked, but now she no longer tries. Mikaela reassures her: these things take time. It will come back. She has never been in a place where there was no need for words. When she thinks of her old life – that other person, in the other city – it occurs to her that there were always words, and never silence. There were promises and lies, but there was rarely the truth.

Spoons scrape against bowls. She notices details like this, the small functional sounds, a swallow or a cough. They eat all of the stew. Mikaela switches on the o'dio. The apartment is full of the smell of cooking, briny and fresh. The woman looks at the empty dish and she is surprised by the peace that settles over her in that moment. She offers a smile to her rescuers and receives two smiles in return. Their lips curve in the same way. She is not sure if it was always like this or if they have become more like one another over time, their gestures merging into one entity, as happens sometimes with those who share lives.

She writes one word on the piece of paper and pushes it towards them. A question. Mikaela Larsson looks at her.

'Because you need us, Ata.'

Weeks pass and they are beginning to depend on her too. Returning from the market with the day's fresh kelp, she feels lighter than usual. She's got a large bag of it, and she's pleased, because she has learned to haggle without words. There are plenty of ways to communicate without speech: the slight contraction of the eyebrows, in surprise at the price, the shrug that denotes indifference. Take my money, don't take it, I don't care. She worried at first that her silence might mark her out, but the truth of it is, everyone has their peculiarities on this side of the border.

When she reaches the door to the apartment she hears voices. Not the o'dio but real voices in real time. Mikaela, and another, male, youngish, and with an insistent whine. She stops at once and listens.

The man says, 'I think you should come.'

'Well. . .'

'No, I think you should.'

'We'll see. We'll see.'

'I helped organize it. Don't you want to know more? Aren't you interested?'

'Of course I am, you know I am. Go on. You tell me.'

'It's a demonstration. Something big, exciting. There'll be a lot of people there.'

'You know we don't go in for that sort of thing.'

'It's important. You should be there. It's about integration. You can't not be there.'

Mikaela makes a non-committal noise and the man repeats himself. 'You can't not be there.'

'Really, I don't think—'

'You don't think? You're right, you don't think.' The man's voice grows louder. 'You don't think about anything other than yourselves. Call yourselves westerners? You know what, you deserve to stay here when the border opens.'

She feels a rush of anger towards this person, whoever he is. How dare he speak to Mikaela in that way?

'We don't call ourselves anything,' says Mikaela. She does not rise to the other's anger and her voice remains gentle. 'We just want to get on with our lives. Be careful, Oskar. You know we worry about you with those people.'

Then she hears the sound of something being hit. The table, she thinks. The table she polished this morning. She imagines the strange man's palm smacking it, his sweat now smearing the clean surface, *polluting it*, and her anger grows.

She hears him say, 'This is a joke.'

Footsteps, hurried, across the apartment. She backs away, alarmed, but it is too late. The door slams open. The young man is in the doorway, his coat buttoned to the throat implying he never intended to stay for long. He stares at her, his face flushed with anger.

'Who the hell are you?'

She backs away, panicked. She can't think. She can't think! She hears Mikaela coming to the door, wants to say *no, don't acknowledge me, don't say a word*, but her throat is stoppered.

'Ata?' says Mikaela Larsson.

The man is still staring at her.

'*Ata?*' he repeats.

Danger, she thinks. *Danger.* Run. Get out. Get out now.

But she can't move. She's transfixed in his glare. The handle of the bag is slippery in her sweating palm. She can feel the damp weight of the kelp.

'This is Ata,' says Mikaela. 'She's been staying with us.'

No. No—

'Since when?'

'Since the night the tower collapsed.'

Please stop – you don't realize—

'The tower—'

'We found her, Oskar. In the water. She was in trauma. Don't raise your voice, it upsets her—'

She sees the change in the young man's face. The hint of recognition, the confusion as he struggles to place her.

'Ata,' says the man again, a disbelieving note in his voice. 'Take those glasses off a minute?'

He reaches out a hand. She doesn't know what his intent is but the movement is enough, it's the impetus her body needs. She turns and runs. Behind her she hears his shout, Hey! and Mikaela Larsson calling after her, but she's already in the stairwell. Her chest is tight. It's hard to breathe. She races down the stairs, blundering into people, ricocheting against the walls, unaware of any pain as she connects with concrete. She can hear the man, Oskar's, voice.

'Hey, *Ata*! Where are you going?'

He's following. Did he recognize her? Could he?

There's a bridge ten floors down. She ducks into a corridor and heads for it. He won't know which way she's gone. He'll have to guess.

She steps out of the tower onto the narrow catwalk that constitutes a bridge this side of the border, clutching at the rusting handrails for balance. The tail of a winter wind hits her face, whipping through the inadequate western clothing and chilling her at once. The sea churns coldly in the waterway below. Ahead of her on the bridge is a young child. She watches where the child steps and places her feet in the exact same spaces. They are agile as birds, the kids here, and it is this that will give her away, any hint of hesitation, the suggestion that she has not spent her entire life balancing on rickety bridges constructed from salvage that might at any moment give way beneath her feet.

Fifty metres to the next tower. She crosses the bridge. She does not look back. She ducks into the tower. The lift is a trap; she takes the stairs to the surface. A waterbus is pulling in and she elbows her way onto it, using the few peng left over from the kelp to pay for her ticket. She goes below, and sits, head down, heart racing. Black spots dance in front of her eyes. The motor starts up, sending shudders through the boat.

Yes, leave. Leave now. Please. Please.

The boat pulls away. She doesn't know where it is going and doesn't care. The place that was safe is no longer safe.

She should never have gone outside. She thought the disguise was enough, but it only takes one person who follows the newsreels, and it's over.

The waterbus reaches a terminus somewhere near the south-western edge of the city. Here there are wide interstices of daylight between the conical towers and through them the sea stretches away into the distance, its grip unbroken except for the occasional fishing or military boat.

Adelaide disembarks with the rest of the passengers. It is only then she realizes the waterbus has remained busy to the end of the route. She looks up at their destination. The terminus appears like any other tower in the west, its drab grey slopes pocked with indents from unidentified sources, graffitied landscapes layered over grime, with no obvious signs to indicate what or who might be found inside.

On the decking westerners mill about, some pushing into the queue for the returning waterbuses, others smoking thinly rolled cigarettes, watching the buses, idly exchanging conversation. She finds it hard to guess the ages of westerners, who often look older than their years, but there is a full spectrum here, from young children clinging to the legs of their minders to old faces furrowed with lines and tempered by the harsh climate. Something jumps into her mind, something Vikram said once, about the average life expectancy this side of the city, and she has to close off the thought quickly, to prevent the whirlpool. She enters the tower with a stream of other passengers.

Inside is a heaving marketplace; a tower full of winding corridors opening abruptly into dimly lit hallways, where walls and ceilings have been knocked through, and partitions lean at dubious angles. She is swept into the flow of prospectors. Vendors grin up at her from the tightly jammed, competing stalls. Their grins seem identical, mass-produced – the grins of toothed fish. At every pace merchandise is dangled under her nose. Salt boxes and other amulets she does not recognize, pieces of mirror, jars of undefined substances, recalibrated scarabs and tobacco pouches with barely concealed slips of milaine inserted inside. She jerks back as something wet and wriggling is thrust in front of her face. It's an octopus, still alive, on a platter. To her right, from the same stall, she sees a bucket full of creatures clambering over one another, their claws gaining the lip of the bucket but never quite managing to escape. The reek is abominable, the smell of rotting seafood and bodies in too-close proximity, a whiff of manta fumes drifting through, everything overlaid with a mask of cheap incense which fills the halls with bluish, hazy smoke.

A woman in white Teller garb and cheap plastic clogs totters down an aisle, grabbing at the clothes of the market-goers and imparting nuggets of wisdom into their ears. Adelaide swerves away as the Teller approaches, but she is not quick enough: the Teller has caught her eye and veers purposefully, inevitably, towards her. She will make herself more visible if she tries to evade the woman. The Teller grabs her shoulder and brings her mouth close to Adelaide's ear. She can smell the alcohol on the Teller's breath.

'Osiris is a lost city,' mutters the Teller. Adelaide jolts back as if struck, but the Teller clings on, nails digging into her shoulder.

'She has lost the world and the world has lost her.'

In close proximity, she can see the hems of the Teller's robe are stained with dirt. The skin of her face is peppered with spots and shiny with grease. Everything about the woman is repulsive to her, and yet she cannot move, pinned as much by the rasping voice as by the need to remain invisible.

'Not dead,' says the Teller. 'Not dead yet.' She laughs drunkenly. With a gesture that is almost tender, she strokes a finger down Adelaide's cheek. 'I can spy a heretic. I can smell them! When did you last perform the salt?' The Teller hiccups, and covers her mouth with a giggle. Her fingers tighten. 'Not lately, not lately. They're not dead yet, the ghosts. They'll deny it, but it's true, you know.'

The Teller darts quick, paranoid glances around them. She lowers her voice.

'Something is coming. The ghosts have roused it.'

Adelaide stares. She wants to ask, what? What is coming? But the words won't come and the Teller now bears a guilty expression, as though she has already said too much. She reels away, reaching out to clutch at her next victim, repeating her mantra.

'Not dead, no, not dead yet. The ghosts are not dead yet.'

The white-garbed figure recedes into the crowd. For a moment Adelaide remains where she is, very still, until the motion of the crowd pushes her too deeper inside.

The sheer volume of people makes the tower unbearably hot, causing her glasses to steam up continually. This is good, she tells herself. People are good, the more the better. In the crowd you can disappear. Everyone here is on the hunt. Their eyes are alert and animated, exaggeratedly so; they seem to her like people on the o'vis, in those old Neon reels she used to watch, alone in her City apartment, dulled by voqua, as though life was difficult, problematic, then. Voqua. She hasn't drunk alcohol since she crossed the border. Not since her father's bodyguard – no. *Don't think about that.* The thought of alcohol glitters. Perhaps it would make her feel something. Perhaps it would give her a purpose, even if the purpose were oblivion. All around her, people are moving. *Not dead yet.* Their concerns are now her concerns; like them, her focus must be to survive, but she will always be an intruder, not wanted here, and reliant on camouflage to avoid detection.

She walks the height of the tower, floor by floor, barely noticing the ache in her feet. She counts the remaining peng in her pocket. There is enough to get herself something to eat. Her stomach churns at the thought of food. She needs to wait, to spin the money out. What is she going to do now? She can't go back to the Larssons. She has no credit, no belongings but the clothes she is wearing. She's alone.

She keeps wandering until the stalls begin to shut down. Evening brings a different crowd, one intent on liquor and gaming. She watches as objects are exchanged, City things, petty there but of value here, and realizes that what she is witnessing is the black market. In one hall there is a pit where huge rats are taken out of cages and set against one another. She can hear the scrabble of their claws and the shrill squeaking and she can see flecks of blood where their teeth sink into haunches and bellies. She stares, transfixed by the vicious struggle of the creatures. Bets are called, money changes hands. There are arguments. Heated words. A rat whimpers in a pool of blood.

She hasn't been there long when a fight breaks out. She is too slow to spot what is coming, or to move; the first thing she knows is the weight of a woman crashing into her. She falls and lands awkwardly. All at once the hall is full of noise and limbs lashing out. She rolls out of the way just in time to avoid a boot in her ribs. The grey blur of a rat scurrying away. Through the commotion she senses eyes upon her.

Dizzy, overwhelmed, she goes outside and manages to sidle onto the waterbus without paying for a ticket. It's getting late and she doesn't know where to go. She stays up on deck and the western towers slip by in the dusk, barely lit, gargantuan and prophetic against the deepening sky. It's cold, bitter, end-of-winter cold. The conductor calls the stops: *Ess-two-seven-four-west, ess-two-seven-five-west.* His voice is hoarse and thick with phlegm. *Ess-two-seven-six-west. Ess-two-seven-seven-west.*

She sees the light from a fry-boat hatch parked at a tower decking, and it is only then that she remembers the kelp. She still has the kelp. All day the bag has been in her hand and somehow she has clung on to it, even during that fight. She scrambles to get off at the stop with the fry-boat, and approaches the vendor, resolute. The vendor is chatting with a customer. She waits for the man to notice her. When she has his attention, she taps her throat, which has become her sign for muteness, and holds the bag of kelp to the hatch. They haggle. The man says it is stale. She shakes her head and squeezes the bag.

She gets half the price she paid for it this morning, but it is peng in her pocket, and the vendor also gives her a bag of leftover weed squares and a few hot squid rings. The transaction brings a glow of pleasure to her cheeks. She holds on to it, telling herself over and over that this is a victory: her first in this hostile new world. She sits on the decking trying not to eat too quickly, feeling faint with the sudden influx of protein. But soon enough the dusk is swallowed into the night. The fry-boat packs up and drives off to another tower, and with its departure her elation fades.

She gazes up at the dilapidated tower. Washing hangs down from the windows, strung from lines, the clothing shapeless in the dark. Its owners are out or they have forgotten it or they are not coming back. She goes inside. There is no security on western towers. Further up, people are sitting in the stairwells, smoking manta, their eyes glazed and sated. She chooses a level with a bridge out so she can run if she has to and curls up, chilled and exhausted, in the stairwell. Now she can feel the deep ache in her feet and calves.

Slumped against the wall, she chases sleep half-heartedly, and through the night she senses other people coming and going. Drunks stagger back from the bridge, uncertain of their footing. There are other homeless, shuffling up and down the stairwells. She wakes from bad dreams, crying, her lips mouthing *I'm-sorry I'm-so-sorry* but no sound, still no sound. She wakes again to find hands on her body.

She lurches upright. Fingers slip from her pockets and the thief darts from her side, but she is too late. The peng she earned from the sale of the kelp is gone.

The thought comes and will not retreat. *He is dead.* He is dead because of her. Vikram is dead. *Not dead yet.* No, but he is. She wants to hit that stupid, drunk Teller, sink her teeth into the woman like a rat from the pit. The whirlpool advances. The floor opens up and she falls into the whirlpool, through all the floors of the tower above the surface and below it, where the ocean sucks you down, down, and the core of the earth opens up to swallow you whole. She stays like this, cheek to the filthy floor, listening to the low, atonal humming of the manta addicts, the restless footsteps up and down the tower, the crank of the lift. Flickering lights emit a static, intermittent burr. After a time it all becomes part of a single disconnected symphony, and her thoughts revolve in kind.

Dead.
Not dead yet.
Dead.
Not dead yet.
Vikram's dead.

She keeps on the move. Sleeping in different towers, never quite in step with the daylight world. More than once she is woken by the pounding boots of skadi soldiers, and the other homeless get to their feet and they shift as one, a loose, amorphous mass, like a shoal ejected from their coral. One day a boy gives her a cigarette, and they smoke together companionably, in silence. Another day her hat is stolen while she rests. She becomes aware that there are striations even within this side of the city. There are towers where the homeless are permitted to sleep. There are other towers where the residents will kick you if you so much as park your buttocks on a step, and each day the residents go doggedly to their jobs at the plants or to queue for a western work party. There is talk of *the shanties*, clusters of boats roped together like a crust of scum over the sea, out near the unremembered quarters, on the very edge of the city. It's a place even the homeless don't want to go.

The days are spent walking, through the towers, over uneven raft racks and swaying, precarious bridges, where the sea glints invitingly below. Everywhere she goes its voice is with her, soft and sibilant. She remembers the horses of Axel's hallucinations, and finds they have a plausibility now that they did not have before. Once or twice she thinks she glimpses them: a white flank, or the turn of a long head, its eye black and portentous.

At twilight she gathers with other homeless at the fry-boats to beg for scraps. At first the corrosive ache in her stomach is at the front of everything, and then it becomes a dullness, always present, but a mundane part of existence. Some days she is too tired to go anywhere and stays where she slept, breathing in the fumes of the manta addicts.

Her movements become furtive. Calculated. Scraps are not enough, so she watches the food of others. Her first attempt at stealing is a disaster. As her fingers close around the food she hears a shout. Faces turn towards her. She drops the food and sprints away over the raft rack, loses her balance and falls into the water. Her heart jerks. The cold is terrifying. She loses her glasses, sees them float for a precious second and thrashes about, trying to grab them. Too late. She drags herself spluttering onto the raft rack. A hand comes down upon her throat.

'Try stealing from me or mine again and I'll fucking cut you.'

The man pushes her back under the water and holds her there until she thinks her lungs will burst. Just as her vision starts to go black, he lifts her out, and up, to her feet. She sees his face, scarred, and his neck, bare, encircled with a tattoo of interlinking chains. Then he launches her from the raft rack. She crashes back, goes under, fights for the surface. The man is striding away. As she struggles back to the rack, she can hear the jeers of onlookers. She grabs the rack, gasping for breath, her heart still racing. A kid ducks close to her and mutters, what the hell you thinking trying to steal from a Roch, are you insane, and she thinks: *I can't afford this. I have to learn faster.*

The second time she is more careful. She watches the western kids. How they do it. The way they watch. She learns to recognize the moment they identify a target. Then the slow nonchalance of the approach and the dash away, quick as sin. She copies their movements. She has always been a good mimic. The first success is a dull thrill. Squid rings. Only a quarter-full bag but she doesn't care, it's food, it's hers. She took it. She stuffs the rings into her mouth, an explosion of fat and salt, aware if she doesn't dispose of the evidence fast enough someone else will take her prize. She turns the paper inside out and licks out every scrap of grease.

Here and there she catches glimpses of herself. In water, in smeared glass, thin slivers, an eye, a limb, a half of her mouth. Her face, at once familiar and unfamiliar, has become her greatest hindrance. She maintains a mask of grease and grime. When her hair starts to grow out, she steals another hat.

Inevitably she finds herself drawn to the border. She watches from the rails of waterbuses and the precarious ledges of bridges. From raft racks and deckings and public balconies where children stare and point at the spectacle below. The angle is different but the view is the same. The conical towers in their emerald and silver casings. Birds drifting in slow spirals above and about their peaks. Sometimes lone pairs, sometimes a flock in sudden inexplicable ascent, shrieking and clouding the sky with their beating wings. She used to be afraid of them. She is not afraid any more, not of birds. Along the length of the border waterway, the netting lifts from the waves as though suspended from invisible hands.

There was a girl over there. A girl who threw parties and sketched gardens and her words were like a charm, even when they were about nothing of importance, which was most of the time. That girl ceased to be real in the moment the City abandoned her, the moment the Rechnovs, her family, gave the order to fire upon the tower, knowing she was trapped inside.

Adelaide, run.

What he told her. She is running now, though there are times when she believes it would be easier to let go. Slip through the gap in a bridge. Lie on a raft rack in the night and ask the stars to freeze her with their great cold hearts.

People look at her in a way she has never experienced before. She is painfully aware of the softness of her own body, of never having learned to defend herself, of being frightened. One night a fight breaks out in the corridor where she is sleeping. She sees a westerner break a bottle against the step and stab the jagged end into the face of another.

Glass shards are strewn across the floor, spotted with blood. The fight blunders away down the hallway, accompanied by crashes and screams and someone shrieking. *What have you done, look at his eye, holy fuck look at it!* She surveys the glass. The glimpses of red. She lets her eyes travel over it until she sees what she is looking for. An edge piece, a long, narrow triangle shaped like a blade. When no one is looking she darts forwards and takes it. Slips the glass into the pocket of her coat. Walks quickly away.

Later, she uses a wall to grind the edges smooth at one end and wraps around scraps of cloth to make a grip. She brings the sharp end of the glass to her face, trying to find the courage to make a cut, rendering her face unrecognizable forever. The point of the glass presses into her cheek. Her hand shakes. She tries to make herself drag the glass down but she can't do it. When she lowers her hand her cheeks are wet with tears.

At night she keeps her fingers locked around the glass and doesn't let go until morning.

She hears the announcement late one night, lying with her ear close to the gap under someone's door so she can listen to the intermittent sound of the o'dio. There will be an expedition boat. The boat is to depart the city, leaving on the first tenable day in the spring, to seek out land.

She hears, with a shock, a voice she recognizes.

Her brother, Linus.

'As you know, this is the first expedition in almost fifty years. Naturally we're excited about what we may discover, but it's equally important to be reasonable about our expectations. The fact is, no one knows what's out there.'

The words flow from him the way life has always flowed for him: effortlessly. The way a Rechnov's life is meant to flow.

'But what do *you* think, Councillor? Do you really think there could be life on land? After all this time?'

Linus's voice is replete with confidence. 'I think we should expect the unexpected.'

After the interview with Linus the o'dio channel switches to Isis 100, and a few minutes after that the person on the other side of the door turns it off completely. She can hear a strong wind getting up outside the tower. Suddenly she can't stay where she is, she has to move, go somewhere, it doesn't matter where. She crosses a low-level bridge to the next tower, holding her hat to her head, because the wind is already whip-fierce. In the next tower there is a late-night bar which has the o'dio turned up loud. She waits and watches until one of its patrons leaves a beverage half-finished, and then she slips inside and takes the seat with the drink and holds it in both hands. You can't hear the wind in here. That's good.

The bar is warm. She sips at the drink. It's warm too. A slow fuzziness wraps around her head. Chatter is idle. Whispers, low and interrogative.

Something is coming. She thinks about Linus's expedition and tries to imagine land and wonders if it is possible that people might be there and what they might be like. The bar quietens. Unasked, the bartender brings her another drink and takes away the empty glass. She remembers Second Grandmother's stories about square houses and flat gardens. Second Grandmother was a westerner. She wonders if Second Grandmother ever sat here, in this place, if she is retracing a course backwards, and if so where it ends. And then she realizes the bar has gone very quiet and she can hear the wind again, and she looks up and the only people left are herself and three men, two of them embroiled in deep conversation, the third sat apart, staring at her intently.

The bartender has disappeared.

She gets up and pulls on her coat. The man stands also, his movements leisurely, but his eyes never leaving her face.

As she leaves the bar she hears his footsteps cross the room behind her. Outside, the tower corridor is deserted. Her heart starts to beat faster.

'Hey, sweetheart.'

He makes a chirping noise in his throat, the way you might call a pet, or a bird.

'Hey, pretty girl.'

She ignores him. Keeps walking, down the corridor, towards the stairwell. She hears his footsteps hastening and speeds up until she's jogging. He's following her, increasing his pace as she does. Why is it so empty? Where is everyone?

She reaches an impasse. Bridge to her left, stairwell to her right. She can hear the wind shrieking. A Tarctic wind from the south, packed with spite. She can't go out there: she'll be ripped from the bridge like a piece of tissue. The man is only paces behind. She runs towards the stairwell, her heart pounding, her hands clammy with fear, and as she starts to descend the steps she hears quick, heavy footsteps and feels a shove between her shoulder blades and she trips and falls.

She scrambles to her feet to find her way blocked.

'Where you going, sweetheart? Don't you want to say hello?'

The man is taller than her. Broader. She can smell alcohol on his breath, sweet and pungent, but he stands quite steadily, his eyes narrowed, travelling from her face to her chest and downwards.

'You are a pretty little fish,' he says. 'I was watching you in there.'

She tries to speak. *Get out of my way.* The words stick; she can't get them out. She tries to move around him. He blocks her.

'Hey, hey! Where do you think you're going?'

She looks desperately past him. No one.

'No point in screaming,' he says softly. 'There's always someone screaming.'

He reaches out and grips her shoulder, pinning her. His hand drifts down her arm and runs over her buttocks and he smiles.

She eases her hand into her pocket. Her fingers clench around the grip of the glass shard.

Once again she tries to speak. Her lips work helplessly.

'G-get—'

'G-g—' he imitates her. 'You trying to tell me something, sweetheart?'

His hand squeezes.

'F. . . f-fuck you!'

She jabs the glass into his belly. Direct, instinctive, like a thrust in fencing. Blood spurts over her hand. He gasps and lets her go at once, clutching at the wound. His face twists horribly. She wrenches the glass out and turns and sprints down the stairwell without a second glance. The glass is wet in her palm. The wind is shrieking. But she can't hear footsteps.

Sick and shaken by the incident, it is only later that she realizes. The words are in there. When she needs them, they are there.

On the day of the boat's departure she goes to watch, because everybody goes, and because she wants to see it leave. And it is an event. There is a curious parity between the two crowds as the boat makes its way down the rows upon rows of well-wishers, a moment when an outsider, perhaps, could hardly tell which way was east and which west.

After the boat has disappeared, an uncertain atmosphere descends. Now we wait. Now we wait, not knowing. We wait. For how long? A month? Forever? A trail of thrown flowers and messages, those that did not reach the boat, float in the water corridor, the white patches of paper and colourful petals an incongruous debris between the crowds on either side. A large boat of Citizens begins to blare out music and soon its decks are bouncing with revellers. A group of westerners, apparently in jest, imitate the moves, and suddenly most of the crowd is moving, infected by the celebratory beat, but the movement is not quite in kilter, and a streak of restlessness, of unconfirmed mockery, weaves like an undercurrent through the westerners.

After a time the skadi begin to urge westerners to move on, and Adelaide realizes that what seemed like a united occasion was only the appearance of one; now that the boat has gone, things will carry on, as they were. This is just another gesture from the City. The founding families, including the Rechnovs, are already surrounded by bodyguards in anticipation of potential assassins. When she looks again, they are gone.

Anger grips her. Nothing changes.

But now she has an instinct for the inevitable violence to follow, and shortly after the Rechnovs leave she extracts herself from the scene.

She remembers Linus speaking on the o'dio and wonders what he made of this occasion. If he orchestrated it. What he meant by it. He always did believe in life outside Osiris, and she had always mocked him for it, but now she feels a flower of hope unfurling within her chest. That he might be right. That there might be something, anything, out there.

Perhaps it is this thought that makes her take a route she has not travelled in weeks. On the waterbus she looks at her hands, marvelling at the layers of dirt, crammed between cracks in her fingernails, embedded in the grain of her palms. It doesn't seem right, to go and see them like this, but she is suddenly so tired, so very tired. The thought of their kindness glows like a lantern over black water.

She just wants a sighting. Ole and Mikaela don't need to see her. She just wants to make sure they are there.

She finds a spot on a tower decking across the waterway from where they live. Scanning the boats parked opposite, she sees that the Larssons' boat, the one Ole taught her to drive with its faded blue stripes, is missing. One or both of them will be on their way home. They were probably in the crowd with her, watching the expedition boat.

She waits. Her stomach is twisting about on itself. She barely notices it these days but she does now, here where she was cared for. She is in the shadow of the tower but she can see the sun on the waves, and refracting against the dirty bufferglass, and for a moment it is possible to imagine that she is somewhere else entirely. She feels herself sinking into the decking. She's so hungry. So tired.

A hand grabs her shoulder. Lips come close to her ear and she feels the warmth of breath as the aggressor murmurs.

'*Ata*, isn't it? There's someone who wants to see you.'

Another hand under her elbow, pulling her to her feet. She stares at the man, testing her body for a reaction, asking. In her pocket is the shard of glass. But as she stands the face of her captor fades in and out of focus. She dredges her memory. She has seen him before. Yes, she remembers now. The son. Oskar.

She looks towards the tower, searching for the boat, suddenly desperate for a sight of those cheerful blue stripes. Oskar says, 'Don't worry about them. You're coming with me.'

On the journey there, blindfolded, she wonders how they will do it. If it will be slow or if they will just shoot her. Maybe they'll drown her, like the City did the activist Eirik 9968. She thinks of his body in the glass tank, the hood over his face. Does it matter how it's done? Soon enough, it will be over. Is that so bad? The guilt will vanish, along with everything else. She won't wake every day knowing Vikram's ghost has been wandering the corridors of her dreams. She won't wake at all.

After half an hour of driving she feels the boat stop, the motor cutting out. They push her out and she feels the decking, uneven beneath her feet. The air temperature rises as they enter a tower and then a lift which bears them upwards. The son, Oskar, leads her into a room and seats her in a hard plastic chair. She waits, expecting at any moment the coldness of a gun against her temple. This must be it. Then she feels hands at the back of her head. Untying the blindfold. She opens her eyes, blinking.

She expected a dripping, burned-out room like the derelict spaces of the unremembered quarters where she was held captive before. But she is in somebody's apartment. Plainly furnished, a kitchen area in front of her, a column of window-wall to her right. Sat in a chair facing her is a thin woman with sharp, intelligent eyes. She is wearing a headscarf and a thick smearing of cherry lipstick. The woman is leaning forwards, studying her intently.

After a minute the woman says, 'Yes, it's her. You can go.'

She hears retreating footsteps and the door closes. She is left in the room with the woman. They appear to be alone.

The woman addresses her.

'It is you, isn't it? You are Adelaide Rechnov?'

There's something in the way she utters those last four words that is difficult to decipher. Perhaps disbelief that this pathetic creature could be connected to the City's most eminent founding family. Or amusement that society's darling, a woman believed dead, a woman worth millions, is seated here before her in the heart of the west.

Adelaide doesn't attempt to deny it. They know.

'Cup of tea?' asks the woman.

She nods tentatively.

The woman rises, crosses the room, fills a pan with water and puts it on to boil. For a minute the only sound in the room comes from the bubbling water. She pours a mug of tea and brings it to Adelaide. It's very hot against her palms. An exhausted part of her registers that were she to throw the steaming liquid into the other woman's face, there might be a chance of escape.

'What happened to you?' asks the woman.

She looks at the floor.

'What happened? You were in the tower, with the rebels?'

The floor is cleanish, with cheap linoleum, peeling away in places.

'I'm going to have to keep asking until you give me a response.'

Adelaide taps her throat, and shakes her head.

'Easily solved. I'll get you something to write with.'

She dumps paper and a pencil in Adelaide's lap. Balancing the tea, she forms the words slowly.

Who are you?

The woman laughs. It is such a surprising sound that Adelaide starts and spills the tea. She lowers the mug to the floor and focuses on the woman's hands, which are strong and capable-looking.

'My name's Dien,' says the woman. 'I'm what's left of the resistance movement. The others are dead. Everyone in Soren's cell. And the folks who had you. Pekko. Rikard. Drake. Nils. Your friend,' the woman allows herself a certain degree of innuendo, 'Vikram. They all died in the tower. They burned there. But you already knew that, didn't you?'

Adelaide looks down. The hand that is squeezing the pencil is trembling. She doesn't need to hear his name. She wishes they would get on with it. Why bother tormenting her, unless it's for revenge?

'Somehow you survived,' says Dien. A note of wonder in her voice. 'Somehow, that doesn't altogether surprise me. Though when Oskar told me his suspicions I didn't believe it. It's only now, seeing your face. . .'

Once again she rises and crosses the short distance to Adelaide. Cupping a hand under Adelaide's chin, she lifts her head gently.

'Incredible,' she says. 'You know, I never in a thousand years thought I'd meet one of you. A Rechnov. But here you are. The Architect's granddaughter, sat in my apartment, drinking my tea.'

Adelaide jerks away. She writes quickly.

Get to the point and tell me what you want.

'That's a good question,' says Dien. 'Much as it pains me to say it, I'm afraid we need you, Adelaide. That face of yours has a value. We need it. We need your name. There's work to be done, and you're going to help us do it. So we're not going to let you die just yet, though I've got to say it looks like you've been doing your best to do the deed yourself.'

Adelaide shakes her head. She writes.

I can't help you.

'It's not a choice,' says Dien. The tone of someone who isn't used to being argued with. 'Stars know you're the last person in the world I'd choose to help me, but I know your worth, better than Pekko ever did. He was an arsehole – yeah, just because he was one of ours doesn't mean we didn't know it. But you – the City will listen to you.'

She has a sudden sense of where this is leading. That nub of anger returns, bright and fierce. She is done with the City. Done with it.

'Fuck – y-you.'

Her words, barely a croak, but with force behind them, catch both women off guard.

Their eyes meet.

'So you *can* speak,' says Dien.

She doesn't see the blow coming. One moment she's staring up at Dien, the next she's on the floor, her jaw a fierce star of pain, blood welling in her mouth. Dien stands over her, clenching and unclenching her knuckles.

Adelaide puts a hand to her throat. She can feel the words, trapped deep down inside her throat. Slowly, haltingly, she calls them up. Blood dribbles from her lips.

'I w— I won't go b-back there. I won't – t-talk to them. I won't have anything – to do – with them.'

Dien gazes at her for a long time, and now her eyes are hard.

'Well,' she says. 'We'll see about that.'

* * *

Dien goes away. Dien returns. She begins a tactical campaign. She starts by speaking softly, sitting on the table with her legs hanging loose and casual in their warmers, speaking about Vikram. With every repetition of his name, Adelaide feels the whirlpool widening. He was important to the west, says Dien. He had ambitions. He started something, something even Eirik was unable to start. He got under the City's skin, that's the truth of it. He was getting people on side, even Citizens. And she knows Adelaide helped with that, even if it was for the wrong reasons, she helped. She knows Adelaide cared about Vikram. She knows they were fucking. After all, everyone saw the newsreel. Maybe Adelaide even thought she was in love. It has a certain romance, doesn't it, the Architect's granddaughter and the poor revolutionary. But now he's gone, and the last things that were said about him made him out to be some kind of criminal mastermind, and worse. Devious, they said. Conniving, treacherous. An eel in the water. Dien lifts her gaze sadly. What kind of legacy does Vikram have now, she asks? Was his death for nothing? Surely Adelaide does not want him to have died for nothing?

Another cup of coral tea. Other people – Dien's people – escort her to the bathroom. They bring her back. They sit her in the chair. Feed her, force her to swallow when she tries to refuse. *We don't want you passing out on us, now.* She wants to scream.

Dien's efforts become more overtly hostile. Adelaide owes Vikram, she says. She owes the west. If not for everything her family have done, and Dien could offer a pretty comprehensive list, Adelaide only has to ask, then how about for the man she betrayed. Make this right, she says. Help us. Help your dead westie boyfriend.

Dien talks on. The mobility of her face becomes intensely familiar: the stretch of her lips, thickly coated in that cheap cherry lipstick, the way her jaw sets at a slight disjuncture when she clenches her teeth. There's a small mole at the edge of her eyebrow, a larger one at her temple. Every action she makes is decisive and set, she moves as if there were no other possibilities of movement; Dien has conquered all of them. She circles the room. She comes closer, pausing at Adelaide's back, leaning in, the smell of her last meal ripe between them as her words drift into Adelaide's ear. Constructed. Persuasive.

Hours pass. The light in the room changes. Dien talks. Adelaide sleeps, or thinks she does. She feels numb with exhaustion. She wakes to find Dien sitting, surveying her, not a trace of weariness in the other woman's face. Dien's eyes shining in the dark. She has no idea how long she has been there. They begin again. Dien talking. Adelaide silent. A dead man and a whirlpool between them.

Daylight. A man enters the apartment with a case. He sets down the case and opens it and from an array of metal tools he selects a scalpel and a tin of salt. The westerners rope Adelaide to the chair and remove her boots and socks and someone takes hold of her ankles, their thumbs digging in, pulling back her toes and presenting the soles of her feet to the man. She clamps her teeth, a fresh flood of pain welling in her bruised jaw. The man takes up his scalpel. His thumb runs over the soft skin in the arch of her foot, his grip tightening when she flinches.

Adelaide looks at Dien. Dien looks at her. She doesn't want to show fear but all of her limbs are shaking uncontrollably at the thought of what is to follow.

'No,' says Dien. 'This won't work. Let's try something else.'

The next time she wakes the room is empty and the door is open. She looks about her, blinking, confused. Is she really awake? She becomes aware of a hot, itching sensation in her groin and realizes to her humiliation she's wet herself. Through the door she sees two figures. A man and a woman, his hand on her elbow in an intimate, supportive gesture. Familiar. So familiar.

The Larssons.

Shame envelops her, that she should appear to them in this state. She tries to stand but she is still bound to the chair.

The Larssons see her.

'Ata!'

Their faces change. They look confused. What is she doing here? Then other figures come into view. Dien. The man carrying the case.

The case. Dien is holding something. She uncurls her hand, letting Adelaide see. A salt box.

Adelaide starts to scream.

'No! Dien, no!'

She can hear Mikaela pleading.

'What are you doing to her? Please, let us see her!'

Dien does not reply. She is staring meditatively at Ole and Mikaela.

'Leave them alone!' Adelaide screams. Ole tries to enter the room, to reach her, but the man with the case bars the way.

'Please—'

Mikaela's face, fraught with distress.

'Ole, Mikaela, get away from them! Get away!'

'Ata!'

'Mikaela!'

'Ata!'

Dien passes the salt box to the man with the case, then enters the apartment and closes the door, blocking Adelaide's view of the Larssons. Panic floods her. She looks frantically to Dien.

'You wouldn't—'

'I would.'

'But their son, that boy – he's one of yours – you can't do this!'

Dien shakes her head regretfully. 'I know.'

'No.' She is shaking. 'No, I don't believe you.'

When Dien speaks her voice is soft, almost caressing.

'Don't underestimate me, Adelaide Rechnov. And let's be clear – I want you to be clear. We're talking about me hurting these people. Your rescuers. Ole and Mikaela, that's their names, right? Which I will do. Do I want to hurt them? No. I don't, of course I don't. I don't enjoy torture. But will I, in order to make you do what we need? Yes. I will. Unequivocally. Because we're at war here, and in war, people make sacrifices.'

Her gaze locks with Adelaide's.

'Don't make these people be one of them. They helped you, I hear.

You might say they're the reason you're alive. I'll leave you to think on it.'

She rises. Walks towards the door.

'Wait!'

Dien pauses. As she turns Adelaide sees the glint of triumph in her eyes, and she understands that this is the end result of a calculation Dien made a long time ago, one whose outcome she has been riding out ever since.

'Yes,' she says. 'I'll do it. I'll do whatever you want. Just please, don't hurt them.'

Dien's crew can't work out how to act around her. They are more uncertain of themselves than Adelaide, who has been treated worse than this, and now that the terms have been made clear she at least knows where she stands. The arrangement is essentially house arrest: they keep her locked in Dien's apartment, but she is free to move around it, as long as someone is there, to make sure she doesn't take a knife from the drawer. Try to stab one of them – or herself.

She doesn't recognize the towers across the waterway. She can usually orientate herself by the graffiti. This must be one of those parts of town where they kick out the homeless and the people have regular work and an assumed air of gentility, where aspirations of crossing the border are not uncommon.

Different people come and go from the apartment. There are only two rooms, the living and sleeping area, and a small bathroom where the taps work if the water meter has been paid. When the westerners mention their plans it is always in hushed voices. After a few episodes like this Adelaide starts to laugh.

'Something amuse you, Rechnov?' asks Dien.

'No, nothing.'

But she can't suppress a smile, and Dien is watching.

'Only, if I'm going to be your figurehead, don't you think it would be useful to know what you're trying to do?'

'I don't think we're at quite that level of trust yet, Rechnov. Shut up or we'll lock you in the bathroom.'

Despite everything Dien has done, she has to admit to moments of liking for the other woman. One of the others glances in Adelaide's direction and mutters, 'The water.'

'You don't think I'm serious, do you? Stars above. Anyway, she isn't going to kill herself. Are you, Rechnov?'

'I'm weighing up my options,' says Adelaide.

Her levity seems to surprise, but not displease, Dien, who every now and then will give her a curious, straight-on look, as though Adelaide is a previously undiscovered species whose behaviour must be constantly monitored and re-evaluated, and Dien is not fazed by this process being transparent. It reminds Adelaide of the way her twin Axel used to examine things, back in the days when Axel's speech was almost entirely composed of questions, tumbling over one another in his eagerness to ask all that he wanted to know.

Something has shifted in her memories of him. The poison has drained away; it is easier, now, to remember Axel at his best, and not in the absent, befuddled state which defined the last years of his life. Axel, she suspects, would have appreciated the ludicrousness of her current situation, and he would not have hesitated to have pointed it out to her captors. But Axel didn't always use his head, either.

She remembers Mikaela's face. She can't trust Dien.

'This is the speech.'

Dien pushes a piece of paper under Adelaide's nose. This is the latest iteration of their plan, the plan Adelaide is not to know, but can guess at.

Adelaide puts a finger on the paper and slides it back across the table. Dien looks at it for a moment, expressionless, then stands, picks up the paper, walks around the table and puts it in front of Adelaide.

'This is the speech,' she says again.

'There is no point in me doing this. Nothing I can say—'

'I'd slam your stupid head into the table,' says Dien, 'but there's no point in beating you up. It won't have any impact if you look like the victim here. But if you don't help us, so help me I will damage your precious friends. That is a promise.'

Mikaela's screams. Ole's frightened, bewildered expression. Her gaze drops to the paper in front of her and against her volition, she begins to scan through the text. After a few lines she frowns and picks up the paper.

'Who wrote this?'

'It doesn't matter who wrote it, you're going to read it, and you're going to read it like you fucking believe it.'

'It matters because it's shit. No one says things like this.'

Dien places both hands on the table, her head thrust forwards, the muscles in her neck taut with tension. Under her headscarf Adelaide can see strands of dark brown hair. She has never seen Dien's hair before. Her own is starting to grow out, but they won't allow her to dye it again.

A vein pulses in Dien's forehead as she clenches her jaw.

'Then write a better one, Rechnov,' she says at last.

She places a blank sheet of paper and a pencil in front of Adelaide, and leaves the apartment. Adelaide hears the key turn in the lock behind her.

Sounds of habitation from the adjacent apartments blur and fade away as she stares at the blank page. The room is still.

Once again she reads through the speech that Dien has provided. She doesn't know if it was Dien who wrote it, but it is bad. Incoherent and inconsistent. Adelaide has food in her stomach and the taste of coral tea in her mouth, and it's good coral tea. For the first time in days her head is clear; she should be able to write what they want in her sleep.

What do they want?

And who is *they*? Who is she meant to be speaking for?

She had thought she understood the west. Its character is imprinted on her mind in a series of inexorable impressions: her journey to the unremembered quarters, bound and blindfolded in the well of a boat, crossing from tower to tower on a fraying rope metres above sea level, a skad beating the face of a westerner into pulp, a girl who showed her kindness falling to her death from a collapsing bridge.

But even these few weeks since have revealed to her a more complex, segmented society than she, and maybe even Vikram, would have liked to acknowledge. What can she possibly say that will convince a crowd of westerners?

After an hour, Dien returns. She looks at the blank paper. At Adelaide.

'Time's ticking,' she says. Her mouth curls in a grimace that might be a twisted smile, Adelaide isn't sure. She looks at Dien, thinking how the old Adelaide would have judged this woman. The slight irregularity of her features. The cheap cosmetics. She would never have seen what lies beneath that exterior, the courage or the cruelty; it would have been beneath her to offer Dien a second glance.

She picks up the pen, and writes a line.

'That's right,' says Dien.

The door slams again.

Adelaide stares at the words on the page.

> I used to live over there.
> I used to live over there, with those people.
> There was a man I knew, a westerner. His name was Vikram.

Dien reads through the speech in silence. When she comes to the end she sits back in her chair and folds her arms, eyes narrowed in the familiar, shrewd expression. Assessing. Reassessing.

'It almost reads like you mean it.'

Adelaide says nothing.

'Good. This is what we need. The meet's tomorrow evening. It'll be busy. You'd better practise.'

'I want to see Mikaela and Ole.'

'The meet,' says Dien. 'And then we'll see.'

She is clearly restless, but Adelaide senses her mood is closer to anticipation than irritation. She takes her chance.

'What did you do, before you did this?'

'And what do you call this?'

'Revolution.' Adelaide looks at her. 'Isn't it?'

'Good a word as any, I suppose.'

'So, before the revolution, what did you do?' Seeing the refusal in Dien's face, she adds, 'I'm just curious.'

Dien takes her time answering, evidently considering the wisdom of engaging in more intimate conversation with a Rechnov, even one undisputedly under her control.

'I was a nurse. Still am, when they're desperate.'

'Seriously?'

'Does that surprise you? Course it does. I threatened to torture your friends. That's not the actions of a nurse, you might think. But I'll tell you something, Rechnov. Nursing teaches you a lot. Like suffering, it teaches you about that. It teaches you about pain, and the thresholds of pain, and when to alleviate it, and when to apply it, and how people behave when they feel it. When you're a nurse you treat whoever comes your way and you don't question what they did to get themselves in that state and whether they deserve to live or die. You just. . . plug the holes.'

For a moment Adelaide sees, very vividly, a shard of glass stuck in a man's stomach.

'I don't suppose you'll have been to the western hospital,' says Dien. 'It's not a pleasant place, that's for sure. It's not a fair place, either. And you might be the most hard-arsed soul in the world, but until you've held a woman's head with half her face shredded while she drowns in her own blood screaming for her mother and the ghosts, you haven't seen shit.'

'Was that what persuaded you? To join the resistance?'

'A lot of things persuaded me,' says Dien evenly.

'Do you hate me, Dien?'

Dien looks to the window-wall, distracted by a passing gull. The bird beats its way upwards, lofting out of view, leaving behind the grey assault of the city. 'I haven't made up my mind.'

From the moment the speech is agreed, the apartment is abuzz with adrenaline as Dien's crew prepare for the meet. Adelaide, always at the edge of someone's eye, now feels almost invisible as they bustle about, tense and distracted. Adelaide herself presents a fresh problem to be solved: Dien is concerned that someone might stab her on the spot.

'Before she has a chance to open her bloody mouth.'

'Is that likely?' Adelaide asks. She tries for a joking tone but no one will meet her eye. Dien takes her aside.

'People are angry,' she says roughly. 'They want to be persuaded. We've had western fighters before but they're all dead, every one of them is dead. We need someone who is immune to the system, and *you*, Rechnov – you have immunity.'

When the evening finally arrives it feels no more real or unreal than any of the strange events that have preceded it. They drive to the place in Dien's boat. She listens to the voice of the sea, trying to make out a message in its whisperings, wondering if fate has an eye to her today. The meet is in a drinking house. Before they go in, Dien tells her that this was where Vikram and his friends Nils and Drake used to meet. Adelaide has no way of knowing whether it is true, or another piece of emotional ammunition to make her perform, but when they go inside she sees their photographs on the wall, pinned up with others, a collage of faces, southerners and Boreal, young and old. Among them is a man whose face is familiar from the newsfeeds, a man she watched drown: Eirik 9968. Beneath the collage is a tin of salt, the metal scratched and tarnished. Dien and the others go to the wall and perform the salt ritual, and Adelaide does the same, the grains falling somewhere behind her, over her shoulder – she can't hear them land above the general rowdiness of the place.

It is a shock to see Vikram's face. In the photograph he looks quietly confident, in a way she struggles to remember now but knows must have been true. The image must have been taken during his time in the City.

The place has a raw, unfinished quality with the upturned kegs and crates set out as seats, the naked bulbs swinging overhead. There are a lot of people here. Dien's people are standing very close to her, all of them carrying concealed knives or handguns, and Dien's flippant remarks about someone stabbing her take on an uncomfortable layer of truth and she realizes she is deeply, fiercely scared in a way she hasn't felt for weeks.

'Ready?' says Dien.

'Don't have a choice, do I?'

'No.'

Dien jumps onto a keg to speak. Her introduction is quick and energetic. She has a natural way with a crowd.

Having caught the room's attention, Dien gets down to business.

'All right. I said I had a surprise for you. And here it is. Or rather, here *she* is.'

Adelaide senses the people surrounding her tense in anticipation. Fear stiffens her spine.

This is it.

She has a fleeting memory, of standing on a podium amid the old-world grandeur of the Council Chambers, beckoning Vikram to join her.

'I present to you our new speaker for western rights – Adelaide Rechnov!'

Dien bends down and with a theatrical, if slightly clumsy gesture, whips the hat from Adelaide's head.

There are a few moments of silence during which Adelaide feels the weight of scrutiny, her face under the lens of a magnifying glass, like never before. Then the room erupts. Dien's people gather closely around her, forming a barrier between Adelaide and the crowd, crushing her. Voices are raised in uproar. Through the barrier of familiar bodies she feels the impact of strangers, lunging to get at her.

If they reach me, I'll be crushed before anyone can even pull a knife.

She hears a glass shatter. She hears Dien shouting above the melee, telling everyone to calm down. Hands grasp at her, pulling her up onto the table. Whichever way it goes she will be exposed. Now she's standing next to Dien, an easy target. Dien has taken up a defensive stance, using her body to shield Adelaide from assault. A splash of liquid catches Adelaide square in the face and splatters over both of them. She can taste the tartness of alcohol on her lips, shocking in its sudden intensity. Dien is shouting and gesticulating with both arms.

'Shut up! Shut the fuck up and listen to what she has to say!'

She shouts into Adelaide's ear.

'Go on. Go on! You'll just have to start.'

A glass flies overhead, narrowly missing both of their heads.

'This is insane!'

Dien shrugs and ducks.

'Do or die, Rechnov.'

Adelaide pulls out the piece of paper on which she had painstakingly written out her speech. She glances at it once, then screws the paper up into a ball. She gathers her breath.

'I used to live over there, with those people.'

'Louder,' hisses Dien.

'I used to live over there,' she shouts. The room reacts with jeers, but others shush them. She says it a third time, quieter this time, forcing the volume of the room to lower, until an abrupt, ambivalent hush settles. The westerners watch her mistrustfully, accusingly.

'I used to live over there. There was a man I knew, a westerner. His name was Vikram. For a while, he lived where I lived. But he was never at home there. You know what they call people who cross over – what we call them. Airlifts. And Vikram – he could never find a balance. He was torn between two places.'

She gathers the courage to let her gaze settle on individuals, forcing herself to meet their eyes. Some look away but others hold her gaze. These westerners. These westerners, who she does not know.

'I understand now how he felt. I don't belong there any more. I can't go back. You're wondering what I'm doing here when the o'dio says I'm dead. Well, I could tell you how but the only thing that matters is that I was rescued, by two of you. Two westerners, who were kind to me. Who didn't know, or care, who I was. They only wanted to help. Only, I've realized I don't belong here either. I don't belong anywhere.'

The room has fallen silent, enough to hear the sound of the wind whining through the shutters, the distant blare of a waterbus horn.

'I'll tell you something,' she says quietly. 'My brother – my twin – he went mad. That's the truth. I didn't want to believe it but it's what happened, he went mad, and he killed himself. I know, I know, I shouldn't speak of it. We never speak about that. But it happened. He believed in horses. He heard them speaking to him. Sometimes I see them and I think I might be going mad too, and then I think, no. It's just this place. This city. What it does to us.'

She wavers. Dien is at her side, nodding encouragingly. She remembers Vikram, his voice falling onto the ears of the Council, his confidence in the face of impossibility. Both their confidence, that they could make something happen. She cannot help glancing at the photograph on the wall.

'I'm here today without any expectations. I can't condone the things my family did. The things I did, without knowing. Or maybe I knew but I didn't care enough to stop. It doesn't really matter which, I did them. And to be honest with you, I'm here because I was blackmailed into being here.

'But now that I am here, I realize I can do something. This city isn't a fair place – but it could be. It could become what it was meant to be, a long time ago. I can help. I can't give you much but I can give you my voice, if you'll have it. I'll fight for you. I'll give you whatever I have left, because I owe it, to that man.' She points at the photograph. 'I owe it to Vikram Bai, who I loved, and never told. And I owe it to all of you.'

She gazes around.

'That's all I've got. There's nothing else.'

In the ensuing silence, Adelaide senses the mood in the room teetering, tipped to go either way with the least bit of provocation. Has she done enough?

A woman with grey hair says, 'Why have you brought her here, Dien?'

Dien answers the question directly.

'Because we can use her.' She glances at Adelaide. 'And because, despite everything, I think she means what she says.'

The room divides into clusters of mutterings. Adelaide hears, quite distinctly, a voice saying, 'We should just kill her now and be done with it.' And someone else: 'What about the prophecies? What if it's her?'

Her life hangs now on her ability to act a part, or to tell the truth, or some convergence of the two.

She waits. Dien waits.

A man at the bar says, 'You haven't said you're sorry.'

'Yes, I'm sorry. Of course I'm sorry. There's a lot of things I regret, that I'd take back now if I could. But you can't live a life like that. Or you're no better off than a ghost.' Even as she speaks, the truth of what she is saying sharpens its focus. This is how she has been living, and from here she too has a choice: a path is being offered to her. She looks at the grey-haired woman who first spoke. 'Well, you have a choice as well. You can use me, or not.'

The room is pregnant with anticipation. Adelaide can hear the breath moving in and out of her lungs. In these moments, she still has her life. How could she have been so careless with it?

The grey-haired woman says, 'I'm with them.'

Adelaide has made enough speeches in her life to know, in that moment, that she has won. It's a bittersweet victory, the kind that is squeezed from ashes and tears, but it is a victory. A binding one. Dien meets her eyes. There is no hugging, no screams of exhilaration. Just a nod of acknowledgement from the other woman, which Adelaide translates as: *You did all right.*

One of Dien's crew comes up and murmurs, just loud enough for Adelaide to hear.

'That little eel Ren snuck out five minutes ago.'

Adelaide notes the shift in Dien's expression.

'What does that mean?'

'It means we've got about five minutes to get out of here.'

Dien jumps up onto her keg.

'All right, people. There's going to be a skadi raid in about five, that's five minutes! So get the hell out of here unless you want to wake up feeling even worse tomorrow than you're going to already!'

No one needs to be told twice. What was boisterous chaos is now a systematic evacuation as punters stream from the bar. As Dien puts a hand on Adelaide's shoulder and steers her towards the exit, she sees hands tearing down the photographs from the wall, all of the west's dissidents, faces gathered up and shoved unceremoniously into a folder. This was just an arena, a pop-up show. Outside, people are splitting, heading either upstairs or down.

'We've got the boat,' says Dien, directing them downwards.

'Is there time – you said five minutes—'

'There's time. Anyway, you should always go the way they don't expect.'

They cram into the lift with a dozen others and drop down through the tower in a series of juddering fits and starts. The raft racks are crammed with people unmooring their boats. Dien leaps into theirs and starts the motor. Adelaide scrambles in after her and Dien powers the boat away at once. Looking back, Adelaide can see other boats moving out, their wakes creating a star-like formation around the base of the tower, licks of white extending over the surface, before their makers duck away into darker corners of the west. For a few moments, the tower appears as dark and desolate as any other western building at night. The air still, the water lapping. Her breath in the arctic night. Then they hear the whine of approaching boats.

Skadi boats.

'Right on time,' says Dien with satisfaction.

Dien is relaxed at the wheel; they are well away now, the tower receding fast behind them. By the time the skadi reach the bar, all they will find is a deserted room with a few empty kegs, and the dregs of beer in tankards.

'So, Rechnov,' Dien shouts above the engine. 'You ready to do it all again?'

'Who's Ren?'

'A snitch. Don't worry. We keep an eye on those people.'

'Will it be like this every time?'

'Worse, probably. Once they get wind something's up.' Dien glances back. 'But you can handle it, right?'

Adelaide nods. The evening is sinking in on her now. As Dien steers expertly through the darkness, she hears again the jeers of the crowd, her voice against theirs. The outcome tonight was as fine as the edge of a blade, and the sense of danger, absent in the adrenaline of the moment, now crawls back to nuzzle at her throat.

When they reach Dien's tower she gets out of the boat first, then waits for the others to catch up. As Dien approaches the tower entrance she calls out.

'Hey, Dien?'

The woman turns. Adelaide takes a step towards her.

'You don't fucking threaten my friends.'

She swings hard and fast. At this range it's impossible to miss; her fist connects with Dien's nose with a satisfying crack. Dien staggers back, hand to her face, eyes wide with shock. When she takes her hand away, blood is dribbling from her nostrils.

Someone grabs Adelaide's arms.

'You little—'

'No!' snaps Dien. 'This is between us.'

Adelaide feels her arms released. Her knuckles sting with the impact of the blow, but it's a good pain, a welcome pain. Dien's people move back, giving them space. Dien wipes her face and shakes droplets of blood from her hand. All of her focus is on Adelaide.

They move warily around one another. At the entrance to the tower and on the far side of the decking, Adelaide is aware of other, shadowy figures, watching the scene unfold.

Dien rushes her, left arm swinging. Adelaide lifts her arms to protect her head and Dien undercuts with her right fist. The blow hammers her stomach. It's Adelaide's turn to reel off balance, winded and gasping. She takes a few unsteady steps backwards before catching herself. Dien moves in, aiming a second punch. She ducks it, darts out of reach. At last she's found a use for all those fencing classes, her feet moving nimbly over the decking as she recalls long-forgotten sequences.

'Come on then,' taunts Dien. '*Rechnov.*'

The use of her name is enough. They come together in a fury. Adelaide relishes the moment of impact. There's no finesse, only passion as she implements every resource she has – fists, feet, teeth, nails – on whatever parts of Dien's body are exposed. Dien's headscarf comes off as she yanks at her hair, hearing it tear, bringing tears to the woman's eyes. Next thing there's a knee in the small of her back and she feels herself retch in response.

By the time they hit the floor, grappling and scrabbling like two rats in a pit, Adelaide knows she's going to lose but she doesn't care; it's about pride now. All she wants is to inflict as much damage as she's capable of. She lashes out indiscriminately and hears a yell of protest, knowing she connected with something tender. Then a blow to the temple sends her vision spinning. She collapses against the decking. Oxygen comes in sharp, jagged breaths. Everything hurts.

'Are you done?' pants Dien.

Adelaide squints upwards. She is grimly pleased to see Dien's right eye is swelling viciously. She hopes she's broken the woman's nose.

Experimentally, she tries to move. Pain flares through her body.

'I'm done.'

Dien digs into her pocket.

'Take this. You're going to need it.'

She throws something down. It's a scarab. An old recalibrated model, undoubtedly stolen. Adelaide looks from the scarab to Dien, hair askew, face a bloody mess, and understands that this is an expression of trust.

From here, she knows, there is no going back.

PART TWO
LAST OF THE PENGUINS

PATAGONIA

The Osirian attaches only one condition to their travelling together: he does not want to be seen. Under this understanding, Mig is the one who goes into the farms and negotiates for food and, on the few occasions when the Osirian agrees they need it, to scout for shelter. The Osirian prefers to stay in the open, regardless of rain or winds, and more than once the pair of them have sat out in the midst of a deluge with thunderclouds clashing overhead, spears of lightning illuminating the flat, miserable land, with Mig curled up soaked to the bones, shivering like he will never stop and cursing himself for throwing in his lot with this casual lunatic.

The storms crash around the valleys, the light a strange yellowish-brown that lifts in the moment the clouds roll away, peeling back like the skin of an orange to reveal clear skies and drenched, sparkling fields. The late spring sun burns the water from his clothes within minutes. Mig is suspicious of these abrupt transitions. It isn't right. It wouldn't happen in the city.

The Osirian, by contrast, seems unfazed, sitting with all the serenity of an acolyte of the Houses of the Nazca, watching the skies as though he was born to do nothing but sit beneath storms and observe their passing. Sometimes, when Mig is pretending to sleep, the Osirian opens his pack and takes out a mysterious object – a shiny black stone, about the size of Mig's clenched fist, but it has no purpose that Mig can see – and sits there, puzzling over it. Mig wonders if having such a close encounter with death has scrambled the man's brain.

Mig has never been outside of the city before. Without buildings, the world seems vast and achingly empty. He misses the narrow streets of Cataveiro, the way the city is always colliding with itself, the noise and the raw stink of it. He can't feel at ease out here. The country is too exposed and there's nowhere to hide, not from the elements, and not from whoever they are running from. Because however calm he might look on the outside, the Osirian – Vikram, as he says Mig should call him – is clearly on the run from someone.

It doesn't matter to Mig who the hunters are. Nothing much matters now, only the terrible crater ripped into his chest by Pilar's death. He could throw himself into the river and all of its stinking water wouldn't be enough to fill that hole. He still has the green feather she gave him the first time they talked, a ragged bit of crap now, its fibres all stuck together with sweat and lint, but he could never get rid of it. In the day he walks with his hand in his pocket gripping the feather, and at night he holds it against his lips, as if there might be something left of Pilar in it, something to soothe the inescapable despair of knowing she is no more in the world.

With each step further south, Mig berates himself. He should have looked for her sooner, that day. No – before that – from the second they heard the broadcast about the outbreak, he shouldn't have let Pilar out of his sight. He should have told the Alaskan to go fuck herself. All those years in her service, running her errands, feeding her and cleaning her, and for what? While Mig and his gang of street kids put themselves at risk, the Alaskan lay on her back like a beetle, antennae twitching, stirring up shit from the safety of her attic. If it weren't for that nirvana freak and her manipulative schemes. . .

He can't suppress a shudder at the memory of their last conversation. A nirvana. *What she is.* Yes, it explains things – like her seeming omniscience, that almost abnormal intelligence that she loves to parade – and it's not like Mig hadn't suspected, but it's different having it confirmed from the source. You can no longer pretend it doesn't exist.

He nurtures his hatred carefully. It gives him something to focus on. Something that belongs to him and him alone. He doesn't know if the Alaskan managed to avoid the epidemic but he would bet on it, he'd bet the last of his stash, the stash that was meant for him and Pilar, the two of them, their future – he'd bet every last peso of it that she's still out there, alive and plotting. The freak is indestructible.

Well, if she is, she won't remain so forever. He, Mig, will find a way to change that. The Alaskan isn't the only one who can cook up a plan.

For now, he's here with the Osirian. Vikram. It's strange that the man behind the door has a name, after all this time. In his head, Mig still thinks of him as the Osirian. Sometimes he wonders what he's doing with the man, feels even a little afraid of him – he is, after all, a man who *should not exist* – but it isn't fear that keeps him at Vikram's side, not that. He couldn't say what it is, exactly. Only that he couldn't remain where he was. Not in Cataveiro. Not where she died. And this man was going south, and Mig has never been south, and why not? Besides, there's something about the Osirian, something – Mig can't think of a better way to put it than *special*. He has a sense. A feeling in his gut. The little kids at the old warehouse would say that the jaguar has passed him by.

Of course, they talk rot. He wonders what's happened to them. Ri, that clown-faced girl, the others. Did they survive the epidemic? He's seen for himself how quickly the redfleur spreads – you only have to touch someone who's infected and it's over. If one of them got it, the chances are they're all dead. It's painful to think about it, so after a while he doesn't. What's the use? He can't do anything for them. His life has changed – he's with the Osirian now. Mig the adventurer. Mig the expeditionary.

As they move further south, Mig finds himself capitalizing on this *special* in order to get what they need. The people who work on the farms are simple. They don't have much, and Mig can't imagine they know much, and that makes them the ideal recipients for his message. The first time it's by accident. He's bargaining with the farmer – she's a tough one, and there are two young kids in the corner, sickly-looking brats wearing mouth-and-nose masks, their eyes peeking over like lizards in a hole. Mig almost feels sorry for them, and almost relents, but no—

'Thirty peso.' He names his price decidedly. It's stolen money, but that's no reason to be bounteous with it.

The farmer drives the price up. Mig pushes back. Eventually they reach an accord. As he's loading up the pack she says, with a hint of sourness, there's enough in that bag to feed a skinny stalk like him for days. Mig replies without thinking.

'My friend needs to eat. He has to keep his strength up.'

'Your friend is sick?' The farmer is instantly wary. She shifts her stance, placing herself between Mig and the two children.

'He was,' says Mig. He shouldn't say what he says next but something propels him on, perhaps the faces of the kids, staring at him like he's a curiosity, a boy fallen from the sky. 'But he survived.'

The farmer is reluctant to pursue the conversation but Mig holds out, allowing a tantalizing silence to expand, and in the end she can't help herself.

'Survived what?'

Mig whispers, 'The redfleur.'

There is the briefest of pauses.

'Get out,' says the farmer. 'You should know better than to joke about that.'

'I wouldn't tell a lie,' says Mig, which isn't true, although in this instance it is the truth. He directs his next words at the kids. 'There's scars on his face and all the way up his arms. The redfleur came for him but he survived, he's as alive as you or me.'

'Enough.' The farmer is angry now, but Mig isn't alarmed; rather he's aware of the weight of what he's just revealed. 'Take your things and go.'

The kids' eyes are round as peaches. Mig feels a peculiar spread of satisfaction as he hikes the pack onto his back and heads out of the farmhouse into the dusty, suffocating heat of the day. The blue sky yawns above him and the fields stretch out on all sides for as far as he can see. Usually his loneliness would fall upon him in this moment, like a curse, but telling the tale has done something. It's staved it off, for now at least. He returns to the Osirian with a swagger in his walk.

'Good haul?' asks the Osirian, with a smile.

Mig nods.

'Good bargaining.'

That night they eat well and it does not rain.

By the middle of the night Mig is overcome with guilt. What was he thinking? He resolves to keep his mouth shut. He is resolved all the way to the next farm where somehow it happens again, and this time Mig does not have the excuse of an accident, this time, he can't resist provoking the farmers, and the sense of importance which fills him in the telling.

Farm by farm Mig embroiders his story. He adds little details. The man is from the ocean. He eats fish raw when he can get it. The scars from the redfleur are in the form of scales, golden, like fish, or like a simurgh from the old tales, yeah, lizards with wings. When he brings back the supplies the guilt returns and he tells himself this is the last time. He'll confess to Vikram; he'll stop this stupidity.

But he can't help himself.

His story garners different reactions. Sometimes people are angry, and he guesses that, like him, they've lost a loved one to the redfleur or some other horrible plague. They don't want to be reminded. Other times they can't get enough. Wanting to hear more, they bribe him with extra food. Perhaps he'd like to stay for supper? They can spare enough for another mouth. . .

Settled in his role as storyteller, Mig starts accepting the occasional gift. A lemon from the groves, its skin thick and waxy, the flesh a bursting tartness on the inside of his mouth. He insists on eating the fruit straight, to the mirth and delight of his hosts. He wants to say to them, you think you get lemons two a dozen in Cataveiro? The next day it's a plate of enchiladas cooked fresh, with seasoning plucked straight from the fields. Then a tumbler of wine. He says no, the first time, knowing it's best to refuse this particular type of hospitality, but at a second entreaty relents and accepts. What's a drink, after all?

The wine tastes rough and acidic and Mig doesn't care for it, can't believe people would drink this stuff for pleasure, but after a few gulps it becomes more tolerable, and by the end of the glass he is feeling faintly light-headed, warm and relaxed and ready for another. Yes, he'll take another. The farmers – a brother and sister, both with the same narrow face and clouded eyes – press him for details about the man who survived.

Mig is in an expansive mood. His inventions grow wilder and less plausible with every sentence, and he watches with satisfaction as they swallow it down. He has found that the kick he gets from telling these tales is exponential to how far his fabrications deviate from the truth. By now he has settled on a style of delivery: a mixture of wide-eyed innocence and bewilderment. When the farmers ask how he came to be travelling with such a man he says he was bewitched, or thinks he was – his head is so foggy now it's hard to remember. After the second round of wine he stands to leave; he really has to go. Won't he take another? they ask. But Mig is firm this time. He has to go. He smiles, thanks them, and heads for the door.

And finds the man standing in his way.

For the first time Mig experiences a moment of panic. He asks the man to let him pass. The man smiles – not a pleasant smile, not any more – and says he doesn't think so. Keep calm, Mig tells himself. Make a dash for it. You're faster than this arsehole. He sprints for the gap between man and door, but either his balance is off or the man trips him, and somehow he misses. Falls. Face down to the dust-clogged doormat, the dust clenching him in a sneeze, and then the man has his arms pinned painfully behind his back. He's dragging Mig backwards into the house, Mig's heels kicking uselessly against the floor. He thrashes in the man's grasp and feels his arms yanked tighter, contorting his shoulders. Mig yelps in pain. The man hauls him up the stairs, Mig shouting and screaming with every step. All the while he's aware of the other one, the woman, closing the front door, watching.

His panic dissolves into terror. What are they doing? What are they planning? He's thrown into a room and the door slams, and locks.

The man's footsteps thud down the stairs. Mig is left in the room, in silence.

He can hear his breathing, fast and ragged. The thud of his own heart against his ribcage.

Fuck, fuck, fuck, fuck. *Fuck.*

He's been duped. He can see it now – feeding him the alcohol – fuelling his stories. The thought comes to him, clear as a rash. The bastards want Vikram.

They want the man who survived.

He should have known this would happen.

His head is beginning to hurt, but maybe that's the blood racing at his temples, a dull, insistent throb. He cases the room. The window is locked. He can see the farm outbuildings, pieces of machinery at a standstill, the pink and white poppy fields and the flat skyline beyond. So empty. Nothing out there, no one to know he is here. The sun is hard and bright and low in the west. He tries to force the window open to no avail. He rattles the door handle, kicks at it, yells, 'Let me out!' After a few minutes the man comes back up and bangs hard on the other side.

'Shut up, you little shit, or I'll make you shut up.'

Mig falls silent, genuinely afraid now. He sits quietly, head pounding, shoulders aching, trying to see a way out.

Minutes pass. Longer. The sun moves lower in the sky. It must be an hour since they locked him up in here. Mig feels a great wash of despair. The Osirian will be wondering where he's got to. What if he moves on? What if he thinks Mig's done a runner? He looks again at the machinery out in the yard. These two could do anything to him, kilometres from any place fit for humans to live. Crush him, chop him into pieces with an axe, grind him into food for chickens.

At last he hears the heavy tread of footsteps on the stairs, followed by the click of the lock. He waits, tense. Ready to sprint. The woman slips in quick as a wasp and locks the door again before he has a chance. She stands, back to the door, regarding him, her face inscrutable.

'Where is the man?'

Mig shakes his head. He has to hold his ground.

'Where is the man you keep talking about?' she repeats.

'I was making it up.'

'I don't think so,' she says. She is very calm, but not calm the way the Osirian is calm. This one is calm the way people are when they have an endgame in sight and are prepared to be ruthless. Like the Alaskan.

He's underestimated the situation. He should have known better. The alcohol is making him slow. Stupid.

'I was making it up,' he repeats, but shakily.

'You will tell us where he is.'

Mig judges it best to keep silent. He wonders, with a flush of dizziness, if the woman is going to torture him. He wonders if he can buy some time by lying, tell her the Osirian is somewhere he isn't, give her a location that is close enough to be plausible but far enough away for Vikram to escape.

The woman reaches inside her apron pocket. Mig tenses. A knife, she's going to have a knife. Or pliers, to pull out his fingernails with. The guerrillas have methods like that. What if this pair have connections?

She brings out a large jar with a metal screw lid.

'Do you know what this is?'

There is something inside the jar, Mig can see. Something thin and coiled with black and red and yellow stripes, something that he's only ever seen in pictures. Involuntarily, he jerks backwards.

'My brother collects snakes,' says the woman, turning the jar this way and that, studying its contents with detached interest. 'This one is a young coral. It's highly venomous.'

She places the jar on the floor, between them, but within easy reach. Mig can see quite clearly the outline of the snake. Its coils, each about the width of his finger, are beginning to unwind in a slow, squirming motion, no doubt seeking to escape. Mig's legs have gone suddenly numb; his bowels feel liquid.

'If I release it, it will bite you,' continues the woman. 'And snakes don't like being confined. It won't be happy when I let it out.'

She's bluffing, Mig thinks. She must be. Why the fuck would they keep one of these creatures in their house? Something that could kill you if it escaped? You'd have to be insane.

He thinks how far away they are from the city. How very far. How isolated. These two, alone on their farm, with their snakes.

'Death by venom is slow and very painful.' The woman reaches for the jar, her fingers wrapping around the glass like a caress, sliding it back towards her lap. Mig is overcome with horror. 'It can take days,' she says.

She looks at him.

'Where is the man?'

His mouth is dry. Her fingertips rest on the lid of the jar. The coral snake's head lifts suddenly, sliding upwards against the side of the glass, revealing the scales of its underbelly. Mig has no idea if she's telling the truth. If it's deadly, or not. How can he run the risk?

'I can't tell you where he is,' he says. 'I can only show you.'

She smiles. For a moment he thinks he's bought himself some time but then she twists the lid of the jar a fraction to the right.

'No!'

There is a knock at the door.

'What?' snaps the woman.

'Open up.'

It's her brother. The woman doesn't say anything but is unable to suppress a frown of displeasure at the interruption. Mig gathers his wits. Now is the moment, when the door opens. He'll rush them both. If he knocks one of them off balance, he might make it down the stairs. He tries not to think about all the deadly objects they could hurl after him, or what would happen if they let the snake loose.

With the jar clutched firmly in one hand, the woman unlocks the door. Her brother is standing in the corridor, a strained expression on his face. As the door opens wider, Mig sees the reason for it. The Osirian, Vikram, is behind him, and he has a weapon pointed at the back of the man's head. A gun.

Mig stares.

'Mig.'

Vikram's voice startles him into movement. He sidles past the woman, whose fingers are trembling with rage on the glass, the snake inside shaken about by the movement, its head switching angrily from side to side. Past the man. Past the Osirian. The gun is not like anything he has seen before.

'Inside,' says Vikram. The man goes in without a word. Vikram shuts the door and locks it. As they go down the stairs Mig can hear the remonstrations beginning between brother and sister. He can't help sneaking glances at Vikram, who wields the gun easily, like he's done this before.

In the yard outside the sun hits him, long and low, the silent machinery casting shadows in the dust. They waste no time in putting distance between themselves and the farm. Vikram is still gripping the gun tightly.

After a while Mig says, 'I didn't know you had that.'

'There's a lot you don't know,' says Vikram, and Mig, taking the hint, shuts up.

'What did you tell them?'

Vikram shows no external signs of anger, but Mig senses he isn't going to wriggle out of this one so easily. He tries anyway.

'Nothing much.'

'Mig. What did you tell them?'

He mutters, 'I told them you'd survived.'

'You told them I'd survived.'

'Yes.'

'Survived the redfleur?'

Mig avoids looking at him. He focuses his eyes on the flat, featureless countryside, everything murky in the dusk. 'Yes.' He blurts out, 'I'm sorry, I—'

'Do you want us to be caught?'

'No!'

'Do you want me to be caught?'

'No.'

'There was one condition to our travelling together, Mig. You remember what it was?'

'I'm sorry,' he says again. He's screwed up. He's screwed up and they both know it. He waits for the inevitable recriminations. 'Are you sending me away?'

Vikram looks at him for a long time, the expression on his face making it impossible to turn away. Under that stare, Mig feels the importance drain out of him until he's as low as a worm.

'If this happens again, I won't have a choice. You're smarter than this, Mig. You'd better prove it to me.'

Mig waits, expecting more, but the Osirian appears to be finished. He changes the subject and talks of other things. His Spanish improves all the time. He asks Mig questions about Patagonia and Patagonian people, questions which Mig sometimes struggles to answer, or answers warily, unsure if they contain some trick or test. Eventually he works up the courage to ask.

'What's that gun?'

'You mean where did it come from?'

'Yeah.'

'It was made in Osiris.'

'Your city?'

Vikram hesitates before he says, 'Yes.'

'And you're going back there?'

'Yes.'

They assess one another. Mig is no longer sure, if he ever had an inkling, of what is going through the Osirian's head.

He is surprised when Vikram reaches into his pack and withdraws the mysterious black stone which Mig has seen him examining in secret on so many nights.

'Do you know what this is?' he asks.

'No.'

'It's a holoma. You've never seen one before?'

'No. What does it do?'

'It's a way of sending messages. It belonged to the Antarctican.'

Mig looks at him uneasily.

'Like robotics?'

'Something like that.'

Mig makes the sign of the spider. He isn't superstitious, not remotely, not like the kids back home, but you can't be too careful with shit like this. Robotics are a breeding ground for demons.

'What do you want it for?'

'I need to send a message.' Vikram pauses and Mig guesses he is weighing up whether to trust him. 'The Antarctican. Taeo Ybanez. He had a partner back home. She deserves to know the truth about how he died. But we should get some rest. We need to make progress tomorrow.'

Mig takes the hint and goes to lie down, but finds it impossible to sleep. As he lies awake, riddled with remorse, listening to the steady rhythm of the Osirian's breathing and the click of night-time insects, Mig wonders what Pilar would have made of this odd man and his faraway city in the ocean. He sees her squatting on the roof of Station Sabado, her hair a tangle of bright dyed feathers, her expression caught between habitual truculence and the quiet bliss that enters her face only when listening to music. He sees her looking down on the plaza with the Cataveiro trams approaching the station, and his heart breaks over again. *He's a madman, Mig.* That's what Pilar would say. *This one's touched.*

Touched or not, Mig sticks with him. But when, after weeks of travel, they arrive at the coast and look out over that same ocean – which Mig has never seen before, an unimaginable, restless thing which fills him with an equal sense of limitlessness and terror – there are things which he does not tell Vikram.

He does not tell him about the hours he has spent daydreaming about how to kill the Alaskan. He doesn't want to have to see the freak's face when he does it – the idea of looking into those cold, soulless eyes as she dies is intolerable – so his options are limited. But there are ways.

He does not tell Vikram that at the last farmhouse he visited, the farmer took hold of Mig's arm and grasped it with the kind of fervency usually displayed by Born Again Mayans.

'You're a traveller, aren't you?' said the farmer.

'I'm going to sea,' said Mig. His revised cover story, dull but safe.

'Then maybe you've heard. On your travels. Have you heard – about the man?'

'What man?'

The farmer's grip on his arm increased and Mig twisted away, annoyed, and knowing what was coming but seeing no way to avoid it. The farmer's eyes shone.

'The man who survived the redfleur!'

'I've never heard of him,' said Mig. 'Who is he?'

'How do you like the ocean?' Vikram asks him.

Mig doesn't want to sound too impressed. He doesn't want Vikram to know that his heart is racing at the sight of the waves, their fierce white caps, the way they crash with such wanton aggression upon the rocks. Or that his only wish is that Pilar could be standing beside him, for him to sweep his arm wide across the vista and say to her, as though he had conjured it, *what do you think of this?* A flock of birds take turns diving at the ocean, the successful returning with some unlucky fish to screech and squabble over. How he longs for wings, or a flying machine like that woman he helped in Cataveiro, to take him away from here, back in time, before it all went so wrong.

'It's all right,' he says. 'Do you like it?'

'It's where I come from,' replies the Osirian. His face is impassive.

Mig licks his lips and tastes salt. He watches a boat move slowly across the water, drawing a white tail behind it. He imagines Pilar is alive and on that boat.

'So what do we do now?'

'We find somewhere to hide.' The Osirian turns away from the sea. 'Come on. We've got work to do.'

TIERRA DEL FUEGO

The Alaskan wheels along the quiet, cool corridors of the island's hospital until she finds the room she is looking for. It is easy to identify: two plainclothes bodyguards stand to attention outside. They eye the Alaskan with suspicion, one moving away from the door, posture shifting in intent, until she holds something up.

'She will want to see me.'

Señorita Xiomara is in a bad state. A web of intravenous tubes push clear fluids into her veins. Her body lies slack, blood-drained, and her luxurious length of hair has declined to a limp black wing against the pillow. Appraising the pitiful sight in front of her, it is hard to believe that this is a woman who controls the country's desalination empire, a woman of wealth and power. But the Alaskan has witnessed many a rise and descent; she never settles on a judgement. People vacillate too frequently for that.

When Xiomara sees the Alaskan, her face tightens in anger. If this were a snake it would spit.

'What are you doing here?'

The Alaskan wastes no time with preambles.

'I went to your house, Xiomara. A delightful abode. And a most impressive stock of medicine you have too. I believe it's this one in particular you're after?'

She holds aloft a box of skin patches. Xiomara's eyes widen.

'Somewhat ironic that you should flee south to escape the epidemic, only to contract something almost as bad,' says the Alaskan, extracting the first patch, which is marked one of thirty. 'Who was it – guerrillas? Dangerous, they are. Rabid sorts. I always heard they kept syringes of jinn-blood, but I've never known anyone fall prey to their ministrations. Until now.'

A bead of sweat glistens in the perfect curl of Xiomara's upper lip. It is the first time the Alaskan has seen the lower part of her face without a mask. Even in sickness, there is no denying the beauty of the bone structure beneath the skin. She lifts Xiomara's wrist from the covers.

'No, don't clench your fist – it's got to go on smoothly, against the veins. You'd better prepare yourself, Xiomara. You're in for a rough time with this. Not everyone survives a treatment for the jinn.'

She presses the skin patch into place.

'There.'

With the brief moment of contact, memory floods the front of the Alaskan's brain. Deep in the Alaskan's past, there was a girl, a Scandinavian girl. The Alaskan remembers her, meandering down the forest track, bare feet making imprints in the mud. Her head turning. A smile, offered as a token, though it seemed like something more.

Señorita Xiomara snatches her hand away, rubbing at her wrist as though to wipe clean the Alaskan's touch.

'I am indebted to you,' she says stiffly. 'What is it that you want? The enclaves, is that it? Access? It can be arranged.'

The Alaskan considers her for a moment. A thousand things run through her head, things which are overwhelmingly uncomplimentary to Xiomara. Past slights. Small setbacks and small victories. She can see that Xiomara is trying quite desperately to read her, but to no avail, and Xiomara should know that by now. She should know that you do not mess with a nirvana.

Eventually she says, 'There is nothing you have that I need.'

Xiomara's frustration is evident.

'Then why are you here? Why now? It's been years, years since you've been outside the city – you've never even left your bed. What happened, Alaskan? Did all of your fetid little slave children run away?'

'I brought you something,' says the Alaskan. 'Just a token. Really, it was quite the bargain.'

The Alaskan takes a battered old radio out of a bag. She places it on the table beside Xiomara, just out of the woman's reach, and switches it on.

'Story time,' says the Alaskan.

The flare of triumph she feels is a gold nugget in her tired old heart. She wheels around, not needing to see Xiomara's face. On her way out, she hears the beginning of the broadcast, crackling over the long-range wavelength.

In the city of Cataveiro there was a man who survived the redfleur. He was a man from nowhere. He was a man without a name, although some say that he had scales like a fish, and could swim for hours underwater without coming up for air. The redfleur had him, and the redfleur let him go. Who can say, listeners, why some are spared? The man lived. . .

Stories on the radio. So many stories in this garrulous country, cart-wheeling like tumbleweed. But stories flower from a seed of truth. The Alaskan thinks about what it means to emerge alive from a brush with redfleur. Redfleur, the virus that always comes back, leapfrogging every advance of the scientists in the north with a newer, more lethal strain. Not that the classification matters here: the Patagonian government can't afford to import Boreal medicine, so redfleur is redfleur, except that the man was in Cataveiro and the Cataveiro epidemic was a Type 9, and not even the northerners have a cure for Type 9.

The man lived.

'Now that is one fish I failed to catch,' says the Alaskan aloud.

Xiomara's bodyguards stare at her disconcertedly. She lets them meet her eyes, knowing how her black irises unnerve the weak. She used to cover those irises, in her own country. She doesn't bother here. Doubtless they would like to know more but she will leave them with the line as it is, a cryptic offering for them to relay to Xiomara when she wails and curses and vomits her way through her medication. If Xiomara dies it is no great loss to the Alaskan. She has been a worthy antagonist but this is the sweetest of victories: revenge in the act of saving. If Xiomara lives, knowing she owes her life to the Alaskan will drive her mad daily.

Meanwhile, the Alaskan has that last elusive fish to pursue.

She missed him once, in Cataveiro. She miscalculated – a rare mistake, but she is not too proud to deny she made one. Now she has a second chance.

The Osirian.

ANTARCTICA

Shri's son Sasha comes home from school with one eye swollen to black and his face tight and closed, and will not say a word to her. She bundles his coat off him, his arms pulling, pulling away from her, to get away from her, and runs instantly upstairs. She hears his feet pound each step. There is a moment when the house seems to hold its breath, and then she hears the door slam, and realizes she was only waiting for that sound.

She looks to Kadi, her eldest.

'What happened?'

Kadi shrugs. She looks resigned rather than angry, which worries Shri more. Kadi goes over to Nisha's pen and climbs inside, offering her hand to the toddler to clutch and play with. Shri trails her, still holding on to Sasha's coat.

'Kadi, tell me. Why has Sasha been in a fight?'

Kadi glances up at her and returns her attention to Nisha.

'Why do you think?'

'Just tell me.'

'Because they found out,' says Kadi, matter-of-factly. 'They found out about Dad.' She turns to the child. 'Hey, Nish. What's this? What's this? Pen-guin. Say the word. Say "pen".'

Shri knows she should ask what they are saying, the other kids, those little shits, but she doesn't have the energy. She can only think about how it was before, when Taeo was first convicted: remembering the names, the daily scrapes and bruises, the puddle of urine on the front step and the shit smeared on the door, having to scrape it off; the smell seemed to linger for days and even when it was gone it was there in her nostrils. By comparison, the humiliation of having to leave her job barely registered. She stands in front of the pen, looking at her two daughters, feeling a sense of panic infusing her body until she can't do anything except force herself to stay upright, holding Sasha's coat tighter and tighter against her body. Nyari Town is the absolute back-ice. How much further will they have to go to get away from this? Where else is left to them?

Kadi gets to her feet with Nisha hanging on to one hand.

'It's okay, Mum. We'll deal with it.'

That is not your responsibility, thinks Shri. She can hear thuds from upstairs which must be Sasha taking out his rage on something, and as happens at least once a day, she is filled with grief that this has happened to her children, and fury towards Taeo that he has *done this to them*.

'I'm going to make Nisha's tea,' says Kadi.

Shri nods, wearily. She slumps on her back on the sofa and gestures up the most mindless of channels (Taeo's cousin would not approve, but Taeo's cousin is not back for at least an hour), fighting the temptation to lose herself in a trashy immersive. She's always scorned those particular genres but lately her brain can't engage with anything more intellectual than *Last of the Penguins*. She's spent hours zoned in to the Adélie penguin colony on the far side of the continent, following them around. It's not like they do anything – walk around, come back, dive into the ocean, come back, catch fish, eat fish. This is what her days are reduced to. She wonders whether it's time to tell Taeo the truth. She's kept the worst of it from him, not even to spare him so much as out of a sense of pride, not wanting to admit that this is out of her control. She can't handle it. *I can't do it on my own, there isn't enough of me.* On a spur of action, she jumps up from the sofa, grabs a holoma and activates the recording. She'll tell him everything. He deserves to know.

She pauses, holoma in hand.

She can't do it.

How many times has she been here, propped up by rage, on the verge of speech? Every time, something stops her. The thought of Taeo, alone, in Patagonian exile, hearing this about his children. She can't do it. She can't. A bomb like this might derail him completely. And even now, after everything they've been through, she just can't bear to hurt him that much.

You're an idiot, Shri, she tells herself.

And she laughs.

'Ha!'

The sound short and compressed. Masked by the inane chatter from the channel.

From the kitchen, she hears Kadi singing to Nisha. A Portuguese song. For a week after Taeo's departure she refused to speak his language of the home, insisting upon Hindi or patois, an act of revenge which hurt only herself and which Kadi and Sasha openly defied, so now they're back to their usual hybrids.

She mutes the holovid and orders the holoma to record. She'll send the singing. She'll send the lie.

Things go on this way, no better, no worse, until the news comes, on a Tuesday late in November. After it comes, Tuesdays will be different, but Shri doesn't know that when she wakes up, in the narrow single bed of Taeo's cousin's house, and checks on Nisha in her cot. Nisha's small agile limbs have managed to twist all the blankets around her, like a cocoon. Her eyes pop open as Shri leans over the railing and she stares curiously up. She has a persistent stare, this one. Stubborn, like her fool of a father. Shri straightens the blanket. She gives the mobile a tiny push and the metal birds dance and Nisha's eyes follow the birds, follow the birds in their many colours. Shri smiles. She tries to appreciate the moments like this – to make herself notice them – stacking up the tiny victories like seeds, as though their multitude might distract her from the greater, deeper gulf of the days. She wiggles Nisha's fingers, wraps her dressing gown around her, pulls on her slippers – it's cold, the heaters are on low to save energy – and goes to wake Kadi and Sasha in the bunk beds.

'Up, you two, up now. Who's first in the shower?'

In the top bunk, Kadi groans and pulls the duvet over her head.

'It's too early. . .'

Shri takes hold of a visible foot and pulls steadily until Kadi begins to slide.

'Up, madam. Haven't you got that test today? Siberian, isn't it?'

'I feel sick. I can't go in.'

'Shower, now.'

Kadi grumbles her way into the bathroom. Shri makes breakfast for the children and they eat like they always do, as if the apocalypse is coming. Taeo always made breakfast. He is a morning person. She is not. Mornings to Shri are things to be endured. Taeo's cousin Felícia eats a bowl of porridge that wouldn't feed a flea and her gaze skims over the family with that vaguely disapproving air that Shri has learned to ignore. Shri checks her son anxiously for signs of resistance, but today he eats his breakfast, face blank as a virgin ice field.

After breakfast, Felícia goes to the lab to work and Shri walks the children to school. It's always a wrench at the gates, seeing their faces drop. She hardens herself. What choice do they have? Their father's actions have already put them at a social disadvantage; without an education, their chances of success will plummet even further.

'Good luck with the Siberian!' she calls to Kadi, who pulls a face, then runs up to a couple of friends. That's progress, thinks Shri. Another seed in the pile. Briefly she scans the other kids, who are mucking about with their snowboards, watching for signs of trouble and wondering which ones are responsible for the now-regular bruises on her son –

Sasha will never tell her. She can't bear to watch his slouching progress into the playground and she turns away quickly, determined not to cry.

She walks back home, hands dug deep in her pockets, boots crunching in the snow. She thinks about what she will do with her day. There are some bits of accounting work that have come in, mercifully, so she can give Felícia some money for rent. She should finish those first. She should contact her lawyer about the appeal. There's been no movement for weeks, and at the amount he charges they are almost bankrupt. She has done so much research she feels like she knows the law better than he does by now.

An official is standing outside the apartment block where Taeo's cousin lives. He's in Civilian Security uniform. As she approaches, unease growing, he says, 'Shri Nayar?'

Shri's throat is suddenly very dry. There is only one reason in the world for Civilian Security to speak to her. Her partner. Taeo.

'Yes. Yes, that's me.'

He says they should go inside. She refuses. Going inside is final, and this cannot be final. Going inside is something that cannot be undone. She will not go inside. She tells the official this: I will not.

She does not really hear the next words. When the official speaks, his breath mists in the air. She watches the mist made by the words *sorry* and *tragic death* and *overdose*. She watches how it is made and how it dissipates. Different shapes from different words. It is cold out here. It is very cold.

The official asks if she understands. She says she does, and then she shouts, surprising herself. What does that mean? What does it mean, overdose?

He says it all again. He gives her a holoma. His blunt, rough-hewn features are scrunched in sympathy. She turns and stumbles away, down the road, holding the holoma. She cannot bear to see the sympathy, or his face, any longer. She passes rows of buildings covered in snow. A plough drives slowly past, clearing the night's fall from the tracks. She staggers out of the way. The driver calls out, asking if she is all right there. She ignores her. Keeps walking. When the tears make it impossible to see where she is going she stops and sits where she is in the street. She takes her gloves off and holds the holoma in her chill hands and activates it.

The projection is a senior Civilian Security official, her uniform marked with multiple signatory leaves of the Republic. Her face bears a stern, resolute empathy. She relays what Shri has heard: that Shri's partner died abroad, in service to the Republic. The circumstances were tragic and deeply regretful. In recognition of Taeo's service, he has been issued a posthumous pardon for his breach of the official secrets act. A statement will appear in the press tomorrow. There is a contact number if Shri has any questions.

Shri cups the holoma in both palms. She feels the cold burrowing into her hands and her feet. It is a terrible thing, the cold, and yet she would happily lie down in it, right now, let it take her, embrace her, encompass her like a lover. She would let it turn her heart to ice, because it would be easier, that way. She thinks of the pile of seeds she has amassed and she knows that all the seeds in all the world will not be enough now, or ever again. But she does not lie down. She sits, her frozen hands cupping the holoma, unable to let go. A part of her is surprised, that the world still exists, that people hurry past, noses in their snoods, that clouds still move in the sky. Around her, fresh snow starts to fall, very gently, carpeting the streets of Nyari Town. In a burst of clarity it comes to Shri, who has always considered herself a patriot, that the Republic is responsible for her partner's death. One way or another, they have killed him.

NUNAVUT, ALASKA

From: Commander-in-Chief Katu Ben
To: President Jo Forna
Date of recording: 23.11.2417

This is Ben. What can I tell you, it's bad here. The white coats have confirmed it's a Type 9. We've informed civilians. Martial law was established within hours of detection and we've set up an airtight perimeter around Nunavut. I can assure you nothing's getting in or out that we don't see, nothing at all. The drones are on a roving circuit and will pick up anyone who isn't trying to use the roads. What else? The usual procedures. Medic unit have begun tests and we've already evacuated the first group who tested negative. There weren't many of them, I'm sorry to say. As we anticipated, the virus is moving at significant speed.

I advise keeping our airships grounded. We can't risk letting anything cross the airspace. And I suggest being frank with our counterparts in Veerdeland and Sino-Siberia. They deserve to be kept in the loop, and besides, we could do with a bailout from the Siberian bank. I heard there was an incident on the Veerdeland west coast but they've confirmed it's a Type 3. Between you and me the Veerdeland security isn't as tight as it could be, but a 3 is treatable and even the Veerdelanders should have it under control within the week.

From: Commander-in-Chief Katu Ben
To: President Jo Forna
Date of recording: 01.12.2417

This is Ben. Day nine of martial law. I've got civilians trying to scale the barricades. It's extraordinary the lengths they'll go to to try and get their face in front of an officer and their kids out the city. Even when their kids are infected. Yesterday a man tried to smuggle himself into the compound inside a rice delivery, honestly it's like the regressed south here. I've taken to wearing my hazard suit all the time, even when I'm sleeping. We all have. We had an unfortunate incident with one of the squad in the northern quarter of the city – had his suit ripped open. He was infected and we had to eliminate him directly. He understood, of course. And it goes without saying it's kinder than the alternative. The troops have been more careful about their suits since then, so at least it's taught them a valuable lesson.

The other thing. I don't have much time but you said it was important. You're certain it's Antarctican? Who's the fellow in the hologram, this Taeo Ybanez, are you sure it's a genuine source? We can't trust those voracious bastards for a second. If it's genuine – well – then we have a scenario. A scenario which if you want my opinion is guaranteed to have Tark involvement. Five minutes, soldier, five minutes dammit! Sorry, sir, as you see we're in the middle of a shitstorm here. My advice – put it out in the open. The Nuuk summit's coming up, make a statement there. Say, I don't know, we've intercepted their technology, something about evidence. "New evidence suggests that the sea city did survive the Great Storm of sixty-seven." That sort of thing. Say we'll get to the bottom of this mysterious disappearance – and I assure you, sir, I will get to the bottom of it. Once we've resolved this crisis, that is. We don't want people thinking we're abandoning them to go play with the southerners. But let's make the Tarks sweat.

From: Commander-in-Chief Katu Ben
To: President Jo Forna
Date of recording: 05.12.2417

This is Ben. Day thirteen. The situation's getting rapidly worse. We've evacuated another five clean groups but the last one had to be terminated – too many people trying to get into the airship field, and to be honest with you, sir, it was messy. Regrettably, there were civilian casualties. Although they may be the lucky ones when this is over.

As you can see from my face, I'm exhausted. My troops are exhausted. We're stretched far too tight. Those in the city are working double and treble shifts – I've had to send dispatches into the neighbouring regions to contain the riots.

I've got the nukes on standby. I await your jurisdiction of course but I strongly recommend that if we cross the seventy per cent threshold we take immediate action. We have to face the likelihood that Nunavut is lost.

Will you do me a favour and give my love to Ellie? Comms have been patchy and I haven't managed to see her face in the last two days. I know she'll be worrying about her dad.

From: Commander-in-Chief Katu Ben
To: President Jo Forna
Date of recording: 12.12.2417

This is Ben. Day – I'm losing track, it's been so long – day twenty? The threshold is at seventy-five per cent. I see no option but to neutralize the affected zone. So, as per your instructions, we're pulling out now. Once we're clear of the fallout zone I'll issue the strike. I'm sorry it's come to this. Remember, sir, we don't have a choice. People will understand that you had to take action.

From: Commander-in-Chief Katu Ben
To: President Jo Forna
Date of recording: 12.12.2417

This is Ben. It's done. I'm flying out. Most of the troops managed to evacuate in time. We should arrange medals for those who didn't – something for the families. I've sent you my statement for the press.

I realize you asked me previously about Tamaruq and I didn't reply – you'll forgive the oversight, I'm sure. My thoughts are this: I know the funding's been reduced but I'm concerned, very concerned, about this Osiris issue. My advice – let's deal with that first, and then look at redirecting other streams. I can't afford to lose any more of my budget. Given the toll of this most recent tragedy, I'm sure you appreciate that.

PART THREE
THE WHITE FLY

OSIRIS

delaide has never been so certain of being recognized as in the
moment she and Dien walk into the Silk Vault. She can imagine
the cameras swivelling in her direction, honing in upon her face
and dispatching a code through the Reef to land screeching in the
earpiece of a Rechnov. The thought induces a sick, hollow dread. It's
not only the prospect of being caught. If her family discover she's
alive, she loses the precious fledgling identity which she has barely
begun to forge. It's so fragile, so easily eroded. To go back would bury
her.

But as they approach the reception she can almost see the City
attendant's mind working, along with his disdain: he thinks they're
airlifts.

'Identity?'

She and Dien produce their papers, which declare them to be two
cleaners working in the industrial northern quarter. If their IDs are spot
checked, Dien has estimated they have around thirty minutes to get
out.

A vault guard escorts Adelaide into the lift, and calls an undersea
level. This is her first trip City-side since that fatal dash across the border,
months ago, and after all the surreal experiences of a journey in reverse,

it is this lift that impresses on her the most the gulf between City and west. The hydraulics are silent, the two-metre cube is plush and mirrored. Adelaide avoids her reflection. The luxury of the building feels oppressive, confirming what she already suspected: the City doesn't fit her any more.

The guard leads Adelaide into a small room with a single work station and an o'screen.

'The vault is in whose name?'

'It's Mikkeli.'

She notes the contraction of the guard's brow. Her anxiety increases. Mikkeli's name is all Vikram told her – what if there was a second name, a code, something he forgot in the panic of the moment?

'Have you accessed the Silk Vault before?'

'No,' she manages.

'Each vault is coded with the DNA of its owner and the individuals permitted to access it. I'll need a blood sample.'

'My DNA?'

'Needless to say, all samples are anonymous, as are their counter matches which we hold on file.' The guard gives a long-suffering smile. 'As I'm sure you can imagine, we have some jittery customers. When you're ready, I just need your finger.'

Adelaide holds out her index finger, pad upwards. She feels a small sharp prick when the tester is applied to her fingertip, and a bead of blood spheres on her skin. It must have been easy enough for Vikram to obtain a sample of her DNA – a stray hair left on his pillow would have sufficed, or a swab from her toothbrush. Strange to think that those little domesticities, so unthought of at the time, should bring her to this place.

The guard takes the tester over to an o'screen and plugs it into a dock. Adelaide watches nervously as the woman scans the results, trying not to think about all the places that screen might lead, about the checks and spyware which could be running on the software, ready to pick up any anomaly – like a dead woman's DNA.

The guard frowns. Adelaide feels a trickle of sweat inching down her back, gathering at the base of her spine.

The guard scratches at the skin behind her ear. Her expression clears.

'Yes, that's a match. Well, come on through, I'll show you the vault.'

'Wait.' This is the gamble, the real reason she is here. 'There's one other.'

'Another vault?'

'Yes.'

'What's the name?'

'Axel Rechnov.'

'Axel Rechnov?'

The guard's voice lifts with surprise.

'Yes.'

Her throat is dry. What is the guard thinking? What does that name mean to her, a dead man's name, a madman's name, the Architect's grandson? Can she recognize Adelaide behind what now seems a pitifully thin disguise?

She waits for the guard to react. To shout or sound an alarm. She reminds herself, I'm not a criminal, playing dead is not a crime. Although now there's the inciting revolution, yes that, that might well be considered a crime. She waits. But the guard returns to the o'screen and dutifully enters the name.

'Yes,' she says. Adelaide can sense the struggle as she tries to maintain a neutral expression. 'That's a match too. But the vault is located in one of our sister branches. Would you like it brought here?'

'How long will that take?'

'As it is a small vault we can transport it here within thirty minutes.'

She fights to keep the dismay from her face. Thirty minutes is far too long. But this may be her only chance.

'I'll wait.'

The guard enters further information.

'I have put in the request. Come with me.'

The guard leads Adelaide further down the empty, white-walled corridor. This is something else she has forgotten: the space, the absence of people. They stop by a numbered door and the guard swipes them into a room that is also empty, except for a single chair and a table.

'Please wait here. I will return once your second vault is on site.'

'Thank you.'

The door closes behind the guard. Adelaide sits, then instantly stands again. She can't shake the feeling that this is a trap. That at any moment the door will burst open and skadi will pin her to the floor, or worse, a member of her family will step through.

It occurs to her that there may be other vaults in her name, in other branches. Her grandfather would be the sort to do that. Heirlooms locked away in boxes, the way he hoarded secrets in the attic of his brain.

Her nervousness increases. She can't pretend she's not scared of what she might find here today. She takes out her scarab, prepared to risk a call to Dien, only to find there is no signal this far under-water.

The next thirty minutes are the longest of her life.

At last she hears the door handle turning. She stands, tense, prepared to fight if necessary. But it is the guard, returning as promised with two slender rectangular boxes made of a lightweight steel, featureless except for the names branded into the metal. Adelaide's relief is crushing.

The guard holds aloft the DNA sample she took from Adelaide before.

'This is your key. You hold it against the activator, here. Push the buzzer by the door when you are done and I'll come and collect you.'

'Thank you.'

The guard nods and departs once again.

Left alone, Adelaide is reluctant to open either box; she looks from one to the other, torn. But she doesn't have the leisure of time. Dien is up there in the foyer, counting the minutes. Alone and exposed. Dien put herself on the line to get them in here, based on nothing but a hunch, a feeling that there is something Adelaide needs to see; and she's already exceeded their agreed time limit.

She opens the box in Mikkeli's name first. It is empty except for a folded piece of paper and a necklace. She recognizes the necklace at once: a shark tooth strung on a single cord. The last time she saw it, the necklace was around her twin's neck.

The letter is a copy. Her brother's handwriting leaps from the page, blotched here and there with frenzied splatters of ink. She already knows what the letter says: Vikram recited it to her word for word. It is Axel's goodbye note.

She folds the letter back and slips it into her pocket. As she activates the key on the second box, she notices her hands are trembling.

What the hell did you find, Axel. . .

Inside is a sheaf of papers, each stamped with a familiar motif. She has seen this symbol before. Six-legged. Translucent-winged.

Operation Whitefly.

She spreads the papers over the table and begins to read.

The papers are in no particular order. They date sporadically from the past fifty years. There are logs of ships approaching the city. Ships from other places. Ships from land. There are execution orders for the crews of those ships. She reads through the list, disbelieving.

Polaris, 14

Cepheus Blue, 11

Svetlana, 7

Draconis V, 21—

It goes on.

Some of the names have scribbled notes against them. *Some resistance encountered. We had to weight them. . .* There are references to meetings. Payments made to certain members of the skadi. Records of Osirians who tried to leave the city, but were incarcerated or removed. There are documents signed by the founding family elders.

The names include Leonid Rechnov, Adelaide's grandfather.

She stops reading, overcome with nausea. Panicking, she looks around the room again. There are no receptacles, nothing but the chair she is sitting on and the table in front of her and the two vaults. She clamps her hand over her mouth, trying to swallow down the rising bile, but her stomach heaves irrepressibly. She grabs Axel's empty vault and vomits into it.

She slams the lid of the box shut and pushes it away from her. Sweat prickles her skin. She feels contaminated, unclean. It isn't just the shock, or even the mounting sense of horror over what she has discovered. Worse than that, she can't ignore the idea that some part of her already knew – or could have known, if she'd only thought to follow the signs.

And now she knows the truth she wishes she had stayed in the west, anonymous, that she had never met Dien, never got sucked into playing at revolution, because that's what it feels like compared to this: a game.

She thinks of her grandfather, slowly ageing in a brocaded room, a glass of octopya clutched in his trembling fingers. She remembers the intensity in Leonid's voice as he muttered something she did not, at the time, understand.

Nothing but the white fly.

And then he said something else.

Don't be too quick to judge me.

He knew, she thinks. He knew I'd find out. Perhaps he knew Axel already had.

The contents of Axel's vault could bring down the city's entire infrastructure. The founding families. Adelaide's family. Regardless of which individuals know what, all of the lines would be discredited. The elders would be stripped of their privileges, put on trial, perhaps even executed under Osirian law.

Her grandfather, who she loves, has signed off on these despicable acts. He's lied to her. He's lied to everyone.

Once again the nausea threatens to overcome her. She presses her hands to her mouth, swallowing.

And yet he's so old now. So frail. She would be surprised if he lived out the year. Does he deserve this exposure, at this stage in his life? Even knowing what he has done, the idea of him being dragged from the Domain and drowned in an execution tank is repellent. Surely he must have believed he was acting out of necessity?

But if Whitefly is still in enforcement, then there must be others who condone it. Her father, Feodor, for certain. Linus? Does Linus know about Whitefly? Linus, who said quite clearly on the o'dio *we must expect the unexpected?*

Linus knows.

The taste of bile lingers on her tongue and at the back of her throat. She is trapped in this room, trapped between the truth and the outside world. What in stars' names is she supposed to do now?

And yet, at the very edge of her fear, barely in focus, there is something else. She felt it before, watching the expedition boat leave. She feels it now. Hope. That because of this – because of this terrible and terrifying truth – there might be something else out there.

There might be land. There might be people.

I wish you could have seen this, Vikram. I wish you could have known.

The minutes count down too quickly as she sits in the white-walled room, wondering what to do.

If she leaves the documents here, and remains silent, she is complicit in a conspiracy that affects every soul in the city.

If she takes them out of this room, the documents will be in Dien's hands, for Dien to do whatever Dien thinks is right.

She knows the western woman won't hesitate to use them.

Finally she takes Axel's necklace and pulls it over her head, tucking the cord under her clothes. The shark tooth nestles against her sternum. Then she stuffs the Whitefly papers back into Mikkeli's vault and calls the guard.

'What the fuck took you so long?'

Dien is fraught with impatience – and something else too. The thirty minutes are long past, and Dien is frightened. She doesn't like being this side of the border. As they hurry outside, Adelaide feels the same fear infecting her. The sleek beauty of the Osirian architecture rings too bright and false; the windows glint, malevolent, screening the players within. She fights to suppress a surge of paranoia.

'Not here.'

They barely exchange a word for the duration of the return journey, but Dien keeps herself as close as Adelaide's shadow. When they reach Dien's apartment, a few of the activists are engaged in a lively meeting. Dien expels everyone but herself and Adelaide. They disperse with reluctance.

'So? Was it worth it?'

Adelaide pulls out the necklace.

'This was my brother's.'

'And?'

She extracts the letter from her pocket.

'His goodbye note.'

'Is that it?'

Adelaide hesitates, twisting the shark tooth between thumb and finger. The enamel is smooth, the shark long dead. She thinks of her brother at the moment of writing, the horses cantering at the back of his mind even as he scripted his goodbye. She thinks of the ships who came looking, their carcasses sunk beyond the Atum Shelf with the weighted bones of the crews; the loved ones on land who would wonder, and after a time would try and fail to grieve, because they could not let go of a chance, an obstinate sliver of chance, that something might come back. She thinks of a burning tower, western hands pulling her from the waves, Mikaela's voice: *because you need us.* A man with a scalpel and a salt box. Ole's silent plea. She thinks of Dien's face, bloodied and swollen, her breath huffing in the icy night, Adelaide's body a mine of aches. *Are you done?*

Dien, who is staring at her now, waiting for an answer.

She could lie, of course. She could tell Dien anything she wanted and Dien would believe her, because somehow, on that strange and volatile night, they reached an accord.

But she is done with lies.

'Sit down,' she says. 'There's something I need to tell you about. It's called Operation Whitefly, and it's been going on for a very long time.'

When she has finished talking, Dien sits with her hands clasped very tightly together, stupefied into silence. Adelaide has never seen her at a loss for words.

'Fuck,' says Dien at last. 'Fuck.'

She stands up, sits down, and stands up again. She starts to circle the apartment.

'This changes everything.'

'I know.'

'This – will bring down the Osiris Council.'

'It would do.'

Dien pauses briefly by the window-wall. 'You have to go back and get those papers, Rechnov.'

'My family would be arrested. Possibly killed.'

'Your family deserve to be killed. They're murderers. Listen to what you're telling me! They've executed entire crews, for stars' sake. They've torpedoed ships.'

'That was a long time ago – most of it happened after the Great Storm. My grandfather is dying.' She keeps her voice firm. Dien will pounce on any hint of weakness. 'He won't last the year.'

Dien shakes her head.

'Justice comes late. But it's still justice.' She nibbles at her lower lip, smudging what's survived of her lipstick. 'It's still justice.'

'Dien. I won't let them take him.'

'You can't sit on this. This is our passport to breaking open the border!'

'You think so?'

Something in Adelaide's tone stops Dien in her tracks.

'Of course it is.'

'You think because you can expose my family, and a couple of other families, that the Council will suddenly open up the border?'

'If we're the ones to expose them—'

'No. They'll clamp down even harder. If they don't claim it's a hoax, they'll twist the whole thing to make out that they were the ones to uncover the conspiracy. They'll make examples of the Rechnovs, the Dumays and the Ngozis. But the rest – the rest will survive.'

'You're wrong,' says Dien. But for the first time, she sounds uncertain. Adelaide feels a flicker of sympathy.

'I know the City. I know how they work.'

'So what? You think we should ignore this? Let your arsehole family get away with it, while you and I carry on as if nothing's happened?' Dien delivers a vicious kick to the bufferglass, and looks as if she's about to follow it up with her fist, before thinking better of it. 'Hell's teeth!' she shouts.

'No, I'm not saying that. We can't do that.'

'Then what do you propose, Rechnov? What the fuck do you propose?'

'We need a meeting with Linus.'

'Your brother?'

'Get him to come to the west. Listen. There's one more thing. The distress signal, the one no one has ever answered? There's a reason for that. Whitefly started blocking it, less than a year after the Great Storm. We need to get that signal back out – let people know we're still here. And for that, we need Linus.'

Dien looks disgusted.

'I need a fucking drink.'

Raqua was never Adelaide's drink of choice, but she savours it now, both the fiery taste on her tongue and the burn that drops right to the stomach. Across the room, Dien sits on the floor, her back to the window-wall. She has switched off her scarab. Dusk is falling but Dien leaves the lights off, and doesn't move, and Adelaide knows better than to disturb her. In the gathering gloom, all the events of the last few weeks seem to bleed together. The days adrift. The man who tried to assault her. Dien. The meet. The gatherings that followed. The crowds of westerners. The vault.

'How did he find all this?'

Dien's voice is low and slurred.

'How did your brother know?'

'I don't know.' Adelaide's thoughts turn with difficulty to Axel. The slow, insidious progress of his illness, the vacancies that had opened up in his mind where before there had been dervishes of thought. 'I don't know when Axel discovered this. I don't know if it was the thing that made him go mad, or if he didn't even know what it was.'

'You said something, at the meet. You said something about horses. That he saw things.'

'He had hallucinations.'

'You said you saw them sometimes too.'

'Maybe.' She doesn't like to think too much about that other woman, Ata. The one who had given up, in a way that seems inconceivable now. 'Or maybe I just expected to see them.'

'There are other people like Axel, you know. In the west. He wasn't unique.'

Adelaide can no longer make out the features of Dien's face, only her silhouette against the meagre light through the window-wall.

'People who have visions,' says Dien. 'People who kill themselves. It happens all the time, but no one talks about it. If people knew there was something else out there – that there was land, something to give them hope. . .'

Adelaide speaks gently.

'You've asked me about Axel, now answer me something. I asked you, before, why you were doing this. You said there were a lot of reasons.'

'And you want to know what they are.'

'I want to understand.'

'I wasn't lying, Rechnov. There are a lot of reasons. But it's not like you're probably thinking. It's not like I can just list them, or there's some dramatic event that changed everything. Here, pass me the raqua, will you?'

Adelaide refills both their glasses, and passes one to Dien. She waits.

'It's – a thousand little things,' says Dien. She takes a gulp of the raqua. 'You know, most people just want to get on with things as best they can, without hurting anyone else. And I was like that. For a long time, I was like that. I had my job and it wasn't easy, I worked long hours, overtime that wasn't paid, but I was good at it. I knew I was good at it. What do you call that, Rechnov? Job satisfaction.' She laughs, but not unkindly. 'Well, you wouldn't know, and that's just what you were born to. Your luck. But yeah. I started noticing things, little things, everyday things. Friends who had run-ins with the skadi for no good reason, just because a skad was bored and wanted to kick off. Having to wait five weeks to get an electrician out, or another patient in the morgue because we didn't have the right meds. It wasn't worse than before, I was just noticing it. And then I couldn't stop noticing it. And one day I turned around and realized I wasn't the person I'd been a year ago, or two years ago, or whenever I'd last – taken stock. But, having got to that point, I did have to admit that there wasn't a reset button. I could carry on doing what I was doing and driving myself slowly mad, or I could do something about it. After that. . . it was only a matter of time before I ended up with this crowd.'

She drains her glass.

'There you go, Rechnov. There's your story.'

'Thank you. For telling me. I needed to hear it.'

Dien laughs.

'You're surprising, I'll give you that. I never expected to tolerate you.'

'You're too kind.'

The stiffness in Adelaide's spine is a deep ache, as though she and Dien have been here for a long time, for longer than logic dictates; for years, decades, they have been in this room, having this conversation.

'Dien. We will expose this, I promise you. But we'll do it together. It's our best chance of reconciliation between west and City. I've trusted you. I've done what you've asked. You have to trust me now.'

'Looks like I don't have much choice.'

'No. You don't.'

She hears Dien sigh, a soft expulsion of breath. The sound brings an unnerving sense of premonition, and she gets to her feet, aware of being drunker than she expected, suddenly craving light.

Her world has changed, and changed again. The gulf of what she and Dien know and what the rest of the city do not. She feels it in everything she undertakes, from a purchase of coral tea from the vendor on Wintervine waterway, to her latest rallying speech to another packed, sweaty bar where the press of crowds is at once exhilarating and terrifying. With the burden of their shared knowledge, she and Dien have become conspirators. However dark the secret, there is a thrill in this collusion, a sense of pitting themselves against the world that reminds her of the early days with Vikram. The comparison is odd and confusing. Dien and Vikram might be from the same place, even share some philosophies, but in all other ways they are aeons apart. A small, insidious whisper at the back of her mind starts and will not be ceased: was it even Vikram she fell in love with? Or only the idea of him, born from the romance of unison, of going to war together?

The other activists treat her now with a wary acceptance. They have invited a shark into their home, one who professes itself friendly but cannot be trusted not to revert to form.

Her speeches are printed on flyers and handed out on the waterways. To the west, she has another name. The Silverfish. One day she sees a new graffiti on the wall of a tower, a leaping fish in metallic paint, and her heart jumps with something like pride.

They agree how they will play it. Dien will act as the Silverfish while Adelaide listens in from the next room. The level of traction Dien can gain with Linus will decide whether Adelaide needs to step in. She is reluctant to show her face; to reveal herself will compromise their position.

Dien has selected a safehouse close to the border with easy escape routes in all directions, each assigned a guard.

Linus, as Adelaide predicted, brings his people to the tower but leaves them outside.

Dien is pacing. She looks nervous. It occurs to Adelaide that Dien would not have let this show in front of her, before.

'You can deal with him,' says Adelaide. 'He's only my brother.'

Dien gives her a look and mutters, 'Exactly.'

Adelaide takes up her assigned place in the next room. Minutes later she hears a rap at the door and the sound of footsteps entering. For a few excruciating seconds there is silence. Adelaide imagines the two evaluating one another. She hopes desperately that her assessment of Linus is correct. If this goes wrong, it is all on her.

'The Silverfish, I believe?'

Even prepared, the sound of her brother's voice comes as a shock. The last time she saw Linus, she was begging him not to leave her alone with their father's bodyguard, while he locked her into the penthouse. The memory stiffens her resolution. Linus is going to help them today. She'll make sure of it.

'That's me.'

Dien sounds calm, assured. Good. She's got a grip on herself.

'You asked me to come here, and here I am. Alone, as requested.'

'You brought your people to the tower.'

'If you know anything about me, you should know I'm not stupid.'

'That's why I contacted you, and not anyone else.'

'Should I be flattered?'

Adelaide can't suppress a smile. So very Linus.

'Not really,' says Dien. 'It's more a case of limited options.'

She hears the scrape of a chair being drawn up. She can imagine him sitting there, one leg neatly crossed over the other, brain ticking away behind a face that can never quite escape the imperious.

'There's something we know about,' says Dien. 'Something I think you know about too. Something that would be. . . very unfortunate, if it came out.'

'Get to your point.'

'Before I do, I'd better tell you that I'm not the only one who knows about this information. If you do anything – if anything happens to me, after this meeting – I've issued instructions for it to be released at once. And trust me, this is going to be of great interest to the public – your side and mine.'

Linus sighs.

'Of course.'

Now Adelaide wishes she could see his face. He must be running through the possibilities. Clearly it is some kind of scandal. Has Whitefly occurred to him? Is he even now mounting his defence?

'Operation Whitefly,' says Dien.

A beat. Another.

'I've no idea what you're talking about,' says Linus.

But there is a rigidity in his tone. She can hear it, even if Dien can't.

'We both know that's a lie, Linus Rechnov. You know a hell of a lot about Operation Whitefly.'

'I'm afraid you'll have to explain yourself.'

'We've got papers,' says Dien. 'Documentation. And, wow, it has some interesting things to say. There's a lot about boats. Boats coming to this city, but never leaving it. People going missing, because they've been shot to pieces by skadi. And it's been going on for years. A whole conspiracy set up to keep us believing there's no one else out there. Names are mentioned, Linus Rechnov.'

Linus laughs. 'It sounds like a spectacular theory.'

Dien ignores him.

'Let me see, who is mentioned? Oh yes. Your grandfather. The Architect, Leonid Rechnov. He features rather prominently. Then there's your father, Feodor Rechnov. Such a beloved politician, isn't he. . .'

'You don't have these papers here, I suppose?'

'If you know anything about me, you should know I'm not stupid.'

Linus does not rise to the barb.

'Again, how convenient.'

'Even if they were a forgery – which we both know they're not, however long you sit there denying it – you're a politician, aren't you, Linus? Don't you know that the story – the rumour – is always enough? To destroy you?'

Don't get carried away, thinks Adelaide. You've got to step carefully. He's clever, cleverer than you think.

'Don't tell me you don't have enemies,' Dien continues. 'I don't believe everyone your side of the city worships the Rechnovs. There must be plenty of folk who'd like to take up the mantle of "founding family"—'

Linus cuts in smoothly. 'I'm very sorry, but if this story is all you have—'

'Get in here! He's going to call for backup!'

That wasn't their agreed signal. Adelaide scrambles to her feet, propelled by the urgency in Dien's voice.

The shock on Linus's face when she enters the room is unmistakable. He is standing, clearly about to make some kind of move, and with a jolt of apprehension, Adelaide remembers the invisible tracker placed on Vikram. Dien's eyes meet Adelaide's across the room.

'Sorry. I couldn't risk him doing a runner.'

'It's all right. You didn't have a choice.'

Adelaide turns her attention to Linus. He's aged. Even in these few months, it's noticeable. There's grey at his temples, and the lines around his mouth and eyes have deepened. Worry lines, she thinks. She wonders if he's thinking the same of her – but then, to him she's a dead woman.

'Hello, brother dear.'

Linus sinks heavily into his chair. His mouth works, seeking words, before he gives up and settles on surveillance, taking in her hair, her face, her attire, a dazed expression continuing to occupy his features.

'Adelaide,' he says at last. And then, 'The Silverfish.'

'Yes.'

She waits.

'I thought you were dead.'

Adelaide waves.

'Surprise.'

Linus's brow contracts.

'I knew something didn't add up. She—' He nods towards Dien. 'She wasn't right.'

'Hey, watch your mouth,' Dien interjects.

'Ignore him,' Adelaide says softly. 'He's trying to remind you I'm from the City.'

'Already? He doesn't mess around, does he?'

'No.'

She watches Linus watching her, noticing the dynamic between her and Dien, trying to work out how he can play it.

'That's why we need him,' she says.

Linus rubs the heels of his hands into his eyes.

'Fucking hell, it really is you. How did you get out of that tower?'

'After you authorized the skadi to blow it up with me inside, you mean?'

'Is that what I'm here for?'

'It doesn't matter how I got out. We're here to talk about Whitefly. Now promise me, Linus – and remember *I know you* – promise me you haven't set us up.'

He looks at her, the incredulity still there.

'No. I came because I was interested. I gave her – you – my word.'

'Good.'

'We can trust him?' asks Dien.

'For now.'

'What the hell are you doing here, this side of the border? We – I thought you were dead!'

'That doesn't matter. And don't tell me anyone grieved for me either, because I won't believe you. Tell us about Whitefly.'

Linus seems to crumple.

'How did you find out about Whitefly?'

'Axel left me some interesting material.'

'Axel was delusional.'

'Yes. But what he found was real.'

Linus doesn't answer.

'It's true, isn't it?'

'Yes.'

The word seems to evacuate him, leaving behind a husk. For a moment Adelaide glimpses the man behind the politician: tired, no, exhausted, a man weary of the world and his role within it.

'How long have you known?' she asks.

'Not as long as you seem to think. Dmitri knows, of course – doesn't bother him. We could be living on the moon for all he cares, as long as it doesn't affect his precious trading. Our dear father didn't see fit to induct me into its mysteries until I started pledging support for the west.' Linus falls into reflection. 'That changed everything.'

'Why didn't you tell me?'

He laughs at that, a brief spark through the weariness. 'Do you really need to ask? Tell you, the most capricious person in the City? I'd be insane.'

'I had a right to know. Me and Axel. We both did.'

'Believe me, you were better off not knowing,' he says.

'He's right about that,' Dien remarks. 'We all were. Because now we have to do something about it.'

Linus's gaze slides to Dien.

'And what exactly do you propose we do about it? If this comes out I might as well write my own execution order.'

'That's why we're giving you an ultimatum. The Silverfish here, and me.' Dien nods to Adelaide. 'Tell him. You're right, he listens to you, fuck knows why.'

'We do have evidence,' she says. 'And Dien will use it, unless you get the distress signal back out.'

'Stars above, you are actually insane. How the hell am I supposed to do that?'

'You're the only one who can. The Facility, am I right? That's where Operation Whitefly runs from. Right above my old penthouse. Ironic, really. Some might even say, sadistic.'

'You were the only person who would never have noticed,' says Linus.

'I've noticed now. Linus, listen to me. I know you're not used to this, but I'm serious. Do you remember what you said to me? When you were trying to get me to help Vikram, all that time ago? You said people needed hope. You said there might be life outside the city. It was you who authorized the expedition boat, wasn't it? Because you knew about this. You were hoping that boat would get out. If an expedition returns, it lets you off the hook. Whitefly could be quietly buried without anyone ever having to know about it. I'm right, aren't I?'

Something tremors in Linus's face when she says the words *expedition boat*. She has hit a nerve. Now's the time to push her advantage.

'I heard you on the o'dio,' she says gently.

'What if I did authorize it?' he mutters. 'Why would I risk everything doing this?'

'You can't live with this, Linus. It's eating away at you. I get it. Me and Dien, we didn't want to find this out either. I know I used to laugh at you when you said there might be people out there. But I want to know now. I have to know. One way or another, this is coming out.'

Linus shakes his head.

'I never thought I'd see the day.'

'What?'

'You preaching right and wrong at me.'

She smiles serenely.

'That day has come.'

'The expedition boat might return,' he says hopefully. 'I know it got out.'

'Have you heard anything?'

'No. But that doesn't mean. . .' He trails off, and for a moment she has the impression his mind is working, he's holding something back. Then he slumps in his chair, defeated. 'No, I haven't heard anything.'

'All right.' Dien jumps to her feet. 'We need to know when you're going to do this. How fast can you move?'

Linus looks at her with bemusement. 'It's been a secret for fifty years. What's the rush?'

'Why wait?' Dien counters.

'I just don't understand what you're hoping to achieve.'

'It has to be broadcast on all the channels,' says Adelaide. 'Otherwise there's no point. Trust me, Linus – get that signal out again, and people will soon be asking questions. And that's all we need.'

'Let's say a week,' says Dien. 'Twenty-two hundred – that's your time. We'll be listening each night.'

He shrugs.

'Have it your way. But don't expect me to come and give you an airlift when the city descends into riots.'

'We won't.'

Linus turns to Adelaide.

'What about you? You're going to stay here like what – some kind of revolutionary?'

'Yes.'

'And you expect me to go back to the Domain and carry on this charade, pretending you're dead?'

'It's a tiny charade in comparison to the one you've been enacting.'

'Our grandfather's dying,' Linus says abruptly.

'I know.'

'His mind is deteriorating. He talks Siberian half the time now, has me reading old poetry to him. He thinks I'm Axel. He asks for you. You always were his favourite.' He states it without bitterness or resentment. 'You should see him.'

'I can't do that. I'm sorry. He has to be your responsibility now.'

At the door, Linus pauses. He speaks quietly, without looking at her.

'I did grieve for you.'

All other plans are put on hold while they wait for Linus to act, and each day that passes without the signal is a day where Dien's mood worsens. Adelaide spends as much time as she can with the Larssons, eating stew together, soaking in their silent warmth and kindness. But by the final evening of waiting her own composure is as brittle as Dien's, and in the end the tension is too much and she takes herself away from the apartment, ignoring Dien's protests.

'What if it's early? What if you miss it? Rechnov, I'm talking to you!'

'Linus is always on time,' says Adelaide.

She goes outside and walks over the raft racks, her balance easy and certain, as far as the local links will take her. Only a few weeks until midsummer. The days are long and there is a wealth of light, almost too much light; it seems inappropriate, when all their movements are so furtive.

She crouches on the raft rack, watching the soft grey dimples, the ever-moving symmetry of the water. In it, the reflections of the towers sway and muddle. People pass behind her, their footsteps hurried over the raft rack, which bows beneath their weight so the water laps against it and against the oiled toes of her boots, and she knows a moment of lost equilibrium where she might tumble forwards. The moment where she could fall feels more real than all the moments of stillness which precede it. They are on the edge of something.

The purple colour of the sky tells her it's nearing the hour. She walks back the way she came.

When she enters the apartment Dien is where she left her, folded in on herself in the chair, legs tucked under her, all of her focus on the o'dio. She doesn't say a word as Adelaide comes in and sits at the table.

Every few seconds Dien fiddles with the o'dio, but the broadcast remains the same – a late-night show, the broadcaster's words dropping into the vacuum between them. The minutes tick by. Twenty-two hundred approaches. Adelaide feels her chest tightening like a spring as the seconds tick down.

And pass the hour.

The broadcast does not change.

'You said your brother is always on time,' says Dien.

'He is.'

'So?'

'Something's happened.'

They wait. Adelaide can feel the disappointment welling around her. *Come on, Linus.*

'Maybe he got caught.' Dien pauses. 'Or maybe he lied to you. We shouldn't have trusted him.'

Adelaide can see the rigidity in her body, the strength required for Dien to hold herself up against this defeat, yet another defeat, another card in the deck stacked against her, all the things she can no longer not notice. But this time, the blame is undeniably with Adelaide.

The o'dio gurgles.

Both women tense.

* * *

This is the City of Osiris calling to all nations. If you receive this message, know that we are at the mercy of the elements and unable to leave the City. Please send help urgently. I repeat, if you receive this message, please send help.

'Oh my stars,' Dien whispers. 'Oh my actual stars.'

Adelaide looks at the clock.

It's twenty-two oh-nine.

ANTARCTICA

The call comes just after twenty-two hundred, when Karis is seconds away from bringing down the Bokolu. He's been hunting the creature for days now; stalking it through the decaying settlements of the outer empires of Tua'pala, along the tortuous path of Ruination Ridge and the dripping black forests on the dark side of the moon, and finally trekking alone across the purple outback, following the creature's tracks in the dust, smelling its pheromones. Throughout the hunt he has glimpsed the Bokolu a mere five times, but those five were enough to memorize the writhing swish of its tail and the wet click of those gigantic pincers. He's sweated and bled and lost companions along the way, one of them to the creature's jaws – he won't forget those sounds in a hurry. There are times when he has tried to climb inside the Bokolu's mind, to penetrate the alien rhythms of its thoughts and senses. Times he's thought he was going mad. And now the Bokolu is in his sights. He has a nano-rifle slung across his body and a submachine gun cradled in his arms. He's ready.

The Bokolu has seen him. It is looking directly at him.

His heart rate trebles. The sub is *heavy*.

And then the call comes through. It's Atrak.

The Bokolu begins to advance.

Seriously? It has to be now?

The call persists. It seems to come from very far away, reaching out to him across the vacuum of space, as though a tether is willowing out from Earth towards Karis on the indigo moon, and when he answers the tether connects to the helmet of his spacesuit with a magnetic snap, jerking him messily, carelessly off-world.

He rips off the sensors and lurches out of the immersive. His head is reeling.

'Yes?'

They won't tell him what it is, which means that it's serious. Ever since the boat got out they've been on high alert. He has a bad feeling.

A taxi is already waiting outside his apartment block, the driver standing in the rain to hold open the door for him. Not unattractive, Karis notices. He climbs inside and the taxi jets away at once. Covertly, he checks out the driver in the rear-view mirror and for a few moments allows himself to imagine that this is a different scenario entirely, that he's out or in the cloud and might introduce himself. The usual disclaimers run through his head – what story can I tell, what occupation, I could tell him I'm from Belgrano, I could tell him I'm from Tolstyi.

'Late call, Commander?' asks the driver, catching his eye.

'Unexpected call.'

He looks away. The bluish lights of the peninsula settlement dapple the streets and splinter through the rain. Karis pushes a sober pill into his mouth, though he hasn't been drinking. As the woolliness of the immersive fades from his body, the light shining through the rain seems less soft, as if it isn't rain at all, but the product of some clinical trial or design, like lasers, or a series of silver darts striking against the earth, darts containing messages from an unknown race in another galaxy, or the Bokolu preparing to unleash its revenge.

* * *

The team at Special Unit Atrak who monitor the city in the ocean debrief him. It's a radio signal. They play it back, and when he requests it, play it a second, and then a third time. The four of them sit there in the room where they have dutifully compiled measurements once a week for the past three years (and before then, before he took this post, others did the same; it's been going on for years, decades even), the room with its computers silently calculating shipping records and energy outputs and wavelengths, all of them now listening to this remote voice and thinking *what the fuck? What the actual fuck?*

Karis asks them to play it one more time. He asks, for form's sake, that they have checked all possible avenues that could suggest this is a hoax. Then he sends a meeting request to the home security chief. By midnight, Karis and Maxil Qyn are in the senate house with a security representative holoed in from each of the nine states.

In the senate house the radio signal is played again. There is an unreality to the recording, a sense that it is crossing not only distance but time as well, although the voice itself is clear and confident. Karis fingers the pack of sober pills in his pocket but doesn't dare take another in front of Qyn.

He is asked for a technical update, and stands up to deliver it, referring to the weekly reports from the past year, reminding them of the shipwreck on the Patagonian coast and the alleged survivor who thus far they haven't been able to locate. He shows them the holoma sent by the exiled engineer Taeo Ybanez before his death. The representatives are not really interested. They are all defenders and their attention is placed on the immediate: the lingering echo of the voice, the radio, the intruder in the night.

Maxil Qyn begins the formalities. The radio wavelength is broadcasting as far as Antarctica, which means it will also have reached Patagonia. There is little they can do to contain it now, not with immediate effect. They are left with a number of possibilities. Qyn presents each one in her usual crisp, pragmatic manner.

Scenario one: they do nothing.

Scenario two: they infiltrate the city of Osiris, deactivate the radio signal, and seek to contain the situation by surreptitious means. (Qyn does not use the word *surreptitious*, but the implication is clear.)

Scenario three: they action a total obliteration of Osiris.

The next few hours are spent in mapping and debating the theoretical consequences of these three scenarios. The representatives of the nine states weave around the issues. They are cautious with their words, their phraseology, but Karis is an analyst by trade, good at reading between lines, and what it comes down to is this:

To do nothing is effectively to issue an open invitation to the Boreals, who can be counted upon to reclaim the lost city at the earliest opportunity. Osiris was a Boreal enterprise; the northern states built it. They might have lied to the world about why they built it, but the fact remains – the city is a piece of equity. In one swoop, they will have regained their military base, and they and their new-age plagues will be one step away from the Republic's shores. (No one in the room doubts the capacity of the Boreals to subdue the Osirian population.)

To infiltrate the city may buy the Republic some time, but the end result will be the same. The Boreals will come to investigate, and take the city.

To obliterate the city will prevent the Boreals from claiming Osiris as a military base, and also increases the chances of deniability with regards to the Republic's monitoring of the city for the past fifty years. Such an action convenes both the Nuuk Treaty and the human rights convention, and would not be popular with the public, who will find out eventually, they always do – but it is likely to prevent further bloodshed down the line. An immediate cost for a longer-term gain.

Karis listens and is surprised when Maxil Qyn turns to him and says, 'Io. Thoughts?'

The others turn to look at him, waiting, a sudden quiet in the room.

The fact that they are not physically present doesn't make it any better. He feels like a specimen.

'You're talking about genocide,' says Karis.

'Genocide's an ugly word,' says Qyn, unblinking. 'We're talking about the protection of the Republic.'

Karis looks at the chief, wondering, as he has wondered plenty of times before, what exactly is the driving force behind that steely veneer. Little is known about Qyn's private life. She has a partner, who appears sometimes at official receptions, but no children. In her office there are no photographs, no paintings, no artefacts of culture or anything to signify personal taste. In their to-date limited dealings, Karis has found her stern but not unfair, and yet she must have made decisions over the years, decisions whose outcomes must by necessity be harsh, unhappy decisions where there are no true winners. Or she would not be in the position she is in today. So is it simple patriotism that motivates her, or something more complex?

'I think there's more to investigate before we make a decision,' says Karis. 'And I don't think aggressive action will play well with the public.'

'We'll deal with the public if we have to,' says Qyn. Karis doesn't doubt it, but he also thinks Qyn would rather avoid a scandal if she can. 'What is there to investigate?'

'Patagonia,' he says firmly. There are nods of agreement from around the table. 'The Osirian shipwreck.'

'That's one man,' says Qyn. 'And we've already sent agents to recover him. In light of this new development, that order will be revised to termination.'

'I think we should get him alive,' says Karis. He is thinking out loud, and with the focus of the room upon him, he can feel beads of sweat breaking out across his forehead. Of all the people sitting in this room, he is the misfit. How is it possible to explain to these people, these veterans of Antarctican wellbeing and security, that his place at this table is more to do with accident than it is to do with choice?

Monitoring secret cities is not a vocation, it's something he fell into, because he was good at it, because he has an eye for analysis, because his predecessor got pregnant and there was no one in their division who had the same expertise, no one but Karis, and because he liked the allure of a life lived behind the secrets act – the mystery he could wrap around himself like a cloak, before it became heavy and cumbersome, before the novelty wore off and he realized slowly that his life was in stagnation. For years he has watched numbers and filed reports. Special Unit Atrak has never been challenging: it's just a job. A dead-end job.

A dead-end job that has lurched horribly into life. And now they're consulting him about genocide? What can he possibly say to Maxil Qyn? Qyn is not someone who can conceive of decisions made outside the realm of duty.

'Alive?' Qyn probes. Karis realizes he has failed to respond, perhaps more than once. Their myriad eyes flicker. He feels the heat rising to his face.

'Yes. We should question him. Find out more about the city.'

The Brazilian-Antarctican rep speaks up. 'If it comes to that, we might as well intercept one of the city's fishing expeditions and make the same interrogation with less hassle and fewer dealings with the technophobes.'

'No, no. You're missing the point.' Karis's thoughts are running ahead of him, running into fantasy, the way they have on so many graveyard shifts, waiting for nothing to happen. Only this time, it isn't fantasy. 'This man. Who is he? He left the ocean city. Why did he leave? No one has come out of that city in fifty years – not alive, anyway. So what can he tell us? Surely he must know something? Listen.' Karis leans forwards, making his case. 'First the shipwreck. Now the signal. Don't tell me those two things aren't related.'

All eyes really are on him now. Including Maxil Qyn's, thoughtful, contemplative.

'All right,' says Qyn at last. 'Io, you've got three days to make initial investigations. Track down this rogue Osirian and find out what he knows.' Her gaze snaps around the table. Karis is already dismissed. 'For the rest of you – assign a detail to Patagonia, have our agents report back on the situation there as soon as possible. I want to know exactly who's heard that radio broadcast. And get me the latest intelligence from our people north of the belt. I want scenarios for getting into the city and shutting down that radio signal as well as our options on its dissolution. We reconvene tomorrow at noon.'

One by one, the nine defenders blink out. Karis finds himself alone at the side of Maxil Qyn in a suddenly too-large room. He hesitates, then plunges ahead. This may be his only chance to get out of this mess.

'Chief. Why me? I don't have field training. I'm just an analyst.'

'You're the Commander of Special Unit Atrak, are you not?' says Qyn curtly.

'Yes, but—'

'Then you'd better get moving, Commander. The clock is ticking, and you have responsibilities. Besides.' Qyn gives a humourless smile. 'If we let you go now—'

'Very funny, sir.'

'It's not a joke, Commander. That city has been a thorn in our side for over a century. Believe me, there is nothing remotely funny about our current predicament.'

'No, sir.' Already Karis is regretting his words. He hurries away.

When he leaves Graham Station, much later that night, he has a keening headache lodged behind his left eye and a sense of having swum far out of his depth, far enough that the shore is no longer in sight. Waves pummel him. The radio signal is still emitting, the voice playing over and over on a loop. The voice of a stranger, dropped into the ether, hoping for a reply.

Please send help.
Please send help.
Please send help.
You poor fools, thinks Karis. You have no idea what's coming.

OSIRIS

O'DIO ISIS 100

Tor Aguda (TA): Politician and founding family member Linus Rechnov has not been witnessed in public now for seven days. The Rechnov family claim that he is suffering from a bad case of influenza and is being treated at home. But when journalist Magda Linn asked for an interview at the Domain (the Rechnovs' glamorous high-view home, rumoured to cost thousands in public taxes every year) she was turned away at the tower entrance. All ways into the tower are guarded. Which leads us to ask: what, exactly, is going on behind the closed doors of the Rechnovs, and what does it have to do with the distress signal? Magda, can you shed any light on this?

Magda Linn (ML): As you say, Tor, there's been no statement bar the initial promise of an investigation from the Council. What we know is this: at twenty-two oh nine on fifth December the city's distress signal was broadcast across all channels, with no explanation for the sudden annexing of public o'dio. Hours later it mysteriously disappeared again. By morning, it was back on the o'dio. Now, we know that Linus Rechnov is famously anti-Nucleite. He has been quite open – some might say heretically open – about his belief in life beyond the City, this despite reports from our most prominent Tellers. And he was one of the strongest advocates for the recent, controversial expedition boat – from which, by the way, we haven't heard a word.

TA: Whatever the answer, it's having a terrible effect on the community.

ML: That's right. Conditions on the waterways grow worse by the hour. Fishing crews refuse to break strike, and the kelp harvesters are threatening to follow suit if we don't get an explanation for the mystery hijacking within the next twenty-four hours.

TA: There have been rumours of a vote of no confidence in the Council.

ML: Unless we hear something soon, I would say that's only a matter of time.

TA: Meanwhile, the westerners are keeping surprisingly – some might say suspiciously – quiet.

ML: That's right, Tor. We've heard that the person they seem to call their leader, the Silverfish, has advised westerners to lie low. What we are seeing is almost unprecedented. This is a west who have no comment to make, who will not be drawn to protest or action. No, the violence is all City-side. It's almost as if the westerners know something we don't.

TA: We shouldn't forget, of course, that Linus Rechnov has had western sympathies in the past, even if those have been mitigated of late. His support for the rebel airlift Vikram Bai is one example. Could this be a western ploy, a complex move to incite unification through rumour and chaos?

ML: If so, it means we have a serious security breach. Osiris's distress signal has always originated from the City side on a secure frequency. So whoever recalibrated it to air on public channels must have obtained high-level access codes. Is this a warning, a demonstration? Should we expect further attacks on the infrastructure? A worrying thought indeed.

TA: We'll be back later tonight with a further report. Until then, take care out there, and mind the ghosts.

ANTARCTICA

>TolstyiStandard
#10:48 30.11.2417
SUPER-SHIPS DELAYED

A Civilian Security spokesman has admitted that reports claiming the so-called 'super-ships' have been delayed are true. The ships were said to be close to completion but have suffered repeated setbacks over the last five years.

This year the project lost one of its major engineers. Taeo Ybanez, recently pardoned for a controversial political broadcast where he denounced his own work, was killed in a tragic accident while overseas in Patagonia. Ybanez's research has been passed on but it seems his particular expertise has not.

There had been hopes that the first ship would be ready for trial by the end of the year. Engineers promise that the new ships, which are being designed specifically to withstand the extreme hypercanes of the tropics, will make open-sea travel a possibility for the first time in centuries.

>TolstyiStandard
#13.02 07.12.2417

SENATE DENIES DISTRESS CALL

The Senate has repeatedly denied claims that a distress call has been received from the Lost City in the South Atlantic.

Communications analyst Jamal Mesay says he picked up the long-range signal late on the evening of fifth December. According to his claims, the message stated that the sea city was in distress and called for immediate help. Mesay says he took a recording of the signal and sent it to his local police. When we asked to hear the original, Mesay told us his personal records have been wiped clean and in addition his flat was raided in the early evening of last night. The recording, he says, has disappeared.

Mesay, 47, is a leading member of a local group of enthusiasts who he says are dedicated to studying the eclectic history of the Lost City of Osiris.

>TolstyiStandard
#21.30 09.12.2417

SEA CITY UNDER THREAT?

An insider who cannot be named for reasons of press protection has leaked a high-level memo from inside the Senate. The memo details costs for what appear to be potentially lethal strikes on the ocean city of Osiris. According to a leading defender's analysis, these would cause: 'immense structural damage, and possibly annihilation, of oceanic architecture.'

The memo would appear to confirm suspicions that the Senate are considering an aggressive attack on the sea city, in direct contravention of the international Nuuk Treaty.

Meanwhile, Jamal Mesay, the analyst who drew attention to the much-disputed 'distress call' from Osiris, has been detained under charges of conspiracy. Mesay's lawyer has lodged an appeal.

>TolstyiStandard
#19.02 13.12.2417

OSIRIS PROTESTORS MASS IN BELGRANO

The biggest anti-strike protest yet took place in Belgrano this afternoon. Protestors amassed at Amundsen's Square and marched through the city to the Senate House, where several thousand are gathered now. Those out on the streets today are campaigning against alleged planned strikes on the sea city of Osiris. They demand transparency regarding the Senate's intentions towards the city, as well as the release of Jamal Mesay (47) who continues to be held by the authorities without bail.

The Senate itself has remained silent since the incriminating memo was leaked, but state representatives have been keen to have their say.

'If strikes are being considered, we can be sure it's a very high-security matter indeed,' said Commander Evie Aariak. 'The only reason such a move would be condoned is to alleviate the threat of a Boreal invasion. And if the Boreals are planning a southern expedition, we're all in trouble.'

OSIRIS

O'DIO ISIS 100

Tor Aguda (TA): Thanks for tuning in, folks – and believe me, you'll be glad you did. Today we have an exclusive interview with the figure everyone's been talking about and no one seems to know. Yes, folks, we have met with the elusive Silverfish. Now if the sound quality isn't great that's because we recorded in the west, under what you might call restricted conditions – as you can imagine, the Silverfish keeps a tight security. So without further preamble – from earlier today: our interview with the Silverfish.

Tor Aguda (TA): First and most importantly, welcome to the show.
Silverfish (S): Thank you, Tor, and welcome to you and your team. We appreciate you coming to see us.
TA: I'd like to start by asking, if you don't mind, about your name. The Silverfish. It's an odd one, because as our listeners may already know, a silverfish isn't a fish at all. It's – well, it's an insect. A kind of bug. Why did you come up with that name?
S: I didn't choose it. Not consciously, if that's what you mean. But you're right, a silverfish is an insect. And insects are hard to get rid

of. Resilient. They keep coming back. I want our movement to be something that it's impossible to ignore.

TA: You are campaigning for unification between the City and the west, is that correct?

S: For unification, yes. And also for each and every citizen to know the truth about our city, and our history. Because I believe we have been lied to. I believe there is life outside of Osiris, and that it is up to us to find it.

TA: Let's talk a bit about your methods. Your words are being cited across the west — clearly what you are saying has struck a chord with westerners. But I have to say what's been surprising to us in the City is how very quiet the west has been over the past few weeks. We've seen an upsurge of protests in the City, strikes spreading as far as kelp harvesters and teachers, Citizens clashing with police in the industrial quarter, a surge of arrests — some western security forces have even been diverted City-side. But from the west — nothing.

S: I think the City is making the case for us right now, and the west is happy to let you shoulder the burden for once. This is an issue that affects us all. Why the sudden visibility on the public o'dio? Why draw attention to something which is meant to have been in place for the past five decades? Unless it was never being transmitted beyond the city in the first place.

TA: That is what you believe?

S: That is absolutely what I believe.

TA: Let me be clear. You're implying that the city's distress call was removed — potentially some time ago — and has only recently been reinstated? This is a momentous accusation. Why would anyone want to cut off our distress call?

S: Why does anyone do anything? Two reasons: fear, and power. Ask yourself who benefits from maintaining the status quo.

TA: We've seen a spate of high-level predictions from the Guild of Tellers. They say something is coming. Something bad. Should we be worried, do you think?

S: I know nothing about the art of Telling, but I know to listen when they're in unison. I think we should be prepared—

[pause]

Prepared to expect the unexpected. I think Osiris is on the brink of change, but there are those who will fight to keep things as they've always been. We have to resist that mentality.

TA: I know you don't have much time. I want to ask you now about your real name. We discussed this earlier and you said you hadn't decided whether you were going to reveal it, though perhaps some of our listeners out there may already have their suspicions. I know that this is a big ask and may place you in danger. But I have to ask – have you decided now?

[pause]

I have to prompt you. Have you decided?

S: Yes, I have decided. I've spent a lot of time thinking about this. There are advantages and disadvantages to revealing my identity. You are right that it may place me in danger but I'm more concerned that it could have a negative impact on our campaign, and may even question its authenticity. However. . . however. I think it's important that people in the City know who I am and why I am here, speaking to you about revolution. So. . .

[pause]

The truth is, I'm a dead woman. According to City records. And if it weren't for two people – two westerners – who helped me when I was at my lowest ebb, I would be dead. My name is – my name was – Adelaide Rechnov.

[long pause]

TA: Adelaide, I have one more question to ask you. It's a question I know our listeners will want to hear an answer for.

S: Yes.

TA: Why are you doing this? Why have you given up all of the privileges you had, to disappear into the west and join the western resistance movement?

S: There are a lot of reasons I could give you, social and political reasons, all of which are valid and important, about which I've spoken at length, elsewhere. But in the end it's quite simple. I carry a debt. A debt of a dead man – a dead man who I loved. He is my ghost to watch now, a burden I will carry for the rest of my life. I'm doing this for Vikram Bai.

'How did I do?' she asks Dien.

'It sounds good,' says Dien. 'People will like it. The romance. They like all that romantic shit, it's convincing.'

'It's the story that counts,' says Adelaide.

'That's right.'

'Is this what you had in mind? When you recruited me?'

'It was a gamble. You were a gamble. I didn't know which way you'd jump.'

'You think I've jumped?'

'You tell me.'

'What I said in that broadcast. It wasn't true.'

Or at least, it's not the whole truth. Or even, necessarily, a large part of the truth. While the City's fishers strike and a long-lost radio signal reverberates around the Council Chambers, Adelaide, the Silverfish, is forging ahead with a dead man's soul. Holding up their fleeting hours together as if they are a shield, or an amulet, or a light that is too bright and blinding to see past or through – anything but what it was: two people who used one another, a liaison like a Tarctic vortex, spiralling to something which neither of them could accept or articulate, at least not then. Only later. Only in absence. Adelaide's penitence has become the west's greatest weapon.

Sometimes she considers a life where Vikram is not dead, where Vikram might return, and the idea is heady, almost intoxicating, and at the same time it is desolate. She imagines their meeting, standing on a pier with the boat drawing closer and closer, the boat pulling in, Vikram stepping out. The two of them, walking towards one another.

There's a blue sky, of course, and the waves are sparkling, and the city is sparkling. His face. Tired but happy. His eyes, meeting hers. The moment closes in.

And there, at the point they come together, the reverie stops. Adelaide doesn't know what happens next. She has no idea what she would say to him.

'The thing is, Dien, I'm not doing this for Vikram – not any more.'

'What do you mean?'

'I mean I loved him. Or I could have loved him. But this – I'm doing this for me. It's the only thing I've ever done that's mattered. It's all I've got left.'

She looks at Dien.

'There. You know the truth now, even if no one else does.'

PART FOUR
THE SCALED MAN

PATAGONIA

The two figures wind steadily through the forestry, the boy moving lithe and silent, the woman in front awkward, clumsy, clutching at branches when she misses a step, not always successfully. A muttered, interrupted litany flows between them: the woman huffing, this way, is it still this way, Mig's reply, yes, yes, keep walking. Now over that way. To the left. *Left*. Occasionally the woman sighs and asks, how much further? Mig: it doesn't matter. The woman: I didn't expect to be walking so far. Mig: what did you expect?

She doesn't reply. The answer is curiosity, of course, but more than that, a burning necessity to see for herself, to know the truth of it. She has always sought out the truth of it. This impulse could not be ignored, although the journey south has been fraught, and she has left things behind that she should not have left, people and work, because of a few words snagged from the radio, hooked like fireflies out of the dark. Because of a story.

They progress. The trees are in full leaf and the light falls in narrow strips between them, reminding Mig of other things, corrugated iron and metal railings, tall, straight pillars in Station Sabado. Despite the absence of human life this place carries an echo of where he used to live. The woman blunders on, making enough noise to alert every wild creature on the island, making Mig uneasy – there might be snakes here, concealed in the undergrowth. Mig insists the woman stays in front. He doesn't trust her.

He doesn't trust any of them. Many have come. They all have to prove themselves. Some of them do, some of them don't. He keeps a knife strapped to his body, the blade a constant pressure against the soft casing of his skin. This woman, with her loose words and awkward gait, does not appear dangerous – but those are always the ones you should watch the closest.

When the trees grow denser, the light more sporadic, the woman slows. Mig senses a tentativeness in her step which was not there before. He nods to himself, satisfied. It is right that she should feel this. After all, she has come for the miracle, and miracles are never cheap. Someone always has to pay.

The forest opens out abruptly to reveal a stream and the woman stops, dazed by the transition in light. For a moment she stays where she is and looks about her quietly. At the running water that splits around a series of rocks. The sunlight bouncing off the current.

Mig scans up and down the stream. The boat is where he left it. No signs that anyone has been here.

'You know, you forget about this,' says the woman. 'You forget it's all here. Where I am. Up by the marshes. The sand. I've been there so long now. I had these ideas. I thought I'd make a difference. All those things. You know? You don't think about it while you're there. It's only here. . . Gods, look at the water. It's so clear.'

Mig is not interested in her rapture, he's interested in keeping both of them out of sight. He indicates.

'We take the boat,' he says. He takes a blindfold from his pocket. 'You wear this.'

The woman hesitates, then closes her eyes. Mig helps her into the boat. When she is settled in the stern he also ties her hands – something he's gained expertise in lately. He could truss up a goat in sixty seconds. The woman's hands lie meekly in her lap, the skin dark, the nails cut short and blunt. Mig looks at them, thinking about what she is. Wondering who she has saved and who has died on her watch.

Neither of them speaks during the remainder of the journey. Both are immersed in their private thoughts, Mig intent upon the careful steering of the boat, alert always to any suggestion of human presence along the banks, but all is quiet, as it should be, only the birds and the wind ruffling the trees, quiet in a way he still finds disturbing to the ear. Since Pilar died he has felt different, like the old Mig was spirited away somewhere, wherever she went, and this place with its emptiness and its salt winds and secretive trees is like a second life, an afterlife. Where the abandoned go. The people who seek them out are pilgrims, earnest and determined, with ideas and things to prove, to other people, or to themselves. He looks at this new one, the doctor from the uninhabitable zone. He is not yet sure which category she falls into.

The woman resists the urge to scratch at her blindfold. Her back aches from the hike but she keeps her spine erect. It is important not to show fear, even to a boy. Is she afraid though? Not exactly. Rather she feels the rush of anticipation, adrenaline pushing through her body. The words from the radio rest against the darkness of the blindfold. Glowing there, tantalizing her. A call that could not be ignored. Her colleagues asked her not to go and she shut all of them out.

On an impulse.

'We're here,' says the boy.

As she climbs out of the boat there are other voices, greeting the boy. She feels hands on her shoulders and back, guiding her forwards. She senses she is surrounded. Ridiculous, really, the idea of her being brought here in blindness as if she were one of those characters from the radio stories about northern spies, who always operate in secret, and practise deceit. She is a smart woman who went away to do something good, and here she is on a remote archipelago island whose name and location she does not even know, being shepherded to see a man who has no name, only a reputation which has spread from the archipelago to Titicaca, and beyond.

* * *

When they remove the blindfold it takes a moment for her eyes to focus. She is inside a small log cabin, rudely furnished and stocked with camping equipment which looks like it's seen better days. There is a table in front of her. A man is sitting in the chair on the other side of the table. He is so still that for a moment the eerie idea crosses her mind that he might be robotized. Then he gestures.

'Please sit down.'

A thin, intense face, not South American. The features are – memory jogs, a flicker of a country in the old world order that she struggles now to recall the name of and quickly gives up trying, because his eyes are fixed on her, studying her, appraising her, and she finds she can't look away. There are scars across his cheeks, evidence of tissue damage. It's the pathway of a consuming virus that blasts through the skin's cells, leaving marks that may not ever disappear. The scarring pattern classic of an older, curable strain, you see it occasionally on foreigners – but the outbreak in Cataveiro wasn't an older strain, and it wasn't curable. By the gods, he is lucky. More than lucky – he is something that should not exist. He is a miracle.

She can feel the acceleration of her heartbeat telling her that she was right: right to leave, right to come here.

She says, 'You're the man that survived the redfleur.'

He doesn't answer her directly.

'Are you thirsty? Can I get you some water? We have coffee, too.'

She shakes her head. She doesn't want to wait.

'You are, aren't you? You're him?'

'I'm told that's what people say. Mig tells me your name's Beatriz?'

'Yes.'

'I can't tell you my name. Not yet, anyway. You understand why?'

His Spanish is accented but confident; she can tell he's a foreigner but she couldn't say how long he's been here. She nods.

'Of course.'

'Where have you come from?'

'Titicaca. The marshes.'

The man who survived redfleur unfolds a map and spreads it across the table, orientating it towards her. The map has the hummingbird glyph in one corner and a signature the doctor recognizes: it is a Callejas map. Once again she feels a tug at her memory, something she heard about the pilot, something recent. Wasn't there talk of a reward? The salt woman was involved, the pilot had gone rogue, killed someone. . . The doctor remembers she came to the clinic once, brought an injured boy for treatment. Didn't seem like the killing type.

She points to Titicaca.

'Up here.'

He studies the location.

'You've travelled fast, to come so far.'

'There was a west-coast ship heading south.' She pushes away the memory of seasickness. 'You're not from this country?' she asks.

He smiles. 'No.'

She sits back in the chair, gazing at him frankly.

'Is it true you survived it?'

'I survived an illness.'

'But the redfleur?' she presses. 'In Cataveiro?'

He doesn't answer.

She shakes her head. 'That was a Type 9. Even the Boreals don't have a cure. This is incredible. If it's true, we need you. I'm a doctor. I work in the outback. There's nothing much up there, and we're lucky, it's never come to us. But I know what it does. I know what happened in Cataveiro. And it's not just here – up in the north as well, it's getting much worse, they say, they haven't had a breakthrough in years.

'We need you,' she repeats.

The man looks unconvinced.

'You mean you want to study me.'

'Yes! Of course I do. I'm not a virologist, but I know people – scientists, teachers, in the university—'

'Is that why you came, Beatriz? You want to persuade me into a laboratory?'

'Do you know how many people die every year from redfleur? If you have immunity—'

'I've heard the numbers.'

'Then come with me,' she says passionately. She cannot believe he would refuse her.

The man gets to his feet and goes to stand by the single high window, looking out. She has no idea what he is looking at. She hasn't seen anything of what there is between the boat and this hut.

'Save your entreaties,' he says. 'You won't persuade me to go anywhere with you.'

'Then what are you doing here, hidden away in the middle of the forest? Where have you come from? Who are you?'

He speaks without looking at her.

'You've heard enough to find me here. Surely you must have some idea?'

She stares at the pilot's map. The familiar, tapering contours of the South American continent. The less familiar outline of the mass below it, and between them, the breadth of blue. She speaks slowly.

'I've heard. . . strange things.'

'You call it the sea city,' says the man. 'Where I'm from. Also the lost city, I believe. Its true name is Osiris.'

The colours on the map seem suddenly brighter, the blue more vivid and intense. She wasn't scared before, but she feels something close to it now.

'You want to take me to a laboratory, cut me open and look at my blood,' says the man calmly. 'But you're asking the wrong question. The question is not what. It's where.'

'I don't understand.'

'If it's true, as you think, that I survived the redfleur, and if it's true that this has never been seen before, then it has nothing to do with who I am and everything to do with where I come from.' Still facing away, the man's voice is low and hypnotic. 'It's the only logical answer.'

She thinks about this, struggling to process the implications of what he is saying. It all seems so impossible.

But you came here because of impossible.

'You mean. . . you're saying there might be others? People like you? People who have immunity?'

'I have no idea. But I plan to return there and find out. If I can find it again, that is.' A touch of irony tinges his voice. 'Which brings its own challenges.'

She is astounded.

'You're going back to—' she thinks the word, but cannot say it. No one says that name. 'You're going back?'

'I'm taking an expedition.'

There are a thousand questions that enter her head. The one that comes out is the least relevant of all of them.

'How are you going to get there?'

He turns back to face her.

'Forgive me if I don't tell you the full details of my plan. You're not the first to seek me out. There are others. Some have left. Others have stayed. The choice is entirely yours. Take a look around, see what you make of us. You're free to spend as long as you wish here. But if you try to leave without an escort, I warn you now you will be detained. As you've already experienced, we keep tight security here. No one leaves or enters the camp without an escort. It's imperative that no one finds out where we are. The day they do is the day I'm dead. If you want any chance for a cure for redfleur, you'll respect that.'

She cannot take her eyes from his face, and she has to speak, she has to say the things that are tumbling around her head.

'You know what they're saying about you. That you're something new. Something genetic. Maybe northern, maybe not. They say you have scales. You can breathe like a fish, stay underwater for hours. I know it can't be true but people talk about it like it's real.'

The man studies her for a moment. He says, 'I know exactly what they're saying about me.'

'I—'

'No,' he says. 'Nothing more. Not now.'

He opens the door, and a surge of bright light spills across the threshold. It is summer outside, and warm. She can hear birds. She stares through the doorway, not knowing what to do or what has just happened. The man holds the door, waiting. She gets to her feet. As she passes him, he says, 'We'll speak again,' and she sees in the harsh clarity of daylight the details of the scarring on his face, the ridges and the discolouring of the skin, where the redfleur has razed, and the redfleur has let him go. She thinks about what is in his blood, tries to imagine the value of the body standing before her, so quiet and still. She tries to guess at his age, and cannot. There is something timeless about him. Again she recalls the stories she has heard, the firefly words on the radio, and she thinks, now I understand.

Vikram watches the doctor go out into the camp. She looks bewildered, passing a hand over her eyes, her head turning slowly from one side to the other as she takes in the site, the people engaged in their various activities, who nod to her as she passes or extend a hand to introduce themselves. If he'd had that effect on people back in Osiris, things might have been different.

He might never have left.

He looks for Mig and finds the boy playing with a piece of rope, alert, waiting. Someone in the camp has taught the boy a range of knots. Mig is a quick pupil.

'No trouble getting her here?'

'Nope.'

'Well done,' he says.

'Is she going to stay?' Mig asks him.

'I'm not sure. What did you think?'

The boy shrugs. 'She's a doctor.'

Vikram guesses he is thinking about Pilar, and does not push the question. The relationship between himself and the boy is a delicate one, webbed as it is with the peculiar circumstances of their meeting: his being alive, Pilar being dead, Mig showing Vikram a way out of the city, Vikram showing Mig the place where Pilar died, as they had agreed. They couldn't go inside – the building had taken on the function of an incinerator. The smoke and stench of burning fat was leaking through the vents, permeating the air for streets around, a smell that Vikram had faced before, at Osirian funerals, but which was new to Mig. He wanted to protect the boy from it, but he couldn't – not that Mig would have let him, even if it were possible.

Sometimes Vikram thinks that Mig must resent him, for having lived. Other times he feels that the boy is more philosophical than he has ever been. At any rate, Mig is here, and since the farmhouse episode has given Vikram no reason to believe that he wishes to be anywhere else, which means he's Vikram's responsibility now. He does his best to keep the boy occupied, not wanting him to brood.

'Have you thought any more about my suggestion?'

'It's a bad idea,' says the boy violently. 'A bad, bad idea.'

Vikram lets it go, but he knows he can't postpone for much longer. Volunteers are all very well in this venture, but soon he will need someone with real contacts. Someone who knows all the ins and outs of Patagonian society, and anti-society. Someone who can pull in favours.

Someone like the Alaskan.

'What about the other thing?' he asks.

'The Tarkie thing?'

'Yes.'

'I found someone for you.'

'Good. Send them in.'

Inside the cabin Vikram examines the holoma that belonged to Taeo Ybanez, passing it from hand to hand, admiring the smooth black surface and satisfying weight of it. The holoma fascinates him. On their journey south from Cataveiro the device has been knocked about in his backpack, thrown carelessly to the ground on more than one occasion, but its exterior remains unmarked. He has seen it operational only once, when Taeo showed him a projection of his partner Shri. He will never be able to forget finding Taeo dead, the holoma in his palm, the projection frozen with Shri in the act of leaning over his body, her presence in the room at once static and shimmering, as if she were there for some form of valediction. Vikram managed to turn it off by wrapping Taeo's fingers around the sphere, as he had seen the Antarctican do before. But the holoma does not respond to Vikram's touch.

Outside the Council Chambers of Osiris there are dozens of objects enthroned in glass cases which, according to Osirian history, were relics and antiques. Vikram does not know whether the Antarcticans possessed this technology before Osiris was built, or have developed it since, but either way, it is a brutal reminder of the reality of the city's schism from the rest of the world. In fifty years, while Osiris has stagnated, others have grown, altered, moved on. Things have appeared – like redfleur. Things have disappeared.

A knock at the door interrupts his thoughts.

'Come in,' he calls.

The man who enters is small and angular, with hair greying at the temples and heavy pouches under his eyes. Vikram recognizes the face: he has been with them for a few weeks. He recalls the man's history. A mechanic, he lost his father recently; it wasn't redfleur, but a sudden fever.

'Mig says you can unlock this.' He holds the holoma aloft, watching the man's reactions closely. Most Patagonians would be horrified by the sight of foreign technology, but this man does not display any unease. He squints.

'I can't unlock it but I might be able to hack it.'

'What does that mean?'

The mechanic comes forwards and takes a seat at the table.

'Can I. . .?'

Vikram passes him the device. The mechanic turns it over in his hands, frowning.

'These things are coded to imprint. There's no way of accessing what's on it, or deleting it. Only an Antarctican can do that. But if you want to use it for yourself, I can do that.'

'I want to send a message,' says Vikram.

'Something wrong with a letter?'

'A letter can be forged. I want the recipient to know it's not a fake. Also, it's a matter of returning some property.'

'All right.'

The mechanic unrolls a cloth and assesses the instruments fastened inside. His fingers are dry and calloused and have a delicacy in their movement which reassures Vikram. He selects a blunt-ended screwdriver and unfastens a small pouch on the bag. From this he extracts a minute, sparkling stone.

'Diamond's the only thing tough enough to break this.'

'You're going to break it?'

'I'll put it back together again.'

Vikram looks from the holoma to the mechanic.

'You fix cars, is that right?'

'And an aeroplane.' He sets the diamond carefully on the table. 'But that was before the pilot – before she disappeared.'

'I've heard a lot about the pilot. You know her?'

'I fix her plane. I guess you'd say I know her.'

'Where do you think she went?'

'Ramona's a friend,' says the mechanic. 'So I'd rather not talk about her, if you don't mind. I prefer to think of her as still alive.'

Vikram gestures.

'I understand. Do your worst.'

He watches the man turning the holoma over in his hands, running his fingertips over the surface, until he pauses.

'There.'

'What is it?'

The mechanic rotates the holoma towards Vikram.

'Feel that?'

When Vikram runs his finger over the holoma, he feels an almost imperceptible dimple in the surface of the little machine. He wonders how he failed to notice it before.

The mechanic places the tiny diamond on the dimple and rests the screwdriver on top, then takes up a hammer. Vikram has a moment of foreboding but before he can say anything the hammer comes down on the screwdriver with a heavy crack. The holoma bisects into two halves as neatly as a melon.

The interior is a cluster of intricate mechanisms fused together in copper and silver and green. Vikram watches, intrigued, as the mechanic deliberates over the device.

'Where did you learn how to do this?'

'An Antarctican spy showed me.'

'Why would a spy show you a secret like this?'

'He'd been here a long time. I'm not sure he was doing much spying any longer. When the Tarkies send people over here, they rarely get to go back, whatever they tell them. And the spies get disillusioned – know what I mean?'

Apparently satisfied, the mechanic takes a pair of gloves and presses the two halves of the holoma together. They fuse back into a perfect sphere. Still gloved, he slides the holoma towards Vikram.

'Hold your hand around it for ten seconds, then let go, then five.'

Vikram does as instructed.

'Should be coded to you now. But like I said, whatever was on here, it's locked away. This is just an override.'

'That's fine. That's all I need it for. Thank you.'

'You're welcome.'

The mechanic replaces the little diamond and rolls up his toolkit.

'Who's the message for, if you don't mind my asking?'

'Someone I owe an apology.'

Once the holoma has been coded to his palm print, Vikram finds it simple and intuitive to use. He records and deletes his message several times until he is satisfied with what he wants to say. It's a wrench to let the device go – but it does not belong to him, has never belonged to him, and every day it remains in his care is a reminder not only of the guilt he feels over Taeo's death, but of a world he does not have the time or liberty to explore. When he decided to return to Osiris it felt like a choice, but the reality is there is no alternative – there never has been – and with each new arrival at the camp comes another obligation, another inescapable responsibility for him to fulfil.

He talks to Mig about the best way to slip the holoma into the Antarctican network, and they assign three camp members to the task. At the last minute, Mig says he wants to go with them. Vikram is reluctant. The boy out of his sight is out of his protection, and Mig is not happy, and therefore he is unpredictable, and that worries Vikram. Then again, perhaps it will do the boy some good to get out of the camp. In the end he acquiesces, and watches the little expedition setting out, walking in single file between the trees until they disappear among the denser foliage of the forestry.

The holoma goes with them, bound for Antarctica, and a woman Vikram has seen but never met. As soon as they are out of sight he is filled with misgivings. He has set something in motion, and there is no taking it back.

Evening falls and the camp members who are not on scout or perimeter duty gather in circles to sit and eat, exchanging stories and histories. Fires are not permitted, for fear of the smoke giving away their location, but torches set into the ground cast a low, white illumination across the clearing. Some groups are content to talk; others entertain themselves with cards or dice games or the radio. In just a few short weeks, the concealed glade with its two abandoned hunting cabins has evolved into a tiny community.

Vikram observes the doctor from earlier today and joins the circle where she is sat. His presence is acknowledged, but the conversation continues uninterrupted. Vikram sits quietly, listening. The camp is used to his ways, and rarely ask questions, except those of practical matters – regarding how their mission is to proceed. That they accept the mission so unquestioningly remains a thing of astonishment to him, but they all have their reasons for being here. Sometimes he is not sure that he can bear the weight of their belief.

It is a rule of the camp that no one raises their voice. The murmurings of the conversations run over and under one another, defined only by the silvery glow of the torches, voices out of the darkness, bled through a crack from another world.

The first speaker is a spice trader; he's been cultivating chilli plants in the camp. He begins slowly. It's always the same beginning. I knew someone. Actually, I didn't know him that well. He was my father. Does that surprise you? We were never close. It was always that way, even when I was a child. He played the violin. Every evening the house would be full of the sound of him practising, not just playing but the technical elements, scales, that sort of thing. I didn't like that kind of music – I didn't understand it. I'd put the radio up loud to annoy him, but when I went to sleep I could still hear those fucking scales, up and down, up and down. After I left home we hardly spoke. The last twelve months we had no contact at all. Then I heard the news. He was in the city, when the epidemic came. Since he died, I've been listening non-stop to the music he liked, but I still don't understand it.

He stops, looks down. An exhalation of breath. Another camp member begins. I knew someone. My mother's auntie. Seventy years old! Her skin was wrinkled as hemp from the sun, but her mind was sharp as a pin. We talked about everything. Then she got the jinn. Ten kilograms she lost in the conversion, but she didn't die. She was tough. She lived another three years. Seventy-three! Then we had a redfleur case in the village. The doctors weren't sure if it was that or something else that took her in the end, but they burned her anyway. These people came, masked, with a truck. They put us in isolation. We couldn't take a shit without saying please. I was almost glad, then, that she went so fast. She would have hated it. The confinement. I don't know where they took her ashes. I'd like to know that. I'd really like to know.

I knew someone. No, not knew, exactly. We hardly exchanged a word, to tell the truth, but there was an accord. Every day I'd take the boat out on my fishing run at dawn and about the same time I'd see this woman driving her boat back to the harbour, dragging her nets. You know how sometimes you can have an understanding with someone, without needing to speak? It was like that. We'd nod to one another and sometimes we'd wave. Sometimes it was misty and I only caught a glimpse of her, hunched over the tiller, the water just drifting like silk below. I never saw her anywhere else. One day I took the boat out and she wasn't there. Or the next day, or the next. I asked about but no one knew who she was. Then I heard there'd been an outbreak.

I knew someone. He sold lemons on the promenades in Cataveiro. We said hello every morning.

I knew someone. A bicycle courier. For years I'd been trying to work up the courage to ask her out, but I never did.

I knew someone. A parrot girl. My parrot girl. I knew someone.

The night deepens and the stories ebb away, leaving only the soft fuzz of the radio hub set up by Mig, which is continually monitored despite the intermittent signal. Vikram sees the doctor watching him from across the circle. He knows that however many people come, he will always carry their stories, because even while they are shared with the camp the stories are invasive, spoken directly to and for him. The one who didn't die. Why him? And how? Is it the coral tea he still sometimes craves? Is it something in his blood? Is it a fucking cosmic joke? And all at once he has a feeling of intense claustrophobia, and has to get up and leave the circle, not wanting to hear, or see, any more.

The expedition returns with news and provisions and a look of distraction, a look which says they have seen something strange and can't stop thinking on it. This is how it went: they wound their way back to Tierra del Fuego, travelling at first through the dusk, using the half-light to mask their journey, and then openly, as a small fishing crew, trailing a net behind them as camouflage, pulling in coils of cephalopods and silver-backed fish, moving in and out of the drifts of island mist, eventually rounding the shoulder of del Fuego to bring their haul to the harbour, where two of them began to haggle with the locals, and the third took the holoma, and went to a bar called Arturo's, where you will meet all kinds of people, and listened and learned some names, and obtained an address.

And meanwhile, the two at the harbour sold their squid at a price not good but not bad, you could say it was fair, and they heard a rumour, which everyone in Fuego is talking about, from the smallest child to the oldest fish-skinner. Some time ago – days, certainly, and maybe even weeks, the time varied according to who you spoke to, but the story is the same – a distress signal was detected. It came over the radio. There was a voice. The voice asked for help. And the word from the harbour front is that it came from the lost city. That's right. From Osiris.

Vikram interrupts. 'Osiris? You're sure about that?'

Yes, they're sure.

He listens with increasing alarm. The news raises a thousand questions to which there can be no hope of answers, not here, not cut off in necessary exile as he is. Where has the signal come from? Who set it off? Who received it? And yet – he dares to hope – could this also be cause for optimism?

Someone in Osiris has managed to get the signal out.

Someone else knows, or believes, there is life beyond the ocean.

While the expedition recount the rest of their tale, Vikram can see that something is wrong with Mig. The boy has nothing to contribute. He stands at a slight distance to the other three, glowering, with one hand in his pocket, clenched into a fist.

Vikram takes him aside.

'What is it? What's happened? Did something go wrong with the holoma?'

'No. It's gone. They left it at the house. The Tarkie will find it.'

'Then what?'

A shudder runs through the boy. Vikram takes him by the shoulders and looks into the boy's face. He can feel the tension locking Mig's skinny frame.

'Mig, what is it?'

When Mig looks up at him his eyes are blazing with hate.

'It's the Alaskan,' he says. 'She's in Fuego.'

At that moment Vikram wants more than anything to tell Mig not to worry, that it will be all right, that Mig will never have to deal with the Alaskan again. But he can't lie to the boy.

Vikram needs her.

ANTARCTICA

'**Y**ou can go in now.'

The defender holds the door for her, a courtesy Shri would prefer to throw back in his face, regardless of his complicity, or not. She hesitates before entering. Her gut tells her that to step over the threshold is to give ground in some way, to accept a change in state not yet perceived, but whose consequences are already preset. Nothing good can be inside.

The stomach of the man holding the door eases in and out as he waits. Shri sets her shoulders and walks inside, hearing the door closed discreetly behind her.

She would have thought a military room would be tidy, but this one is not. The work station and the comms desk are grubby, littered with holomas and stray pots lined with coffee grains which are adding, she suspects, to the tinge of mustiness on the air. A room that has the sense of having seen, lately, a lot of the person who now occupies it. The man sitting behind the desk is African-Antarctican. He wears a Republican security uniform with a high-level insignia at the collar. The uniform is sharply cut and suits the slim figure of the man, but the material is rumpled. He looks tired. Thinking of the distress in her children's faces as she said her goodbyes, Shri cannot help but feel glad as she notes this.

I hope you've had as many sleepless nights as I have.

The man waves at a chair in front of the desk. A piece of amateur artwork has pride of place upon it, something Shri suspects is meant to be a penguin, clearly the work of a child.

'Come in, take a seat.'

Shri does not move.

'Sit down, please.'

She senses the man suppressing his irritation. Slowly, Shri comes forwards and settles in the chair, placing her feet neatly together, hands in her lap. These days (*these days?* She cannot comprehend that the path of her life should have led to this conclusion, how it could *be this way*) she has the sense that if she does not hold herself physically together, it will all be too late. Too late for what, she is not sure, but she doesn't want to find out.

'I'm Commander Karis Io,' says the man behind the desk. 'Thank you for coming.'

'Is this about my partner? I've been trying to speak to someone in Civilian Security for weeks. No one will tell me what happened. They say he overdosed.'

'I'm afraid that's the case.'

'They won't tell me how, or why – no one will tell me anything—'

'Citizen Nayar, if you'll let me explain why you're here. . .'

'Yes?'

'My remit is Special Unit Atrak, which monitors the ocean city known as Osiris.'

This is not what she was expecting. She stares at him, confused.

'What does this have to do with Taeo?'

'You have been sent a holoma,' says the commander. 'From a man who calls himself Vikram Bai. An Osirian.'

'I haven't received it.'

'I'll show you now.'

He retrieves a holoma from the collection on his desk and activates the device. Shri waits.

The hologram that appears is not her partner. It is a man she has never seen before. A slender man with Indian features and scarred cheeks who speaks in careful, oddly accented Spanish. This is a message for Shri. He says he is from the sea city, Osiris. Two months ago he landed on the coast of Patagonia. He was rescued by her partner. Taeo tried to help him. He says her partner told him about his family. Shri and Kadi and Sasha and Nisha. He says Taeo would have done anything to get back to them. Taeo had a plan. They intended to return to Antarctica, himself and Taeo, together. He says that Taeo was a good man. He says he is sorry.

'Oh. . . oh shit. . .'

She can feel the tears pricking at her eyes and she does not want to cry. Not here. Not in this office, in front of this man.

'Who is he?'

'Someone we need to find.'

'He's – Osirian?'

The word sits uncomfortably in her mouth. With it come to mind other, disturbing associations, like that man in the news who says he detected a radio signal. Masay? Mesay? She can't remember. She's been distracted. Now she thinks about it, haven't there been protests? The lost city, always unspoken, is suddenly thrust into the spotlight, and this man is saying her partner was caught up in it. *Why did you have to get caught up in it, Taeo? Why couldn't you leave well alone?*

'So he claims. This holoma belonged to your partner. It contains messages sent by yourself. It's been hacked, evidently, and has fallen back into the Antarctican network. Now you see why you are here?'

'Yes – no. So he sent me a message. Why couldn't you just forward it to me?'

'This man, Vikram Bai. Like I said, he's someone we need to find. I've watched the recording several times. I'd like to know what you make of it.'

Shri feels a spark of anger at the idea of her personal correspondence being analysed and discussed by others. She wonders how long this Special Unit Atrak had the holoma in their possession before she was even allowed to see the damn thing. She presses the heels of her hands tightly against her knees, striving for control.

'What do you mean, what do I make of it?'

'This man is a fugitive. But he made a great effort to ensure that this device reached Antarctica, and more specifically, you. What do you make of that?'

'How the hell should I know? You've watched it more than I have. You saw what he said. What more is there to say about it? I don't know what he wanted. I don't know anything about him.'

Shri senses the commander's gaze on her, an assessor's gaze, judging the likelihood that Shri will fall to pieces, disintegrate on him like paper in water. He weighs up his next words.

'It seems he felt the need to reach out to you. To make a connection. We think that's interesting.'

Shri wishes Commander Karis Io would get to the point. The sooner this is over, the sooner she can go home.

Home.

Nisha is too young to understand catastrophe, except perhaps in the mood of the house. But the elder two – Kadi and Sasha – their reactions so different, Kadi hard and proud, refusing to speak about it, so very like Taeo – Sasha a storm of grief, tears soaking the sheets, tears Shri felt like pushing her own face into and howling.

'We think it's likely that Vikram Bai would talk to you,' says the commander. Shri looks up, startled. Meet the Osirian? The prospect hangs before her, abrupt and unexpected.

'He's in Antarctica?'

'No. He's somewhere in Patagonia.'

Shri's heart, raised a moment ago, now begins to sink.

'I don't understand,' she stalls.

'We need you to help us find him.'

Shri drives the balls of her feet harder into the floor, pressing down, feeling the muscles of her thighs tense in response. The commander's words continue with cold inevitability.

'It will involve a trip,' he says. 'We'll need you to go to Patagonia. Once you're there, you'll be open about your reasons for travelling, letting anyone who asks know your intent. You want to find the Osirian. You'll have back-up, naturally. I suspect we'll find that he may come to you, rather than us having to find him. The aim is to get you in and out as quickly as possible, so don't worry, you'll soon be back home.'

That word again. Shri can feel a ringing in her ears. The air thickening around her. She has a flash of memory: her mother's warning hand, a pressure on her shoulder, exerted many times, a voice: *Calm down, Shri.*

'Bait,' she says.

'I'm sorry?' There is a surprised inflection in the commander's voice that Shri is certain is a fake. He knows exactly what Shri is here for. An unpleasant thought occurs to her. If they hadn't concocted this plan, would she ever have seen the Osirian's holoma at all?

'You want to use me as bait.'

'You misunderstand me.'

The last of Shri's nervousness trickles away. She can feel her rage blooming. The warm haze of it heats her face and neck, encompassing her, armouring her.

'You want me to leave my children? This is what you're saying, isn't it?'

'I'm sure you realize it would be far too dangerous for them to accompany you. We couldn't guarantee their safety.'

'They've just lost a parent!'

'And I'm very sorry for your loss. But you must understand, you are now needed, elsewhere.'

'No. I'm needed by my children. I'm needed by Kadi and Sasha and Nisha. My baby, she's not even two years old, and you want to take me away from her?'

'We'll arrange the best care. I promise, you won't have to worry about them.'

Shri feels giddy with anger. She knows she is going to shout and there is no way of preventing it.

'Are you insane? Are you listening to what I'm saying? This Senate sent my partner away. You did this to him. *You.* And now he's dead. Taeo's dead in another country and I can't even see his body. And you want to take me away from my children? You have no right – no right—'

'Perhaps I haven't made myself clear.'

The sudden coolness in the man's voice sheets Shri like meltwater. The room quivers and settles. The commander sits in his crumpled uniform, behind his desk, appearing unperturbed by Shri's outburst. He continues speaking in the same hard tone.

'This is a matter of national security. You represent the strongest lead we have to this Osirian character, and it is vital that we find him as early as possible. This is your duty, Shri Nayar, as a citizen of the Republic. It's your civic service.'

The words *civic service* fall with an inescapable weight.

'Are you going to refuse?' the commander asks.

'What happens if I do? I could go public with this. I bet the media would be fascinated to hear my story, especially after that memo came out.'

But she knows the bluff is pointless. She has seen first-hand what happened to Taeo when he chose to speak out.

The commander holds her gaze.

'That hasn't been the best move for your family in the past.'

'You mean you'll take me there by force.'

A heavy silence descends. Commander Karis Io's face is very still, and whereas Shri's first impression of the man had been of someone tired and worn, even a little slovenly, now she senses the steeliness, an ability to box and compartmentalize, and she realizes even if this man did have any empathy for her, in the end it wouldn't matter: he would do his job. That is who he is, someone who does his job.

At the same time it comes to her, clearer than ever before, that this has always been the source of tension between herself and Taeo. This dichotomy between civic duty and what he called ethics, a gap as long as time and just as twisted, and she begins to laugh.

'You find this funny?'

Shri raises a hand in supplication. She can't explain. It's too much, the irony of finding herself here, being coerced to do the exact thing she had always exhorted to Taeo – protecting their fucking country – and finding that in doing so she relinquishes her fundamental reasons for believing it a necessity in the first place. She is to abandon her family. It is not funny, not really, not at all, but having started, Shri cannot stop. Her ribs ache. She feels tears sliding down her cheeks, liberated at last. The face of the commander, at first startled, then taut and pinched as he waits for Shri's delirium to subside, only adds to the absurdity of the situation.

The commander stands and crosses the room, returning with a glass of water. Shri sips it slowly.

'You'll go, then,' says Karis Io.

'I don't have a choice, do I?'

She senses his relief. It's sour.

'You have belongings with you,' he states.

'Not much.'

'We'll provide what you don't have. Do you have any more questions for me?'

Shri shakes her head. 'You've told me everything I need to know.'

'You leave tonight.'

'Tonight?'

'You can speak with your children through a secure portal. Say your goodbyes. I can't say for certain how long you'll be away.'

The commander folds his arms, indicating that the meeting is over.

Dismissed, Shri rises. Before she leaves the room she points to the child's artwork on his desk, incapable of restraining herself.

'Think about how you'd feel if someone took you away from your child. You should be ashamed.'

When Shri Nayar has left, Karis Io looks at the penguin sculpture, courtesy of his niece Grace, and considers contacting someone. His parents – fuck no. Friends – no one he could trust with this. His sister, Bia?

Bia, he'd say. Do me a favour and imagine this. Imagine there's an anthill in your back yard. An anthill, sitting there quietly, with the ants coming and going but no one really noticing because they go about their business, carrying scraps of leaves back and forth or whatever it is they do. One day, someone comes into your back yard and kicks over the anthill. And suddenly, out of nowhere, they're everywhere. The ants. They're swarming all over the place, getting in your shoes and socks, climbing up your legs, heading straight for your pants. You had no idea there were so many of them. And the only way to get rid of them is to apply poison, and you'll need a lot of poison, to the anthill, to the yard, to all the hundreds of thousands of tiny ants. What do you do, Bia, in this situation?

The guilt is getting to him. He could resign, of course. His career in civilian security would be over – fuck, his career might be over completely. He wouldn't be able to explain his reasons. He'd become the failed eldest child, looked at by older relatives with pursed lips, a cluck of disapproval accompanying his entrance into any family scene.

But he wouldn't be a part of this.

He moves a holoma blocking the comms and puts in an encrypted request for a Tolstyi account. After a few moments, he is connected, and Bia's face materializes in front of him, her mouth hanging slack, mid-word, a child's yellow rucksack slung over one arm. Bia blinks once and redirects part of her focus, the smaller part, to Karis.

'Karis, is that you?'

'How are you, Bia?'

'Yeah, you know, it's the holidays, isn't it? We're all go here – what is it?'

'It's—' He hesitates. 'Have you got a minute?'

'Not really, I've got to get the kid to practice. Is it important?'

'No – no, it's not important. I'll catch you another time. Give my love to Grace.'

'I will do.'

Bia's face and the yellow rucksack blink away. Karis is left staring at the rectangular frame of the door through which Shri Nayar had walked, her shoulders hunched and locked with rage.

Karis hadn't always lied, because he hadn't always had this job, and secrecy had not been a part of his contract with the Republic. But he had found it easy, at first, at any rate. And soon enough the lies expanded into other areas of his life, not just where he worked but his home, his past, the things he had seen and done. He enjoyed it at first. It tasted sweet. And now, truth be told, he can't remember a time before the making up of things, can't get a feel for that other man.

Ants. Thousands of ants, scurrying about in confusion, unaware of their peril. A Bokolu is lurking nearby, but a Bokolu has excellent camouflage. By the time it strikes, it's far too late.

PATAGONIA

The Alaskan is unperturbed by the blindfold. Darkness is contentment, roaming the intricate labyrinth of her own thoughts while other senses test for the mood of those around her. It is always the little giveaways, molecules of sweat, sour to the nostrils, or a primitive, hormonal waft of excitement, that tell her what she needs to know. She can hear the effort in the shortened breaths of the man pushing her chair, and reclines back further into it, having no inclination to give her driver an easy ride.

When they remove the blindfold she finds herself in a rustic cabin opposite the man she has come to see. The cabin is warm and she can smell coffee. The Osirian is brewing a pot on a camping stove. Dark and skinny, he is. A face that might have been considered good-looking before the redfleur had its way with him, and by the looks of it the virus has had quite the party. She has a sense about him straight away: a sense that he has done things, morally ambiguous things, a man familiar with violence. The Alaskan's nose tickles uncontrollably. She snorts and pulls a crumpled handkerchief from her sleeve, blowing vigorously into it.

'Went to visit a friend of mine in Fuego Hospital and I've picked up a dozen bugs. They love me. The bugs. They like to feast.' She lets the word linger, savouring it, considering its implications. 'But you don't need to worry about that, do you?'

The Osirian laughs. A relaxed laugh, which surprises her. She realizes she expected him to be more like Taeo Ybanez, the Antarctican, whose desperation was never quite concealed despite his evident intelligence. Taeo Ybanez had never had to struggle. This one is different. This one screams trouble at fifty feet. The Alaskan likes that.

'Don't worry,' says the Osirian. 'I've caught plenty of colds. Plenty of – bugs, as you say.'

'Survived them all, did you? Never stopped to wonder why? Never stopped to think you might be a genetic freak?'

Her directness does impress upon him this time, she thinks. The Alaskan laughs herself then, long and hard, rocking forwards and back in her chair, the phlegm coagulating in her throat as she fights for her breath. The pollen, she thinks. It's the fucking pollen.

'If you are, by the way, I can give you some advice,' she adds, when the convulsions have stopped. Her eyes are streaming. She extracts the handkerchief once again and swipes it across what is left of her eyelashes. 'I don't doubt Mig's told you some nice stories about nirvanas. How is my boy? Proud of yourself for stealing him off me, are you?'

'He never belonged to you,' says the Osirian evenly.

'That's where you're wrong. He did belong to me. You look like someone who should know about debt, Señor Nameless. Don't think I'll forget this any time soon.'

'He came of his own accord.'

She notices the slight stiffening of his body. Interesting. He cares about the boy.

'He betrayed me,' she says.

'And you look like someone who should know about betrayal,' he replies.

'Touché.'

She laughs again. The laugh forces an ache to her ribs. She isn't used to so much movement. Her muscles are in remission.

'I don't care what you are,' says the Osirian. 'Nirvana, or whatever it's known as. It's not important.'

'Easy for you to say, of course you don't. You're from a place that shouldn't exist. Common word has it you're a cannibalistic fish. Why should you care if my ancestors survived the Blackout?'

'Cannibalistic?' He sounds curious.

The Alaskan nods solemnly. The absurdity of it, she thinks. The dreads of the uneducated never change, and yet they are right. Deep down, when it comes to the dark spaces, the distillation of the soul, what is left but the animalistic? Hunt, eat, fuck, shit. She taps the arm of her chair.

'That's a tidy little collection of lunatics you've assembled. What are you going to do with them all?'

'I think you probably have some ideas.'

'You are correct. I do. Antarctica, that's one of them. And here's another: back to where you came from. There's no reason for you to go anywhere else. Which is it?'

He smiles. 'Perhaps we should discuss why you're here before I tell you that.'

'I thought I was here at your invitation, Señor Nameless.'

'And you accepted the invitation.'

'I did. I admit, I was intrigued. This is an old country. Everything is old here. It's an excursion back through time. Have you ever wanted to travel through time, señor? Ever been curious to see how we got ourselves into this kind of world? What lies did they feed you, shut away in your lost city for all those years? What did they say to make you stop using your heads?'

The Osirian elects not to answer, either because she has insulted him, or because he is smart enough not to respond to provocation. She hopes for both their sakes it is the latter. You would have to be smart, she thinks, to get out of a city that has retained camouflage for half a century. Smart or lucky.

She watches as the Osirian removes the pot of coffee from the stove and pours two mugs. He pushes one towards her.

'Do you want to work with us?' he asks.

'What are you offering?'

'You left Cataveiro,' says the man. 'Mig tells me you haven't left that city in decades. There must have been a reason. I think you want to go somewhere new.'

The Alaskan shrugs. 'An easy assumption, but lazy. Cataveiro has nothing more to offer me. For now. Besides, you might have heard, it wasn't the most hospitable place to be just lately.'

'So come with us. Help us find a ship.'

'I can't find you a ship if I don't know where it's going.'

The man meets her eyes candidly and he says, 'It's going to Osiris.'

'Ha! You want to take me to what's about to become a war zone?'

'You'd find it an interesting place.'

'I might, if I weren't dead.'

'I suspect you'll find a way to escape being dead. You seem to have managed well enough so far.'

The Alaskan wriggles in her chair, trying to find a position of equal discomfort between the competing aches in her ribs, her spine, and her pelvis.

'You're a fool if you don't think the Antarcticans won't bomb your city into the seabed. If they haven't already, after that signal went out. They won't wait for the Boreals to come and reclaim it.'

'They'd cause an international incident if they did that.'

The Alaskan jabs a finger at the Osirian. 'Not if you are dead,' she says. 'It seems to me that you're wanted by a lot of people for a lot of different reasons. Perhaps I should have acted sooner instead of letting you slip through my fingers. This little hidey-hole won't stay secret forever, you know. However loyal your disciples might be.'

The Osirian looks troubled. 'I need to leave soon,' he says. 'It's true, the longer we wait, the more difficult it will be. And I need a ship. I know you can help me.'

'Everyone knows I can help them. Not everyone knows what they can do for me. Such is the regrettable inequality of life.'

'I can't do anything for you,' he says. 'Except for this. I can take you somewhere new. I can give you the chance to see something you haven't seen before. And. . . you could help save lives.'

There's sincerity in his voice, she can't deny that. But sincerity is a low currency.

'Is this an appeal to my better nature? Business is business, Mr Bai. Yes, I know your name. Of course I do. You think I've been sitting around twiddling my thumbs in Fuego? Now, I'll tell you my offer. I want Antarctican citizenship. I want a ship to take me to the new world, and a nice house waiting for me when I get there. Do whatever it takes to get me that, and I'll consider helping you.'

'Why would I have leverage with the Antarcticans?'

The Alaskan tests the coffee. It's tolerable. It could use a helping or three of sugar.

'If you are what they say you are, you'll have leverage with a lot of people. When you go to Osiris, what do you intend to do? Deals will be brokered. I will need to be a part of that.'

'Regardless of whether I have leverage or not, I can't do anything until this is over. The ship has to come first.'

'We can call it an IOU,' says the Alaskan.

The Osirian's face closes down when she says that. She's stumbled upon a sensitivity.

'You have a problem with this?' she says coyly.

He shifts his shoulders uneasily.

'If it's the only way, it's the only way.'

'Then we have a deal. And don't think if you renege on it I won't find a way to have you brutally terminated.'

'I believe you.'

'You should.'

The Alaskan allows that to sink in. Now that they've had a chance to chat, she is getting a sense for a deeper layer to the Osirian. Calm on top, oh yes, but there's depths beneath. Troubled depths. He knows he is running out of time.

'It's a shame the pilot's fled,' she remarks. 'Callejas could have flown you back to your precious city. Might have appreciated the commission now she's got a wanted sticker on her back.'

'Who wants her?'

'A very nasty woman who likes to drop people into ravines.' With a glint of pleasure, she recalls Xiomara's wan, angry face as she applied the skin patch. 'Oh, and the government. Her employer.'

'And there's no way we can contact her?'

'She's disappeared,' says the Alaskan. 'Last seen in Panama. She's probably dead. Brutal types, in Panama. They don't like being crossed.' The Alaskan waits a beat and adds, 'We have some things in common.'

'I've been looking at the captains of the Patagonian fleet—'

'No, no, no. No one legal. That's no use. There's only one ship good enough to take you where you want to go without being caught.'

The Osirian waits. She watches him push aside his impatience, as if he were a rock around which water swerves and parts. It occurs to her that he has learned this, that it does not come naturally to him, and she wonders what it would take to propel him back to the other side. The idea fills her with a sense of glee.

Still, there's no harm in throwing out a name.

'El Tiburón,' says the Alaskan. 'The shark.'

The stories about El Tiburón are enough to keep a grown woman – even a nirvana – awake at night. El Tiburón takes his, or her, inspiration – no one knows for sure and it is said that whoever El Tiburón really is, he, or she, uses doubles – from the pirates of centuries before. Pirates who shot the kneecaps out of their own crew and practised keelhauling as an artistic form. But El Tiburón also likes other toys: things acquired from the north, nerve gases and substances that worm through the brain and change behaviours, identities, the very concept of self. El Tiburón has had enemies dancing on the prow of his, or her, ship like monkeys, naked and sunburned, bleeding from self-inflicted wounds, prattling nonsense to the open seas until they topple to their drowning. El Tiburón likes to fish out the bodies from the water and extract some manner of trophy, which is then hammered to the superstructure of the ship until it begins to decompose.

These are the things that are said, and the Alaskan knows that it does not matter if they have happened or if they are mere rumour – the idea is sufficient. She has never had direct dealings with El Tiburón, but their paths have veered very close. Certainly, El Tiburón will know her name. It would be logical to be afraid, or at the least wary of such an approach, but it is a long time since the Alaskan felt fear. She is not sure she would even recognize it.

After her meeting with Vikram Bai, the Alaskan wheels out into the camp, and selects a spot at the edge of the clearing, where she can retreat into the shade if the heat becomes too much. Twinges of nerve pain prickle her arms. She does not know how long she can keep up this level of exertion. The Osirian is not the only one running out of time.

Vikram Bai's acolytes go about their business with a quiet focus. There are men and women in equal numbers, of varying ages, although she notes there are no children younger than Mig; this is an adult venture, albeit one the Alaskan cannot bring herself to take entirely seriously. She hears jokes, and occasional laughter, but mostly they are absorbed in whatever activities go on within the shelter of their tents or their hideaways deeper in the forest. Evidently they are self-sufficient. There is food stored on the site; they must have a regular chain of supply. She sees maps laid out on the ground, personal weapons being discussed and compared – she notices they all carry rudimentary arms, and does not doubt it is for the Osirian's defence as much as their own protection.

Her boy Mig is nowhere to be seen.

After a few minutes Vikram Bai comes out of his cabin. His followers act like children around him. Everyone wants a prophet, thinks the Alaskan sourly.

It is different for nirvanas. A nirvana has no choice but to relinquish dependency. Forge her own path through the world.

She watches the Osirian move from group to group, noting how careful he is to exchange at least a word with each individual. She observes how their faces transform, the eagerness and deference they exhibit. She looks critically at the women. Some of them are pretty. In any case, fervour animates a face, lending a flush to the cheeks and a sparkle to the eye. Probably, these women look prettier than they are. None of them compare to the Scandinavian girl.

Most of these people have lost someone to redfleur. They are here for redemption. To be absolved for having survived. She wonders, now, how much the Osirian truly knows. How aware can he be of the ripples his presence is creating?

She hasn't told him everything. She has told him about fish and cannibalism but she hasn't told him about the strange following he is accumulating across the archipelago, and further north into the uninhabitable zone, perhaps even beyond it. She hasn't told him about the shrines reputedly springing up in homes or the sea-worshippers that stride out into the cool Patagonian waters, letting the waves swirl about their calves and scouring the horizon for a glimpse of a fantastical city. She hasn't told him about the boats that have already left in search of this strange place, one of them returned smashed to pieces on the shoreline in the wake of a storm, another intercepted, the boat stripped to its skeleton and its crew thrown overboard by pirates, probably El Tiburón. These things, she keeps to herself.

The summer sun is warm against her slack skin and the metal spokes of the chair wheels grow hot to the touch, but the Alaskan keeps touching them nonetheless, her fingers drawn to the searing heat. There is something familiar about this climate. Familiarity is dangerous, provoking memories best left boxed, but the Alaskan allows herself to succumb to this one, very carefully, only thinking about the weather, the soft warmth, nothing more.

After she has been sitting here for a while, people wander up to her.

They say hello and introduce themselves. The Alaskan does not offer her own name. No one presses her, but they don't appear afraid, which makes her think the Osirian has told Mig not to reveal her identity. She can imagine very well how she must present to them: an old woman shrunk against a wheelchair, folded in on herself like a lemon rind squeezed of its juice, a creature already in negotiation with death. Carried here, transported, with no will in the motion, perhaps for one final crusade. Her family, they will think, with sympathy. She's lost her family and this is all she has left. Empathy rolls off them, the Osirian's acolytes.

It is a question worth asking. Why is she doing this? What's in it for her now? She wasn't joking when she told the Osirian his city would become a war zone. For all they know, the Antarcticans have already made their decision. So why would the Alaskan even consider taking a trip into the throes of the South Atlantic Ocean? Is she exercising some manner of previously unsuspected death wish? Has she, in fact, had enough of this warped and peculiar world?

The Alaskan sits in the sun and watches the acolytes, industrious as ants, and considers these questions.

The nirvana faces away from Mig in the bright light of noon. For two years in Cataveiro he ran her errands, aware of the power that she wielded from the squalor of an attic bed, and yet he never feared her in the way that he does now. The chair is new, and alarming. Like that snake in the jar, at any moment she might spring from a state of stillness into something diabolical.

He takes the piece of rope from his pocket and twists it between his hands, knotting and unknotting, seeking to calm himself. They cannot trust the Alaskan: this is clear to Mig and should be clear to Vikram, but Vikram has not listened. Instead he has invited the Alaskan in. He's even given her the second cabin to sleep in. However, Vikram's failure to comprehend the truth brings Mig an opportunity.

Revenge is now within his grasp.

He will have to plan carefully and pick his moment.

If he stares at the Alaskan for too long he finds that his breath becomes short and his vision speckled and so he takes himself away, to the other side of the camp, to occupy himself with the radio hub. The Alaskan is not the only one who knows how to get information.

He holds on to Pilar's feather in his pocket. There's not much left of it now, other than the spine and a few sticky strands, but he won't let it go. When no one is looking he wraps it in his palm and whispers to it.

'It won't be long now. I'm going to get her. I promise.'

Shri isn't sure what she expects of Patagonia. Something – oh, she doesn't know – *different* to Antarctica. Something hot and arid, and the people, not struggling exactly, but not flourishing either, a sullenness about them. She doesn't expect prosperity. It's summer, a gentle, temperate summer, and the climate feels like an affront. The country where Taeo died should be in turmoil, slabs of ground literally tearing in two, the sea walls under assault. The thought is absurd, and yet she cannot think small. Only extremities are left to her.

Shri steps off the boat alone. The commander, that cold-hearted son-of-a-bitch, explained it had to be this way. *You won't be alone. But it needs to look like you are.* The harbour is busy with Patagonian fishers, small boats, small ships, buildings with walls in red and pink and blue, the mountain behind, a quaint air to everything like this is a toy town, a fakery. She struggles to imagine Taeo in this place.

A little further out from the harbour, she sees a flock of gulls wheeling and screaming, their circle interrupted by the occasional swoop to the surface, where more of the fishing boats are gathered. There's something in the water. Something long and grey, streaked with pink. It's a whale, she realizes, and it's dead. The thick grey skin has been sliced into and peeled back to expose the rosy flesh, a hint of white beneath, blubber or bone, and the whale's blood is leaking into the surrounding water. The fishing boats are herding the carcass towards the shore, presumably to butcher it. *Whalers.* Shri turns away in disgust.

She looks back at the town. Now she's here it is tempting to cut and run. Track down the man – the Osirian – for herself. But she knows the Antarctica network will have eyes on her, and besides, there's the children. She can't risk any screw-ups.

Strange how you can live within a regime, entirely unaware of the anatomy which underpins it, until one thing happens. And then all at once the bones are visible and you realize it has been there all along.

At the harbour front she asks for directions to the Facility, speaking pointedly, as instructed, in Boreal English, until someone who can understand the language directs her up the mountain. She sees a steep path winding uphill, away from the town – that way? She receives a brusque nod. She starts to make her way through the streets of the harbour town. There are no vehicles, everyone is on foot, and everyone seems to be looking at her, not in a friendly manner, and she begins to feel anxious. She hasn't got very far when she notices a man hurrying in her direction. Towards her? Yes, he's definitely heading for her. She slows, alarmed by the thought that he might be dangerous, but on the narrow street there's no avoiding him. As he reaches her, the man puts a hand on her arm and guides her to the side of the street, shielding their conversation from anyone passing by. She can see the consternation in his face.

'You came off the boat? The Antarctican boat?'

He speaks in home patois.

'Yes, I – I just got here.'

Shri is thrown. She did not expect to be accosted so immediately, even by a fellow Republican.

'You shouldn't be walking alone in the town. Who sent you here? Who are you? We're not expecting a visitor.'

'My name is Shri Nayar,' she says. 'My partner was stationed at the Facility.'

The Antarctican recognizes her name. She sees pity creeping into his face and she carries on before he can say something, *I'm sorry*, or some other useless platitude.

'I'm looking for someone. He's known as the Osirian. I need to find him. Can you help me?'

The man's expression changes. Surprise, this time. He darts a look up and down the street and she has the sense that he is afraid.

'Come with me. We can't talk here.'

He makes coffee at his house. The space feels strange to her, cluttered with physical artefacts which she takes to be of native origin. A large fabric hanging with stylized drawings of animals – a spider, a monkey, a hummingbird, and a whale – decorates the length of one wall. The coffee is dark and bitter to taste. The Antarctican's name is Ivra, he tells her. He was her partner's – he was Taeo's bodyguard. He goes on quickly, perhaps afraid she will lay blame. Taeo was a good guy, but headstrong, he says. He had his own ideas. There was a shipwreck, the Osirian boat, then the signal – well, everyone knows about it now, and he assumes that's why she's here. Why else would she be looking for the man? Taeo went to investigate, alone. The next thing anyone knew, he was in Cataveiro, in the middle of a redfleur epidemic, with the rogue Osirian. She knows Cataveiro? About the redfleur? Fuck, what a mess. What a catastrophe. He's lived here ten years and this is the second time it's struck. The death toll was worse this time. Nearly ten thousand people. They've only just contained it. A brooding expression settles on Ivra's face and he stares into his mug of coffee.

Shri nods and then shakes her head. She has a vague concept of redfleur, as something that happens *over there*. Over here, she thinks. Over here. She should feel something. The sheer number of casualties should affect her, but all she has is a niggling impatience that Ivra is talking about this, this other catastrophe, when she has come here to investigate her own tragedy.

'The Osirian,' she reminds him.

Ivra cradles his coffee mug. His hands engulf it. He's a big man and the whole house seems too small for his frame.

'What do you know about him?'

Shri tells the truth.

'He sent me a message.'

'A message?'

'A holoma.'

'That's strange,' he says. 'He shouldn't have been able to work a personalized holoma. Unless. . . unless Taeo gave him access.'

He falls silent, either unwilling to or wary of speculating further. Shri ignores the implication.

'I don't care how he did it, I need to find him. I want to speak with him. You knew my partner. You'll help me, won't you?'

Ivra is distracted. He says she will hear some things, some strange things, about this Osirian. There are stories, he says. People are – well, they're becoming obsessed, with the idea of it, of him, that's what's happening, but no one will believe it back in the Republic. Stories are powerful things and it's foolish to underestimate their currency, the way they grab at hearts and minds, especially hearts open to listening, and in this country. . .

Ivra laces those large hands nervously. He says he's worried the Republic will do something foolish. Or they'll do it but not quick enough and before you know it the Boreals will be on the doorstep.

Shri decides not to mention the protests back home in Belgrano. She doesn't want to divert him further. She wants facts. She wants to know where the Osirian is. Ivra says the rumours are he's still on the archipelago, but no one knows where exactly. Or even which island. People go to find him and most of them don't come back. Those who do return are interrogated by the Patagonian government, but it's like they've been bewitched, and still no one knows anything. The route to the Osirian is fiercely guarded and there are no identifiable geographical clues or markers from the actual hideout to suggest his whereabouts.

Still, says Ivra, it can't go on forever. Sooner or later he'll slip up.

'So what happens to these people? You said most of them don't come back. Is this man dangerous?'

'Dangerous? Of course he's dangerous.'

But there are lots of ways you can be dangerous. This is what he means when he talks about the stories. The Osirian is an idea. The most dangerous kind of dangerous. But perhaps Shri doesn't know – he might as well tell her, if he doesn't, someone else will. Ivra's voice drops a level. The Osirian *survived*. He survived the redfleur, that's why everyone wants to find him. Ivra hesitates and then he says, *he's a miracle*, the tinge of sarcasm in his tone not entirely eradicating the suggestion that he might believe it.

Not for me, thinks Shri. Not unless he can bring people back from the dead. And she feels a surge of rage that this Osirian should survive when Taeo did not.

Ivra drains his coffee before speaking again. It's unlikely the Osirian is killing people off, if that's what she means. More likely he's assembling them.

'Like an army?'

Ivra doesn't know. Maybe.

Shri can't decide what to make of this. In coming here she has not really considered the Osirian's motivations – she only wants to see him, and gain the opportunity to interrogate him. Vikram Bai is the last piece of Taeo that exists in this world. She was told that his body was burned. The ashes buried, in haste and without ceremony, in a foreign piece of ground which she will never see or know. It's been strictly impressed upon her that under no circumstances should she attempt the journey to Cataveiro.

Ivra, left in silence, now turns the questions upon Shri.

'You've come here alone?'

'Yes.'

'Do the Republic know?'

Shri's moment of hesitation is enough. He slumps.

'Of course they know. You've been sent here, of course you have. That's how they do things.'

'I'm only just realizing how they do things,' says Shri. 'I have three kids at home. They've just lost their father. Do you really think I'd come here on a whim?'

Ivra seems curiously deflated by the realization. She wonders if he would have preferred it the other way, the romantic notion of her deserting her family, fleeing across the ocean to find the place where her partner died. And yes, it is romantic, but romantic for someone who is not a parent. Who could willingly leave her grieving children hundreds of kilometres away with no assurances, no promises of return, to fling herself upon the hope of a grave and bury her face in the dirt.

Romantic, yes. But an impossible luxury.

'I don't know,' says Ivra. 'I don't know anything about you except what Taeo told me. And he was mostly drunk when he talked.'

She senses he regrets the words as soon as he has uttered them, but there is no way to retract the statement. She looks at Ivra and sees a man who is unravelling. Who somewhere along the line has lost faith and sense and is now struggling to restore something, anything. And instead of pity, she feels the need to punish him. She wants to make someone else hurt the way she is hurting.

'You should have gone with him,' she says. 'You were meant to protect him. That was your job.'

Ivra stares at her helplessly.

'Don't say you're sorry. It's too late for that.'

'What can I do?'

'You can help me find this man. The sooner I can find him, the sooner I can go home.'

The room where Taeo was housed is a concrete box. The bed has been made up and the space is clean and empty, awaiting a new occupant. Another Antarctican exile. One tiny window offers a bleak view of the mountainside. Bare rock and dense, forbidding forestry. Shri puts her nose to the glass and breathes out and imagines how Taeo must have hurt, standing here, how a room like this must have felt like a prison. Of course he drank; his loneliness must have equalled hers, exceeded it – at least she had the kids. Only for him that's all over now. He's left her behind.

Downstairs they give her a box with his personal effects. There isn't much inside. He didn't take much with him. That was her fault.

By the time she returns to Ivra's house he has found them a guide for the first stage of their journey. She leaves the box of Taeo's things in the house. The same day they depart Fuego and head out into the archipelago. As the boat drives out she looks back once at the toy town, assuming the commander's people are following, but if they are she sees no sign of them. After all her months observing the Adélie colony, she is now the endangered animal being watched.

El Tiburón sends the co-ordinates for their meeting place in a sealed envelope which also contains a dead scorpion. The creature's body is crushed and its blood has smeared over the paper, but the deadly curl in its tail is still evident. Vikram shows the Alaskan, who raises an eyebrow but says they should not be alarmed; this is simply El Tiburón's way of making sure they keep their counsel. Vikram doesn't tell Mig. The boy is already angry over the Alaskan's involvement; he doesn't want to add to his doubts.

The pirate has chosen a remote location out to the west which no one in the camp has ever visited. On that side of the archipelago, the land fragments into hundreds of islands, some densely forested, others barely more than rock, all of them difficult or impossible to access and largely uninhabited by human residents. The steep sea channels are littered with the carcasses of boats run aground. El Tiburón's ship must have a hiding place among these treacherous coves; it probably has many.

It is the first time that Vikram has departed the camp since they found their site, and he is nervous. He doesn't like leaving people behind. The camp feels exposed, as though by removing himself he is removing its implicit protection. He doesn't like the idea of placing himself in the pirate's power either, but events have backed him into a corner. Every day that passes is another day lost, another day where a signal drops into the ether and the Antarcticans might choose to invade Osiris, or worse. Throughout the short summer nights he lies awake, tormented by visions of the place he called home, besieged, the people he knew consumed in flames or drowning in the waterways that sustain them. So many have died already because of his actions. He can't be the arbiter of any more death; he isn't sure he could survive it.

Only a handful of people come with him. Mig. The Alaskan, reclining on a crudely constructed stretcher. They are relying on her to negotiate with the pirate. A couple of long-term camp members, both expert sailors. They leave at dawn. Crossing the island terrain to the sea is difficult with the stretcher, and their progress is slow, the many obstacles in their way causing the Alaskan to be bumped and jolted about. If the uneven movement causes her pain she gives no sign of it, and when Vikram glances back to check on her, her peculiar black eyes meet his with assurance, almost defiance.

He puts Mig in the lead. The boy is a good scout, and it keeps the Alaskan out of his sight.

It is a relief to reach the sea. From here they can travel by boat. It isn't a good day for it – a grey and ochre sky overhead forebodes storms, and the water is rushing swiftly through the channels, flecked with hostile foam. The journey takes them the rest of the day, leaving the party tired and jumpy. At the forefront of Vikram's mind is the knowledge that if they run aground, or capsize, the Alaskan will not be able to swim. But the two sailors guide the boat to their allotted co-ordinates without incident.

They find themselves alighting on a steep, rocky beach on a small island hemmed in by larger and higher land masses, which cast the beach in shadow. Cave entrances riddle the side of the cliff face. They pull the boat up high onto the beach and prepare to wait. Vikram scans the sea, the slopes of the surrounding islands, but can see no evidence of human life, or any other kind of animal. Only the birds have made their nests here. Their keening cries reverberate across the water. If anything happens to them in this lonely place, only the birds will witness it.

The two sailors stick together, talking skittishly about the tides, before their discussion drifts to other, darker things. Mig's attention is caught.

'What are you talking about?'

'Monsters,' says one of the sailors.

'Monsters, aye.'

'I thought you were talking about serious stuff.'

'Who says it's not serious?'

'Go on then. Tell me.'

'Did you know a race of giants used to live here?'

Mig laughs. 'Giants? Is that supposed to scare me?'

The sailors exchange a glance.

'They're long dead, it's true. But there's other things. Things you don't see. A spirit in the straits, long, skinny thing with a head like a cat and a tail like a shrub. Doesn't like people trying to cross the water. Stops them. Drowns them. Comes from below.'

'Or from above,' says the other, swooshing an arm towards Mig's head and grabbing a handful of his hair.

'Oy!'

'A flying snake that sucks your blood. Changes shape when you're looking the other way.'

'Like a pirate.'

'Aye, like a pirate.'

'You're talking shit,' says Mig.

'Maybe, maybe not.' The first sailor casts a sombre look skywards, where abrupt, orange rays of light pierce the clouds to reveal a lowering sun. 'When they buried my grandfather, he looked like a lemon that had shrivelled up in the sun. Not a drop of blood left in the old carcass. Something got to him.'

'All right then. If your water spirit's so dangerous, why didn't it stop us?'

The first sailor pulls something from a pocket. Something furred and bloody with tiny feet curled in on its belly. Mig peers. A dead rat. He can see the incision where its throat has been opened up.

'You have to appease it,' says the sailor.

A purple gloom descends across the archipelago. Mig, fascinated by the caves, wanders over to investigate. Vikram watches, wanting to call him back but knowing it will only annoy the boy. Mig ducks in and out of visibility. Each time he is lost to sight Vikram feels a renewed tug of anxiety. He remembers the scorpion. What if those caves are a trap?

'Feeling responsible?' says the Alaskan. Her tone is sardonic. Vikram joins her by the boat.

'It was his choice to come with me.'

'When he made that choice I don't suppose he knew quite how dangerous a person you are to be around.'

'What am I supposed to do, send him away?'

'Don't ask me. You can't train kids like him. They're sweet as syrup until the day they betray you.'

'You're still angry,' he says.

The Alaskan laughs, then sneezes. Her eyes start to water. Vikram half expects the moisture to be black too.

'Angry? No, not angry. Just amused.'

Vikram looks at her.

'How are you holding up? The journey here was rough.'

She sniffs.

'What do you care?'

Mig has disappeared from view for several minutes. Vikram scans the row of cave entrances worriedly.

'Mig! Mig, get back here!'

'If I were you I wouldn't speak quite so loudly.'

Vikram whips around. A figure is striding towards them across the gloom of the beach. They have not come from either of the directions Vikram anticipated – the sea or the caves – and the only other way of reaching the cove would be by clambering down the sheer face of the cliff. Apparently the pirate has accomplished this in silence, surprising all of them.

The pirate approaches. They are dressed in leathers and camouflage, pistols clearly visible at each hip and a rifle slung over the back. A tricorne hat shadows the face. As the figure draws closer Vikram glimpses tinted glasses and a face that is smooth and androgynous, the sort of face that could, from a distance, be mistaken for a woman. But the faint shadow across the chin and the breadth of shoulder would appear to confirm El Tiburón's much-disputed gender.

The pirate comes to a halt a couple of metres away. His head turns slowly, taking in their motley crew.

'You make a lot of noise,' he says at last. His voice is a light tenor, soft and persuasive. The two sailors shift uneasily on their feet, and Vikram wishes he had asked them to wait at the other end of the beach. Out of the corner of his eye he can see Mig picking his way back across the rocks. He moves slightly to place himself between the pirate and the boy.

The pirate steps across to the Alaskan.

'You, I know.'

Unexpectedly, he drops to one knee and kisses the Alaskan's hand.

'Flatterer,' she says.

'Flattery is deserved,' replies the pirate, rising. 'And these?'

Instinct tells Vikram to answer with absolute honesty.

'My name is Vikram Bai,' he says. 'These are my associates.' He names the two sailors and Mig, who has reached them, and is eyeing the pirate closely.

'You are the Osirian.'

'Yes.'

'A lot of people desire your head.'

'Probably.'

'A wanted man.'

Vikram says nothing. He feels the pirate's eyes behind their glasses, roving over him. He stands his ground.

'You come to me for assistance,' says the pirate.

'I need a ship.'

The pirate gestures.

'There are many ships in Patagonia.'

'I need a ship that isn't afraid of a challenge.'

'So.' The pirate takes a step closer. His right hand, gloved, curls around the holster of the pistol. 'I am not interested in bravado.' He points to the Alaskan. 'She is why I am here. Her message piqued my attention.'

The Alaskan displays no interest in this statement.

A shout from above interrupts them, startling Vikram and the others. It sounds like a warning. El Tiburón turns and barks something back in a language Vikram does not recognize. Then, with no warning, he sprints across the beach, drops to one knee, tosses aside his hat and takes the rifle from his back, aiming the weapon out to sea. Vikram follows the line of sight and can just make out the bobbing light of a small boat.

The pirate fires a number of precise, soundless bolts. That's not Patagonian technology, Vikram thinks, unsettled. It is too far away to see whether the pirate has hit his mark, but somehow Vikram does not doubt it. He senses the jitteriness of Mig at his side and knows the boy will have questions later about the company they are keeping. He cannot let Mig know he shares the boy's fears.

'What was that about?' he asks the Alaskan quietly. He doesn't want to ask the obvious question. If they have made a mistake, there is no getting out of it now. The shout from above made it clear the pirate is not alone.

'A warning, I suspect,' she answers.

'To them?'

'To us.'

'How many warnings do we need?'

'A lot of people would like to execute El Tiburón,' she says. 'Perhaps even more than would like to get hold of you.'

El Tiburón waits a moment, despatches one more round, and rises, returning his hat to his head. The pirate proceeds to walk calmly back to where they are waiting, strolling along the water line. Vikram can hear the ocean lapping at the beach. The tide is coming in. Within the hour, this cove will be flooded.

'Who were they?' Vikram asks.

An expression of surprise crosses the pirate's face.

'Should I know? They threatened this meeting.'

'Did you kill them?' asks Mig.

The pirate gives him a haughty glance.

'Certainly.'

Vikram keeps his face carefully neutral.

'El Tiburón, the Alaskan tells me you are the only captain who can help us. What can we do to persuade you?'

'I will take you.'

'You will?'

Vikram looks to the Alaskan, and catches her in the midst of re-arranging her face. She's as surprised as me, he thinks. She was expecting to bargain.

'I haven't said where I'm going—'

'It is not hard to guess. You are correct, I am the only who can take you to Osiris. Any others will fail.' The pirate extends one gloved hand. Cautiously, Vikram takes it, and they shake briefly as people do in this country in greeting or farewell. El Tiburón tips his hat in a salute that appears ironic, and turns on his heel.

'How we will know—'

'I'll send word. Via the nirvana.'

The two sailors are jolted by that. They stare at the Alaskan, then drop their gaze uncomfortably. The Alaskan laughs hoarsely.

'Thank you for that, El Tiburón.'

The sailors begin to push the boat towards the tideline, conversing between themselves, clearly disturbed by the revelation, or the pirate, or both. Mig stares after the retreating pirate. His hand is in his pocket, squeezing the length of rope he carries with him everywhere. Blurring into the dusk, Vikram sees the faint outline of El Tiburón scaling the cliff, moving hand over hand like a gecko. He blinks, and the man has vanished.

'There were bones in the caves.' Mig's voice at his side is very quiet. 'Leg and arm bones, all stacked up together, in rows. I never saw bones like that. I never saw so many.'

'It's probably nothing to do with El Tiburón,' says Vikram.

'Then why did he want to meet here?'

Vikram doesn't answer immediately.

'You have to trust me on this, Mig. It's our best chance.'

It's too dark to see Mig's expression, but his disbelief hangs between them, and the boy heads back to the boat without another word.

Another day. Another island. Shri has lost track of how many they have visited. They all look the same. The dancing trees and the sea and the insects at night and when the insects finally stop the silence, a different calibre of silence to the deaf and blind swaddling of Antarctica, one full of hidden things and things withheld. Then there was a storm, abrupt and terrifying, that almost blew them out to sea, and lost half of their provisions. The physical hardships she could manage, if it weren't for the children's absence, eating away at her like a sore that refuses to heal. She can't connect to them. She can't see their faces or hear their voices. She can't protect them from those little shits at school. She's been cut loose.

Meanwhile, their goal remains frustratingly elusive. Ask an inhabitant of the archipelago and they'll nod and hum and swear they know and yet reveal nothing. The man who survived redfleur? Oh yes, we know who you mean. He's on this island. No, that island. No, the one after that, for certain. Go west, five kilometres, say? Maybe six. You'll find it. There's a cliff whose face is marked with the shape of the parrot. There's a tree with its branches burned to a stump. You'll know it when you see it. You'll know it for certain.

'I'm beginning to think they're all lying to me,' she says to Ivra. 'No one wants me to find this man. What if we can't find him? What if he doesn't even exist?'

'It's not lying,' Ivra says. 'It's the Patagonian way.'

'I hate the Patagonian way. No one tells you anything. They never answer questions with an answer.' This doesn't seem adequate to express her frustrations, so she casts about for something more concrete. 'They kill *whales*.'

'What do you mean?'

'I saw a whale, in the harbour, when I arrived.' Shri remembers vividly the mammal's blood leaking into the sea. The water turning to red. 'It had been slaughtered.'

Ivra's expression clears.

'That's not the case. That whale came in from the ocean. It tried to swim into the archipelago. It was dying.' Ivra pauses. 'It was fleeing from something.'

'That's ridiculous. Face up to it, your precious Patagonians are whalers.'

'It was fleeing,' Ivra insists. 'It had been attacked. The ocean's changed, you know. We don't know what's out there any more. The whale is an animal of the Nazca, no Patagonian would ever harm one. But have it your way, if you want.'

He turns his back, clearly offended. I'm pushing him away, thinks Shri. But I can't help it. I can't stand this place. I have to find the Osirian, and soon.

The message from the daily scout report is unambiguous. Taeo Ybanez's partner is in Patagonia, and she is looking for the Osirian.

This unexpected development throws the camp into turmoil and presents Vikram with a new quandary. He had anticipated there might be repercussions from the holoma, but not this – not the woman in person. And it appears she is travelling with someone: another Antarctican exile, a man who has been in the country for over a decade, whose loyalties are questionable, to say the least. Shri's presence, and the openness of her mission, creates a new danger. The longer she is out there, asking questions, making herself visible, the greater the possibility of attracting attention to their camp. She has already veered close to their island.

Vikram gives instructions to leave her looking. They have a departure date from El Tiburón. They don't have to hold out for much longer. He tries to shut out memories of Taeo, dead on his back, the lingering fumes of opium, the hologram of his partner, frozen. But they refuse to go quietly.

'Please eat something,' says Ivra. 'I'm worried about you.'

'I'm not hungry.'

'You have to eat. I can't let you get sick.'

'I'm not hungry, Ivra. Anyway, we should conserve what we have. Please, just leave me in peace.'

She is thinking of Tuesday. That Tuesday, now the only Tuesday which matters. The word they used was accident, not suicide, but accident is easier to say: blameless, requiring no interrogation. How is she to know the truth? The truth is that Taeo changed, and she did not see it. She can only guess at when and how the process began. Was it standing in the room at the Facility, a space with four walls but in every other way the antithesis of home? Was it this whispering, allusive climate that did it? The way the trees communicate at night? Or exile to a place forgotten and insignificant where it is possible to become forgotten and insignificant, or realize that you always were, or at least come to believe it.

Or further back: perhaps in the moment of crossing, the moment over water, caught between two countries. Or the morning of waking, to discover anew what he had done, the morning she stood over him and said *tell me this is a terrible mistake, Taeo, tell me* and even as he opened his eyes, bleary and bloodshot, she knew it was not and that the consequences would be severe and brutal. Or at the point of composing, drunk but in a state of what he claimed was clarity. Or before that. When he put his DNA to the super-ships contract. When they moved into the central, more affluent part of Vosti with credit from a job in Civilian Security. When Kadi was born and they looked at their tiny daughter covered in blood and mucus and felt for the first time the weight of responsibility for a lifetime beyond their own.

She finds her thoughts turning to Cataveiro. When she first arrived in Patagonia the idea had seemed absurd, a lunatic's cause. Now she can see how one might, suddenly, take flight, embark on the lunatic mission. That this might bring her closer to him.

Ivra is studying her worriedly.

'At least have some water,' he presses.

'They must be following us,' she says. 'Civilian Security. Our defenders. They said they'd be right behind me. But I've never seen them. Not a glimpse, not even during that storm. We might have died. Perhaps something's happened. Perhaps they don't need me any more and they've left us out here. Have you thought of that, Ivra? Have you considered that they've abandoned us, you and me both?'

'Oh yes,' he says absently. 'I used to believe in the Republic, you know. Then I realized they'd fucked over this country as much as the Boreals. Though the Boreals might still be worse. You know they have treatments, for what people here call the jinn, for the older redfleur strains? Price they put on it, you've got to be a tycoon to import that stuff.'

She watches the wave caps ruffling the strait below.

'You've got a thing for the Patagonians, don't you, Ivra?'

'I just see things how they are.'

'You ever think about where you come from?'

'My home town?'

'I mean your family. Your ancestry, the old countries.'

'Not before I came here. Then, maybe. But Brazil's a desert now. I went once, to the edge. It's true I felt something there, a call, I can't explain it. Like I could walk out and keep on walking, like if I gave up my life for the desert it would give back something so. . . exquisite, it wouldn't matter that I was dead.'

'I don't understand you,' she says.

'That's all right,' he says. 'Nor do I.'

'This country makes you think too much.'

'It does something.'

'She's on the next island,' says the scout. 'She's been there for the past twenty-four hours, on the beach. Just sitting there.'

'She's a problem,' says the Alaskan. 'You need to deal with her.'

'You can't bring her here,' says Mig furiously.

'I didn't say bring her here,' says the Alaskan. 'I said deal with her.'

'So you want to kill her?' Mig turns to Vikram, his eyes bright with rage and hurt. 'That's what she means. It's what she does!'

The Alaskan rolls her eyes. Mig can see what she's doing. Bending them, playing them like cards. Don't listen to *him*, she seems to say. *He's* only a boy. What does he know?

'Nobody's going to kill anyone,' says Vikram. 'She's not to be harmed. That's an order.' He sits in thought. 'If she's still there tomorrow I'll go to her. But not on the beach. Get her somewhere out of sight.'

Mig slouches away. This is a ridiculous plan. He goes to sit by his radio hub, an activity which usually calms him, or at least offers a distraction. He fiddles with the dials, trying to find a better signal. There is never a good signal here. He misses the music stations, the samba and the tango and the drums. You can't get a murmur out of Station Cataveiro. He has spent hours trying to trap a station that might play the recording of Pilar's last fado, but he's never heard it, not once, though he knows it's out there and others have, have spoken of the beautiful voice, a voice of angels, like nothing you've heard before. Is this Pilar's last laugh? Her voice is like a spirit that loiters just behind your shoulder but disappears in the moment you turn, giggling to itself, pleased with the joke.

He hasn't been long at the hub when he hears the unmistakeable sound of the Alaskan wheeling across the ground towards him. Mig stiffens. He keeps his back turned and concentrates on the radio he is working with.

The Alaskan rolls to a halt.

'What a neat little setup, Mig,' she says. 'Funnily enough, it reminds me of the one we had in Cataveiro.'

Ignore her, he tells himself fiercely. Ignore the freak.

'And how are you enjoying being the Osirian's shrimp?' she continues.

How he hates that voice. He shouldn't respond, he knows he shouldn't – but he can't help himself.

'I'm not his shrimp.'

'As you say,' says the Alaskan. 'As you say.'

Mig resists the urge to get the rope and throttle her there and then.

'I'm working,' he says instead.

'And I'm sitting.'

'You can sit somewhere else.'

'I'm nicely accommodated just here, in this. . . charming patch of dirt.'

Her eyes glint, the way they do when she is sparring with some unfortunate in her debt. She is enjoying his discomfort.

'You left me alone in Cataveiro, Mig,' she says. 'Left me to die, like a rat in a trap.'

'You didn't though, did you?' he says savagely. 'You didn't die.'

He turns his back but there is no point in trying to work the radios with the Alaskan lurking a pace away; equally he does not want to move, to leave the radios in her proximity and concede that she has won, so he sits in seething silence, making a show of listening to the spluttery signal, until he notices someone is watching them. Watching, but pretending not to. It's one of the sailors who came with them to meet the pirate.

Deliberately now, Mig gets up and goes to join the sailor.

'Is it true, what the pirate said? That she's a. . .' the sailor hesitates. 'A nirvana?'

'She told me herself,' says Mig. 'You should stay away from her.'

'Vikram trusts her.'

'Vikram doesn't know her. I do.'

The Alaskan remains by the radios, her head tipped back to absorb every available ray of the sunlight. A smile on her sagging face.

'You think she'd betray us?' asks the sailor.

'Those monsters you were talking about? The blood-suckers?'

'What about them?'

'That's her,' says Mig. 'That's what she is.'

Shri Nayar. Vikram recognizes her straight away, although she looks different from the woman in the holoma, lesser somehow, drained and exhausted. She is barely able to sit upright. The Antarctican exile hovers protectively nearby.

'I'm Vikram Bai,' he says. 'I know you're looking for me.'

Her eyes raise slowly to meet his. She has the gaze of a woman who is broken. He sees the depth of despair there and recognizes her loss for his own. Too quickly he remembers Taeo's corpse, with the bruises he had inflicted upon the other man still visible on the rigid flesh. He remembers the hologram of Shri, how Taeo's last thought had been for his partner back home.

'You can't stay here,' he says. 'You're a danger to us. I've come to ask you to leave.'

Shri does not answer.

'You need to leave – today,' he says. 'You're putting my camp in danger. You may not realize it, but you are.'

'No,' she says. 'They've abandoned us. There's no one out there.'

Her gaze slides away.

'There's no one,' she says.

Stars help him but she reminds him of Adelaide, Adelaide as he found her in the unremembered quarters, barely alive, those last few hours they spent together. He knows what it is to lose someone you love. With difficulty, Vikram resists the comparison. He reminds himself of the blood tracker they used in Osiris. What if the Antarcticans are using something similar?

'Shri. Please understand. I can't help you. I can't bring Taeo back to you. You need to go home.'

'What happened to him?' she whispers. 'What happened to my man?'

'He missed you,' says Vikram.

She starts to cry.

'Please, take me with you,' she implores. 'Please.'

Vikram debates. Everything that is logical tells him it's madness to let this woman near the camp. But in thirty-six hours, they'll be meeting the pirate. He'll be off the archipelago, the camp will disperse. What is more dangerous, to take Shri with him or to leave her here? Sometimes, he thinks, you just have to go with what your gut tells you.

'I need to check you're not carrying anything,' he says.

She nods. The women in the party take Shri aside and strip-search her while Vikram and the men search Ivra. He submits resignedly. The women shout back – 'She's clean!'

Reassured, they give the two Antarcticans fresh clothes. Everything they are wearing or carrying is confiscated. Vikram instructs one of the sailors in the team to take the bundle out to sea and dump it.

Thirty-six hours. Thirty-six hours, and he'll be on his way. Vikram wishes it were tonight. They can't afford to wait.

The camp is chaotic with preparations. A select delegation will be travelling with Vikram to Osiris; the others are free to stay or move on, but most have elected to maintain their small community, although Vikram has advised them to relocate. The atmosphere is excited, almost delirious with a sense of imminent discovery. Osiris will have the answers they seek. The agreement with El Tiburón has only reinforced Vikram's status and the Alaskan's role in securing it seems to have outweighed the revelation of her secret identity. Mig has seen her, laughing and joking with the inhabitants of the camp, with all the insouciance of a woman without a past, a woman who has never owned a book of those in debt to her, or arranged the release of mass murderers from prison.

Only Mig does not share in the enthusiasm. He can't.

As if it weren't bad enough having the Alaskan on site there's now the Tarkie woman as well, who arrived with a Tarkie spy in tow, a man who upon seeing the camp looked like he might burst into tears, a man so obviously broken Mig can only think of him as a liability, and he told Vikram so – told him explicitly that Mig wouldn't have him in any crew of his, wouldn't task him to pickpocket a five-year-old. But Vikram barely listened. He was too distracted by the woman. They entered the camp together, something protective in the way Vikram showed Shri around, shielding her from questions.

Mig doesn't like it. He doesn't trust the Alaskan and he doesn't trust the murdering bastard of a pirate with his too-soft voice and he doesn't trust this woman, Shri Nayar. Mig is beginning to wonder if he's backed the wrong man, if that sense of *special* that first drew him to the Osirian is going to turn out to be nothing more than Vikram's downfall. Back when it was just the two of them, Vikram would have listened.

The Alaskan's words gnaw at him. Mig isn't anyone's shrimp.

And soon enough, she'll find that out for herself.

Vikram lies on the cabin bedroll running every last detail through his head. Everything is in place for their departure. El Tiburón is to collect them at dawn. He can think of nothing he has missed.

He is desperate to get going. The camp has been a strange place, not unhappy, but a place where he has struggled with himself, where he still struggles to reconcile a destiny over which he feels no control. There are moments when he has felt himself enjoying the sense of authority, and if it weren't for the odd combination of Mig and the Alaskan to keep him grounded, he might have found himself a little too comfortable. A false king in a false empire.

Despite everything Mig has told him of the Alaskan's misdeeds, he feels an affinity for the old woman. He is still in two minds about what to do with Mig. It feels wrong to take the boy with him, on a journey whose only certainty is danger and where there is no guarantee of survival, even if they make it back to Osiris – but it feels wrong to leave him behind. Or is he just being selfish? Knowing he wants to keep the boy with him, when the responsible thing would be to make Mig stay in Patagonia, in safety. But is it fair to deny him the choice?

He is never going to sleep. There is too much anticipation in the air. All of the hopes and worries of his renegade camp seem to crowd the atmosphere, leaching out the oxygen. His chest feels as tight as if he is standing at the top of an Osirian tower.

Resigned, Vikram gets up and pulls on his boots, shutting the cabin door gently behind him. He walks through the camp, passing the tents at the edge of the clearing with their sleeping occupants, and moving into the trees. The forest canopy filters out the starlight, and it is almost completely dark, but Vikram doesn't need light. The Alaskan's cabin, with its untrustworthy occupant, is still and silent.

He has no way of knowing whether she has told him the truth. He only knows what he has seen: the acquiescence of the pirate. They are not people he would choose to ally himself with, but he lost the luxury of choice a long time ago.

He goes beyond the camp, slowly treading its perimeter. He feels a wave of gratitude towards the forest, which has been kind, granting them refuge, keeping them safe at a time when they had nothing. The forest has allowed him to regroup. To build something. Some of the camp may stay, but not forever, and once they have departed it will return to what it was, silver-barked, murmuring trees and the undisturbed floor of the forest, soft with mulch, gently composting. There will be no trace of the nights that have passed here, the impassioned discussions, the plans, the uncomplicated fervour of those who found him, who found in this place a mission to distract from their own grief. All that will be gone.

Vikram stops to exchange a few words with the sentries, who seem unsurprised to see him. Their mood is quiet but confident. He wonders what they will do when tomorrow is over, and when he – if he – is on the seas, bound for Osiris. A part of him wants to ask but he holds back, acknowledging the transient nature of their meeting, the way lives cross and have importance to one another and then move on, with nothing known of before or after, and no likelihood of meeting again. He leaves the sentries to their posts.

He has an irrepressible urge to see the sky as he would see it from the sea, uncluttered by the topography of land. He clambers up into a tree not far from the clearing. The sensation of lifting himself into this growing thing remains one of his greatest pleasures: one of the rare and treasured moments which feels like it belongs solely to him. He climbs as high as his weight permits.

The southern constellations are bright and clear. The upper part of the tree lofts in a gust of wind and for a moment it is possible to imagine himself back in Osiris, lying on a raft rack or a western bridge with the sea moving somewhere beneath him, the constant, ever-shifting motion of the waves. A memory comes to him: his friends Nils and Drake, both drunk, supporting one another as they staggered over a bridge, the southern lights radiating above them, Drake pointing up to the sky.

Aurora australis.

How do you know? he had said, or something like that, not realizing, having no inkling of just how much they did not know. Of a world they had imagined only in ground-dreams. If Vikram succeeds in returning to Osiris, his mission will not be confined to redfleur: he intends to find out what they did not know. To discover who has told them these lies. He will fish the culprits out, one by one, at sea or on land. This he promises himself. This he will do, for Nils and Drake. For Adelaide, the woman he loved. For Adelaide, who never knew the truth about the city that killed her.

Lost in thought, it is only because of his vantage point in the tree that Vikram notices movement in the camp. The flap of a tent peels open and the Antarctican woman crawls out, moving with slow and clearly deliberate stealth. She doesn't zip the door to the tent closed, and Vikram realizes she must have left it open all night, precisely so as not to alert anyone with the distinctive sound. As he watches, the woman straightens, hugs her coat around her body, and sets off into the cover of the trees.

Vikram drops silently to the ground and follows her.

Mig waits until Vikram has left the cabin and then he goes inside and finds the Osirian's pack and retrieves the gun. He holds it in both hands, getting used to the weight and heft of it, the strange rounded contours, the coldness of the steel that slowly warms within his hands. With the weapon finally in his grasp he feels a flood of relief and triumph, even as he notices his fingers are trembling. But that's all right. It's all right to be scared. He always told his crew that. It means you're ready. Once the barrel of this thing is up against the Alaskan's head, he won't be trembling any more. He rests one finger lightly on the trigger.

Now is the moment.

The Alaskan sleeps in the other cabin. Mig knows she was unarmed when she entered the camp because all of her belongings were searched, and they confiscated the pistol she used to keep under her pillow in Cataveiro. But he wouldn't put it past her to have secreted a knife, or some other implement, into her possession since she has been living in the camp. Nor does he doubt that the Alaskan has other things, things Vikram's people wouldn't have spotted, wouldn't have known to look for, things which are fatal. Mig will remain at arm's length, and ensure the Alaskan keeps her hands within his sight. If all else fails, he has the rope in his pocket. He hopes he won't have to use this. The gun will be quicker.

As he approaches the cabin he rehearses his opening line. She may scream for help, so he won't have much time. But it doesn't matter if they all come running. It only takes a second to shoot someone. The freak is lucky. She'll die fast. It wouldn't have been like that for Pilar. His parrot girl had a slow, agonizing death. She was alone. There was no one there to hold her hand.

Pilar's dead because of you.
He'll begin with that.
You killed her.

In the forest gloom Vikram can barely make out the outline of Shri Nayar, but despite her efforts to keep quiet, she's making more noise than he. They can't have country like this in Antarctica, or at least, she's never had to move through it in silence, in the dark. Shri is fumbling with something in her hands, something too small to see. Vikram moves closer. He sees a minute speck of light between her cupped hands. Realization floods him.

He sprints forwards. She looks up, startled, but reacts too late. Vikram knocks her hands apart, grabbing her around the waist with one arm, and clamping his other hand over her mouth. Shri struggles in his grip, kicking out and biting at his hand. Whatever she was holding has fallen to the floor, and the light has gone out. Vikram drags her awkwardly back through the trees, swearing under his breath. He can feel her shaking with suppressed shouts.

A sentry comes running as he enters the clearing, quickly followed by another. Vikram relinquishes Shri into their care.

'Get her inside the cabin, and keep her quiet! And find the other one, Ivra - he may be involved.'

Shri Nayar continues to struggle as the sentries haul her across the camp. The disturbance has woken more than one person. Vikram follows the sentries inside before anyone can ask him questions and closes the door.

'What the hell were you doing out there?'

The woman is breathing heavily. She looks at him with fierce, accusing eyes. One of the sentries is binding her to the chair.

'I wasn't doing anything.'

'You snuck out of the camp. I saw you. What were you doing?'

'As if I'd tell you,' she sneers.

Vikram draws up a chair and sits facing her.

'Don't make me ask again.'

'Are you going to interrogate me? Torture me? What would your precious followers make of that?'

'If you've threatened this camp, there isn't a soul here who'll lift a finger to save you. Now you're going to tell me – what were you doing out there in the forest?'

She glares at him defiantly.

'Fuck you.'

'Have you betrayed us?'

'Why did my partner die? Tell me that. Tell me what happened to Taeo!'

'Your partner was an opium addict.'

He sees her wince.

'Show me your hands.'

The sentry forces her to place them on her lap, fingers splayed. On the fingernail of her right index finger, Vikram sees a slight stickiness, like a residual glue.

Outside he can hear a commotion. Quick footsteps followed by a banging at the door.

'Vikram – you'd better come – it's the Alaskan—'

He swears.

'Keep her here! And search the forest floor where I found her – you're looking for something robotic. Something very small, as small as a fingernail.'

Mig eases open the Alaskan's cabin door and pushes it gently, silently, shut. It's dark. Her breathing is shallow and gurgling. As if there are things in her throat. Demons, he thinks. From all the people she's had killed.

The gun is solid in his hand. He takes a step towards the bunk. She breathes in and coughs. He freezes. He can hear her hacking, the phlegm sticking in her throat. Her breathing pauses. If she'd only choke herself to death he wouldn't have to do this. Then it evens out. Regular. In. Out. In.

He will need the torch to be sure of what he is doing. He'll have to move quick.

His own breathing is rapid now. He's scared, horribly scared. What if she has powers he hasn't yet witnessed? What if her nirvana mind can somehow overcome her spine and she'll crawl from the bed, breaking out like a creature from a shell, seize a hold of his ankle—

There's no time for deliberation. He needs to act, now.

He flicks on the torch, blinks in the light, stumbles to her bedside. The gun in his hand. The gun in his hand, rising, the barrel pointing, the muzzle of it, up against her temple.

The Alaskan's eyes snap open.

Black. Pitiless. Soulless.

Her lips part. Her jaws work, chewing, and then her gums bare in a grimace. He can smell the cloying sugar that she loves so much. It makes him gag.

'Mig,' she says.

'You killed her.'

'Who did I kill, Mig?'

'You killed Pilar!'

'I have no idea who Pilar is. Who is she, and why do you think I killed her?'

'Stop it!' He is trembling. 'She's dead because of you.'

'Oh, she's dead because of me? Because you said I killed her, before, and they're not quite the same thing. Especially as I don't even know who you're talking about.'

'I'm talking about Pilar! My girl Pilar! Just because you never asked, you never cared. I didn't tell you everything, you stupid freak.'

There's a power in using that word, a sense of victory, that swells up inside him. He says it again, with more force.

'You fucking freak!'

'I know, Mig. I know you had secrets. And yet I did so much for you. Didn't I pay you well enough? Didn't I let you run your crew, just as you liked, no questions asked? Didn't I give you a life, Mig?'

'Stop talking. Stop talking now!'

'I can stop talking when I'm dead, I might as well talk while I'm not.'

'I'm going to kill you.'

'If you need to announce it, you're not much of a killer. Not much of anything. A nothingness, Mig. A shrimp.'

'I'll do it!'

'Then go on.' The Alaskan grins at him. Yellow teeth in a dry mouth. Sugar smell, overpowering. 'Go on then, shoot me.'

Mig's finger rests on the trigger. His arm is shaking so much he has to grip it with his other hand to steady himself. The muzzle of the gun knocks against the Alaskan's slack skin. In the torchlight he can see the veins running across her forehead. The blood pulsing within them.

She raises her voice.

'Shoot me!'

'You deserve to die,' he says, shakily.

The Alaskan grabs the pistol and pushes it into her mouth. Her lips work around the barrel.

'Shoot – me.'

He closes his eyes and pulls the trigger.

Nothing happens.

He pulls it again, eyes open. Nothing. What's wrong with the gun?

The Alaskan seizes his wrist and pulls the gun from her mouth, forcing his arm aside.

'Nirvana!' he gasps.

'That's no magic, boy. The gun's all out of charge, as any amateur can tell.'

She tugs on his wrist, pulling him closer to her. Her strength is terrifying. Her face is inches below his.

'But now you're a killer, Mig. Just like me!'

'Stop saying my name!' he howls.

The Alaskan laughs. The sound of her laughter, cackling on and on, enrages Mig. His vision is blurry. She's jerking on his arm, manipulating him like he's a puppet. He can't think straight. He can't think! There's still the rope. He can't back out now. The rope – in his pocket—

He lets her jerk one more time on his arm. In the moment her grip slackens, he pulls back with all the strength he has, and lets himself fall from the bed. She tumbles after him with a shriek. On the floor they tussle, but now Mig has the advantage – the Alaskan can't move her legs, writhing on the floor like the squid he saw plucked from the nets in Fuego. He gets the rope. Her eyes widen. She shrieks.

'Help! Help now!'

She pushes at his chest with one hand. Her breathing is laboured. Mig stretches the rope across her neck and lets his weight lean in. The cords of her neck jerk and tighten.

'You killed her,' he whispers.

The Alaskan gurgles.

The door bursts open. Vikram runs inside, flanked by two camp members.

'Mig, get away from her! Get away from her now!'

Vikram, shouting.

Mig pushes harder. She has to die. She has to.

The Alaskan's face is changing colour.

Hands grab at Mig, pulling him away from his prize.

'No! No, no, no!'

The Alaskan draws in a sharp, ugly breath. She rubs at her throat, continuing to make those sounds. Mig can see where the abrasion of the rope has left its marks. His eyes mist over.

'You see, Osirian,' croaks the Alaskan. 'You have a snake in your midst. He betrayed me – it's no surprise that he would betray you too.'

Vikram's hand clenches on Mig's shoulder.

'What are you thinking? She's our only way out of here, our only way back to Osiris!'

'She killed Pilar.'

'Pilar was infected days before she died! That's how redfleur works. You know that, Mig. You *know* that.'

He has never seen Vikram so angry. The man's rage is like a force, rippling against him. He staggers back. He wants to crawl into the ground and die.

The Osirian curses in his own language. Someone helps the Alaskan back onto the bed.

'He broke my wrist,' she says. Mig can see it, her hand bent at a horrible angle, the flesh swelling up. Somehow it is worse than seeing her dead.

'I don't have time for this,' says Vikram. 'Keep them apart. I need to find out what the fuck the Antarctican woman's done.'

Shri wriggles helplessly against the ropes. The more she wriggles, the tighter the bonds seem to become. Her allotted guards, people who have shown her kindness in the past couple of days, are looking at her as if she's an abomination.

'I'm not the one who's abducted and trussed someone up in a chair!' she says, but they look at one another blankly. They don't speak Hindi. She says it again in Portuguese, Taeo's language of the home. They ignore her, conversing in their own Spanish dialect, low-voiced and too quick for her to comprehend. They seem to be debating something. Now it's she who doesn't understand.

'For fuck's sake.'

She doesn't know what to do. She's angry and frightened and worse than that, she's caught. It was meant to be simple – sneak out of the camp, activate the tracker, sneak back in, and go back to bed as if nothing had happened. Come morning the camp would be breaking up. Shri could go on her way, and no one would ever be the wiser. By the time her countryfolk moved in, she would be kilometres away, safe with the Antarcticans.

She's waited longer than she should have done to act. If she'd followed orders, the camp would have been exposed within hours of her arrival. Instead, she's given them time.

Vikram returns, his body rigid with fury. For a moment their gazes lock, each reassessing, adjusting to this new awareness of one another. When she left Antarctica he was one person: the man who had last seen her partner alive. The man who apologized. Now he is something else: a saviour, a piece of political dynamite, survivor of a disease which has the potential to wipe out every living person in the Boreal States. She wishes she had never seen these other faces.

'I trusted you,' he says. His voice is tight with compressed rage. She can see him struggling to maintain control. 'I let you in. The people here, they trusted you too, because I asked them to.'

'It's stupid to trust people,' she says dully. 'They always let you down.'

'Tell me what you've done.'

'I waited,' she says quietly.

Vikram takes up the position he left, facing her.

'Go on.'

'I was meant to do it as soon as I found you.'

'Why?'

'The Antarctican government sent me.' The exhaustion she has felt for days returns in force. 'I'm the bait,' she says.

Vikram looks at her. She senses his thoughts rippling beneath that scarred face, the growing comprehension of her position, and she hates him a little for it. It would be easier to be enemies. Gradually, the fury drops away from his face, leaving only sadness.

'And Ivra? What about him?'

'He knew why I was here. He didn't know about the tracker.'

'How long do we have?'

'I don't know. An hour? Hours? I don't know how close they are.'

Vikram stands, wipes his hand across his face, stops where he is. The others ask a question in Spanish. He responds. She sees the alarm spread across their faces. They stare at her in horror. Vikram gives an instruction and they leave at once.

'What will you do?' she asks.

'Evacuate. Now.'

But he doesn't move immediately.

'Can you untie me?'

He does so without comment, but says, 'You might be safer staying in here.'

She assumes he means the other camp members. It occurs to her that Ivra, too, may no longer be on her side. The realization of danger to herself is sudden and shocking. She cannot orphan her children.

'You said Taeo was an addict,' she says.

'He was.' But she senses Vikram is no longer with her. He's already thinking ahead. 'He missed his home,' he says. 'Like I told you.'

His hand drops. He moves with sudden decision. She watches as he throws a few things into a pack. He has a knife but no firearms. At the door he pauses.

'If you'd told me the truth—'

He appears to collect himself. He shakes his head.

'It doesn't matter. Keep your head down.'

And then he's gone.

The camp has descended into pandemonium. All about him, people move in a frenzy, rushing to strike their tents and gather up belongings in the dark, only switching on the torches for brief moments of visibility. Those who have just woken run up to Vikram.

'What should we do? Where do we go?'

'Go into the forest,' he tells them. 'Get as far as you can from here and hide. Get off the island if you can. Take the boats. You know where they are.'

Some disperse at once. Others linger, worried, frightened, seeking reassurance. He repeats his words, trying to stay calm, to fight a feeling of rising panic. He's fucked up. *He's fucked up.* One person, that was all it took. One person to flatter him. He's fallen victim to his own guilt.

'Go,' he urges them. 'Now, quickly. Get away. We don't know how long we've got.'

Those who are due to make the journey to Osiris gather round. He tells them to fetch the Alaskan and make for the meeting point. They'll have to carry her; it's the quickest way. Mig isn't with the party. They tell him the boy ran off after he tried to murder the Alaskan. Vikram works his way through the camp, waylaid at every step, shouting for the boy.

Then he hears it.

A low, droning sound passes overhead. Like the wings of an insect, multiplied a thousand-fold. He freezes.

There is a moment's respite and then the droning thing makes a second sweep.

Bright lights burst overhead, breaking through the canopy of the forest to illuminate the camp in dazzling shafts. It's some kind of machinery, flying at speed, exposing their camp, exposing the clearing, the cabins and tents, the people, paralysed with shock.

'Run!' he bellows.

Those who remain scatter. Vikram runs from one side of the camp to the next, desperately searching for Mig. He can't see the boy anywhere. The lights sweep overhead. People lurch in and out of the shadows, running. He can't tell if they're his own people or hostiles.

'Mig! Mig, where are you?!'

The drones pass over again.

'Mig!'

He draws a breath and inhales something bitter. He starts to cough. At the next sweep of light he sees a yellowish mist is creeping through the camp. The Antarcticans have dropped something.

He runs in the opposite direction. The gas is making him tight-chested. His eyes are streaming and disorientation is setting in. Strange shapes move in front of his vision. A figure rushes past, screaming, he can't see who, too tall for the boy.

It's the gas. There's something in the gas.

'Mig!' he shouts hoarsely. 'Mig! Mig, where are you? Mig!'

The gas is spreading, billowing outwards like smoke. He can't go into it. He has to move away. He can't see anyone now. His chest burns.

He's on the wrong side of the camp to the Alaskan's cabin. He doesn't know if the Osiris party got her out in time. He moves into the trees and as he does he hears the crack of a shot striking against something, the cabin, or the trunk of a tree.

He drops to his belly and starts to crawl. He can't see a soul, ahead or behind. Something sears past his ear and hits the tree to his left. He crawls painfully into the undergrowth, expecting any second to feel the burn of a shot in his flesh.

A hand grips his shoulder and Vikram suppresses a shout.

The pinpoint light of a torch flicks on. He is face to face with El Tiburón, belly to the ground.

The pirate's face, streaked with paint and merging with the bushes, is a startling sight. El Tiburón extends a hand and says, 'Come.'

The torch flicks off. They are in darkness again. The drones whir overhead. A pillar of light passes behind him.

'I can't leave these people—'

'You have to leave if you wish to make it off the island alive.'

'No, I—'

'You have one chance,' says the pirate. 'I will not offer it again.'

Another shot whistles overhead. Vikram ducks his head, swearing, but the pirate does not move.

'To clarify, your options are these,' says the pirate. 'Stay and be killed, or come with me and live.'

Vikram lies helplessly, unable to force himself to move. What the fuck is he meant to do? Mig is out there. Mig, and everyone who put their trust in him. The Alaskan—

'I can't leave the boy—'

'Make your choice. Quickly.'

'I have to find him—'

'Then I have to leave you.'

He senses the pirate beginning to move backwards. The Antarctican raid continues behind him, the yellow mist drifting outwards. The camp is lost. If he's caught, it's all for nothing.

'I'm coming with you.'

'Good.'

The pirate finds his hand. Vikram takes it and allows himself to be lifted to his feet. It is only with that brief contact that he realizes something is wrong. The size of the hand is smaller than he remembers – much smaller. In the next sweep of light he peers at the face and despite the paint and the briefness of the light he can make out a slenderness that does not fit with the man they met on the beach.

'You're not who I met—'

'Nonetheless I am El Tiburón,' says the woman – it is a woman, listening again, Vikram is sure. 'Come with me, or take your chances with the Antarcticans.'

She turns her back and starts to move away at speed.

'Wait—'

He doesn't understand what's going on, but behind him is a massacre and to go back is capture or death.

He follows the pirate through the forest, struggling to match her pace. They have covered a few hundred metres when the pirate turns, pushes him down and draws a gun. An Antarctican is a short distance behind them. She shoots the soldier in the face. She moves on. Vikram tries not to think about what is happening in the camp. What happened to Mig, whether he got out in time – if the boy ran away he might have escaped before the Antarcticans moved in – the fading screams and gunshots as members of the camp disperse through the forest, pursued by Antarcticans.

I should have given myself up—

This is your only chance to get back to Osiris—

As he stumbles after the pirate his mind turns numb. His lungs are burning with every breath.

A small boat awaits them on the water: no light, no motor, only the hint of a figure at the oars under the starlight. El Tiburón steps lightly into the boat and turns to offer her hand to Vikram. He takes it dazedly, feeling once again the slenderness of the fingers beneath the glove. The boat rocks with his weight. They are on the move at once, pulling smoothly away from the shore, out into the inky blackness of the archipelago, with only the sound of the oars dipping and lifting, and his own inhalations as he tries to settle his breathing.

Behind them, at the heart of the island, he can see a flock of distant lights circling above the trees.

Vikram senses rather than sees the ship: a source of darkness more eclipsing than that which surrounds them already. He feels the impact of their boat against the hull. Invisible signals are exchanged and he hears the faint mechanical whine of something extending down the side.

'After you,' says El Tiburón.

He climbs the ladder, rung by rung, with no idea of its height until he feels the weight of a hand under his elbow, guiding him onto the deck. Moments later El Tiburón jumps lightly over the rail. El Tiburón says something, too quietly for Vikram to hear, and then the pirate's hand is on his shoulder once again, shepherding him expertly around invisible obstacles on deck and below, until he finds himself inside a cabin. Only then does El Tiburón allow a light.

It's a low, reddish glow that projects deep shadows around the room, and under it, the planes of the pirate's face look like something from an ancient depiction of purgatory. Her attire is identical to the man they met, down to the pistols at her hips. The pirate goes to the sideboard, pours a single glass of liquor from a decanter, and offers it to Vikram. There is something in this small gesture of luxury – the chime of the decanter, crystal – that seems striking to him, but in his stupefied state he couldn't explain why or how. He is only grateful for the liquor, whatever it is, which burns down his throat and makes his eyes water even more. The pirate does not drink. She is fiddling with a console, trying to find a radio signal.

'Who was that – on the beach – if you're El Tiburón—'

'That was Gus.'

'Gus?'

El Tiburón does not reply. The static from the console wheezes into words. The signal sounds faint and distorted, as though the voices are coming from a long way away. Vikram takes another gulp of liquor. He has an overwhelming desire to be drunk. As drunk as possible, drunk until he is sick.

The pirate taps the console, apparently satisfied, and straightens.

'This happened today,' she says.

Vikram looks at her without comprehending. It is only now that the words clarify – it is not the lilting Spanish he has become accustomed to hearing, but Boreal English, strange and, to his ear, formal and stilted. What he is hearing is a broadcast.

From Osiris.

The city of Osiris. The subsidiary state city of Osiris.

Vikram stares at El Tiburón, and his world upends for the second time that night. The pirate's face bears no discernible expression, except perhaps a mild curiosity as to how he is taking the news.

'I thought you should know,' she says. 'Your city has been claimed by the Boreals. They entered Osiris last night.'

PART FIVE
SILVERFISH

OSIRIS

A shark has entered the city. The Boreals let it in. They don't know about the ring-net, you see, they just arrived, opened the city up like a ribcage, and the shark slipped through, soft as a knife in the dark. It's a giant, as long as a raft rack from nose to tail. Pale-bellied, dark-backed. Teeth on it like a set of shivs, teeth that can tear you piece by piece and limb from limb.

The shark is hungry, yes, but not for meat. This is not a shark like other sharks. It's not interested in eating us. Then what is it after, you ask? Perhaps your question should be, *who does it want?*

This shark has morals, you see – no wait, listen, cut me some slack here. You think this is just a tale but there's more to it than that. The shark has ideas about who should live and who should die. This is something old, older than we are by far. It's been in the ocean for millennia, its belly resting on the seabed, tail a-twitch, sleeping. Dreaming whatever it is that sharks dream – of shadows and hunts and blood. It rouses when times are bad. The Blackout. The Great Storm, it was seen then. Who by? Plenty of people. Ask anyone.

And now it's back, and it is very much awake.

You don't have to believe me.

But I'll tell you how it goes. The shark's sense of smell is so sharp, so incredibly precise, that it knows its target from half an ocean away. It can distinguish the exact aroma of one human being from another. There's something about us, like pheromones, or maybe the shark just knows something else, that puts this shark in a murderous rage.

Having identified its prey, it moves. Slicing through the water, metres below the surface, torsional and direct, silently and at speed. It is in range. With a swipe of the tail, it rises. It has your scent. It's coming for you.

In your last moments you see the nose, rising from the water, the vast breadth of the jaws, opening, a yawning pink aperture fenced with teeth. The shark in this moment is nothing but a mouth. You have an uncanny sense about it, a feeling that everything is inevitable, because the shark had marked you, perhaps from the moment you were born. The shark always had you in its scent.

The shark strikes.

It never misses. It takes its prey down deep, and it begins to demolish.

A fisherman is the first to see the ships, and claims that notoriety later, although there are many who will claim it, later. His name is Erlyn Tako. Late in the afternoon under a white sky, his nets trawl behind him as his boat moves sluggishly through the sea. When he winches in the nets, a large squid squirms against the ropes, wet and translucent. The catch is bad today and Erlyn does sums in his head: how much will this trader give him, or that one, are there any good fish to pull out, fat ones with scales bright and clean to push under the wind-burned noses of buyers, make the catch look more valuable than it is. He is further from the ring-net than he usually goes; he swears these days the fish are fewer, and the city grows no smaller, though when he looks back today it seems small, a collective of tapering shapes that merge into one single shadow.

Most of the time he doesn't think about the peculiarities of it: this housing of souls wedged between the flat lines of sea and sky, nothing to be found as far as anyone has travelled, just the water, and the city, and the boats. There are some who think too much, and you see what happens to them. You see them gazing out, and you see the way indifference steals away curiosity piece by piece. Erlyn is wary of such a fate. So today, out in his boat, when he glances back at the city he thinks nothing of it, only notices the height of the waves and the velocity of the wind against his face, things you have to notice, things that can save your life.

The ships appear with no warning. They emerge out of nothing, from beneath the waves, colossal things, larger than any ship he has ever seen, the long backs pushing against the membrane of the ocean surface before breaking through in a cascade of foam. Rising steadily upwards, they tower over his tiny boat.

Erlyn stares, his initial shock blossoming into incredulity as the fleet assembles. He remembers stories of ghosts and monsters. He remembers the expedition boat that left the city of Osiris over three months ago. Is this the result? What did it find, that boat? Ghosts or monsters?

The news wings through the city, from the westerners' fry-boats to the marble vaults of the Council Chambers, where austere men and women argue in purple surcoats. Residents begin to gather outside, standing on raft racks and leaning over balconies and the rails of the waterbuses, looking, searching for what is rumoured to be seen.

Seagulls settle on the roof of a fry-boat in a squawking chorus. A homeless kid whose eyes are too large in a malnourished face gapes at the vendor as she hands over a parcel of kelp squares, extra squid rings thrown in because she feels sorry for this one – sorry for them all, but sometimes she can't not act on it. The kid says: they've come to save us. She says, what's that then, and the kid is standing there holding the parcel, staring at her with those big anime eyes. The boats, he says. The boats are here to save us.

A diver in the aquarium tower swims close to the glass where her partner presses both hands, fingers splayed, against the tensile barrier. The diver waits, reads the other's lips and forgets for a moment to breathe. In the adjacent tower, a psychiatrist named Radir frowns and turns up the o'dio. The investigator Sanjay Hanif cocks his head, crouched over the corpse of a young man with two gun wounds in his upper torso, and looks impatiently at his sergeant and says: Yes? What now? A skad swings her rifle like a stick, the gun falling in a satisfactory arc, and she laughs. You think we're going to fall for that? What planet are you living on? An old man known as Mr Argyll grips the matted hair of his beard and yells Osuwa! Osuwa! Turn the lights out!

The city's leaders confer in hastily gathered committees, while military vessels rush from the waterways of the city towards the ring-net, manned by disbelieving skadi forces. A lone bird follows the wake of a speedboat, tracing its path overhead. The submarines await them silently.

On the fifty-first floor of a western tower not too far from the border, a group of activists sit in heated discussion. The o'dio crackles. Dien raises a hand, frowning, and the conversation ceases abruptly. They wait. The silence is leaden.

Then a voice begins to speak.

It is not an Osirian transmission. It is not a voice any of them have ever heard before.

'The Boreal States of the north reclaim the subsidiary state city of Osiris believed lost in the year of twenty-three sixty-seven. From hereon, this city is under our governance.'

The reaction in the room is one of strange delirium. Hands run through hair, glances exchanged, a smell of sweat, a hostaging of breath. Moments pass before tentative voices begin to rise.

'We're not alone—'

'I always said—'

'What do they mean, governance?'

Adelaide Rechnov, the woman known as the Silverfish, stares at the o'dio, immobile. In the seconds that follow the broadcast, time seems to slow, and within its hand she watches all the things she has hoped for rise and crash back around her, debris from an act of her own conjuring.

'It means they've come to claim the city.'

* * *

On the first day, the Boreals surround the city. Their submarines gleam with a sleek, effortless health. They enter the ring-net, ploughing through the Osirian waters, pushing aside the rusting hulks of ships in the abandoned harbour as easily as plastic.

Adelaide and Dien remain glued to the o'dio, piecing together events from the panicked reports of journalists across the city. The Osirian defence is brief, disorganized and swiftly crushed. Strikes attempted against the submarines barely dent their superstructure. After the initial retaliation, a submarine dives and disappears. Another seems to vanish where it rested. The Boreals target a City tower and give its residents fifteen minutes to evacuate. The last boat of civilians has only just departed when they issue their counter-attack. The screams on the o'dio sound distant and unreal. Then the reporter's voice comes through, taut and panicked – *there's people in there still, there's people trapped—*

They hear the screams echo on. Adelaide remembers the burning tower in the west, the flames at her back, her terror as she jumped. She doesn't know what Dien is thinking. She looks at her hands and finds they are shaking. She has done this. Shortly after that, the Council declares a state of emergency and the Boreals move into the city.

Their first act is to requisition Osirian weapons and replace their operators. Skadi boats are commissioned into Boreal service. Then the Boreals seize the Osirian o'dio stations and the Reef falls suddenly, shockingly silent.

The Boreals issue a summons to representatives from the City and the west. The new arrangements for the city will be discussed in the Council Chambers, at ten hundred the following day. The western summons is handed to a skad who hands it to a fishing vendor who hands it to a raft rack engineer until eventually it reaches the woman with many names, the woman known as the Silverfish.

Adelaide Rechnov reads the summons without comment. She looks at Dien, who has not said a word all day.

'Do you want to read it?'

Dien doesn't reply.

An unnatural hush descends upon the city. People remain inside, gathering in the stairwells, adults whispering, children alert for clues that will demystify this new, unexplained state. It begins to rain, a soft persistent drizzle. The rain streams over the solar skin of the towers and the bufferglass window-walls and the armoured sides of the Boreal submarines, soaking into the newly mounted Boreal flags.

Sometime between the hours of two and three in the morning, an explosion rips open the night. Orange flame bursts skywards, blazing brightly for several minutes before receding. Smoke drifts upwards and dissipates in the rain. The explosion occurs on the far eastern side of the city, where Adelaide Mystik once hosted her annual Rose Soirée at the Red Rooms. In the laboratory above the apartment, a row of exquisitely crafted telescopes is blown into shards.

Adelaide enters the vaulted dome of the Council Chambers unaccompanied. Today there are no glamorous accessories, no statement white suit or tinted spectacles to antagonize or distract her spectators. Her footsteps fall sombrely with each step, the sound seeming to sink rather than echo, and she can feel the creak in the waterproofing of her western boots.

The Chambers are almost deserted. Without the Council present, the skeleton is exposed, the wood and marble that were shipped from land nations and the ceiling frescos which are so painstakingly maintained, the rows of empty chairs bearing the impressions of those who are usually seated here. She has the sense of standing in a place that has not heard a human voice in years.

Except there are people: a single row of occupants, men and women, none of whom she recognizes. The Boreals regard her with curiosity rather than interest. Their attire is foreign, though some are dressed in what she takes to be military uniform, with insignia at their breasts or collars. Their faces are smooth and plump and strange to her. Even as she surveys them, a part of her can only marvel that they exist at all.

The mouth of one of the Boreals, a woman, curls in a sneer. Adelaide can imagine how she must appear to them. Unkempt. Bedraggled from the rain. Not much of a leader.

There is one other Osirian in the room.

Her father, Feodor Rechnov.

The contrast between them could not be more marked. Feodor, perhaps under advisement from his colleagues, has dressed austerely, even conservatively, but he has retained the purple surcoat of the Osirian Council. Everything about him speaks of affluence, from the protein-rich skin of his face and hands to the immaculate creases of his trousers.

Of all the people they could have sent, it had to be him. Feodor, who has so much to lose. She knows exactly how he would have bullied and cajoled to ensure his name was first on the table, employing every last scrap of his influence in the Council, the way he has used it to keep Linus out of sight. Seeing him standing there brings a wave of despair almost greater than the sight of their invaders. She cannot think of anyone more damaging to represent their case.

An usher leads Adelaide to a seat. She can see the terror in the young man's face, and she murmurs to him, 'It will be all right.'

A brazen lie, for quite clearly, it will not be all right. But the usher's hands steady; he backs away and at a nod from the foreigners, he leaves.

Feodor looks her up and down. He laughs, an unmistakably bitter sound.

'So it is true. I didn't believe Linus.'

'You should have listened to him.'

'Listened to a traitor?'

Adelaide drops her voice.

'I heard you torched the Whitefly headquarters.'

For a moment she sees the scene: Feodor's lackeys entering the laboratory with hammers and explosives, smashing up data drives and telescopes, sloshing fuel over the monitoring equipment, an excess of it leaking down in oily puddles. She sees again the tail of the explosion and she wonders if there was any warning for the people in the tower where she used to live.

'I don't know what you refer to,' Feodor says smoothly.

'Of course you don't.'

They are both placed facing and below the Boreals, she on the left, Feodor on the right. At the centre of the row of Boreals is a large man whose uniform is heavily decorated. His lips lie slightly apart, revealing the upper front teeth and giving him an expression of incongruous merriment. He addresses her father first.

'You are Feodor Rechnov?'

'That is my name. You can refer to me as Councillor Rechnov. That is the capacity in which I represent the people of this city.'

'And you——' The Boreal glances down. 'You are known as the Silverfish.'

'That's correct.'

Feodor laughs again.

'That is my daughter, Adelaide Rechnov.'

'Familial relations do not interest us.' The Boreal looks at Feodor. 'You represent the eastern side of the city.'

'I represent the City,' he says contemptuously. '*Our* city.'

The force of Feodor's will has a physical weight. Adelaide has felt it before; in the past it has swayed entire Councils to Feodor's way of thinking. Now she senses him consciously directing it towards these strangers. Difficult to say whether she wants him to succeed or not: they don't yet know which way the current flows.

The smiling Boreal turns his attention to Adelaide.

'And you represent the western side of the city?'

'I do.'

Feodor cannot restrain a snort. Adelaide resists glancing across at him. She is his weakness; this is clear to her now in a way that it never was before. But he should know better than to reveal it to these outsiders. The city's only hope for survival may be to work together, which means she and her father have to co-operate, however much each of them detests the prospect.

'I am Commander-in-Chief Katu Ben,' says the Boreal leader. 'I represent Alaskan interests. You should note my colleagues Luciana Tan, representing the Sino-Siberian Federation, and Marc Bernier of Veerdeland. We'll be leading the transfer of jurisdiction. We understand the city is divided, which is why we've brought you here today – to work through the practicalities of Boreal governance.'

'The city of Osiris is an independent state,' says Feodor forcefully. 'It was declared as such in the year of twenty-three forty-six. Your presence here is unlawful.'

'On the contrary.' Katu Ben gazes at Feodor with a clear, unblinking stare. 'The City of Osiris may have declared itself independent, but independence was never formally granted by the Boreal States – which, I'll remind you, paid for every cent of its construction. You remain a colony of the states of the north.'

Feodor squares his shoulders, making the most of his imposing frame. He adopts a leisurely, benign smile.

'You have not set foot in the city for over fifty years. What right do you think you have over its citizens?'

'A legal right,' says the Boreal calmly. 'But the fifty years is, as you say, pertinent. Fifty years is a long time for a city to disappear. A very long time. Wouldn't you agree?'

'It's not our fault if you ignored our distress signal,' interjects Adelaide.

'There was no distress signal.'

'You're mistaken. Or your technologies failed to intercept it.'

'There was no distress signal,' Katu Ben repeats. 'Or have you been colluding with the Antarcticans this past half a century? For that, I have to point out, would be an act of treason against the Boreal States. If treason is proved. . .' He trails away, looking at both of them with apparent surprise.

Feodor tenses in genuine outrage.

'The Antarcticans have been as lax as yourselves in coming to our aid. We've had nothing to do with them. On the contrary, we've been left to rot. You want our city? Well, here it is. Take it, and pay for the repairs while you're at it.'

'Feodor, for stars' sake—'

'I mean it!' he shouts. 'They want it, they get it all, including your little western crusade, Adelaide.' Feodor is on his feet now. 'So I hope you've got the resources to patrol a border and keep down terrorist attacks. I hope you've got the solar skin and the bufferglass to patch up the leaking towers and pump dry the flooded ones, and fix the ring-net too while you're at it – I hear one of your submarines has already ploughed through the northern barrier and now we've got a rabid shark cruising around the waterways. There's a reason we keep that ring-net in place.'

'Local governance is your concern,' says the Boreal. 'We are here simply to oversee. So – this is how it's going to work. You will report to us. The city will be economically viable, and pay tax to the Boreal States like any other colony. My advice: take the time to read these directives – at your leisure, of course, but not too slowly. Take them back to your Council, and explain to them how the administration will work from hereon. That is the extent of your role. No more.'

His voice carries a note of warning, but Feodor does not heed it.

'And if the Council refuse, as undoubtedly they will?'

'They should not refuse.'

'And if they do?'

'If you refuse to comply with our entirely reasonable demands, the Boreal States will have no choice but to enforce them.'

'Now we come to it,' says Feodor. He folds his arms. 'All bullies are the same at heart.'

'Just so we're clear, what exactly do you mean when you say "enforce them"?' asks Adelaide.

The Boreal leader looks at her, and while he speaks his mouth remains in that perpetual upward curve. Nothing, says that smile, could delight him more to be in this room on this day, dispensing these orders.

'Let me tell you something.' He leans forwards conspiratorially. 'I have had to obliterate cities of my own people under the eyes of the world to preserve the Alaskan state. Don't make the mistake of thinking I'm a man of empty threats. Do you understand me?'

'I understand you perfectly.'

The blandness in Katu Ben's voice terrifies her.

'I hope that you do.'

'Threats don't go so nicely with your policies of governance, if I may say so.'

Katu Ben lets his gaze rove over the empty Chambers. Adelaide can almost read the calculations as he evaluates every aspect of the wealth on display.

'When it comes to rogue states, we aren't left with much choice.' He nods to his left and right. 'As I'm sure our neighbouring nations would agree.'

A Boreal officer rolls over a trolley.

'It's been so very, very long, no one was sure what level of technology you were working with,' says Katu Ben. 'We have made the relevant documents available in various formats.'

'Too kind.' Feodor's voice is thick with sarcasm.

'We'll leave you to absorb these in your own time. Well,' Ben consults a device in front of him, 'within the next twenty-four hours. We've arranged a handover ceremony to take place tomorrow evening, when the city's new governor will be announced. You can put your DNA to these documents then.'

'And the city's new governor?' Adelaide asks. 'Am I right in assuming that's you?'

Katu Ben inclines his head.

'In the transitional stage. Until we find someone more permanent. Believe me, none of us wish to spend any more time here than we have to.'

'Should have guessed,' she mutters. 'Should have fucking guessed.'

'Now do you see? Now do you see, you stupid girl? Where your idiotic, thoughtless schemes have led us?'

'Shut up, Feodor, they're probably bugging us—'

Feodor's hand tightens on her wrist. She shakes it off.

'The Chambers are a sacred site!' he shouts.

'Not any more, they aren't. Let's get out somewhere we can talk, for stars' sake.'

They hurry back to the aquarium lifts of the Eye Tower. Adelaide takes the lead, leaving Feodor no choice but to follow her, taking the lift to the seventieth floor and walking briskly through the tower until they reach the private shuttle platform reserved for Council use. Adelaide calls the shuttle pod. She can hear rain pattering on the roof of the tunnel. It hasn't stopped since yesterday. Feodor pays it no attention; he is apoplectic with rage.

'You are so very ignorant, Adelaide. You always have been – wilfully so. Why do you think you were never told about Whitefly? I couldn't trust you. And now you see why it was necessary – now those monsters have come to shit all over us!'

'You could never have kept it up, Feodor, it was a stupid plan. Think how everyone in the city feels now they know they've been lied to. Do you think they'll trust you now?'

He looks impatiently down the tunnel.

'It was the only viable plan.'

'It doesn't matter now. It was only a question of time, and now your time's up. What the hell are we going to do about this? Have you thought about that?'

'You think I'm going to discuss this situation with you like a rational individual?'

'Don't forget I represent the west.'

He snorts.

'Of course, you're all for terrier rights now.'

'For some people, Boreal governance might be a whole lot better than life under the jurisdiction of your precious Council.'

Feodor's cheeks redden, emphasizing the fine capillaries running through his skin. She can see the tic working in his cheek.

'Better?' he explodes. '*Better?*'

'We're both negotiating here. You for your side, me for mine.'

'If you do this to spite me, you'll be condemning the entire city.'

'It's not about spite. It's about survival.'

She stares at the spotless white platform.

'Do you ever think about all those people whose murders you authorized, Feodor? All those lives? Boreal lives, some of them. I'm not surprised you burned that laboratory.'

'Your problem, Adelaide, is that you never look at the bigger picture. You've spent your entire life playing with your heritage as if it were a toy. You've never been put in a position where the only options are impossible ones.'

She looks up then, looks at him straight on.

'I might have done that once but I'm not playing now. Work with me here.'

Feodor ignores her.

'The fact is, I did what I had to do to protect this city and I'd do it over again.'

'You make me sick.'

'And your grandfather? Does he make you feel the same way? You should talk to him. Ask him why he initiated this. It might give you some perspective. We're a small fish in an ocean of sharks, Adelaide. Our only hope was camouflage. I didn't create Whitefly – I inherited it.'

'Why don't you send Linus in your place? He knows how to negotiate. He and I could work together. We might have a chance.'

'I can't trust Linus any more than I can trust you.'

'What have you done with him, anyway?'

'He'll stay out of sight. Out of trouble.'

'Put the bodyguard on him, have you? How is Goran these days?'

She turns away, too angry to continue. How can he remain so blinkered, after everything they've heard today? The call light on the platform is flashing, but there's no sign of the approaching pod. Outside, the towers loom as dim, indistinct shapes through the translucent tunnel walls and the misty rain.

'There has to be something we have,' she says. 'Something we can offer them, to leave us alone.'

'Are you out of your mind? You heard what I said in there – Osiris can barely cover its repairs. You know the only way this city stays afloat is by keeping the west in its place. With a proper decision, taken with care, we might have found a way to contact land – the Antarcticans, perhaps, or the Solar Corporation. Maybe.'

His voice drops. He might be talking to himself.

'It's too late for that,' he says. 'You've doomed us.'

Adelaide looks at him. She can see the tiredness, the dejection, and for the first time she thinks there might be something behind that draconian exterior, some hitherto unsuspected emotion driving her father's actions. But she cannot sympathize. She knows that nothing she could possibly say would convince him to see things differently. He might make a show of it now, but Feodor would never have made contact with land. The idea is outside of his lexicon.

'Where's this fucking shuttle?' he snaps.

'I don't think it's coming. You'll have to walk.'

She leaves him alone on the platform, peering into the tunnel, as if by sheer force of will he can conjure up the pod. If they can't work together, they'll have to work apart. He to his people and she to hers.

Unless, she thinks. Unless there's another way. If I can only get hold of Linus, we might have a chance to redeem this mess.

Twenty westerners and Adelaide Rechnov gather in an undersea room of an old warehouse tower. Dien. The gang lords: a Roch leader, the chain-link tattoo lurid around his bare neck. The leader of the rival Juraj gang, resurrected by his niece after Juraj's assassination last year. The shadow-figures behind the manta trade, the black market. A table. A conference where guns are laid down in front of their owners and bodyguards hover at the exits. They talk. Lay out the possibilities, unfolding each like a piece of silk wrapped around a jewel. They let the possibilities shine, clear and unambiguous. Assassination. Rebellion. A strike on a Boreal submarine, knife to the heart, show them some southern steel. Dien argues. We need the City now. Over there they have firepower; stand together and we have a chance. A Roch counters: but then again, what if we're better without them? What if we use them, what if this is our chance to set the City straight? How can we trust *her*, the Silverfish, a Rechnov? Why should she represent our interests?

Adelaide shrugs. You can go, she says. You can go, but know this. Your interests are tiny to theirs. They come from a bigger world, a world where cities are pieces in a game of dice. We're krill to them, and they don't care if we put a name to this article or not, but if we don't I can promise you one thing: they'll burn us to the Atum Shelf.

After the meeting she takes out her scarab and enters the code for her brother Linus. She can hear the whisper of static as the scarab attempts to connect with the Reef, but there is no response: the Boreals must be blocking the channels.

Let's do it western-style, then. She dispatches one of Dien's crew to the Undersea, bound for the City with a handwritten note. The Boreals might have their submarines, but they can't monitor every one of the city's security points.

In Dien's apartment she lies awake, haunted by thoughts of the Boreals: the memory of their cold eyes and soft hands, the smiling one impassive at their centre. Questions run through her head. Who are these people? Can she use them? Should she use them? Is she on the side of the west or the side of the City, or on the side of Osiris? How can she advocate for one without the other?

The schism between themselves and the Boreals seems insurmountable. The northerners have not sent diplomats to negotiate; they have sent an army to conquer. She knows, with absolute certainty, that they will never understand what it is to be Osirian, and they will not try to. They will never know the desolation of believing themselves the last. They will never feel the siren lure of the water, a call to abandon, to drown because there is nothing else, only this glittering, decaying, impossible city. They will not throw salt over their shoulders or raise a glass to the ghosts. They will not press wrists in greeting. To Adelaide, so often scornful of these customs that run through the fabric of Osirian society, they now seem infinitely precious. And she feels strongly, fiercely Osirian in a way she has never conceived of before.

But she has nothing. Her hands are not only tied, they are empty. What can Osiris offer the might of the Boreal nations? The City is already in turmoil, torn between the ungiving will of her father and the evangelical fervour of her brother. The west has been poised to spiral into gang warfare for months. Even if we unite, she thinks, what do we have?

'Rechnov. Are you awake?'

Dien's voice is soft as a feather.

'Yes, I'm awake.'

'I can't sleep.'

'Nor can I.'

She senses Dien feeling for words, battling with the thing she has been battling with since the Boreals appeared.

'It wasn't supposed to be like this,' says Dien at last.

'I didn't expect it either.'

'I can't help thinking. . . that it's my fault.'

'If it's your fault, then it's my fault too. I was the one who suggested activating the signal. We sent a cry for help, not invasion.'

'All my life I've dreamed of what might be out there. Do you have ground-dreams, Rechnov?'

'Of course I do.'

'There's one I get over and over. It's land, but there's towers, just like in Osiris, with raft racks running between them even though there's no water, not a drop in sight. I'm on the ground, and I'm running, following these footprints in the ground, golden footprints – and whoever made them, I know I'm trying to catch them up but I can't, however fast I run, I can't get a glimpse. I keep running, keep following those footprints. Until the city ends. And there's this flower field, flowers as tall as me, taller. I can hear something crying inside. A horrible cry. I know I'm meant to go in, under the flowers, but I can't. I'm too scared. And that's where I wake up.'

'You think it means something?'

'That I'm scared to go in the fucking flower field? I don't know. Fear, fear of something. That's the usual explanation, isn't it.'

A minute passes before Dien speaks again.

'I never told you this, Rechnov, but I used to want a kid, I really, desperately wanted a kid. And I got pregnant. But I couldn't bring myself to go through with it, because all I could think was this kid was going to have the worst, the most shitty life, and I knew I couldn't give her anything better. There was a choice, I thought, and this choice was irresponsible. So I had the operation – in the western hospital, obviously. Only something went wrong. And afterwards, they told me that was it. There wouldn't be another chance.'

She falls silent. Adelaide can hear her breathing, shallow but sharp, the breathing of someone trying not to cry. She gets up and crosses the room. Dien doesn't resist when she puts an arm around her shoulders.

'I'm not giving up, you know. Not this time. And you can't either. My great-grandfather built an extraordinary city. I know there must be something here that we can use.'

On the afternoon of the second day of occupation, unidentified strikes are launched against a Boreal submarine, killing two crew members, and at dusk the Boreal-conscripted skadi line up a dozen suspected perpetrators at the border and they bring out the Osirian execution tank. From the back of a subdued western crowd, Adelaide and Dien watch as the tank is filled and the suspects are drowned, pair by pair. When it's done, the bodies are dropped into the sea. The Boreals forbid their recovery. The bodies float, at times apart, then jostled against one another by the motion of the waves, a head against a foot or a shoulder to a knee, and after a time the circling gulls descend and perch upon the dead and begin to open up holes.

Not long after the gulls descend, one of the bodies disappears. No one sees what took it, but elsewhere there are sightings: a fin, passing through the city. A silken shadow below the surface. By the end of the day, all twelve bodies have gone.

In the evening of the second day the Boreals announce an investigation into the purposeful concealment of the city. They introduce curfew. Those who break it are detained. Those who are suspected of having a role in the concealment of the city receive a knock on the door in the night. Some of them are witnessed to leave their homes and do not return.

On the third day of occupation the city of Osiris signs an unconditional declaration of surrender. The signatories are Feodor Rechnov, City Councillor, and the Silverfish. After they have signed, Feodor Rechnov goes back to the Domain and does something he hasn't done for a long time: sits at the bedside of his father, the Architect, and listens to the old man babbling in Siberian, not sentences, just fragments, although even if he were speaking in sentences Feodor Rechnov would not understand a word. He's never spoken Siberian or tried to learn it. This is the new world. Now the old is shouldering in. He pours himself a glass of vintage raqua and downs it and pours another. A larger dose. He looks at it and considers forcing the contents down his father's throat, this measure and another and another, until the babbling ceases and there is silence. He drinks the measure and pours another. He tells the old man, slowly and without sparing any detail, what has happened today. The Architect blinks, but does not acknowledge. It's not our city any more, says Feodor. You hear me? We've lost it. He slams his glass against the table. *You've* lost it. The Architect blinks. Siberian words slip from his lips. His hands flutter at his sides. Feodor should have burned the old man in the tower with the rest of Operation Whitefly. It would have been a mercy.

Later that day, by which time Feodor is very drunk, his bodyguard Goran comes to find him. There are people at the door, he says. Councillors. Shall I let them in? Feodor shakes his head. He pulls himself upright. Hears the old man's ragged breathing. Still alive. Slowly he makes his way to the entrance of the Domain.

There are ten of them. One of them is his younger son, Linus. He can see it in their faces before they speak. Cowards, the lot of them. He hasn't represented their interests, they say. They had to release Linus Rechnov from an underwater cell. There's been a vote. Feodor's resignation papers are here. They'll leave them with him. He knows the procedures.

'Fuck you all,' says Feodor Rechnov. And closes the door.

At twenty hundred the Boreals sound an alarm for curfew. One by one, Osirian boats pull into deckings and their occupants retreat inside. In the City, the external lights of the rotating towers power down; there will be no patrons tonight. Somewhere below the surface, the shark glides silently between the city's foundations, its nose tormented by competing scents. This one? Or this one? Where does it begin? Tellers link hands and murmur to one another: it's here. It can't be stopped. We said it was coming.

When it begins it's past curfew, and Adelaide is out on the waterways.

A pulse of light appears in the sky over to the east. In its brief, fierce effulgence the city is visible for a moment: the western towers outlined against the clouded night sky, the shadow of other boats on the water, moving slowly, furtively, dreamily through the darkened waterways. The light vanishes, and the dull boom of an explosion echoes in its wake.

Adelaide waits, unsettled by the strange display. Sounds that were barely audible before now register insistently. The murmur of boat motors, tuned discreetly low. An oar lifting and dropping in the water. The patter of feet, swift, over a raft rack. The west have turned off their lights, and the darkness brings with it the feeling of a silent consensus within the city, although of what and what it means remains to be resolved.

As her eyes readjust, Adelaide senses the driver turn her head, away from the direction of the light.

'What was that?'

'I don't know,' she answers.

'The Boreals playing games?'

'I can't see why. Maybe it was one of ours?'

'Maybe. . .'

Adelaide can hear her own uncertainty reflected in the driver's voice.

'Are we going on?' the driver asks. They are meant to collect Dien, who has been working at the hospital for the past twelve hours, before heading to another illicit meeting of western leaders. Adelaide hesitates. She doesn't want to keep them waiting. But this – this is something new.

'No. Head over that direction. Where the light was,' she adds unnecessarily.

The driver obeys. They switch course, gliding between the lightless western towers, easing past boats who are also breaking the curfew, their passing without acknowledgement, although Adelaide feels a surge of camaraderie with each fellow transgressor. The new regulations are easier to enforce in the City, where the glow of night-time towers and the guiding lights of the waterways lay malefactors bare. Westerners, accustomed to skulking, have the advantage in this transfigured Osiris.

Adelaide gnaws at the chapped skin of her lips. The light worries her. What was it and where did it come from? They know so little about the Boreals. Once again she thinks: there must be something Osiris, with all its ingenuity, can offer their invaders to make them go away. And if anyone would know, it would be Linus. . .

She takes her scarab from her pocket and enters the code for her brother. She waits impatiently, but there's still no signal.

'Hell's teeth,' she mutters. Without communications, they have no hope. The Boreals know that, of course. The Boreals are not stupid. But then again, the Boreals have never had to live like westerners. That's another advantage.

They have just skirted the perimeter of market circle when another pulse illuminates the night. This time she counts: one, two. It vanishes. The light seemed closer to the city this time, and brighter.

A boat moving down the waterway in the opposite direction alters its course and heads across to them. One of the two passengers leans over.

'Hey, did you see that?'

'We saw it. Hard to miss it.'

'What was it?'

'I don't know—'

'You're heading that way?'

'We're going to take a look.'

'We'll come with you.'

Adelaide directs her driver eastwards, taking a route near the edges of the western quarter, using the outermost towers to maintain their cover. The driver maintains a moderate speed, not dawdling, but not moving fast enough to warrant attention from any patrolling forces, Boreal or skadi. The other boat tails them. As they pass another tower, Adelaide feels a sudden anxiety to be as far as possible from the city's architecture. At this moment, the sea feels like the safest place to be, despite the terror of the roaming shark who is already rumoured to have snatched several people from the deckings.

As they near the border, a third, much closer light blooms in the sky, gleaming against the blanket of cloud cover. This time, Adelaide has a clearer sense of its origin. The light seems to emanate from a region outside the city, but within the perimeter of the ring-net.

Again, the sound of an explosion follows the light, but there is no accompanying evidence of fire or smoke. What the hell is going on?

'Take us outside the city,' she says impatiently.

'Silverfish, are you sure? The curfew—'

'I need to see what's going on. If we see skadi, we scarper.'

'All right, all right. . . But don't say I didn't warn you.'

'I won't.'

Cautiously, the driver eases the boat out from between two towers.

'I've got your back,' Adelaide assures her.

Adelaide listens to the open waves ahead, but she cannot hear a single skadi patrol boat. The night is bound in the same muffled quiet that has defined the past few days.

They skirt around the sweeping path of a searchlight and head directly south, tracing a course parallel to the border, moving out towards the southern side of the ring-net. As they clear the city's grip, Adelaide has a view of not only the glimmering towers beyond the border, but also of the Boreal fleet, anchored to the east.

'Bring us nearer to the border,' she requests. The driver does so, and cuts the motor to idle. The boat rocks freely with the waves until the driver throws a hook, securing them to the mesh. Adelaide weaves her fingers into the border netting and pulls her face close until she can see through. She blinks, confused. Half of the Boreal fleet seem to have disappeared.

'That's weird. . .'

'What is it?'

'I think they've moved, but it was so fast—'

She waits, confused but expectant. Minutes pass.

'See anything?' asks the driver.

She shakes her head.

'Not a soul—'

A pinpoint of light ejects from one of the Boreal submarines still visible and arrows away, quickly pursued by a second bolt. Moments pass, then a fourth flare, apparently reacting to the Boreal bolts, identifies a lone ship situated between the Boreal fleet and the ring-net.

'There's someone out there,' breathes Adelaide.

'Who? Who is it?'

'I've no idea. Another ship. Not a submarine—'

She is still watching, her face pressed against the ring-net, when the game changes. A missile from the outer ocean hurtles upwards and arcs across the sky. Adelaide doesn't see where in Osiris it hits but she feels the impact as a physical shock. A white fireball blazes over the eastern side of the city, before a vast plume of smoke obscures Adelaide's view of the fire.

The aftershock ripples through the border. Adelaide and the driver can hear the wave before they see its approach – an ominous rushing, then the white tidal crest racing from east to west, directly towards the border—

'Hold on!' yells the driver.

The wave slams into the border, drenching them instantaneously. The boat rocks violently and for a terrible moment Adelaide thinks they are going to capsize, the boat lurching in the wake of the wave, water slopping in the well, before it regains equilibrium.

Adelaide hauls herself to her feet, spitting saltwater. She looks back east. She can see the glow of fire, red and sinister.

'Help! Help over here!'

The boat that was tailing them has not been so lucky. Adelaide can hear the two passengers splashing about in the water, trying to right their stricken craft.

Her driver steers the boat in their direction while Adelaide grabs a bucket and starts to bail, already consumed with shivers. The douse of Tarctic water cuts to the bone. They reach the capsized boat and help the passengers on board their own.

'Something touched me – in the water.' The man's voice is fraught with horror.

'It must have been kelp—'

'It didn't feel like kelp—'

'What the fuck *was* that, anyway?'

'I saw a ship,' says Adelaide. 'I don't think it was Boreal. I think it was attacking us.'

They begin the precarious drive back, still bailing water, the boat riding dangerously low. To the east, the sky pulses with the light of now recurrent explosions. There is something about the play of the light that is eerily reminiscent of the aurora australis, something almost beautiful but far more deadly that transfixes everyone in the boat. Once again Adelaide tries to contact Linus. Once again, the signal is jammed.

As they move back into the cover of the towers, she can see fragile, intermittent lights blinking on across the west. The deckings are crowded with westerners who have been drawn outside by the flares. The traffic on the waterways has doubled. Adelaide and the driver drop off their two passengers. They are reluctant to leave, begging Adelaide to keep them with her, but she has no notion where the night will take her, and cannot risk them being caught up in it. As they drive away from the tower she sees their faces, anxious, receding, swiftly swallowed up in the mass of other spectators.

'The hospital,' she instructs.

They head on, back through the west. She hears footsteps running over the connecting bridges, voices shouting from tower to tower. Fragments of renegade o'dio broadcasts spill from open windows.

'This is going to be a bad night,' says the driver.

'I know.'

The restlessness is palpable. A mood that could turn so quickly and irreversibly to panic, and from panic to anarchy.

She tries one more time to contact Linus and to her surprise she gets a connection.

'Linus? Linus, are you there, can you hear me?'

'Adelaide? Is that you?'

His voice is faint and the signal is producing intermittent static.

'Linus, what's going on?'

'Adelaide, I can't—'

'Linus!' she shouts. 'Hell's teeth.'

'Adelaide, where are you?'

'I'm in the west, where else would I be?'

'Good. Good, stay there—' There's a delay, and then he says. 'They're bombing us.'

'Who? Who is it, Linus?'

'The Tarcticans—'

'Tarcticans? *That's* who's attacking us?'

In the background of the call she can hear noises: frenzied voices, thudding feet.

'Adelaide—'

The sound of an explosion, shockingly loud. A scream. Then moments of silence.

'Linus! Linus, are you still there?'

She hits the scarab. A buzz in her ear and she hears his voice, quick and urgent.

'Adelaide, there's something I have to tell you, I should have told you. Vikram was on the expedition boat. He was on the boat—'

'What?'

The scarab falls abruptly silent. Frantically, Adelaide tries to reconnect, but the signal has now gone completely.

'What did he say?' asks the driver.

'He said – he said it's the Tarcticans.'

But she is not thinking about the Tarcticans. She is thinking about what Linus just said. What she thought she heard him say—

The driver is silent for a moment. 'Tarctica,' she says at last. Both a finality and a wonder in the tone. 'I've had ground-dreams about that place.'

Vikram was on the expedition boat. He was on the boat.

That's what she heard.

'Are you all right?' says the driver.

Distantly, Adelaide hears herself reply.

'I don't think they're here to rescue us.'

'Doesn't seem that way.'

They reach the hospital in silence.

'I should stay with the boat,' says the driver.

'I'll be quick.'

She hurries inside the tower, suddenly worried that Dien may not even be here, that she's left already, ventured out into the night on her own, to investigate – that would be like Dien. The waiting area is rammed and the hospital staff look grim and harried. Adelaide scans those on duty. She can't see Dien anywhere. She pushes through a set of doors into the area for emergency treatment. No one stops her. Patients are doubled up on beds with more laid out on the floor or propped against the walls. Finally she spots Dien, dressing a nasty-looking head wound on an elderly woman. Dien looks up as she approaches.

'Fuck, Rechnov! You were meant to be here hours ago!'

'No time – we need to get out of here. Linus said the Tarcticans are attacking.'

And he also said—

'The Tarcticans?'

Dien's hands keep working, pressing layers of gauze into place, although her face is frozen in disbelief. 'Why would they attack us?'

'You know as much as me. Are you coming?'

'Let me just finish this – is the meet still on?'

'I don't know.' She drops her voice. 'But I don't want to be inside.'

Dien finishes her bandaging and complies wordlessly, pulling on her coat, grabbing her scarab.

'When you say attacking,' she says, 'you mean they're attacking the city, or the Boreals?'

'Both. Or the Boreals, but they don't care if we get in the way.'

As they exit the tower, a team of paramedics are rushing inside with a body on a stretcher. Dien lingers, clearly torn, then follows Adelaide. The driver has moved the boat a short distance away from the tower. Adelaide realizes why when she sees the crowd. Those without transport are endeavouring to beg, coerce or steal a ride. Where they want to go is unclear, but it does not matter: they want to get away from the tower. At the back of Adelaide's mind is the collapsing tower in the unremembered towers; the night Vikram—

Did he really get out? Could he be alive? Is it possible?

'So?' she asks Dien.

The other woman looks at her, back at the tower, at their driver muscling the boat towards the decking. She realizes Dien doesn't have a plan any more than she does.

They fight their way through. She can feel the force of the surging crowd, some injured, some not, pushing and pulling, the edge of the decking a perilous place to be, shifting underfoot, the looming blackness of the water as they teeter on the edge, struggling for balance. She sees something tall and narrow, slicing through the water.

'Shark!'

The cry cuts through the crowd. Adelaide strains to see. She tries to push back, where was it, she saw something, it was there, but now it's gone, or dived, in preparation, they come from below—

'We're going to have to jump for it,' yells Dien.

The boat is coming in. The crowd's eagerness turns towards it. Someone grabs Adelaide's shoulder, intending perhaps to use her as a launching point. She shoves back. The boat curves, side to the decking, in a throw of spray. Dien leaps expertly on board. Adelaide follows her and lands, rolling into the well, and the boat is already powering away, accompanied by shouts and curses, and Dien has a manic smile on her face, but it is not a smile that's reassuring in any way.

'Where to?' asks the driver.

Dien looks at Adelaide and Adelaide looks at Dien.

'The City,' says Adelaide. 'I need to get over the border. Find Linus.'

Dien shrugs.

'Why not? I doubt anyone's left guarding it now.'

'And I want to check on the Larssons.'

'Do it.'

The driver calls back to them.

'If you're going east you're on your own. I've got to find my kid.'

'You go,' says Dien. 'Find her.'

The driver jumps out near the desalination plant and Adelaide takes the wheel.

'How much charge have we got?' asks Dien.

She checks the gauge.

'Enough to get us City-side.'

But only just enough.

The sound of the battle between the Boreals and the Antarcticans ebbs and falls as it moves around the city with the oscillating lights. They check the Larssons' tower first, but their boat is gone and the apartment is empty.

'They'll be safer out,' says Dien.

Adelaide nods. 'The City, then.'

For a few blocks they progress without incident. Then Adelaide notices a disturbance in the water ahead.

The waterway between the two towers begins to froth and seethe. The two women watch, incredulous, as something gargantuan pushes at the surface of the water. For a moment Adelaide expects the razored mouth of a monster to emerge. Then the water sluices away, revealing the glossy hide of a Boreal submarine. The submarine rises majestically, a storey high, two storeys. Caught in the displacement of the water, their boat skids outwards on a tidal wave.

'Look out!' shouts Dien.

Turrets swivel on the submarine. It begins firing. They hunker down in the boat, arms covering their heads. The submarine's shots are directed at an Antarctican ship that has breached the western quarter, but stray bolts catch the walls of western towers. All around Adelaide can hear the shower of breaking bufferglass and the impact of firepower against steel. The sudden heat in the air burns against her face. A return shot strikes the submarine. Fire blooms and almost immediately dissipates, the submarine seeming to suck in the fire, ready to turn its energy back on the aggressor. It appears immune to destruction.

The Antarctican ship is being annihilated. Adelaide can see it listing; the ship seems to shudder with each additional impact, isolated fires bubbling up and jetting from vents, shades of grey and blue and green rippling over its superstructure in complex, nauseous patterns. Crew members scramble over the doomed vessel, fighting to escape. Some topple into the water. Dien is shouting, *let's go let's go!* but she's mesmerized, hands clenched to her head, she can't look away, they're trapped between ship and sub. Over the groans of the sinking vessel she hears shouts for help. The sub refocuses, fires again, concentrated bursts. Some of those still on board the ship manage to get a lifeboat out, but in the efforts to do so others are lost to the waves. She hears a piercing shriek. A crew member that was treading water vanishes. Moments later, a yawning mouth breaches the surface and fastens almost delicately around the torso of a screaming Antarctican.

Adelaide stares. It's the last thing she witnesses before an explosion temporarily wipes her vision and her hearing.

Next thing she knows she's on her back in the boat. Her ears ringing. Hot sparks stinging her face. Debris hitting the water all around. The air clears slowly. Something is wrong with the scene in front of her. The submarine is—

The submarine is gone.

Dien is standing over her. Dien's mouth opens and closes. She can't hear a word. Dien repeats whatever she is yelling and Adelaide reads her lips.

Get us out of here!

Dazedly, she levers herself up, takes a hold of the wheel. They push the boat onwards, away from the forsaken ship, the obliterated submarine, back into the city. She struggles to collect her thoughts. Even if they make it east, soon they'll need to recharge. And then what? What's going to be left there, how far have the ships penetrated? She thinks of Linus. The sudden silence. What he said. She tries his scarab, expecting and making no contact.

'Nothing from your brother?' asks Dien.

Adelaide shakes her head.

'He'll look after himself. You know he will.'

They pass a converted waterbus whose upper deck is ablaze with fire, adorned with drummers who are half-naked, their upper bodies glistening with grease. They appear immune to the flames and the immediate danger they have placed themselves in, and are shooting flares into the air. Their voices lift in guttural, harmonic chants. The boat proceeds slowly, imperiously through the city. The drummers wail. The drums beat on.

'The Rochs,' says Dien, gazing after them. 'The gangs are going to war.'

'At a time like this?'

'What better time? There's no place to hide tonight.'

'No.'

They drive on.

As the battle moves into other parts of the city, they have company. At first Adelaide assumes people are trying to get away from the fighting zone. But as they draw closer to the border, she realizes something else is happening. There's a unity to the movement, a direction.

Boats packed with westerners brandishing banners and weapons alike are swarming as one towards the border. Their shouts urge one another on. Boat by boat noses ahead, taking turns to lead the procession, Adelaide and Dien caught up in the flow. As they draw closer to the line between west and City, the westerners resemble a small army going into battle.

'Oh my stars.' A look of wonder arrests Dien's face. 'They're going for the border.'

The same idea has occurred to Adelaide. They look at one another excitedly. This is something unforeseen.

Adelaide and Dien let the boat drift with the throng and stand side-by-side at the prow, hoods thrown back, both caught up in the momentum and careless of being recognized. A cheer goes up when they are spotted. Someone shouts, the Silverfish! The chants resume.

'Down with the border! Down with the border!'

Adelaide joins in.

'Down with the border!'

She hears Dien laugh beside her, a joyous laugh. Searchlights wash over the netting, illuminating the faces of the protesters, the rippling banners with their printed slogans. She sees a banner with the sign of the Silverfish and her chest warms with pride. A Teller is balanced astride two boats, her greying robes flapping in the breeze, her text a hybrid of prophecy and political apocalypse. The metal links of the border clank with the disturbance in the water, as if it is breathing. Adelaide has never been so aware of its physical presence. This close, draped with kelp strands and crusted with salt, the netting looks at once immutable, and strangely fragile. It looks – the word comes to her. *Biological.* As though it has always been here, since before the city's creation, since the birth of the ocean itself.

It's survived this long because it's a living thing. A thing that grows inside minds, feeding off thought.

At the edge of the mass, only metres away, Adelaide is aware of skadi boats lurking with idling motors. She thinks of their guns and their paralysis gas and her heart shrinks, but then a great roar goes up from the crowd and her fear falls away – yes, they can attack, but more western boats are arriving every moment, massing on the water, carpeting this part of the ocean as far back as there is light to see.

The boats part to make way for Adelaide and Dien's boat, drawing them deeper into the safety of the pack. People reach out as they inch forwards, wanting to touch them, to press wrists to theirs. She sees pinches of salt tossed into the air; this isn't just for them, it's for those who have come before, those who have died seeking justice. The chants coalesce around them. Adelaide's head tingles with it. She feels the scent of danger – the skadi-turned-Boreal moving closer – and braces herself. Whatever is coming, she is a part of it. And at the same time she is aware of an incredible exhilaration, a sense of momentum so over-powering it makes her head giddy.

A ladder extends upwards from one of the boats and clatters against the border. A woman begins to scale it. Searchlights converge on her body, so small and slight, and Adelaide's breath stalls, waiting for the inevitable shot.

Then she hears something. Voices, raised in unison.

Singing.

She sees, on the far side of the border, a conglomeration of City boats. They too have banners. They too are headed directly for the border.

'Fuck!' Dien grasps her arm.

'No – no, it's all right – it's all right!'

She points.

'They're here for the same thing!'

They exchange incredulous looks. The sound of voices reaches an apex, shouting and singing, yelling encouragement to one another. As one, the two crowds draw together to attack the border. She sees axes hack at the metal links; laser cutters usually applied to dismantling ice sheets rent through the netting. Two hands from either side clasp together and the crowd cheers. The rent widens, stretching until it is large enough to accommodate at first a small boat, then a waterbus, which powers through into the City. Others are scaling the netting, waving torches and banners aloft.

Adelaide looks at Dien and is shocked to see the other woman is crying.

'Don't fucking stare at me, Rechnov.'

She puts an arm around Dien's thin shoulders.

'I never thought I'd see the day,' says Dien.

But Vikram did. And he might be alive—

A firework whistles upwards and explodes overhead. People who have never before exchanged a word are embracing like sisters.

The two collectives continue to attack the border, tearing down segment after segment. Adelaide and Dien push closer. Adelaide gets her hands to the meshing, feeling it come away in her fingers. On the outskirts of the city, pulsing lights mark the ongoing battle. The skadi boats slink away, or ditch their guns and join in. Dien clutches a fragment in her hand, rolling the metal links about her palm as though she never intends to let go.

'That'll be worth something one day,' says Adelaide. 'You should put it somewhere safe.'

Dien smiles dizzily. She seems incapable of speech.

'You know this is only the beginning.'

Her friend nods, but the smile remains on her face.

'I know.'

'We might all be dead this time tomorrow.'

'I know.'

They grin at one another deliriously. On either side, figures hang from the border-netting, backlit by the explosions that ripple through the sky, bathing the city in molten colours. Under this peculiar light the figures appear to Adelaide like ghosts torn from another world, where a rift has opened up in the stratosphere above Osiris, disgorging souls. And even as westerners and Citizens reach to embrace, it seems to her like the last gesture of souls damned years, even centuries, before, who have waited all this time to receive their particular retribution.

Amid the chaos she sees two familiar faces. A man and a woman, a little older than the average protestor, but joyful, jubilant, as they steer an old blue and white striped boat on a careful path towards what remains of the border. Adelaide's rescuers, who pulled her from the waves. She raises an arm in greeting, shouts their names. Mikaela Larsson's face lights in recognition. She touches Ole's shoulder, and he turns, surprised. Adelaide waves again. The Larssons return the gesture. She indicates she will head over to join them, and steps up, balancing on the edge of the boat.

There is no warning of the shot. It hits her in the chest, straight on. She sways, arms limp at her side, before folding backwards into the well of the boat. She hears screams and does not at first comprehend why. She sees Dien's face, very close to hers, frozen with shock. Dien's voice. Saying her name. Her name. What was once her name. Rechnov! *Rechnov!* Blooming in her chest, the pain a thing too complete to register or to comprehend. Dien's voice, urgent, full of horror. *Adelaide!*

Flashes of light sear across her vision. She wants to say something to Dien. It is important, to say something, in this moment which she realizes with surprise must be a departure. *The* departure. She wants to take Dien's hand, to hold it tightly, reassuringly, as others have done for her, but she can't move. She wants—

The lights on the backs of her eyelids grow dimmer. The voices fade. She can't hear anything.

And then the lights too, slide away, and there's nothing.

PART SIX
THE POLAR STAR

THE PILOT

I t's dark. Not the thick, clotted darkness of the city, or the crystalline infused darkness of the desert at night. Darkness complete, undisturbed except for a tiny, greyish column of light through a minute hole drilled into the upper wall of the shipping container. Ramona Callejas holds on to that. She puts the back of her hand against it, although if there is movement in the slender airstream, she doesn't feel it. It's her only air vent.

She hears the sounds of the docklands machinery moving closer, and then an ear-splitting clang reverberates through the shipping crate as the gantry crane deposits another one-and-a-half metre cube on top of the one she is hidden inside, the crate connecting and locking into place, its weight undetectable as a physical force but she senses it, pressing down as if she is being buried. All around her crates from the Panama Exchange are being dropped, stacked up on the container end of the *Polar Star*. They carry the poppy harvest, solar cells for reconstitution, and a runaway pilot without a plane. The column of light from the air vent grows dimmer as the rising crates block out the dawn sky. She fights down panic. What if they've blocked her in? What if she can't get out?

The machinery subsides.

Ramona waits.

Around her, she hears the papery slither of boxes shifting as she adjusts her position. The rasp of her shorts against her thighs. Her sweat dripping on the floor. The rap of her knuckles, hesitant, against the wall of the crate:

tap tap.

The sound tumbles away into nothingness.

After a time, there comes a deep groan that could come from hell, if you believe in hell, if you believe in an afterlife, which she doesn't; the too-soon deaths of her younger siblings quashed any thoughts of life beyond life. The only family she has left is her mother, who is somewhere on this ship, in the custody of an unknown perpetrator. She doesn't know who and she doesn't know why, but she will find out. That thought is the only thing that keeps her from screaming.

That sound again. The bowels of the ship, girding into action.

Motion. Slow and ponderous. She feels it through her entire body, a tremor that thrums against her coccyx and up the length of her spine. Creaks and scrapings, cargo straining against its moorings. Motion. She feels it with a crash of relief and a wash of pure, unadulterated terror, because this is the moment, the line, the belt between north and south, and she has committed herself and there is no turning back and if anyone finds her who shouldn't, they will probably kill her on sight.

At last the Boreal ship begins the long crawl which will take it across the gulf and up the coast. Inside the crate, Ramona Callejas sweats and shivers like she has a fever. It's sweltering. The equatorial sun is soaking into the metal and Ramona knows her time inside the crate has a stamp upon it. She has to trust that the truck driver at the Exchange told the truth, and if he didn't, she will have to shoot the lock off the hatch to get out and hope by all the Nazca that it opens. She doesn't have much ammunition left.

Listening, waiting, she doesn't know how much time passes. The sweat runs off her, collecting in body hollows: crook of elbow, small of back. Soaking through her clothes. Her bladder is painfully full, pressing against her abdomen.

Only now does she switch on the torch.

Flash of light, skipping over the interior of a metal cube, blinking as her eyes adjust. Boxes of papaver tea piled high above and around her. She sees the cut-out of the hatch.

After what feels like hours, she hears the dull thud of approaching footsteps. She tenses, backing up against the papaver boxes, readying herself, crouched with the gun in one hand. She flicks off the torch.

The footsteps pause. She hears the sound of something scraping over the hatch of the crate. Gently, she releases the safety catch on the handgun. Her breath is shallow and every gulp of air is like swallowing soup.

There is a clunk as the hatch opens and dim light floods the crate.

Framed in the hatch is a Boreal man in a functional ship's uniform. His gaze falls upon Ramona, and for a moment she sees herself as he must see her, a desperate, terrified southerner in tank top and shorts with a gun clutched in her hand, ready to shoot at a second's notice. But the crewman's face remains impassive. He must be used to border hoppers. He points to Ramona, and speaks in strongly accented Spanish.

'Bring your things. Don't talk.'

She jams the gun into her waistband, grabs her pack and squeezes out into a narrow corridor between two towering walls of crates. The Boreal crewman waits for her, then closes the hatch. From the exterior, she can see the minuscule air vent and marvels that she could have been so reckless with her life.

But she's here.

Made it.

For now.

Glancing up, she sees the crates are stacked in rows ten high. A ribbon of sky is visible high above, shocking in its blueness. She can see the glint of refracted sunlight and from its direction she guesses it is midway through the morning.

The crewman is already moving down the line of crates, checking each one. She realizes they must be marked: there is a system at work here. The crewman pauses. Ramona keeps her distance as he opens up a second crate, and a wild-eyed man crawls out from the hatch, babbling in Spanish. He seems to fall forwards, clutching at the crewman, but the Boreal steps away, out of reach. He repeats the same instruction he gave to Ramona.

'Bring your things. Don't talk.'

The Boreal continues to the end of the corridor, the second stowaway hurrying closely behind, Ramona following, maintaining a gap between herself and the others. The Boreal does not check any other crates. He opens a door leading out of the container cell, and stops, listening to ascertain there is no one nearby. Ramona can't hear anything except the faint groan of the superstructure, and a level humming noise – a motor or engine.

The other stowaway begins to talk. Where are the others? There is one more crate. Are they going there now? What about his family?

The Boreal sailor shuts the exit door abruptly.

'I said don't talk.'

'But what about—'

'I have two numbers. You see? Two crates. Her.' He jerks his head towards Ramona. 'You.'

'There's another! You're mistaken! You have to get them out!'

The man is frantic. Ramona glances back at the cell of containers and her heart sinks. What chance is there of identifying another crate?

The stowaway turns desperately to Ramona.

'Help me!'

'He says there's another crate,' she says.

The Boreal crewman regards them coldly.

'You want to come with me, or go back in your boxes?'

The man attempts a few more words of protest, then subsides.

The Boreal indicates they should follow. He leads them down into the ship, moving with ease through the constricted spaces, the other stowaway struggling to emulate his movements, Ramona following silently behind. The gun is a snug pressure against her lower back. A reassurance, but also a last resort. Unlike the soundless Boreal tech used by the raiders, hers is a weapon that will draw attention if used.

The crewman switches on a torch and brings them down into the unlit hold of the ship, below the water line, where smaller crates and boxes are stowed. He shows them a stash of basic provisions. Packs of bottled water. A bucket with a lid.

'You piss here. Stay out of sight. At Scotia, I will come for you. By then you are over the border. A boat collects. You understand?'

Ramona nods.

'You keep quiet.'

The Boreal makes to leave but the other stowaway protests once again.

'What about the others?'

'I have two numbers,' says the Boreal. He jabs a finger. 'You. Her.'

'No, no, there's another crate.' The man fumbles in his pocket. He pulls out a crumpled piece of paper and holds it up. 'Here!'

The Boreal looks at it.

'I don't have that number.'

Once again he turns to leave. The stowaway grabs his arm. The Boreal lashes out, pushing the stowaway off balance. He staggers back a couple of paces and trips over the bucket. The Boreal has a gun pointing at him.

'No trouble,' says the Boreal.

When the Boreal has gone, the stowaway turns to Ramona.

'Please, you have to help me. My family!'

'Why were you in a different crate?' she asks.

'I was meant to go first across the belt – they should have taken the next ship, they came early to Panama. It was all a rush but we got on board. The driver promised, he promised me there would be spaces. Please!'

'I've got my own people to find,' she says.

'Please!'

He looks desperate enough to do something dangerous, she thinks.

'All right. Let's wait a few minutes, make sure the Boreal's gone. And don't piss him off, all right? You anger him, that makes trouble for me too.'

They make their way cautiously back to the cells containing the crates. As she passes the crate of her own transportation, now closed, Ramona notes its strategic placement at the front and bottom of the stack, so that the hatch faces outwards. It would only have taken a mishandling, a word awry in the immigration chain, for the crate to be facing the other way, sealing her in her own tomb. She pushes back nausea. She's out. She's alive.

She helps the man check the numbers on each of the crates they can reach, but none of them match. He starts to call for his family by name, low-voiced at first, but becoming more and more agitated as he fails to locate the crate. Ramona is worried now. He's going to compromise her.

'Keep it down,' she warns him. 'You're going to bring him back.'

They move into the next cell, but have no more luck.

'I'm sorry,' she tells the man. 'You're on your own from here. Maybe they're on another ship? Come and get me if you find them.'

Alone, she begins the search. Below the water line there is no light except for the brief, occasional flicker of the torch; time is slippery, uncatchable. Someone has her mother. *Who are you? Do you know I'm coming? Do you know I'm going to find you?* The mantra keeps her moving. Gradually the ship makes itself familiar. Ramona is always one step ahead or behind, perpetually alert to the footfall of a crew member, the possibility of discovery. Watching them, sometimes from afar, sometimes very close, close enough to spit. She makes herself like the dust again. Hating and learning, but exerting herself to put her hate aside, because it gets in the way of learning. There will be time enough to reclaim it later.

She grows accustomed to catching a hatch in the moment before it closes. Clambering from compartment to compartment, watching and listening, committing every exit and cubby and ladder to memory. All her life she has made maps. Now the humid belly of the ship becomes a three-dimensional labyrinth in her mind.

It is strangely devoid of life. At the stern, the large shipping containers sit snugly within their cells. Aft, the ship's solar sails tilt towards the sun, tracking its passage across the sky as the ship creeps up the coast. She knows it is night when the ship powers down and sometimes she thinks she can hear the pummelling of the sea around them.

The crew are quartered below deck. Each time she sees a new face, Ramona commits it to memory. She counts seventeen faces. Once or twice she spies the Boreal crewman who opened up the crates, but she always keeps herself out of sight. The crewman does not come to check on her and the other stowaway, or if he has, she wasn't there, and he has left no sign of a visit.

It is not until the second day that she finds evidence of the kidnapped Patagonians.

She observes a woman who is clearly not a member of the crew going to the upper decks. Unlike the others, the woman goes barefoot, and is not in uniform. She wears camouflage trousers and a tank top and a flashlight on a string around her neck, and she is armed: a handgun clearly visible at her hip. The woman passes several crew members, but not one of them acknowledges her, or even meets her eye. They act as if they haven't seen her.

Ramona has no doubt that this is her woman.

She waits for the woman to come back from the upper levels. When she returns, her hair is wet and she smells of soap. Ramona follows. The woman leads her down a flight of steps, along a corridor, and through one of the below-deck holds, packed with smaller crates, situated on the opposite side of the ship to where Ramona and the stowaway were taken. The woman climbs backwards down a ladder to reach another level, switching on the flashlight to guide her. No one else is down here. It's dark and hideously hot. They are still in a storage area, a long and narrow compartment, but the engine room must be nearby because the noise is louder.

Loud enough to mask any upsetting sounds.

The woman stops abruptly. Ramona drops to a crouch and freezes. The woman waves her torch around what appears to be a makeshift living area, with storage shelves and a slung hammock. She selects things from the shelves, cans of food and bottles of water, and loads them onto a tray, humming to herself. She picks up the tray and continues for another twenty paces, until she reaches a hatch at the end of the storage compartment. Then she sets down the tray, takes hold of her gun, and slowly rotates the wheel of the hatch.

In the few moments while the hatch is open Ramona can see the compartment on the other side is small, perhaps three metres square, and dimly lit. She glimpses figures huddled against the walls. The woman – the handler, she thinks – slides the food inside.

'Lunch,' she says.

Hands reach for the food.

Ramona creeps closer.

To the left of the compartment is a familiar figure, small and shrunken. A figure hunched over on herself, back to the wall, rocking with the gentle rhythm of vacancy.

Ma.

The relief and anger together are almost too much. Her first instinct is to shout out, *I'm here!* She wants to rush into the room, scoop her mother up in her arms and run. But there is nowhere to run. They are stuck on this ship, together, but not together. The crew, up there, the prisoners, down here, the two layers of the ship a dual consciousness that is never acknowledged, and if it is never acknowledged, it cannot exist. These people have already been vanished.

The handler closes and locks the hatch, cutting off Ramona's view. She ambles back to the storage area and pulls on a kind of robotic headset, with goggles and earpieces and wires. Then she settles herself in the hammock.

Ramona remains where she is, trying to control her breathing, the shaking in her hands. The impulse to act without thought.

The handler fiddles with the headset and lets out a long, satisfied sigh. Minutes pass. From time to time the handler makes noises – a grunt of satisfaction, or a shout of annoyance, which seems to correspond with a blinking light on the headset. Her hands clench and relax at her sides.

Ramona watches. She weighs up the options. She could kill the handler. The opportunity is before her: the handler is exposed, her bare neck offering a tempting target, and Nazca keep us Ramona would find it easy to end this woman's life. But where does that leave her? With a room full of prisoners and no way of getting them off the ship without being seen. Even if she could, they're advancing up the coast of the northern uninhabitable zone. There's nowhere to go between here and Alaska. To get her mother out, she needs help. She needs the co-operation of the handler.

She thinks about the handler's movements. This woman never interacts with the crew. They don't look at her. They don't speak to her. If asked, could any one of them describe her?

Slowly and very quietly, Ramona retreats back the way she came. She needs to think, and prepare.

For the next twenty-four hours she follows the handler's movements, memorizing her routine. The handler feeds the prisoners three times a day. She takes their waste up on deck and returns with an empty bucket. She goes to the crew's quarters and returns with wet hair, smelling of soap. But Ramona never once observes her speak or interact with a single member of the crew.

Ramona returns to the stowaway compartment and raids her pack for the things she will need. She chooses her location: a small hold near to the engine room. The confined space is dark and claustrophobic, there are pipes, and most importantly it's never visited by the crew.

The next time the handler takes food to the prisoners, Ramona waits for her to close the hatch, and wheel it locked. Now the handler will proceed up on deck to take some air before going to the crew's facilities to wash. Only this time she won't make it as far as that. Ramona follows silently, gun in hand. As the handler reaches for the ladder she makes her move.

She leaps forwards and strikes the back of the handler's head with the barrel of her gun. The woman staggers, but does not fall. She turns. She's taller than Ramona, and stronger too by the look of it, but she's temporarily disorientated. Ramona clouts her again, hard across the temples, putting all of her strength into the blow. The handler slumps and Ramona lowers her to the floor.

She resists the desire to beat the handler's head to a pulp.

Now Ramona works quickly. She drags the handler backwards. The woman is muscled and heavy. Her bare feet slither along the floor. When she reaches the holding place, Ramona strips her of her trousers, leaving the woman in the tank top and her underwear. She takes the nylon rope from around her waist and trusses the handler to the pipes, drawing the bonds tight and finally fixing in place a gag torn from her own clothes. She can't risk any screaming.

She fights the urge to go and check on the prisoners straight away. She has to be here when this one wakes.

While the handler remains unconscious, Ramona runs the torch over her, checking the woman's body for any identifying marks and the pockets and linings of the clothing she removed. She removes a knife and a pair of handcuffs, which she puts to use to shackle the handler's ankles. Like the Boreal kidnapper in the highlands, this woman has no birthmarks, tattoos or other identifying markings. She carries no identity papers. Her body is honed for action, with strength in the arms and thighs, and her hair is cut short, out of the way of her eyes.

Ramona sits and waits. Her entire body is sticky with sweat; it's been over seventy-two hours since she was able to wash and she probably stinks. She wonders how far up the coast they are now. She wonders how the hell she is going to get her mother off the ship and back to safety. For the first time since boarding she allows herself to think of Félix, who she left in a papaver-induced slumber, Félix's horror on waking up and finding her gone, Félix's worry, Félix's anger that she's undertaken this mission without him. From childhood friends to inter-mittent lovers, they've always led their own nomadic paths, but put herself in his position and she knows she would feel the same worry, the same anger. She hopes he hasn't done anything stupid, like try and follow her. Ramona's life is hers to gamble with; he shouldn't be dragged into her mess. Félix has to understand that, even if he doesn't agree.

Despite their long history, there are instances in her life that she has never shared with him, and doubtless he with her – things they have seen or done, acts too strange or shameful to speak of. Observing the handler's shallow breathing, it occurs to her that this trip is likely to be one of them.

When the handler begins to stir, Ramona speaks softly.

'You're in a part of the ship where no one will come looking for you. There is no point in shouting or trying to scream. If you do, I'll kill you here. I'll cut your throat.'

She draws the edge of her knife gently along the handler's bare leg, not hard enough to cut, but enough for her to feel the blade.

She hears the handler's breathing, shallow and ragged. She switches on the torch. The handler's eyes squint in the sudden brightness before settling on Ramona with a clear, steady hate.

'Do you understand me?' Ramona asks. 'You speak Spanish?'

The handler nods.

Ramona sets the torch upright on the floor and loosens the gag, taking care to avoid the handler's teeth.

'Now you're going to talk. Who are those people you're guarding?'

The handler stares at her contemptuously. Ramona considers her for a moment. She has met people like her before, people so inured to violence you could shoot their best friend in front of them without them flinching. But most people will fight for their life when it comes down to it. The handler has to feel the thread her life is dangling on.

Ramona backhands her, and a thin line of blood trickles from the corner of the handler's mouth.

'Who are those people?'

'Scum,' says the handler. 'Lizards. They're nobodies.'

'Where are you taking them?'

The handler spits. Ramona strikes her a second time, and feels a crunch in the soft tissues of the nose.

'I said, where are you taking them?'

'North.'

'Where north?'

'To a place where they can be useful.'

'What place?'

The handler doesn't answer. This time, she gets up and puts her boot into the handler's stomach. The woman folds over, groaning. It's a miserable sight. Ramona reminds herself: this woman has her mother captive.

'What place?' she repeats.

'How should I know? It's in the middle of the fucking desert.'

'The desert?'

'Yes, the desert.'

'In Alaska?'

The handler sneers.

'If you'd ever been north you'd know the answer to that.'

'I haven't been north. You have. You're going to tell me what's there.'

'I don't know what's fucking there. It's the North American desert. It's outside the border. There's nothing there. Just sand.'

Ramona's mind works quickly. The desert. Outside the border. This is something illegal. Something outside of Boreal jurisdiction.

'You're not going through all this trouble to dump a bunch of southerners in a different desert,' she says slowly.

The handler licks her bloody teeth.

'I need water.'

Ramona gives her a small sip. The handler spits blood.

'More.'

'Later. Tell me how the process works. Tell me exactly how it works and maybe I'll let you live. Did you kidnap these people, in the highlands?'

'No. That's not my end. The batch is delivered to me at Panama. At the Exchange. And then I tell them the new quota, and they go back to where they get them from.'

'The batch?'

Ramona is trembling. The handler's eyes dart away, perhaps in self-preservation, alert to the emotions she is inducing.

'That's what they call it.'

'And then?'

'And then I bring them on board. It's always the same ship. This ship. I guard them. I feed them and keep them alive through the journey. There's a halfway house where the ship makes a stop and someone comes to pick us up. The crew are all paid off. They pretend they don't see anything.'

'Where's the drop point? How far from here?'

'I'm not telling you any more.'

'If you don't tell me what I want to hear, I'll fucking kill you.'

The handler's lip curls. 'You're no killer. I can always tell.'

'Do you want to test that? Do you know who you've got in there? In your batch?'

The handler says nothing. Her tongue flicks out, seeking moisture, but finding none. Ramona leans closer and speaks softly.

'My ma. That's who you've got. My ma.'

She places the bottle of water on the floor in front of the handler, just out of reach. Then she places a second bottle next to it.

'One of these is drinking water. The other is saltwater. Which of these I leave with you depends on your answers to the next question. I said I'd kill you. I didn't say how. Now. How far is the drop point from here?'

The handler's eyes dart from bottle to bottle. Ramona can see the conflict in her face. She moves the drinking water backwards.

'Six days,' says the handler quickly. 'Maybe five, without storms. Depends on the weather, doesn't it?'

'How do you know you've arrived?'

'A crew member comes for us.'

'And what happens when they drop you off? You stay with these people?'

'There's an aeroplane, sea and land, it can land on both. It takes us inland. If there's no sandstorms, that is. Sometimes we're waiting for fucking days. It's a joke.'

'So you do go all the way. Where do they take them? Look at me. Look – at – me. Remember what I said to you. Where do they take them?'

'I don't know. It's a compound. Some secret place, mostly underground. Camouflaged. I've never been inside. I only take them as far as the door. Maybe I get a meal and a shower. Then I go back to the halfway house with the plane, and when the ship comes back down the coast they pick me up.'

Ramona sits back on her heels. The handler dips her chin towards her shoulder, trying to wipe away the blood at her mouth. Ramona doesn't help her.

'This compound. What are they doing there? What do they need people for?'

'Are you listening? How should I know?'

'How long have you been running this rig?'

'Couple of years.'

'And in all that time, you've never wondered? Never asked? Never thought about where you're taking these people?'

Just for a moment, she sees something close to fear creep into the handler's expression. But it quickly returns to defiance.

'They're northerners, aren't they? You think I want to know what the fuck they're doing? Nazca keep us.'

Only now does the realization hit Ramona. A horrible, nauseating realization that trebles her rage.

'You're not even Boreal. You're fucking Patagonian!'

The handler shrugs.

'What the fuck do you care?'

'You're Patagonian and you're trafficking these people.' She squeezes the gun. 'I should kill you right now.'

'Everyone's got to make a living.' A gob of saliva and blood dribbles down the handler's chin. 'I know your type. Righteous. Deluded. The world's full of fools like you. So judge all you like but you don't know shit about me.'

Ramona gazes at her with cold anger.

'No. But I can leave you here to rot.'

Taking her time, she deliberately pulls on the handler's trousers, then takes up her knife. The handler watches her uneasily.

'What are you doing?'

'What do you care?'

Ramona takes a handful of her own hair and lifts the knife. Gently she saws back and forth until the hair comes away in her fingers.

'Almost like yours. Don't you think?'

She moves both of the bottles out of reach, and rises. The handler wriggles in her bonds.

'Hey, you can't leave me here. I've told you what you want. I've told you everything! What are you doing?'

Ramona stuffs the gag back into the handler's mouth. She can see the woman's lips working around the gag. *You can't leave me here!*

'Oh, I can leave you here,' says Ramona. 'Or, I can take your place. Don't think I haven't been watching you. You said it yourself – the crew pretend you're not here. No one on this ship acknowledges you. They don't look you in the face. I doubt a single one of them could describe you. So all I need to do is borrow your clothes and. . . when the time comes, you can take the place of one of your victims.'

She watches the handler's eyes widen under the torchlight, a genuine fear now visible, a fear that in any other circumstances, Ramona would be compelled to try and eradicate. The look sickens her. Her own actions sicken her. She tells herself: this is necessary. Then she switches off the torch, plunging the handler into darkness, and walks away. She can hear the woman's muffled voice, trying to shout or plead. She ignores it. *This is necessary.* Now's the time to let her simmer. Let her think that all is lost. When the handler is nearing the level of despair of her prisoners, then, and only then, Ramona will introduce the next phase of her plan.

At the hatch she hesitates, then berates herself for her own fear. She wheels open the lock. It's heavy, and takes some effort. She steps inside and pulls the door to, but wedges it ajar as a precaution.

The compartment is thick with the stench of human waste and sour sweat. There is a single, dim light set into the ceiling. The prisoners are sat around the room. Each is cuffed and they are roped together. Their faces are dirty and soporific and they barely react to Ramona's entrance.

Ramona's mother is sat to one side of the room.

Inés stares at her, eyelids blinking ever so slowly, perhaps trying to decide which cycle of her unconscious mind has just delivered up this vision.

'Ramona?'

The uncertainty in her mother's voice breaks Ramona.

'Ma, it's me. It's really me.'

She stumbles forwards, sinking to her knees and pulling her mother into an embrace. She can feel the terrible thinness of Inés's body under her clothes, how much weight she has lost, the ribs protruding like sticks against her own chest, the shoulder blades sharp beneath her hands. She sees the scalp through the thin grey hair, smells the pungent oils that have accumulated through lack of washing facilities but can't quite eradicate the smell that is Inés and Inés alone, a smell that reminds her of stones on a terrace and clean pots and light streaming through the shutters of the shack. She clasps her mother to her as though if Ramona were to let go, even for a second, Inés might dissolve in her arms. Ramona can't bear it.

'It's not really you,' says her mother, a note of suspicion now creeping into her voice. 'It can't be. Not my girl, not here.'

'Ma, it's me. I promise you. I'm real. Hold on to me. Hold my hand. It's me. I'm here. I'm going to get you out.'

She releases her embrace and takes her mother's face in her hands. Inés gazes at her, still mistrustful.

'Ramona?'

'It's me, Ma. I swear, you're not dreaming.'

Tentatively, Inés raises her own hand, her fingers curling around Ramona's.

'A vision would say that. I should know.'

'Ma—'

'My lucky one.' She says it with a kind of pride. Ramona can imagine the internal monologue running through her head, her mother struggling to reconcile her own eyesight. She must have dreamed of rescue, or that she was never on this ship, and is now unable to trust the reality before her, afraid she will wake, to find herself alone again, lost again.

'I'm here. I'm here.' She repeats it, over and over, gently squeezing the bony fingers. 'I'm here. I'm real.'

Slowly, Ramona becomes aware of the others in the room, stirring from their stupor, watching her. Their faces frightened, uncertain. Hopeful. The sight of those faces is like a knife twisting in Ramona's stomach. She came here for one purpose, but how can she leave these people behind?

When she speaks to her mother again she speaks to them as well.

'I'm going to get you out. I promise.'

There are six in total. Three women, one man, a teenage girl and an adolescent boy. She recognizes two of the names. They were taken from the village raided in the highlands, where Ramona landed in the midst of the storm, when she first suspected something was wrong. She doesn't tell them she was there. They crowd around her, offering their stories.

'I was putting out the washing—'

'I was going to visit my uncle in the next village—'

'They came in the night, in the middle of a storm. They set our house on fire—'

'They fired a dart into my belly.' Inés's voice, weak and tired. She begins to chuckle softly. 'Didn't know they'd picked themselves a dead one, did they?'

'What are you going to do? How are we going to get out?'

'I have a plan,' says Ramona. It's half true. She has half of a plan. But she can't tell these people that. She has to give them some semblance of hope, however slim. However unlikely the outcome.

When she's replenished the food and water, Ramona speaks to her mother aside.

'Carla told me what happened. Her niece saw the kidnappers take you. And Carla told me about the jinn. Ma, I thought I'd be too late. I thought you'd be dead before I could find you.'

A flicker of amusement enters her mother's face.

'I might as well be dead, my lucky one.'

'Oh shush, Ma. You're alive. And I'm going to help you.'

'Not for long. This jinn is a malevolent one. I can tell.' Inés slaps the loose folds of her stomach. 'It's been squashed inside here wishing me ill for a very long time, yes, and now it's got its wish. This jinn is happy, I can tell you. Happy and fat.'

'Ma, you're not listening. Listen to me. I've got medicine. It won't be happy and fat for long. We're going to get rid of it.'

Inés tuts impatiently.

'I don't want medicine. It's northern anyway, don't tell me it isn't. Why would I put that poison inside me?'

'Because it will save your life. Simple, isn't it?'

'How do you know it will save my life, eh?'

'Because – I know.' Her hesitation is only momentary, but it is long enough for Inés to pounce.

'Ha! You don't know at all. Someone told you a thing and you believed it. Let me guess, this medicine makes me worse before it makes me better.'

'How do you know that—'

'Because I've been in the world, Ramona. Maybe you forget this. You think of your ma all weak and frail, like a used-up yam you think of me. You forget where I've been. I've been to some places. I've been about. Did I tell you the story about the jaguar? I saw that cat with my own eyes, did I tell you this?'

It is the closest Inés has ever come to alluding to her fugue years, even if it is a barefaced lie. All those days lived far from home, disappeared for months at a time, a lost, wandering soul, her past a blank, no future except the day ahead, the road, her last remaining child forgotten. Or so Ramona imagines; only Inés can know the truth. It makes her at once terribly sad and terribly angry. Why does her mother have to leave everything to the last minute? Why now, when they have less time than they have ever had, and maybe no time at all?

'You never told me where you went, Ma. How am I supposed to remember if I've never been told? I don't know where you went or what you saw or what you were told or if you saw a jaguar or if you're making up some story to pacify me now.'

'Eh, don't get cross on me. What's the need to know everything? I went places. I saw people. These medicines, they've been around longer than you think. Rare, yes, very rare, but that doesn't mean it's a secret.'

Ramona sighs. 'If you know they exist, then you know they could save your life. I went through a lot of trouble to get this. To find you. Félix as well. I'm indebted to him.'

'Oh, that boy adores you. Always has. He'd do anything for you. Don't you love him too?'

'I'm not with him, am I? I'm here. Look. It's a patch a day for thirty days. We'll start today.'

Inés pats her hand.

'Ramona look at me. No, look at me. I can't take this medicine now.

Not here, not on this ship. It will kill me. And why waste it if I die anyway? You tell me that, eh?'

Ramona looks at her mother and knows, inescapably, that she is right. If she takes it now, in this state, she won't make it. Ramona puts her hands on her mother's shoulders. She's wearing an old blouse that might have been red once but now is a dirty faded pink. She's had that blouse for thirty years. The sight of it here in this hellish place breaks Ramona's heart. She squeezes Inés's shoulders gently.

'Ma, you have to promise me something. Promise me if I get you out of here, you get back home, you will take this. I'll help you through the course. Me and Carla will, together. You can get better. You have to make this promise. You can tell me all the stories then, Ma. About the jaguar. All of that.'

Inés doesn't say anything.

'Ma!'

'All right, all right. Won't give me a moment's peace, will she, even when I'm all but in the ground.'

'I need to hear you say it.'

'I promise.'

'That's something.'

'But, Ramona. How are you going to get us out of here? Look at this place. So you get rid of that other one, that bitch. That is only one. You say you have a plan but I know you, my girl. You left your luck behind, didn't you? There's no luck in this place.' Inés glances around the cabin, at the huddled bodies, the other prisoners pretending not to listen to their whispered conversation. 'This is a place for the already dead. It's a coffin, my girl. And I don't want you in it.'

She leans close to Ramona and drops her voice.

'You should go. Leave us. Get off. Where's that flying machine of yours? Fly away while you still can.'

'It crashed, Ma. You're right. My luck did run out.'

Inés sighs.

'It happens to us all.'

'Doesn't mean I'm giving up, though.'

'Well, you always were a stubborn one. What was I to do with a one like that? Eh?'

'Help me to figure this out.'

Inés looks at her shrewdly.

'I thought you had a plan.'

'I mean after – after we get off this damn ship.'

'What are you plotting, Ramona? What are you trying to fix this time?'

'Nothing. I'm just thinking out loud. Will you help me tidy up my hair?'

'It's a mess,' says Inés critically. 'What's this great hole here? You lost a chunk.'

'I don't have scissors. You'll have to use the knife. I need it short. Make me look like her.'

'Yes, I see. All right.'

Inés's fingers curl gently around the knife handle, then grip it tightly. She begins to shear the remaining sections of hair, tutting to herself. *Such a shame, all this good hair, it won't suit you so short, still it's greasy as butter, maybe for the best after all.* Shanks of hair fall to the floor around her. There's something soothing in the muttered litany, the light but firm touch of her mother's fingers against her scalp. If she closes her eyes she can almost imagine herself back in the shack above the sliding city, with the sun streaming through the shutters and the earthy scent of peas steaming in a pan.

'There,' says Inés, squinting. 'The worst haircut I ever give you.'

She goes through the handler's possessions. There is a Boreal rifle, and an untouched stash of paralysis darts with a dartgun. She counts them: twelve in total. She sets some of them aside to give to the prisoners. Then she finds the peculiar headset which was entertaining the handler on that first night. Boreal. She tosses it aside in disgust, then changes her mind. What if it's important?

Cautiously, she pulls on the headset.

It's like falling backwards into quicksand. The ship disappears and a three-dimensional world springs into life around her. She's in a forest, but like no forest she's ever seen – the trees sprout colossal black and purple leaves in the shape of tongues, leaves which are dripping with some thick, poisonous-looking unguent. She can hear the noise of animal life, unearthly screechings, terrifyingly close. There are figures spread out in a line to left and right. They are all masked and helmeted and armed to the teeth. One of them is carrying a mauled head – a human head – fingers interlaced in its hair. The figure closest to Ramona turns its head and looks straight at Ramona and through a slit in the mask says, 'Are you ready, soldier?'

Ramona rips off the headset and hurls it from her. She clamps a hand over her mouth, retching, the bile corrosive against her teeth. *Boreals and their robotics.* Whatever it is, she's already seen enough.

The other stowaway finds her while she's loading up the handler's rifle. It must be the torchlight that gives her away – with only two of them creeping about in this part of the ship, the light would have drawn him. Ramona moves to hide the gun but it doesn't matter: the man's eyes are wide and crazed, he's not interested in what she's found. He says he's located the crate.

She follows him through the underbelly of the ship up into the container cells. Already she has a bad feeling about this, and when they reach the crate, her fears only intensify. He shows her the hatch.

'You see – it needs two of us.'

She helps him to lever it open. When a crack appears she hears the hiss of air escaping – and with it a smell, something rotten and pungent. Something bad.

'Oh god,' the man is saying, loudly, too loudly. *Oh god. Oh god oh god oh god—*

Cold with apprehension, Ramona shines her flashlight through the narrow aperture. The light falls upon figures, adults and children, balled or clinging together. Limbs entangled, features rigid in some last contortion – a prayer, a curse. Skin a colour skin should not be, a greenish hue creeping in. The fingernails of the adults are broken and bloody where they have tried to open the hatch. Their enabler lied, or something went wrong with the lock.

It could have been Ramona.

Close it up for god's sake close it up.

She pushes the hatch closed, sealing them back into their tomb. A part of her numb with anger.

Who brings their children—

The other part raging with despair.

How far must you be gone to—

She thinks of the north, the Boreals whose infinite wealth fuels this shipping route by stripping an impoverished country of its sole valuable resource, who have need of nothing except a window on the south and its unaccounted people.

What were they thinking, those unfortunates in the crate? What were they hoping for from a life north of the belt? Did they expect to find kindness there? Because the Boreals show no kindness, no mercy that she can see.

You have some things to answer for.

They get away with it, she thinks. They're answerable to no one except their own insatiable greed. They get away with everything.

The stowaway man is rocking back and forth, groaning. As his sobs escalate, Ramona's anxiety deepens. She cannot afford discovery, not now, when every day is a step closer to the halfway house and the plane.

'Come on.' She tugs at his shoulder. 'Come on, there's nothing you can do.'

He looks at her, utter desolation in his eyes. He moves suddenly, and begins to scale the side of the crates with an agility she had not expected, manoeuvring himself up and between them, clambering gecko-like from crate to crate. Ramona watches, helpless, knowing even if there were something she could do, it is not her place to. The man's life is his own to do what he wishes with, to discard if he feels fit. When he reaches the top she sees his figure in relief, a black shadow against the pale ribbon of sky, before he disappears from her sight. She doesn't need to hear the splash to know what happens next.

In a dreadful way it is a relief. Nothing she could do or say could ever assuage his grief, and she does not like to think what else he might have done.

Ramona has lost weight. It's not surprising, really – the stint in the desert, followed by her all-too-brief recuperation in Panama, and now she's probably sweating off what's left of her physique. But with her newly shorn head, she has to hope no one will notice the handler's trousers are cinched a few notches tighter at the waist.

The first time she makes her way up through the decks of the ship her heart is pumping so fast she feels light-headed.

Just once a day, she reminds herself. *Just for appearance.*

A crewman approaches. Ramona holds her breath, then pushes it out, forcing herself to breathe naturally. Hold your head high – don't look at him – he's not looking at you. He's close now. Just keep walking.

The crewman seems to suck himself to the wall as he passes, avoiding any possibility of contact.

Ramona's vision is spotted. From here she doesn't know the way. From here, it's guesswork.

She keeps walking. Passes a canteen. Several crew members are eating breakfast. The smell of coffee meets her nostrils. A moment later it hits her stomach and she feels woozy again. Keep walking. A crewwoman passes her, averting her eyes over Ramona's shoulder.

She reaches the washrooms. There is another woman in there but when Ramona enters she departs immediately. Ramona goes into a cubicle, shuts the door and locks it. There's a shower. She finds the switch, turns it on and strips off her clothes. Her legs seem too weak to hold her; she crouches under the running water and masked by the sound she starts to cry, her whole body shaking. There is no timer on the shower. The water runs on and on, sluicing off her skin in sheets, and the wanton excess of it only serves to intensify her rage.

She pulls herself together. A box on the wall dispenses soap. She washes her newly cropped hair and dresses and goes back the way she came, barefoot.

Later that day they hit storms and the ship comes to a frustrating halt. In their weakened state, the prisoners are badly affected by the rolling motion, vomiting until there is nothing left to evacuate, and even Ramona feels ill. The handler is also in a poor state. There is a strong stench of urine. The woman has pissed herself.

Ramona switches on the torch. The handler flinches. Ramona gives her water. Some of it dribbles down the handler's swollen face.

'Listen to me. It's time to decide what happens to you. Are you listening?'

The handler's eyes peel open. She nods.

'Option one. I kill you now. Option two. I swap you out for one of your batch, and you can face whatever happens to these people on the inside. You're wondering how I'll get away with that one. Well, to be honest, it probably wouldn't work, but more importantly, I don't think your employers are going to think much of a handler who's coming in as one of the batch, do you? So they'll probably sign you up with the rest, regardless of what happens to me.'

The handler's eyelashes flicker, and again Ramona sees that trace of primitive fear. The handler does not want to go inside the compound.

'Option three: I think you'll agree this is the best pathway for both of us. When the time comes, I let you go, and you continue in your role as if nothing has happened. You smuggle me in with the batch. I'll be armed, of course, and you won't be, because I can't trust you not to turn on me. So I'll have a gun on your back all the way. But if you get me on board that plane, I swear I won't hurt you, despite what you've done. I'll let you go. What do you say?'

The handler's lips work, but no sound comes out. Ramona brings the water flask to her mouth. The handler sips slowly. She tries again.

'What are you going to do with the plane?'

'Did I mention I'm a pilot?'

The handler looks at her with resigned animosity.

'Doesn't seem like much of a choice.'

'No,' Ramona agrees. 'It isn't.'

'I'll do it.'

'Good. Now tell me about the plane. Who else is on board?'

'Just the pilot and the co-pilot.'

'Do they see you coming on board? Do they count your batch?'

'They're in the fucking cockpit,' says the handler.

'But do you interact with them?'

'Not unless there's a storm, and we're grounded. No one knows anyone else. No one *sees* anything. That way no one can recognize you.'

'The pilots don't know who you are?'

The handler hesitates. Ramona tips the water bottle, allowing a few precious mouthfuls to dribble onto the floor between them.

'If you betray me, I will kill you. That may mean I end up dead too, but then we'll both be dead, and that doesn't help anyone, does it?'

'They know my face,' admits the handler.

'Walk me through it. I want to hear every detail.'

For six days the ship remains grounded by storms. Ramona is terrified someone will come and check on the prisoners, but no one appears. Each day she takes their waste upstairs, showers and washes her hair. Each day she takes a ration of food and water to the handler, and watches the woman gobble up the food like a rat while Ramona fights back her own self-loathing.

'What could the Boreals possibly offer to make you do this?' she asks on one visit.

'I like their lifestyle,' comes the reply.

'Their lifestyle? This?'

The handler licks water from her upper lip.

'Their stuff. Their robotics. Their country, one day.'

'They don't keep their promises. You know that, don't you?'

'There's more to life than Patagonia,' says the handler.

She worries about Inés too, but of all the prisoners her mother seems the least affected by seasickness. She says the jinn is the only one who has power over her stomach. What's a storm at sea compared to that?

Ramona is restless.

'They can't get away with this, Ma. Everything comes back to them. The poppy harvest. The jinn. This. No one stops them.'

'When we take the plane home, you can tell your high-up friends,' says her mother drowsily.

'What friends? The Facility?'

'These people you know. They can investigate.'

'And what if it's too late? What if we escape and the Boreals realize something's wrong and they shut it all down?'

'Then it's shut down. And I can sit on my veranda until the jinn eats me up and I'm a dead woman and then you can sit on my veranda.'

'They won't stop taking people—'

'Let it go, Ramona.'

'I can't stop thinking about it.'

'Just drop it.'

The storms pass. They recommence the slow crawl up the coast. She goes to fetch the handler and begins the process of unbinding her, cautious all the while as to the potential of a counter-attack. Ramona hands her back her trousers, a clean set of underwear and a top. When she steps back she keeps her gun trained on the woman.

'You'll have to change here.'

She watches the woman's movements closely, trying to ascertain whether the handler is as weak as she appears, or whether there is some greater deceit at work. Certainly, Ramona can't imagine that anyone, however robust, would fare well after more than a week in the sweltering heat with barely enough water to stay alive. But the handler will have been chosen for this job for a reason. She'll be resilient.

'And by the way,' she adds. 'I'd behave if I were you. Those darts of yours – I've given them to the prisoners. You won't want to upset them.'

The handler gives her a look of hatred, but says nothing.

As night falls and the hour approaches for the ship to make its appointed drop, the atmosphere in the compartment grows ever tenser. Ramona can sense it: the brittle nerves of the Patagonians, the brooding resentment of the handler. Whichever way she looks at what is to be done there is no good outcome. She came all this way to save her mother, but now she's here, she faces a far worse dilemma. If she overpowers the pilots mid-flight, she could get them all away, and her mother out of danger, but then she will never know why the Patagonians were taken, or what is happening in the desert. There will be a short delay, while the break in the chain is identified and another handler found, and then the residents of the desert will start their raids and the whole cycle begins again.

But if she does what she is thinking of doing, there's no guarantee anyone will make it back.

At last she senses the motion of the ship slowing. The engines wind down and quieten. The ship comes to a halt. Ramona nudges the handler, reminds her she has a gun on the woman.

'No tricks.'

The handler goes outside of the compartment and waits. Ramona shoulders her pack. In it she has the handler's rifle, her knives and the dartgun. Her own handgun is concealed at her waistband. The other prisoners are carrying provisions of food and water, and each of them has a dart.

'Stay with me, and act as you would with the handler.' Ramona makes her tone as reassuring as she can. 'It's going to be okay.'

It isn't long before she hears footsteps approaching. No words are exchanged, but the handler comes to open up the compartment. At the other end of the narrow hold, she can see a crew member standing.

'This way,' says the handler. 'You follow him.'

The prisoners file out, Ramona at the back, keeping close behind Inés. All the way up to the deck of the ship she is intensely aware of the handler at her back, the woman's snuffling through her broken nose, the measured pace of her step, the too-short distance between Ramona and the handler, which the handler could so quickly breach.

When they reach the deck, the air is clean and blessedly cold on the back of her neck. After a few moments the thinly dressed prisoners start to shiver. They huddle together. Ramona puts a protective arm around her mother, keeping the gun shielded from view between them. We're north, she thinks. We may be on the coast of a desert, but this side of the belt it's midwinter, and the nights are bleak.

The deck is deserted except for the crewman who brought them up. But across the water, Ramona can make out faint lights from a few isolated buildings on the shore. This must be the halfway house.

The handler directs the prisoners into a boat lowered over the side. Ramona helps her mother struggle into the boat, half an eye on the handler, ready to counter any unexpected move. The handler climbs in after them, then the crewman. Ramona lets her hand rest at her side, where the gun is concealed, and makes sure the handler is aware of it. The crewman, at the head of the boat facing away, mutters an order and the boat is lowered until they hit the water with a soft splash.

The crewman starts up the motor and steers the boat towards the shore. As they draw closer, Ramona counts the lights of three distinct buildings, set back and at some height above the waterfront. She guesses one of them is a small desalination plant. Now she can hear the shoreline, waves lapping against land. There is a landing stage marked by a single lantern.

The boat moves steadily towards the stage. The prisoners, ostensibly roped together, sit in silence. What are they thinking? What if one of them panics and uses the darts?

No doubt sensing her anxiety, Inés reaches back and squeezes Ramona's hand. The contact gives her some comfort.

The boat knocks against the landing stage. The handler jumps out.

'Come on.'

She tugs on the rope and one by one the prisoners climb awkwardly out, until they are all standing on the landing. The boat departs at once. Ramona hears the whine of the receding motor, but looking back, she can't make out the outline of the ship at all.

There is no sound from the buildings of the halfway house. No evidence of habitation.

'This way,' says the handler.

She takes the lantern and leads them along the landing stage. And then Ramona sees a sight that despite everything about their predicament makes her heart lift.

An aeroplane.

It is much larger than *Colibrí*, built to carry passengers, rotund and sturdy-winged without the refined elegance of Ramona's surveillance plane. It is nestling in the water, just offshore. A gangway extends from the fuselage across to the landing. The plane is waiting for them.

The handler sets down the lantern at the bottom of the steps and they board the plane, still roped together, the handler following close behind.

The prisoners take turns to keep watch on the handler through the night. Ramona is awake and alert at first light, the answer to her dilemma no clearer than it was before she slept. She can hear the two pilots in the cockpit, both of them men, talking to one another, and although she cannot make out the exact words she guesses they are running through a pre-flight check. Inés has fallen asleep with her head resting on Ramona's legs. Her breathing is shallow but steady. Ramona twists her upper body to try and see out of one of the small windows without disturbing her mother.

Except for the buildings of the halfway house, the landscape she can see is flat and barren and entirely desolate. The remains of a road lead inland, and some way off she can make out the ruins of what must once have been a coastal town or city. An ashen light slowly lifts to a clear blue sky. She sees no signs of life.

Opposite Ramona, the handler is also awake. Her expression is impossible to read.

In the cockpit, one of the pilots is whistling. The other says something and he stops and they both laugh. Ramona bites down on her hatred. Her relief when she senses the aeroplane powering up is immense. If the pilots were to check the batch, she is certain she would stand out, and they'd have questions about the state of the handler too.

The other prisoners wake with the movement of the plane gathering speed over the water surface. As they take off Ramona feels a peculiar lurch in her stomach. She isn't used to being a passenger. The others peer through the windows, reporting on what they see, and the handler doesn't bother to stop them. The coast is receding. There's a huge desert! How huge? Endless. As far as you can see. To the end of the world. The small pleasure they take in the newness of flight is a source of both gladness and sorrow for Ramona.

Inés wakes. Her eyes rest on Ramona's face, questioning. From time to time the prisoners remark on things, and Ramona doesn't need to see to picture the landscape they are describing: the derelict cities drowning in sand, the stumps of bridges that once suspended roads, a dried-up river bed swirling across the sand like a desert snake. Echoes of another era, reverberating back on themselves because there is no one left to answer. The voices of Boreals before they were Boreals, before they went north, pushing into places not previously their own. Once or twice she glances out of the window and sees that the plane is moving faster than *Colibrí*, perhaps at twice the speed. Then she looks away. She remembers the crash. The desert frightens her.

If they get out of this alive, she will have to make the return journey south, crossing not one but two uninhabitable zones in an unfamiliar aeroplane.

But she can't think of that. Not yet.

'Time to act, yes?' says her mother. 'You need some help with those men?'

Ramona looks down at her, torn. The deluge of thoughts keeps coming;

she can't shut them out. She's in a plane over an unknown desert and she's on her knees outside the empty shack, with the dawning, anguished knowledge that her mother has been taken. She's flying an injured boy to a medical unit in Titicaca, to have his foot removed. She's with the poppy farmers and the packers and the stevedores, she's northbound on a ship with the harvest while morphine supplies in the Patagonian centres run dry. In a crate with a family, suffocating. With a father climbing to the top of a cell and throwing himself into the ocean, at the handler's side as she mumbles: *their stuff, their robotics, their country.*

'Ma—'

'I don't like that look on your face, Ramona. I know that look.'

'Ma, I have to know. I have to know what they're doing.'

She lifts her chin, catching the eyes of the others, speaking quietly.

'I know the plan was to get the plane away but if we all leave now, this will never stop. I have to get into the compound.'

Inés's eyes close, shutting out Ramona's face, her speech, and for the first time Ramona thinks she understands the meaning of the word crusade. The intransigent force behind it, the impossibility of turning away from it. She remembers her transportation through the desert. The feeling that the jaguar was walking at her side. She had a sense, in Panama, that the desert had altered her. Is this the proof of that? In crossing the belt has she crossed another line, of awareness that can no longer be ignored?

'None of you have to come in with me. None of you should. When we land, I'll overpower the pilots. The handler will get them to open the hatch. We'll take them out. We'll get out the plane, like she says they always do, but that's as far as you have to go.'

She waits. The handler starts to laugh.

'Of course. Of course you turn out to be a suicide mission. What else?'

'It's not suicide,' says Ramona. 'I'm going to get you all out.'

Her mother's eyes flicker open. Whatever was fleeting through her mind, she is clear-sighted now.

'Yes, my lucky one. I am with you.'

'Do you understand?' Ramona addresses the others. 'If I don't find out what's happening, all of our families and friends remain at risk.'

One by one the prisoners meet her gaze. She hates herself, in this moment, but she hates the Boreals more. They will be accountable.

It's one of the youngsters, the girl, that speaks first, and savagely.

'You should kill them all.'

The cabin heats as the day progresses, and the prisoners fall drowsy. The handler passes round water. After that initial outbreak of mirth her face is closed off and Ramona can't read her thoughts. One of the pilots is singing to himself. His voice is brash and cheery and fills Ramona with disgust. She runs through everything the handler told her about the compound. She thinks about the paralysis darts and debates whether she should apply them both herself or get one of the other prisoners to do the second. In the end she decides to take responsibility for them both. She'll have to be quick as a scorpion.

Inés reaches up and shakes Ramona's shoulder.

'Sleep an hour. I'll watch for you. You need to be ready.'

She nods. Lets herself drift. Never fully asleep but not awake either, imagining herself suspended above the sand, facing down, unable to move in any direction, and her skin begins to sweat.

She wakes. Inés is patting water against her cheeks.

'I think it's near the time,' she says.

Ramona blinks. She can feel it too. The plane is slowing. They have been flying almost all day. The reality of their situation, the decision she has made, slams back into the front of her consciousness.

She beckons the handler.

'As soon as we land, you need to knock on the door. Get them to open up. Say it's an emergency. All right?'

The handler nods sullenly.

Ramona waits. Her ears pop as the plane begins a spiralling descent. There is no singing from the pilots now. They are going through the landing check. The prisoners are alert and nervous. The teenage girl's gaze is locked on Ramona. She tries to relax her own face into something reassuring.

As the plane touches down in a series of small bumps Ramona's heart begins to pound. She motions the handler.

Get ready.

The handler moves into position, Ramona just behind her, a dart in each hand. The plane's thrusters kick in, slowing the aircraft's momentum. They coast to a halt.

The handler bangs on the door and begins to shout.

'Open up, open up! Emergency! Open up, quickly!'

'What is it?'

'Open up! Now!' The handler's voice rises to a panicked shriek.

The connecting door opens and the co-pilot leans out.

'What—'

Ramona springs forwards and jabs the dart into his neck. His eyes glaze over and he slumps at once. The other pilot, seeing what has happened, tries to pull the door shut. Ramona jams herself between the door and the frame. He changes tactic, hands reaching for the console. She lunges, grabbing both of his arms, but in doing so drops the second dart. She lets go of one arm and aims a punch at the head instead. The pilot ducks to the side and her blow glances off his skull. The pilot swats at her. She can't see where the dart landed. A blow lands in her gut, knocking the breath out of her. Then she sees him reaching down beside the seat, scrambling for something, a gun—

He gasps and his mouth falls slack. Ramona looks up.

The handler has stuck him with the dart.

'Thank you,' Ramona wheezes.

The handler says nothing, but goes back into the cabin. Ramona climbs out, retrieving the pilot's gun and stepping over the unconscious body of the co-pilot which blocks the open door. She gets her breath back. She looks at the terrified prisoners.

'All right,' she says. 'This is it.'

She points to the unconscious bodies.

'Help me bring them in here.'

They drag the pilots into the passenger hold. Ramona arms herself. She's never carried so many weapons: the handler's rifle, her own handgun, knives strapped to her body, and the dartgun, fully loaded.

'Remember what we talked about. You've got more darts, use them if you have to. I need you to stay calm. Once I'm inside, you can retreat to the plane.'

She looks round at them. They're so scared. And so is she, scared of what she's done and what she's about to do, but she can't show it.

'It'll be okay,' she says. She meets her mother's eye. Inés nods.

They step out of the plane into intense, blazing white sunshine. Ramona pauses at the top of the steps, shielding her eyes and squinting against the onslaught of light. They have arrived in the middle of the desert. Dunes slope away on either side, reaching to the edges of a panoramic blue horizon. The plane has alighted in front of a collection of low-rise buildings, all linked together by domed, connecting corridors. The buildings are the same colour as the sand, and as Ramona looks at them the walls seem to ripple disconcertingly, and she realizes they are clad in the same technology that camouflages *Colibrí* and the aeroplane that has brought them here. A high wall runs around the edges of the compound, but there is no one in sight, no visible guards or security, which corroborates with the handler's report. She supposes there is nowhere to run. The primary purpose of the wall is more likely to keep the sand at bay during the desert storms.

'This way,' says the handler. She casts an apprehensive glance up at the cockpit.

'Don't look there,' says Ramona. 'Act exactly as you would normally.'

The handler herds them towards the first of the buildings. Ramona keeps to the back of the group, the rifle concealed in her pack, the dartgun tucked into her waistband, beneath her top. As they approach, two figures exit the building and hurry outside, one male and one female. Both are clad in loose clothing and bear broad, beaming expressions. The sight of those smiles fills Ramona with trepidation.

'You're early!' says the man in accented Spanish.

The handler stops. She clears her throat.

'Yes. We made good time.'

'Welcome to Tamaruq!' says the woman.

The eyes of the pair rove over the group of southerners. Their smiles do not falter.

'Now let's get you inside and comfortable,' says the man.

'You must have had a long journey,' the woman chimes in.

'You'll need a rest, and a shower.'

'And remove those ropes, there's no need for that.'

The woman's eyes settle upon Inés, then the younger girl, before drifting further back to Ramona. Her brow contracts.

'You're over quota?'

It's enough. Ramona lifts the dartgun and shoots the woman in the stomach. She falls backwards and hits the dust heavily.

One of the prisoners screams.

The scream seems to roll around the desert for an intolerable length of time before the handler hushes them.

The second Boreal, the man, stares at Ramona in shock. His hand moves towards his wrist. She tracks the dartgun to his torso.

'She's not dead. Not yet. Put your hands where I can see them.'

He lifts them slowly. The prisoners toss aside the ropes. Ramona can see how they are trembling. Inés pulls Ramona's rifle from the pack and slings it across her daughter's body.

'Ma, check if there's anything on her.'

Inés does as instructed, going through the pockets of the unconscious woman, who stares up at the sky, lips parted, eyes closed, the silver dart sticking out of her belly.

'Just like the one they shot into me,' says Inés meditatively.

Ramona comes forwards, never moving her gaze from the remaining man, who stands mute and quivering.

'Move the woman out of sight,' she instructs the others. 'Then everyone get back on the plane.' Without looking at the handler she says, 'You can go with them or come with me.'

'I'll stay with them. I'm not going in there.'

'Can you fly that plane?'

'How should I know—'

'If I don't come out, you get them out of here. Figure it out.'

Inés attaches something to Ramona's belt.

'This looks like a thing you may need.'

'Ma, take the pilot's gun.'

She accepts it without hesitation, causing Ramona to wonder whether her mother has used a gun before, but she doesn't have time for anything more than a brief, 'Stay safe.'

She waves the rifle at the man. 'You. Inside.'

As she steps through the entrance, the man walking slowly in front of her with the muzzle of the rifle pressing between his shoulder blades, Ramona can hear the sound of the prisoners dragging the woman's body across the dusty yard.

They enter an empty, windowless foyer: a holding area, she thinks. The air is cool after outside and the hairs on Ramona's arms raise in response to the drop in temperature. Two sealed doors are in front of them, heavy steel doors that remind her of the robotics laboratories at the university in Cataveiro. Doors designed to keep things in. Ramona can feel the shakiness in her limbs. She is afraid in a way she has never been afraid before: afraid of what she is going to find. Afraid that her body will let her down, and the people she has put at risk by coming here.

'You speak Spanish,' she says to the man.

'I'm the welcome,' he replies. She can hear a different kind of fear reflected in his voice: the fear that she's going to hurt him. A justifiable fear. 'I speak many languages.'

'You're going to take me inside. Show me what is going on here. I spared that woman's life, but if you scream, if you do anything, I will shoot you dead. Do you understand?'

'Yes.'

'How many people are in this place?'

'I don't know—'

'How many?'

'Maybe twenty. No more.'

'Who are they? What are they doing?'

'Staff,' he whispers. 'Scientists.'

Coldness injects her body.

'What about southerners?' she asks. 'People like them? How many?'

'I don't go to those levels—'

She can see the sweat gathering at his hairline, trickling down beneath his collar.

'You don't go there? Then you're no good to me. Shall I kill you now and be done with it?'

'I'll take you.' His voice quivers. 'I'll take you.'

Ramona looks at her belt where her mother attached the device belonging to the unconscious woman. A pass. She looks to the door and sees a blinking red light at waist height. She presses the pass to it and the doors slide open.

Two corridors lead off in opposite directions. The walls are painted a pale, innocuous blue, and are empty of adornment. The floor is grey and carpeted. Seed bulbs are planted in the ceiling, offering an unobtrusive light.

A corridor you might find anywhere. A corridor that makes her think of data drones in the Facility, a life without the sky. A prison.

'Where are the southerners?'

He points to the left.

'Move,' she orders.

They proceed down the silent corridor, passing a number of doors marked with signs. *Library. Immersives. Canteen.* Ramona pauses by the canteen, sniffing, but can smell only the faint, dry antiseptic that lingers in the corridor.

She keeps one hand on the rifle, her other squeezing the dartgun.

At any moment she expects to come face-to-face with a group of guards bristling with weaponry.

'Where are all your people?' she demands. 'Your security?'

'It's not like – we don't need—' He stops. 'Please, let me go. I don't know what you want but I can't help you. I just work here.'

Ramona pushes the rifle into his back.

'Move.'

Garden. Gymnasium. Showers.

As they pass each door she tenses, listening, alert to movement. But there is nothing. The corridor ends in a lift.

'Where now?'

'D-down.'

'Call it.'

As the lift doors slide open, she hears talking, calm and leisurely. There are two people in the lift. One male, one female. Both dressed in overalls, a mop and bucket between them. They pause their conversation and shuffle over, waiting for the others to enter. They register Ramona. The dartgun and the rifle. Panic crosses their faces.

Ramona fires the dartgun twice. The first hits its target, the second glances off something, a buckle or belt. She reverses the rifle and clouts the woman over the head. Her hostage moans.

'Get in there!' She pushes him inside and hits the close button. 'Which floor?'

'Lower four,' he whispers.

She looks at the options, where a red light blinks steadily. Lower four is not the last level.

'You're lying.'

She swipes her pass and pushes lower six.

The lift starts to move. The two cleaners are slumped insensate where they collapsed. A trickle of blood makes its way down from the woman's temple.

Lower ground one. Lower ground two. . . The lift judders to a halt at lower ground six. Ramona lifts the rifle in anticipation. The doors slide open. Another empty corridor, pale and benignly lit. Where is everyone? She orders the hostage to drag one of the unconscious cleaners halfway out so that their legs jam the lift doors. On her way out the woman starts to stir. She sticks the deflected dart into the woman's neck, where a vein pulses. Only three darts are left.

The man said there were twenty staff, but this compound must have the potential to house many times that number. Is he lying? Or is something else going on? It feels too easy, like a trick. But his fear is genuine, of that she is certain.

She's here now. She has to keep going.

The hostage leads her down a passage of numbered laboratories. At each door she listens. Behind one door she can hear the faint sound of voices in discussion, and hurries on.

Finally the hostage stops. They stand outside Unit 4. The sign on the door is plain, simply marked, with nothing to indicate what they might find on the other side. Ramona glances back. The corridor is silent. The other doors remain shut but there are people down here. Scientists. She can feel her heart knocking between her ribs. The rush of blood in her ears.

'This is where they are?'

The hostage nods. He looks petrified.

Ramona closes her eyes momentarily. She does not want to go inside. She wants to turn and run. Get out, get away, as far from this place as the Earth and an aeroplane can take her.

Slowly, she forces down the feeling of sick dread. She lifts the pass, noting the tremor in her fingers, unable to stop it.

She swipes and enters, pushing the hostage before her.

They are inside an airlock. On the other side is a second door, with the now-familiar blinking red light. Ramona has never wanted to do anything less in her life than open that door.

The hostage turns to her.

'We shouldn't go in, I'm not meant to be here, this is wrong, please—'

Out of his fear she dredges up the reserves of her strength.

'In,' she says coldly.

She swipes the pass. The light turns green and she pushes him through and follows after him.

They are standing in a long room with a series of large glass windows running down each side. Instinct, soft and cruel, tells her this is the place.

'Why don't you look first?' suggests Ramona. 'I think you should look.'

The hostage shakes his head. He is close to tears. She nudges him with the rifle. He walks to the first window.

'Look,' she says.

He looks and a shudder runs through him. He stumbles away.

Equally unwillingly, Ramona approaches the first window.

On the other side of the glass a man lies on a bed. His body is perforated with wires and tubes, feeding in translucent liquids, or transporting blood in and out of his veins. It is impossible to tell whether he is young or old, or anything about his features, because his skin is infested with redfleur.

It's in the most advanced stages. He is hairless. The head and neck are a tessellation of raw and seeping ruptures. The man's eyes are closed, or gone, it's impossible to tell. An oxygen mask covers his mouth. It looks like it is glued there; to take it away would take the man's flesh, his mouth, with it. The only indication of life is the shallow rise and fall of his chest, and every minute or so, his torso beneath a plastic sheet, twitching in a sudden violent convulsion. If it weren't for his feet sticking out the end of the plastic sheet, the soles weeping, you couldn't say for certain that she was looking at a human being.

Ramona stares at the man for a long time. Distantly she is aware of the hostage, who is sat hunched over on the floor in the centre of the room, perhaps hoping if he pretends he isn't here she will forget about him. As she stares at the diseased man in the glass unit, a creeping numbness invades her body, her thoughts seeming to slow to absolute stillness, because to let anything take form, any thought, emotion, acknowledgement, will be catastrophic. She will not survive it. She lifts her hand to the glass, pressing her fingertips gently against it. Gradually, she registers the nervous breathing of the hostage. She ignores him.

The woman in the next unit is naked and completely encased by a glass dome. The skin on the left side of her head has been peeled back and a section of the skull the size of Ramona's palm removed so that the brain is exposed, grey and slick. Her face beneath the intrusion is intact, but Ramona can see bubbles of the virus swelling under the skin all over her body, ripe to burst. Every few seconds a nozzle pumps a misty gas into the dome. Ramona sees the woman's chest expand in a shallow breath, and realizes with a shock that she is still alive. As she watches, the white-clad, gloved arm of a scientist comes into view, reaching down through an opening into the glass dome.

Ramona jerks backwards, but the scientist gives no sign of having seen her. The glass must permit onlookers to see in, but not for the experiments to see out. The scientist, who is fully suited, adjusts a wire curling around the woman's head. The woman twitches.

She makes her way down the row. At each window she stops, and looks inside. Each room is the same. Securely sealed. Bufferglass dividers. A southerner – she has no doubt they are all southerners – on a bed. They are in various stages of redfleur. Some display no symptoms that Ramona can see, but they are already hooked up and sedated. One woman is conscious, but clearly disorientated. She looks confusedly about her, scanning each corner of her prison, poking at the sheets, coming up close to tap at the glass. Then she returns to the bed and rolls to her side, hands pushed against her belly, kneading, as though trying to alleviate acute pain.

Ramona tries the handle of the door.

'You can't go in,' says her hostage. 'They're contagious. They have the Type 9 strain of redfleur. We'd both be infected.'

The door is locked, in any case. Ramona looks at the foetal figure of the woman. She doesn't look Patagonian. Her face bears Asian heritage.

She turns back to the hostage, who speaks many languages, who is the welcome. She thinks about opening the door and pushing him inside and sealing it.

The last few units are empty.

Each contains a bed with immaculate white sheets. A pillow. Medical machines standing still and silent. Ramona pauses by the last empty unit. She looks at the bed. She thinks of her mother in her faded red shirt, with the jinn lodged inside her, eating away at her immune system, ready to deal a fatal blow at the first whisper of an infection. She feels like her heart has been torn out of her chest.

They exit the opposite end of the laboratory through a second airlock and find themselves in front of a lift. Ramona calls it. Her vision is not quite right. She blinks and it steadies itself.

'Who is in charge here?'

The hostage's face is greyish in colour and damp with sweat.

'D-Davida Kvest is senior.'

'Let's find Davida.'

The doors slide open and a tall, silver-haired man in a laboratory suit steps out. He stops in surprise.

'You don't have clearance to be down here—'

He sees Ramona. In the instant alarm enters his face her hand goes to the dartgun, then releases it. She lifts the rifle, levels it, and pulls the trigger. The gun, a Boreal gun, shoots soundlessly, but at such close range it blasts a hole into the man's chest. He is thrown back a metre before he falls. Blood begins to spread from the wound in his chest, soaking into the grey carpet of the exterior corridor. Ramona advances. She shoots him a second time, then a third. The body jerks with each shot. Only the thought of the others in the building stops her from pulling the trigger on repeat. She needs to conserve her ammunition.

The hostage drops to his knees by the silver-haired man, moaning in horror.

'My god, that's Yoseph, what the hell are you doing—'

'Davida,' she says.

'Why should I take you to her? You'll kill me anyway – you'll kill her too.'

'Which floor?'

'I can't tell you, I can't—'

She rests her boot on his shoulder and jabs the gun into his chest.

'Which floor?'

'Lower ground one—'

This time, as the gun jerks in her arms, she feels nothing at all.

The lift doors close on the two dead men and the lift begins to move smoothly upwards. Ramona cradles the rifle. She can feel blood spattered over her face, Yoseph's and the hostage's, and she knows if she sees anyone else, she will not be able to walk away. Not now. She wishes they would all come, that the lift doors would open and the lot of them line up in front of her so she can dispense the justice they deserve. Except it wouldn't be justice. Not a clean death. Not even close to justice.

As the lift reaches each floor she holds her breath, preparing. But it continues without stopping to lower ground one. She steps out, and checks up and down the corridor. No one. This level of the compound is devoted to offices. Like everywhere else, the doors are neatly signed. How long has she got until someone discovers the bodies downstairs, or the cleaners blocking the other lift? She walks briskly down the corridor, checking each door until she finds the one she is looking for.

Dr Davida Akycha Kvest.

She knocks on the door. A voice calls impatiently in Boreal English.

'Not now, not now.'

Ramona opens the door and steps inside.

A woman in a baggy sweater and trousers is gazing intently into a luminous swirl of digits. Letters and numbers are strung together in cryptic combinations, hovering at head-height, and the codes seem to swarm in the air about her like a horde of fireflies. Her face is lit by the projection, her eyes are open, blinking, taking in information. She has grey hair, pulled up into a knot at the back of her head. Socks but no shoes. As Ramona closes the door she turns in irritation.

'I said not now—'

Her face shifts. After the initial shock her expression alters again, rippling through emotions. The surprise remains, but there is something else present too. A kind of recognition. As though she has been expecting a visitor like Ramona for some time now.

She swipes a hand and the projection disappears, leaving a small woman the age of Ramona's mother, or older.

'Who are you?' she says.

Ramona understands the question, but does not have the words to respond. The scientist studies her for a moment.

'Hindi? Español? Afrikaans?'

'Español,' she answers. 'You speak many languages too, I suppose?'

'I've had the time to learn,' replies the scientist. 'And I find it helps, to hear a language that is familiar.'

Ramona understands that she must mean the batch. The people down there in Unit 4. The man with no skin. When she next speaks, it feels like she is tearing the words from her throat.

'What is this place?'

'What do you think it is?'

'I can guess. But I don't want to be right. I want you to tell me I'm mistaken.'

The scientist massages the back of her neck with one hand, her face wrinkled with discomfort.

'I could do that. I could tell you anything, seeing as you have a gun to my head.' She shrugs. 'It might not be the truth.'

'You're very calm, considering the position you're in.'

'If I lose my calm I'm more likely to be dead, don't you think?'

Ramona feels the trigger of the gun, warm beneath her finger. The need to do damage is at the front of her brain, but she has to have answers. She came here for answers.

'What is this place?' she repeats.

'It's a medical development centre.'

'What does that mean?'

'It means we are trying to find a cure for redfleur,' says the scientist. 'Type 9 redfleur, at the moment, which as I assume you know is fatal.'

'You're infecting these people.'

'That's part of the process.'

'You're killing them.'

'Some of them die, yes.' The scientist looks at her steadily. 'Most of them, it's true. Most of them do die.'

There is a howl of fury building inside her, a rage which wipes out all other thoughts. All the years of anger and resentment towards the Boreal States, the knowledge of her country's exploitation, her frustration at its reliance, and now this – this inconceivable abuse – have found a channel through this one woman in her sweater and socks. Never has Ramona wanted to hurt someone more. She wants to maim, tear the scientist into pieces and slather her face in the blood.

If Ramona's emotion shows in her face, the Boreal gives no sign that it affects her. This is a cold one, thinks Ramona. Cold as an unmarked grave.

She slides her finger back from the trigger. Answers. She must have answers. She owes that to her mother, to everyone inside the plane and everyone who has died here.

'There is a law,' she says. Her voice sounds wrong, tight and high, but she cannot right it. 'An international law. What you're doing is illegal.'

'Yes. Technically, it is.'

'Technically?'

'The Nuuk Treaty bans the experimentation of medical drugs on non-consenting humans, yes. And what humans would consent to be infected with redfleur? You're right – volunteers would be hard to come by.'

'Do the Boreals know you're doing this?'

'They believe we use chimpanzees.'

The scientist's expression remains quite calm. Perhaps she is only waiting for backup. How long has Ramona been standing here? How long until the dead and unconscious are discovered?

'The people in the basement.' She sees the woman under the dome. The man with the ruptured face. 'You take them from my country?'

'Yours and others. Southerners aren't counted in any census.'

'We're easy,' says Ramona softly.

'You're untraceable,' the scientist says.

'You're a monster.'

'Some might call me that. I might call myself that. Unfortunately the world needs monsters. Let me ask you something. How old are you?'

Ramona stares at her.

'What does that have to do with anything?'

'But you're here, you've come all this way, so hear me out. How old are you?'

'I'm thirty-six.'

'Redfleur first appeared around the time you were born. Your entire life, it's been a part of this world. A spectre following you about, year on year, outbreak after outbreak. Strain after strain. Every time we think we have beaten it, another version evolves. I don't suppose you have ever thought about how these viruses are overcome?' The scientist pauses. 'How it is that you are still alive?'

Cold. Cold as snow. Cold as nitrogen.

'You can say whatever you want but you won't make me tell you that this is necessary. Not this. Not those people down there.'

The scientist rests her hand on the back of a chair. 'You don't mind if I——? I have very low blood pressure. Can't stand for too long.'

Ramona nods and the scientist sits, her hands in her lap. Neatly clasped, no rings, the knuckles very slightly swollen with what might be arthritis. For a moment she is still, lost in contemplation. When she begins to speak her voice is quiet, almost musical, and the words come slowly.

'It's funny. I shouldn't even be here. I was meant to retire. I always thought I'd get a place in Veerdeland. That's home. If the place where you are born means home. But I'm here still, in the middle of the desert, thousands of kilometres from civilization. I don't know why I'm telling you this. As if you're my conscience. My confessor. Probably because you're going to kill me. You are going to kill me, aren't you?'

Ramona looks at her for a long time. Cold, she reminds herself. You'd have to be so very cold. But even through the haze of her fury, the tapestry of the other woman's thoughts is discernible – the regrets and fears, the days of doubt and those of belief, and other things – memories – the ones that make Davida Kvest laugh or smile or cry.

No, that can't be right. There wouldn't be tears. A person who cried could not do this.

She raises the rifle and slides her finger forwards to the trigger. She is shaking.

The scientist lifts her head.

'I'd like to make a final request, before my execution.'

Ramona does not trust herself to speak. She nods.

'I've kept a diary. I'd like you to hear it.'

'You don't deserve that.'

'Deserve it or not, it's my request, and you'll honour it, because you're the one that came. We don't always get to choose our burdens. It's in the drawer. I can get it, or you can.'

'Where?'

I'll take it, she thinks. I don't have to hear it, whatever it is. And I won't understand it anyway. She's a Boreal.

The scientist points. Ramona crosses the room, keeping the rifle trained on her. She opens the drawer.

'You'll find a small device in a blue and white case.'

Ramona extracts the diary cautiously. She places it in her pocket.

'Thank you. I can see you're a woman of your word. I know you'll listen to it.'

Ramona does not move.

Long seconds pass. She has to act.

'You are not really a killer, are you?' says the scientist. 'But if you don't shoot me, I will have to press the alarm. If that helps.'

She stands, reaching towards a set of controls on the wall.

With a gasp, Ramona squeezes the trigger.

The scientist flops back into the chair, clutching at her shoulder. Blood spreads between her fingers and begins to soak into the sweater.

'Up,' orders Ramona.

The scientist gets clumsily to her feet. Her face is sweating.

Ramona grabs the scientist's unhurt shoulder and marches the woman in front of her. All at once she is intensely aware of time.

'We're going outside.'

As they proceed down the corridor a man puts his head out of another of the offices.

'Davida, I was after you—'

He sees Davida, bleeding, Ramona behind her, the gun.

'Fuck—'

Ramona shoots. The shot ricochets. The man scrambles back into his office. Ramona moves faster, pushing the scientist ahead of her. Time, accelerating. Moments later she hears the alarm reverberating throughout the building. The hiss of doors sealing. She calls the lift, cursing with every moment she has to wait. A woman in a white coat appears, running down the corridor towards them. She sees Davida.

'Don't move or I'll kill her!' Ramona yells.

The woman stops in her tracks, a look of horror etched onto her face.

The lift arrives. Ramona backs into it and jabs the button for the ground floor.

'Come on, come on!'

'They'll lock down my pass,' says the scientist. 'You won't be able to get out.'

'Shut up.'

She still has the welcome woman's pass.

At last the lift begins to rise. It seems to take an infinite amount of time to move between the two floors. Ramona tenses, her grip on the scientist's shoulder tightening. Ground level. The doors slide open.

Three overalled technicians block the way between Ramona and the exit doors. Two of them are holding guns.

'Move aside or I'll shoot her!'

She is shouting in Spanish but she has no doubt that they take her meaning. The technicians hesitate.

The scientist begins to speak in her own language.

'Shut up! Don't say another word!'

The scientist continues to speak, delivering instructions quickly and incomprehensibly. Ramona lowers the gun and shoots her in the leg. The scientist yelps and doubles over in pain. Ramona hauls her back up. The technicians stare, indecisive, a naivety suddenly clear in their faces. They've never had to deal with an attack, she thinks. She pushes the gun against the scientist's head.

'Move! That way, all of you!'

They move. She hustles the injured scientist forwards, keeping her body as a shield between herself and the pair with guns. She swipes the welcome woman's pass against the door. Nothing happens. She grabs the scientist's pass and swipes that but it too displays a red light.

'You! Open this door!'

'He can't,' says the scientist. Her body is slack, the full weight of it leaning against Ramona's chest. She is losing blood from the leg wound fast. Bright red footprints track the carpet behind them. 'He doesn't have those privileges.'

The others begin to press forwards, scenting an advantage. Frantic, Ramona slaps the pass again. It has to work. It has to—

The door moves aside suddenly.

Her mother is standing on the other side, holding the handgun which Ramona entrusted to her. Ramona drags the scientist through and Inés swipes the door shut again at once.

'How did you—?'

'Get to the plane,' says her mother sharply. They back out of the final set of doors into the courtyard. A blast of desert light and heat hits her. Two security guards are lying prone on the ground. One has had his throat sawn open. Another is sprawled with his legs at odd angles to his body. There is blood, a lot of it, in pools all over the courtyard. The bodies of the pilots have been pushed from the aircraft. One of them has had his stomach ripped open and the intestines glisten wetly under the blazing light. The handler lies beside them. A few metres away is the woman Ramona first shot with the dartgun, now face down with a knife in her back.

Ramona releases the scientist, who falls groaning to the ground.

'Quick, Ma, the plane—'

Her mother raises the handgun. She considers the scientist for a moment.

'Ma!'

Inés pulls the trigger. She turns and walks calmly ahead of her daughter. Ramona stares at her in shock.

'Move,' says Inés sharply.

They run to the plane, Inés now gasping for breath, Ramona helping her along. Ramona pushes her up the steps and pulls the door shut with a bang. She is aware of the prisoners, sat together, trauma monopolizing their faces, the blood all over their hands, their clothes, one of them – the youngest girl, the teenager – still clutching a knife. She climbs into the cockpit, pushing aside the welling horror which now threatens to swamp her. She has to stay calm. Look at the controls. It's an aeroplane. Here's the console. Here, look. Different but familiar, just like *Colibrí*. Let your muscles remember. Don't use your brain.

Whatever you do, don't think.

The plane hums into life. Her hands grip the controls and settle. She steers the aircraft around. The wheels bump over something – someone. Ramona points the aircraft the way they came and rolls forwards, building up speed.

She has done this a hundred times before.

The aircraft lifts into the sky and the compound falls away behind them. Ramona focuses on the yoke, the blinking console. The horizon.

The device given to her by the scientist fits into the palm of her hand. When she curls her fingers about it there are shallow dimples where her fingertips rest. She presses at random until she feels a slight warmth in the device. Abruptly, the scientist's voice begins speaking, filling the cockpit with its guttural, foreign syllables.

'I can't understand you anyway,' says Ramona aloud. 'For fuck's sake.'

The recording pauses, and then a robotic voice says: 'Language detected: Español.'

'Yes,' says Ramona uncertainly.

There is a pause. She senses the machine thinking, and wants to hurl it from her, hurl the scientist out of her head, along with everything else she has seen today. The voice that continues speaking is not the scientist's own, but it is now using a language that Ramona understands. The translated speech is dehumanized, without cadence or differentiation in tone, and there are times when the structure of the sentences sounds unnatural. But she understands it. She listens for a few sentences.

I'll switch it off in a minute.

Any minute now. After this.

THE SCIENTIST

March 2392

I start this diary at a crossroads, a point of uncertainty in my life – on the brink of a journey, you might say. Oh, for fuck's sake, that sounds pretentious already. The fact is, I don't know where the next few months – or longer – may take me. And this is unusual, because I always know what I'm doing and where I'm going.

These musings are something of an experiment, then. The last time I recorded my thoughts I was in the knowledge schools. It's safe to say education and I had our differences. Here in Veerdeland we are supposed to revere it, knowledge that is, but that's done nothing to eradicate a culture of bullying as old as time. Sadly I was too smart to be ignored. That was the story then and I suppose it is the same story now, although I'm not yet sure what, at the age of forty-seven, lies ahead of me now. Back then I just wanted to get the hell away. I wanted to be somewhere where a thirst for knowledge was appreciated.

I stumbled across those self-indulgent old journals on a vacation between advanced semesters and I deleted them, all of them. Looking back, do I wish I'd saved them? Is there any point in retaining bad memories? Does it really build character, as people like to say? I'm not so sure. I can't say I miss that naive, zealous young girl. I like to think I wear the last few decades well.

I haven't even said my name – not that anyone will ever hear this but me. I'm not used to keeping a personal account. The records I keep are notations, observations, scientific discourse, theories, and occasionally breakthroughs. So here we go: my name is Davida Akycha Kvest, and I'm a senior microbiologist and virologist for the Jeysson Group. Well, don't be modest about it, Davida, tell the truth – that's what you're here to do. I run the department of microbiology and virology. We have the best team in Veerdeland. I'd go so far as to say the best in the Boreal States. And me – I'm at the top of my game. Which, I suppose, is why I'm in the position I'm in now.

I was approached at a convention in Nuuk and until that moment I hadn't thought about going anywhere. I'm happy at Jeysson. I love my work, it's challenging and rewarding – a rare enough combination. Why would I move? But within this one conversation, the prospect of *going somewhere* moved from an undreamt-of notion to a genuine possibility, and I realized I still had – I still have – an itching. In my sphere there's always more to interrogate, not to mention all we have to recover from before the Blackout. A virus is the smartest thing in the universe, smarter than us by far, even when it is engineered by *homo sapiens*. A digression: I can't pretend that I – like so many others – haven't spent idle hours wondering who exactly was responsible for releasing the Blackout virus. Was it a nation, a splinter group, a religious zealot, an Earth child? Who would have had the resources to engineer death on such a colossal scale? Who wanted us back in the dark ages? And was that always the intended outcome, or did it go wrong? More importantly, perhaps, who would have had the balls?

We can ask these questions – and I have, and the theories are multiple and fascinating. But in the end it's history.

Anyway, I'm digressing. The point about a virus is, you learn to respect its prowess. You even come to admire it for its resilience. And you always remember that when placed against it, you are insignificant.

The man who approached me in Nuuk was small and one of the palest people I've ever seen, and he looked nervous.

He said, 'We have a proposition for you.'

Classic, really. There was nothing to identify who 'we' was. Not then, and not in the interviews that followed. All I know is I'm going west, to Alaska, to work on a government-level project which goes by the name of Tamaruq. Classified, of course. It's not military – I have my ethics and I made it clear I wouldn't be involved in any kind of weaponry development, although I hope – I do believe – the Boreal States wouldn't be so foolhardy as to risk a second Blackout. Not with the world in the shape it's in – I mean, even virtual's a problematic word these days. We all know about the illegal implant ops out there – this is the problem with criminalization: sooner or later whatever it is falls into the hands of an elite, and rarely for a good purpose.

We have more worthy work to do than that.

The posting will be quite an upheaval from my life here in Qaanaaq, but I've been to the Alaskan territories a number of times before – a few conventions and summits, and once on vacation. My English is good enough. I don't suppose they'll speak any Scandi, although the mystery man hinted that Tamaruq are an international bunch.

I'll find out soon enough. Tomorrow, we transfer from the capital out west. Travelling by zeppelin, very fancy. There's a calm-wind window coming up.

I've a good idea what this is about. In all honesty, there's only one thing that would compel me to leave Jeysson, but – I don't want to count newts before they hatch.

Last week I had leaving drinks with the team. They said kind things. Claimed they'd struggle without me – not true. I'd had my qualms about leaving, especially halfway through a study, but at that moment I thought, they'll be just fine, and maybe without me clipping their wings they'll fly. I knew then I'd made the right decision.

Anyway, I told them, it's only six months. Officially, I'm on sabbatical.

March 2392

The last few hours of the flight they restricted us – me and my minder, the same ghostly man – to a windowless cabin. But I could tell we were going much further than had been implied in the brief. I wasn't anxious, but it did reinforce my suspicions – what kind of project would take such pains to conceal its whereabouts and more importantly its purpose? When the zeppelin set down there was no escaping the fact that we were in the middle of a desert. Nothing but sand as far as I could see, not even a buckled old Neon highway to give a clue to our geographical location. I said to my minder, this is old American territory, isn't it? He wouldn't confirm it but he didn't say no either.

So, somewhere south of the Alaskan circle, mid-continent, I assume. We're deep into the uninhabitable zone. It's a high-security compound, on a topographical rise in the landscape but extensively climate-reinforced. Walls and solar panels and a geodesic greenhouse – diamond, at a guess. African tech. The outbuildings and the zeppelin all use camo. Blink and you'd miss the place entirely. The majority of the facility, though, is an underground warren where they've burrowed into the hill.

I was shown my room and a private bathroom, and they brought dinner to me there. The food was cooked fresh, so the greenhouse and a good supply chain must meet their needs, despite being in the back of beyond. My induction's tomorrow. I haven't met any of my colleagues yet.

March 2392

I was right. It's redfleur.

It had to be, really. What else would need such extensive secrecy and isolation controls? If you think about it rationally – as a casual observer, I mean, not as a scientist – the idea of cultivating these viruses borders on the insane. There's no disease more dangerous in the world. But of course the precautions are suitably intensive.

They have excellent facilities. This part is a joy. The best laboratories I've ever seen, all funded by the knowledge banks. There's a bit of everything – recovered Neon tech alongside state-of-the-art innovations from the past twenty years. The team of scientists is small but they are the best in the world – people whose findings I've read and admired and actually been sick with jealousy over. Biruk Oliyad is here, for god's sake! I thought he was in Dakar. Even the lowest-level technicians are ridiculously qualified. The staff are thoroughly international – a few Alaskans, some from the Sino-Siberian Federation, Biruk representing the Solar Corp. I wanted to speak to him but he was standoffish with me, really quite arrogant. I hope my impressions are wrong: I want to get on with him. I want to work with him! I'm the only Veerdelander, but they all seem to make at least a token effort with languages and there's the translation filters when we need them.

I've seen the labs and the computing facilities but there's levels deeper down and they haven't shown me those yet. I assume the testing labs are down there.

So far they've talked around the testing – my induction process has been very regimented and the staff have obviously been briefed not to mention the details – but the chimp gen-tech centre is established knowledge in our community, and it stands to reason that a good percentage of the crop is directed here.

April 2392

I'm settling in. I found the underground life difficult at first. It's not advisable to go outside – the sandstorms can whip up out of nowhere, and despite our elevation the compound's been buried in the past. But they do a lot to alleviate the mental strain of such a strange habitat – there's a gym, a good immersive library, even a kind of garden where the technicians like to play at botany. Orchids are the latest project.

And I really think Biruk Oliyad is starting to like me. We have regular arguments, but they're jovial, more like banter. I'm curious about Biruk. The Solar Corporation has always remained mysterious. A plutocracy built out of shattered countries. They're cash rich and wading in energy but there's barely any habitable territory. We have the Knowledge Banks but our land is poor, hard to cultivate. The Antarcticans have it all, and hoard it, greedy to the heart. None of them here, of course. They've never had to suffer the spectre of redfleur.

May 2392

Today I saw my first subject. The name tag read Luisa.

I wish they didn't give them names because a name makes this area of my work that much more difficult to approach. The worst thing about handling a live subject is the eyes. Regardless of species. A snake has no voice, and no eyelids, but it feels pain like any other animal. However long you've been working on clinical trials, that part doesn't change.

Luisa was sedated and her eyes, for the most part, were glazed. There was a moment when they weren't – when they were quite conscious, blinking and moist with liquid. For the first time I'm grateful for the cumbersome hazard suit which offers some form of barrier between us and them. Otherwise—

But it's pointless to complain. I knew this area of the work was coming and I knew what it would entail, or I thought I knew, and when I think about it, about the way everything has been handled – am I surprised by the specifics?

I'll try and be clinical about it. That's my job: that's why I'm here.

The subject is a female adolescent without history of prior infection or exposure to the redfleur virus. State of health has been bolstered since time in the facility (they give them good care and nutrition before bringing them down to the lab) and the subject is currently in robust shape. We'll be injecting the original strain of redfleur first, a Type 1 which we do have a cure for, and monitoring the period between infection and first symptoms. The team have been working on a new treatment which they hope will reverse the virus before it first presents.

May 2392

I tried to be rational in my last entry but the truth is, I almost lost my shit that day, when they presented me with Luisa – even while some compartment of my mind refused to be surprised. If I'm being honest I should say that. I mean – the Nuuk Treaty. I almost walked out of here and demanded to be sent back home.

Biruk talked me round. I was in the gym, pounding the treadmill. I'd called up an immersive and I was running over the surface of an asteroid, a bleak scene, the ground black-pitted, the stars going out one by one, but that wasn't cataclysmic enough, so I switched to a landscape of molten lava, volcanic matter bubbling and exploding all around me, and then Biruk appeared, standing at the head of the treadmill. I thought he was going to tear a strip off me. But actually he just stood there, while I ran, the sweat flying off me, and after a while he asked how I was. I told him to fuck off. How did he think I was? He said he knew exactly how I felt.

He's been here for two years. He laid out the arguments and although I had an answer for every one, in the end I acquiesced. I said I'd ride out the six months, and then I'd see.

May 2392

Today I was out in the courtyard for an illicit smoke and as I went back inside I noticed again the sign over the interior entrance. It hadn't occurred to me before to think about where the name came from but seeing it there I found myself wondering.

I asked Biruk about it. Why Tamaruq? (I've learned since that the place is more commonly referred to as 'The Sorting House', or simply, 'The House'. Unsurprisingly, the people who work here have that particularly dark breed of humour most commonly shared with doctors and pathologists.) Biruk wasn't sure. I asked him if he knew anything about the history of my country and he said no. Then I told him that the name of the compound is close to another word which means wolf, in a language which was once spoken in my country.

Biruk liked this idea. He began expounding upon species characteristics (Biruk, of course, is a geneticist by trade, and in the way I have a casual interest in etymology, he has a casual interest in extinct wildlife). Wolves were exceptionally resilient creatures, he said. Beasts of extreme stamina, and capable of withstanding great pain. I said I thought they were vicious predators and Biruk corrected me, quite emphatically: wolves were sociable animals with a strong familial hierarchy, he said. They've been misunderstood, demonized. So of course we then had to have a full-on debate about wolves and the ownership of biological records and historical narrative in general. Biruk said we have a duty to the extinct, to tell their story as they no longer can. I said we have a duty to empirical science. Really, Biruk is too much of a romantic to be a geneticist. I've heard mathematicians wax lyrical over the beautiful solution, but he regards code as poetry.

But anyway, he said, no one really refers to this place by *that* name. I said I was aware of this. I didn't mention the Sorting House. To do so feels. . . it's an acknowledgement, I suppose. Which I'm not quite ready to make. I will, but not yet.

Still intrigued, I had a look into the records and after some digging I found the information I was after, which turned out to be more banal than I might have hoped. The major founding donor of this site was one Yulia Tamaruq, a Veerdeland philanthropist with substantial holdings in the knowledge banks and a passing interest in science. In particular: medicine.

For a while, every time I walked through the entrance on my way back from a smoke in the yard, I played a game with myself, trying to imagine what this Yulia might have been like. For example: a woman with an old Inuit-influenced name, genteel, interested in heritage and abstract concepts, pulling strings behind the scenes. Or a woman who wears her name like a badge, an armour, those strong syllables demanding attention whenever she takes to the podium. Or a woman who doesn't care for rhythm, has no music in her soul at all – only a head for acquisition and investment. Or a dreamer, an idealist. A palaeontologist of wolves. Which woman was it who left their mark, Yulia? Who were you to fund such an enterprise? Did you even know, or care, what you were developing? And why does it matter to me, when I'm here and you're not and for all I know you're dead in the ground? You must be dead by now. Mustn't you, Yulia, the reason I'm here?

Yulia Tamaruq. The money.

I like Biruk's idea though. It's nice to think that we could learn from those mythical, ill-fated creatures who once roamed the northerly plains of the Arctic circle, absorb something of their natures into our own.

June 2392

Eight days since Luisa was exposed to the virus. As yet the subject has shown no symptoms and remains in health. The team is excited – seven days is the previous record. I am cautiously optimistic.

June 2392

I lost Luisa.

It happened very fast.

She held out for a record ten days, but after the symptoms showed it was a matter of hours. During that time we pumped her with a number of treatments for Type 2 which are in very early-stage development, one after the other – she showed no response to anything. Then we gave her the Type 1 cure, but it was too late – she'd already relapsed into crisis. We have to keep them conscious for effective monitoring, but after three hours of this I insisted on an assisted exit. The lab technician offered to do it but the responsibility was mine. I administered the dosage myself and through my technician's gloves I felt the moment where her pulse stopped.

Feeling very low tonight. Drunk a lot of vodka.

Once again I'm questioning whether I'll be able to stick the job.

July 2392

I'm recording but now I'm here I find I've nothing to say.

Nothing I want to say, anyway.

I probably should say that a replacement batch has come through. Luisa was not the only casualty. Her unit now has a resident and so we begin again.

July 2392

I forgot to add – it seems that some of the others choose to spend time with the subjects before they are brought downstairs. They asked me if I wanted to do the same but I can't bring myself to do that. It feels too much like deception.

I'm not looking forward to the next few days.

November 2392

I had another interesting talk with Biruk about the history of this place. Before redfleur appeared, it was used for something else. Something that had been going on for much longer.

It started with the Blackout. The polar communities were still young back then, and far more vulnerable than they are now. Even as we evolved with the climate the fear remained – fear we'd run out of space, fear there would never be enough room – squashed up like we were against the north pole. That's where the House came in. Originally, Biruk tells me, it was used for geo-engineering. The intention was to develop the human immune system – make it tougher, hardier, more resistant. Capable of surviving in all of those plague-infested, barren places we could no longer populate.

The part I find intriguing is that there were a number of ancillary centres. One was over in Sino-Siberia. Something happened there, and they had to eradicate the site. Biruk didn't offer any detail, but – well, it seems one of the experiments got out of control. I didn't ask for more information. I can imagine the scenes.

There was another site in the South Atlantic sea city. It must have been the perfect place to conceal a renegade project like that, and the extremes of life at sea would have presented a whole other kind of challenge for the engineers (the way he talked about it I could tell Biruk had fantasized about life on the ocean). Biruk says that after the Great Storm, the House tried to make contact with the sea city. . . but to no avail. Whatever advances those pioneers might have made, the research has been lost to the waves forever.

The overarching Osiris Project – this whole geo-engineering initiative – was funded by the Osiris Knowledge Bank. Most things, when you look back far enough, lead to the knowledge banks.

I asked Biruk if any of the ancillaries were still going but he said everything north of the belt was abandoned years ago. The emergence of redfleur overtook events. It became the priority. Well, there's not much point in engineering a superhuman when there's a virus out there that can knock you dead in a week. I was secretly relieved. It's like the back-room implant ops – it feels ethically wrong, too close to weaponry for my liking.

Now our focus is entirely upon Type 2 redfleur.

January 2393

I didn't like to think about this when I started my work here and I confess to a slight anxiety even to record it in private – but these are the facts. A lot of my colleagues are dead in the outside world. I almost said 'the real world' for a moment there. Yoseph was actually reported as deceased. Others are retired, or have allegedly changed careers, or their presence has been erased in some other way. I wonder what they have said about me, to my team? I haven't asked. Some things you don't want to know.

Today I found myself thinking about Jeysson for the first time in a long time. It was a strange feeling, remembering the little jokes we used to have, teasing Saamik about changing his hair every two minutes, or just casual gossip about the latest immersives. I suppose they were the friends I never had, and yet I never identified them as such, I always said, 'my colleagues'.

I had a dream that I tried to explain to them what we do here, and as I talked, my tongue twisted around on itself – my tongue had grown as long as my arm – and the more I talked, the more it twisted, like a plait of hair, like a worm. And they sat there and stared at me and didn't say anything at all.

February 2393

We are so close to a cure. So damned close! I can hardly speak for the excitement. Biruk is making final adjustments to the treatment now. I told him today that he's an extraordinary scientist and it's a privilege to work with him. He said he felt the same. A neatly mutual circle of appreciation.

April 2393

Today is a historic day.

Today, a subject has survived.

Further trials in the next week – if all goes well we begin mass production of the treatment as soon as possible.

Today, everything we do is worthwhile.

January 2394

We've received reports of a new strain. The treatment has been out six months. We'd refined it, we'd just begun working on a vaccination.

Six goddamn months.

I don't know what to say. What is there to say?

What?

July 2399

I've been remiss with these updates. Five years remiss, by the looks of it.

I see, listening back, that this was meant to be a truthful and honest account.

The truth is, the person who stepped into that zeppelin back in ninety-two is not the same person who is speaking now.

I've left the compound twice in the past seven years. Vacation. They insist on us taking them, but next time I will refuse.

Out there, life continues, innocent and undisturbed.

I went to a resort on the north British islands. I spoke to a young waiter – she couldn't have been twenty, all fresh skin and sparkling eyes and ambition – she wanted to be a marine biologist and she'd taken this coastal job, god help her, to be close to the sea. I looked into that face and I saw the dreams I'd had and I felt a rush of – of *everything* – hope and despair and bitterness and rage and a horrible, sneering condescension that I can't explain, and instead of congratulating her on her ambition I wanted to say to her, *you do not understand the world. You have no idea what keeps you alive, and if you knew, you would never sleep again.*

You're a fucking idiot.

That's what I wanted to say.

That *is* what I said. I said it not even realizing I'd spoken aloud, until I saw the young waiter staring at me like I'd slapped her in the face.

It seems I can't be around people. Not those people, those innocents, not on the outside.

There are the staff here and there are the subjects and they, from hereon, are the focus of my life. I used to want acclaim. I dreamed about honourable mentions, prizes, an international platform, but I don't care about that any more. I don't care about anything but redfleur.

In the past seven years we've beaten it twice and twice it's evolved. We run through subjects. I used to keep track of their names but I can't remember any longer, even with the name tags, I'm blind to them. Every couple of months or so we get a new batch.

But I won't give up hope. I know more now than I ever did before. I know more about redfleur than anyone on the planet, except Biruk Oliyad, and I don't begrudge him that particular accolade.

I won't give up.

January 2400

So here we are in twenty-four hundred. A new year, a new century.

The last night of twenty-three ninety-nine was a turbulent evening with the threat of sandstorms to come. Despite the wind speed the four of us — myself, Biruk, Sara, and Yoseph — sat in the yard in our desert robes drinking vodka and listening to music. There's no exterior lights of course — nothing to give away our location (like anyone would ever think to look here — it's ridiculous, really). We might be lost in time, for all I know. In the dark I could hear the sand moving. The wind getting up, whistling and thumping against the solar panels and the domes. Grit was making my eyes water and I kept the vodka lid screwed on tight between sips. I could imagine the storm building in the distance, the way you see them in the day sometimes — dust devils whirling across the horizon, banks of sand raised up like it's alive. Makes you realize how alone we are out here.

Except we're not alone, are we? We're never alone. The subjects are here too, locked in their wards, in the ether realm of semi-consciousness, deep below ground. They're always with me, whatever I'm doing, from taking a piss to dropping into an immersive in outer space.

A security guard came to get us — said it was too dangerous out here — but it was quarter to midnight and we insisted on waiting. I've noticed there are fewer security than there were when I first arrived, and I swear the kids get younger. Well, it's not like we need security. The funding's better spent elsewhere, and so Biruk told them. Anyway, I couldn't bear to go back inside. Even though there was no light, only the touch of Sara's hand, next to mine, the glass of the bottle against my palm.

As everyone was in a relaxed mood I took the opportunity to quiz Biruk about the Corporation's space programme. Is it true they're planning to go off-world? Biruk humoured me for a while, yes of course, he says, the Corporation currently occupy one of the most uninhabitable places on Earth, why wouldn't they want to decamp to an even more hostile location? But when I pressed him he wouldn't be drawn, and when I think back on the conversation I can't say for sure what might or might not be true of it.

None of us feel much of a tie to our homes any more, but in some ways, Biruk is African through and through. I swear the Corporation encourage all those old tales of witchcraft and alchemy; it's a self-perpetuating smokescreen.

When Yoseph's antique watch beeped we gave a sort of half-hearted cheer and Biruk said, 'To the downfall of redfleur,' and we all repeated it together, and then we went back in.

Happy fucking twenty-four hundred.

July 2405

Last night I got drawn into a conversation about ethics with Biruk and a newcomer, Malina. Knew I shouldn't have responded but I couldn't help myself. A new batch had just come in — that's what's triggered it. We're starting to pinpoint what we ask for now — factors like age and race and so on, see if that makes any difference. I think secretly we're all hoping for a natural immune, however implausible that may be. What I can't stand is the way Malina's acting like no one's ever made these points before, as if we haven't all battled with our own consciences a thousand-fold. There she sat, quoting Nuuk at us like it was our first day in medical school.

'You're meant to be using chimpanzees,' she says, sanctimonious as they come.

Yes, there was a time when I too believed the myth about the chimp farm, but I know better now. All that was lost in the Blackout. What remains is a useful cover story. Now, every time there's a new advance, medical science thanks the lab chimps, and no one complains. They were extinct already, so why should anyone care about their survival now?

In addition to the blanket ethics, Malina also has issues with where we get the subjects.

I let Biruk explain things to her, and as he sat there, speaking very calmly, his words very measured, the way he always does, I heard him delivering the exact same speech to me all those years ago.

The fact is, southerners aren't censused. And yes, of course we have people north of the belt who fall out of the system. Just because we're the most advanced nation on the globe doesn't mean there aren't holes in society. Five years ago there were movements petitioning to use criminals – it might be a speedier solution, people said. But that would directly contravene the Nuuk Treaty, wouldn't it, Malina? And once you're a Boreal citizen, there's always a way of tracking you, always. Southerners, on the other hand. . .

Southerners are untraceable.

The first case of redfleur was documented twenty-three years ago. That's most of Malina's life (she's a prodigy, if you didn't guess, and an insufferable one at that). Year on year, outbreak after outbreak. Strain after strain. Every time we think we've beaten it, another version evolves. Maybe we get six months' grace. Sometimes it's a couple of years. But there's one thing you can promise about redfleur: it always comes back.

For every person who dies here, thousands have been saved. I know the moral arguments. I know the value of one life should be incalculable. Maybe somewhere in the universe there's a perfect world where that's true but, Malina, this is not one of them.

April 2408

Biruk, Biruk, my old friend.

What have you done?

What were you thinking?

I can hardly bear to record this. But he deserves the truth.

On the twenty-first of April Biruk Oliyad injected himself with an enhanced superstrain of Type 6 redfleur. He did it in the lab, under sterile conditions – exemplary to the end. He sealed himself in there and insisted that we observe him.

Even when we'd broken in he refused the morphine. His eyes

were wild and the vessels had already burst. I could see the pain he was suffering and I knew – with all the expertise of the last sixteen years at my disposal, I knew exactly what was happening to his body. His neural pathways. God help him, his nerve endings.

I lost my control then. I took hold of his shoulders and I shook him like a misbehaving child.

'What the fuck have you done, Biruk?'

I didn't know it at the time but I was screaming. They said afterwards it was frightening. *I* was frightening. But this was my friend, my ally, my counsellor. Yoseph was holding me back, or I might have ended it there and then. I would have snapped Biruk's neck. It would have been kinder.

Biruk grabbed my arm. I could feel the strength of his grip through the suit, that last surge of adrenaline – and he looked into my eyes with what was left of his. I thought of Luisa. I couldn't help it, I thought of her, that young girl. My first subject. A teenager. Maybe he was thinking of his first. He spoke so only I could hear.

'Davida, I couldn't live with myself any longer.'

We had to strap him down to administer the drugs. Malina said he'd gone crazy and we should accede to his wish, but I couldn't let him die like that. Not Biruk. Not my colleague, my friend.

I am not that much of a monster.

June 2408

We burned Biruk like we burned the rest of them. His ashes were driven out to the desert and buried there. I've spent so much time wondering what pushed him, what little thing sent him over the line. It's always a little thing. Some word or gesture or twist of expression or formation of clouds or message in the night or dream or just a name that has a significance entirely unimaginable to anyone else. That is known only to the individual psyche. What was Biruk's monster? I have no answer and I think I may spend the rest of my life asking this question.

What is my monster?

The ability to forget.

Names, they all have names. So many names. I try but I can't remember any of them. To me, every one is a Luisa, and that's what I call them, as I administer our experimental cocktails into their veins and I smile and say, 'It will be all right, Luisa. It will be all right. It will be.'

Sometimes I feel like they gave this place the wrong name. They should have called it after qalupalik, the sea creature who stole away children. Sometimes I feel like I am qalupalik. I am the terrible thing in the story, the monster who has a name but nothing else, no other characteristics worth noting, who is the purest distillation of evil. Sometimes I think about a different life. What it might be if I had made other choices. If I had stayed with my team. Ignored the call of Tamaruq. I try to imagine a woman without this great burden. I have an image, an idea, but it's shapeless. There are no details, or the details seem blandly generic, an idea of an idea, an idealist's idea of what a life should be. Would I have partnered? Considered adoption? These are only details – facts – in and of themselves they tell me nothing about this other, fictional, Davida. The moment I release her she slips away easily. No doubt glad not to be me.

In my country, there is a famous mountain where people once went to end their lives when they felt themselves of no more use to family or society. This was not viewed as a crime, but as an act of honour.

I wonder if Biruk felt honour, or only shame.

I've decided to stop recording.

March 2412

After seven days of tornados it's safe to go outside. Smoked a cigarette in the yard, watched the sunset – red and cloudless, almost peaceful. I saw a sandstorm swirling on the horizon but it was moving south, away from here.

I was glad of a few moments alone. The latest reports have frightened me, more than I like to admit, enough to break my hiatus from here. There's been a spate of outbreaks across the Boreal States, and worse, it's infiltrating south. Thousands in the Patagonian capital, one of the Indian enclaves entirely wiped out. We're told to keep our spirits up, the work is valued, but when I ask for more funding, there is none. Are the banks losing confidence in the project? Are we hearing the full truth, or do they pacify us, like children? Has it reached an epidemic, a pandemic? Only Antarctica and the Solar Corporation remain unaffected since inception; up in the Arctic Circle our borders are too porous, the virus slips through like a devil in the night.

Remote as we are it's easy to feel that we're indestructible, that nothing can touch us here. The deliveries keep coming. We continue the work. We occupy our minds. Some of us pray, some of us drink. But on days like this it's all too easy to imagine an alternate scenario: one in which we send our weekly report, and nothing comes back. We wait. We tell ourselves some other crisis has delayed the response – an airship crash, an assassination, the Africans squeezing the energy line, it could be anything – we tell ourselves we'll hear back soon. Days slip by. Weeks. We wait. Eventually we can't ignore it any longer, the absence of contact, the diminishing supplies, and we have to admit to ourselves what none of us wish to admit. No one's coming.

There's one explanation. The redfleur took them, every one; there's no one *left* to come.

Just us, and the desert sky.

And them.

There would be a certain irony to that.

June 2417

It's the early hours of the morning, hot as hell despite the aircon, and I can't sleep. What's the date – I should say the date. Second of June, twenty-four seventeen, there you go. My name is Davida Akycha Kvest and I'm a redfleur virologist. I'm the only one left, actually, except Yoseph, but Yoseph's given up, I can see it in his face. He should leave but he doesn't know where to go. What would he do? He's as institutionalized as I am. They keep promising me replacements. I'll believe that when I see it.

I've got into a bad habit – sleep for a few hours and then wake and lie here, sweating and turning in my bunk. Thoughts revolving round my head like a bloody carousel. Nights when I can't help thinking about how my life might have been different, if it weren't for this one fucking bug that we just can't beat.

I might sleep better for a start.

I was meant to retire a year ago. Strange to reflect on old notions: always thought I'd get a place on the coast back home. Lead a quiet life, fishing, music, good food, good wine. Watching the Arctic shipping fleet go by. I do believe I've earned that. But I'm still here. Holed up in a laboratory in the middle of the desert, hundreds of kilometres from civilization.

Somehow I can't leave. It's as though the rest of the world operates on a different time stream, one that I slipped out of years ago, and even if I wanted to, there is no way of rejoining. The dislocation is too great. Life is mutable, yes, and selves change, but there are some lines that cannot be undrawn.

Here, there is us, and there is the redfleur. Me, and my nemesis, to give it a fictional terminology. The redfleur is as tied to me as if we're stitched together. Every day we rise to do battle at dawn. We lose, we win, we lose. We fight a greater war.

Often on these nights when I can't sleep I make a cup of tea and go and sit outside the compound. On a clear night the stars reveal a strange, shadowy, denuded landscape. On other nights it's black as a void. I'd say it feels like world's end, except at the end of the world there should be silence. The desert is never silent. You can hear things. You can hear the sand moving. You can hear the wind. You can always hear the wind, even if it's a way away, howling gently, a hint of wolfish voices tucked in its call, like a promise.

THE PILOT

The door to the cockpit opens. Ramona's mother climbs through and settles herself in the co-pilot seat. She has changed out of her own clothes into some of Ramona's spares, which are too big for her, but at least they're clean. They sit in silence. Below, the shadow of the aeroplane skims over the dunes, as wave after wave of desert passes by. Ramona keeps the plane steady and an eye to the skies to east and west.

'How far is it to the south?' asks Inés.

'I'm not sure. There are maps here, but there's nothing to indicate where that place was. We just have to keep heading south.'

'So what shall I tell them back there? Days, do you think?'

'Yes. Days. Maybe weeks. We'll have to stop at Panama for supplies. Maybe in the highlands too.'

'I'll tell them,' says Inés, but she doesn't move. 'They were scared,' she says. 'And angry.'

'I get it.'

'It's every person's right to take revenge.'

'I know that.'

'Then why are you angry? I don't know what you saw inside that place. Not yet. But I can guess.'

311

'I don't want to talk about it, Ma.'

'You think it's worse for a daughter to see her mother kill someone than for a mother to watch her daughter do the same?'

'I don't know.' She fights back the tears. 'I don't know.'

She does not know how to explain that if the deaths lie with her, she can reconcile herself, or at least she can see to a future where she can reconcile herself. That the prisoners took their revenge should not be any different; why should they not, even the youngest? But she can't erase the scene in the yard from her mind, any more than she can shake the image of the experiments behind the glass. It's her fault, for choosing to go there. For choosing to ignore that this was a possible outcome.

She changes the subject.

'Why didn't you tell me about the jinn?'

'What is the point in telling you?'

'I would have come home. I would have looked after you.'

Her mother puffs air.

'You know I would have, Ma. But you didn't tell me. I had to find out from Carla instead.'

'So, every little thing I should write to you now? If I step on a snake, and my ankle swells up, shall I write? If a mosquito bites me, shall I write? If I fall and scrape my hands, shall I write?'

'Don't be ridiculous. This is different. This is the *jinn*. What if you hadn't made it through the conversion? What if you got a fever, the next day? I might never have got to see you again. Don't you understand how upsetting that is?'

'You say that like it's a bad thing.'

'Ma!'

Inés gazes out of the window, her eyes following the ripple of the dunes below.

'I don't like goodbyes.'

They collapse back into silence. Ramona wants to say something more, but her tongue feels clumsy in her mouth; everything she says will be wrong.

'The skin patches,' she says at last. 'You promised.'

'When we're south.' Inés replies without looking at her.

'All right.'

She reaches over and squeezes her mother's hand.

'I know you don't like goodbyes. But it would have broken my heart.'

'You have a strong heart, my lucky one. You would have survived. You will survive, when the day comes.' Inés points to the west, where a bank of mustard clouds is building between the desert and the sky. 'What is that?'

'It's a sandstorm, Ma. We'll need to land.'

Ramona's eyes itch with tiredness. Her heart is sore and she wants nothing more than to curl up in the hold of the plane and sleep for days. But they aren't safe yet.

'I can't promise you we'll make it home,' she says. 'I can't promise them.'

'All your life I tell you this, my girl. I would have liked to protect you from it.' Inés sighs. 'But not everything is possible.'

PART SEVEN
BOKOLU

OSIRIS

A motor boat breaks from the escalating chaos of the city, streaking across the long stretch of open water towards the waiting ship. Confusion breaks out on deck. Medics rush to the rail, shouting, cables whir as platforms are lowered to the surface. Karis is shunted to one side. He isn't prepared for what comes back – the bodies, lolling on stretchers, moaning, the mess of blood, the places where limbs should be and are not. The medics converge. He hears snatches of conversation. A super-ship has sunk. It takes a moment to register. The Boreals have sunk one of their fucking super-ships. And something else. A shark. There was a shark. Past the medics, glimpses of eyes vacant with shock, of shredded, ribboned flesh. Impossible to unsee. The medics abandon one of their cases. In the minutes Karis has been standing here, she's died.

'Can we clear some space here!' a medic yells. Karis feels a hand on his shoulder, another officer.

'Go below deck, Io. Nothing you can do here.'

In his windowless cabin, the bombardment continues. Every moment he thinks himself on the verge of sleep another distant rumble drags him back to alertness and a humid, breathless fear. He wakes uncertain how long he has slept, or if he has slept at all. His body in the narrow

317

confines of the bunk feels mummified, like he's lain here for centuries, slowly calcifying but conscious throughout. It is a gargantuan act of will to raise his knees, swing his legs over the edge of the bunk, and switch on the light. He waits, listening for the sound of detonations. He can't hear anything of that now. Only the creak and hum of the ship, sounds that cause him a different kind of alarm, persistent and niggling. Everyone knows these ships aren't ready for ocean faring. But here they are. Here he is.

He goes to the communal wash area to splash water on his face. The beard on his chin is at a week's growth now. It feels unnatural to him, but there seems no point in shaving. Who cares what he looks like here? He makes his way to the officer's mess, then changes his mind and goes up on deck, unable to ignore the heavy silence any longer.

When they arrived last night there was little to see, except for the sodium mass of the city rising out of the ocean, imposing but mysterious, like a figure beneath a veil in the mist, whose intent is yet to be revealed. The ship carrying Karis is a standard defence vessel and it stayed clear of the action, retaining camouflage, until the wounded came in. It was a super-ship that first broke through the metres-high chain fence encircling the city and proceeded to attack the Boreal fleet waiting on the other side.

Today the sky is overcast and the sea looks hostile, turbulent, to Karis's untrained eye. It makes him nervous. Two of the surviving Antarctican super-ships are visible, as are the outlines of several Boreal submarines moored by the nearest Osirian towers, which means both sides have reversed camouflage, at least for now, and some form of ceasefire has been agreed. Or some of the fleet have reversed camouflage, but not all, and this is just another element in the game. Karis does not doubt that at this moment other wars are under way, invisible wars of wavelengths and espionage, as each fleet attempts to ascertain what and who the other is carrying. Ostensibly, both sides are adhering to the Nuuk Treaty. Karis doesn't like to think about what might happen if that changes.

Parts of the city continue to smoulder. The sky is grey and the smoke is grey and the city is grey and the churning sea is grey. It looks like a place that has long been forsaken, a place from which there is no coming back. A place like Ruination Ridge, he thinks, picturing the Bokolu's dripping pincers, and then he remembers those maimed bodies on deck. Not for the first time, Karis wonders what the hell Maxil Qyn was thinking when she issued the command to retaliate.

Then Karis thinks about the Boreals, about those sleek, deadly submarines which arrived in stealth and were meant to be years from completion. He imagines a torpedo streaking through the water from below. He imagines being blown up, the ship coming apart, his physical body obliterated in the explosion, or worse, scattered in unidentifiable parts. It seems a terrible thing, to come apart. All of a sudden the deck feels less solid, and Karis hopes the other wars, the invisible wars, *are* being fought. There is still blood on the deck, dark and congealed.

A couple of defence officers whose names Karis has been told but cannot recall wander up to join him at the rail. They nod a good morning. Both have the faces of the exhausted, eyes bloodshot, mouths pinched and dry. Karis assumes his own appearance is equally unsavoury.

The first officer gestures in the direction of Osiris.

'Apparently the place is in uproar. One of their leaders got shot last night.'

'Who was that?' Karis asks, although the name will be meaningless to him, and to these two, seeing as they know nothing of the internal politics of the city.

'Not a name, a pseudonym. Was it the Silverfish? Something like that.'

'I thought it was Rechnov,' says the other.

'No, that's the east side. They have ruling families, apparently. It all sounds a bit pre-Neon.'

'Whatever, the name's irrelevant. The fact is she's probably going to die. And they're not happy. The Osirians.'

The officer doesn't add what Karis assumes all three of them are thinking: that the entire situation is one massive fuck-up.

'How many did we lose?' he asks.

'Still waiting on the report.'

'People are going to hate us when we go home,' says the first officer. Her tone is matter-of-fact.

'Not if we win,' says the other, who has a nice, muscular physique, a physique Karis appreciates more than usual against the apocalyptic backdrop facing them. 'Then it will be a liberation.'

'And if we don't?' he asks.

Neither of the officers reply. If they don't win, it will be an even greater fuck-up. And they will have shown the Boreals their hand. Karis thinks of his family back home. Bia. His niece Grace. He would like to ask the other officers whether they share his fears, but to express such doubts would be unwise. His position here is tenuous enough as it is.

'Look over there.'

The first officer points. She is looking away from the city, towards the open ocean. Karis squints, unclear as to what she is indicating. Then he sees it, still some distance away on the horizon, but drawing steadily nearer. A ship, making no attempt to disguise itself. The reverse in fact, it is approaching with solar sails fully extended, daylight refracting and glancing off the skin, so that the ship at times glows entirely white. As it draws closer, Karis can make out the colours of the Pan-African Solar Corporation and the International Nuuk Alliance.

'Mum's come to give us a scolding,' remarks the first officer. The second laughs.

'Good luck to her.'

She is on the ocean bed. She is lying on the ocean bed and all around her are the bones of the ships who came. A long time ago. The ships who sank. A ship weighs upon on her chest. There are faces. With skin. Drifting down. She is in a room. She is in a room and there are faces.

Slipping in and out of focus, down through the water. Faces should come with attachments, with tags and memories, but there are none. However hard she looks, there is nothing.

Pain in her chest, dull and deep. The faces loom and recede. It is important, she realizes, that they should not leave altogether. And a feeling of panic suffuses the ocean bed and the bones and the room and wherever the hell she is.

She locks on to the first face.

I know you.

Something else. She waits, bewildered.

Voices.

I can't stay any longer, I've got to be there in half an hour—
You go, we'll stay—
You'll find me – if anything changes—
A slam of recognition.

I know you.

She dredges her consciousness.

'Dien,' she croaks. 'Wait.'

The emergency summit is called in the Osirian Council Chambers. Representatives are ferried into the city under a Solar Corporation guard, and as the Antarctican delegation passes through the city's idiosyncratic waterways, all of them deserted, Karis senses they are being watched.

Their destination, the Eye Tower, is situated in the centre of the city and has so far escaped harm. Karis is taken aback by the undeniable beauty of its interior, the tall fir trees and the twin columns of the aquarium that wrap around the lifts that rise through the building's core. Osirian staff direct them through the building. No one will meet Karis's eye, though when he looks away he senses the Osirians watching him, covertly, with fascination, as though trying to decide how he has been put together and why. After scrutinizing the city's outputs for so many years, it's hard not to stare back. Have these people been complicit in Osiris's disappearance, or is this clashing of cultures as much a shock to them as it is to Karis?

The Chambers are in the shape of an amphitheatre. Everyone has an assigned place. Overseeing, and leading on the negotiations, is a team of ambassadors from the Pan-African Solar Corporation. Representing the city of Osiris are two individuals: a man, sharply dressed but with the slack, greyish face of someone who has not slept for weeks, and a shabbily clad woman in a headscarf.

Karis taps the shoulder of the woman seated in front of him, an immaculately turned-out military type he knows as Evie Aariak, and speaks in patois.

'Who are the Osirians?'

She replies without turning.

'That's Linus Rechnov, a member of their so-called founding families, and the woman is known as Dien. She's from the west – the rough side of town.'

'Dien?'

'She doesn't have another name.'

Karis can't read Aariak's tone, and so he isn't sure if she disapproves of this unconventional titling or whether she simply doesn't care. He looks to the other side of the room, where the Boreal delegation are seated. He's never seen a Boreal before, and never expected to do so. He can sense the animosity from the northerners, like a toxic chemical substance leaking out of them and trickling its way across the room. One of the Boreals has suffered a head wound, a fact that gives Karis some small pleasure.

'And them?' he asks Aariak.

'The central three are the ones we need to worry about. One Alaskan, one from Veerdeland, the other from Sino-Siberia. They sent everyone. We know something about Katu Ben, the man from Alaska. He was responsible for containing the recent redfleur outbreaks. He has a reputation for ruthlessness.'

Karis considers the round, almost cherubic face of the Alaskan man.

Burly and round-shouldered, his teeth protrude slightly, raising the upper lip so that even in repose he gives the impression of a man who at any moment will break out into a display of beaming joviality. He could easily have had that corrected, thinks Karis. But he's chosen not to.

'I know, doesn't look like much. But don't be deceived,' says Aariak. 'This is a man who incinerated an entire city of his own people.'

'Is it that bad up there?'

'It's bad,' she says.

'And the other two?'

'Luciana Tan from the Sino-Siberian Federation and Marc Bernier from Veerdeland. Let's just say none of them would hesitate to shoot your firstborn.' Aariak sits back and folds her arms. Her face is set like bufferglass. 'Then again, if it was a Boreal, neither would I.'

Across the Chambers, Luciana Tan tilts her head to acknowledge something Katu Ben has said. She smiles. A cat's smile. Karis looks from face to face. The city's fate, and Karis's with it, now lies in their hands.

He is relieved when Nkem Sosanya, leader of the Solar Corporation delegation, begins the proceedings. Sosanya rises, and without any obvious gesture manages to convey that everyone else should do the same. With the room on its feet, she thanks them for their attendance. She has a beautiful head, thinks Karis incongruously, the sort of head that would have sculptors in ecstasy. The smooth shape of her skull is accentuated by the close shave of her hair, speckled in black and grey. The face is experienced, commanding, a face to which Karis would probably apply the vague descriptor of wise, and a face which gives him cause to hope.

The Corporation leader speaks in her own language, and there is a rustling as everyone inserts their receivers, some glancing mistrustfully at the African technology. The Corporation have set up a translation chamber, with a row of receptor cubes set in a semi-circle in front of the delegates. There is a second's delay and then the mechanical voice of the translation murmurs into Karis's ear, speaking Boreal English.

The foreign language, with its clipped northern enunciations, has a strange effect upon him, a distancing from the room and the people in it. He has a surge of longing to hear Swahili, his own language of the home, or patois, or any common Antarctican language.

Sosanya speaks and the translation follows.

'We are now in session. Be aware that any words you voice from this moment will be picked up by the translator and exported until the session end. Please raise your hand to indicate your understanding and agreement.'

Hands raise, some with obvious reluctance. Sosanya inclines her head. She puts forward the situation. What has happened here is a direct contravention of the Nuuk Treaty. Both parties have used illegal weapons of force, against each other, and against the Osirian people. Hundreds of innocent civilians have already died in the crossfire.

Despite her measured address, Karis has the impression that Sosanya would like nothing better than to bash together the heads of everyone in the room; that the perilous journey across the sea from the Solar Corporation has been a matter of deep inconvenience, a matter which has taken the African away from more important, pressing, never-to-be-revealed matters.

'There are a number of legal issues to address,' she continues. 'Firstly, the legal ownership of the city of Osiris. Secondly, the reason and responsibility for the city's disappearance in the last fifty years. And thirdly, whether crimes against humanity have been committed by the parties to my left and right, that is: the Boreal States of the north and the Republic of Antarctica.'

Aariak stands. 'We wish to put forward a fourth issue.' She looks pointedly at the Boreals. 'The question of why Osiris was built in the first place, and so conveniently close to Antarctican waters.'

Sosanya consults briefly with her peers. 'Intent will be considered. We have a lot to unravel over the next few days. I expect the full co-operation of everyone in this room.'

The Boreals respond with outrage. The translation babbles in Karis's ear. Voices overlap, the words fusing together, too quick to make any sense. Sosanya calls for order.

As the day goes on, Karis feels the hope prompted by Sosanya's presence gradually seeping away. Glancing around the room, he can read only anger and resentment. There is no will here for resolution. Rather, the Boreals and the Antarcticans are relishing the chance to finally come together, out from the shadows of a war long fought but never acknowledged.

It all comes back to the fucking knowledge banks, he thinks. The Corporation has energy, but the north maintains its monopoly on medicine. They guard those banks as jealously as emperors. We're self-sufficient and they can't bear that; they can't bear to be excluded from anything. Because of our independence, we have to be punished.

'Is it – ready?'

'Almost, Ms Rechnov – Silverfish—'

'Just Adelaide.'

The technician makes some final adjustments. She watches silently. The small, bluish eye of a camera is trained on her face, a microphone positioned by the pillow. If she concentrates on any one thing in the room for long, it blurs into senselessness. People materialize who she knows are not there. Others take on appearances that are not their own.

'You don't have to do this,' murmurs Mikaela Larsson at her side. Ole squeezes her hand in agreement.

'I do. It may be. . . the last useful thing. . . I do.'

Ole's grip tightens. She senses him shaking his head. *Don't say that.* With difficulty, she turns her head to the nurse. Lifts a hand to point.

'I need you to take that away.'

'That's your morphine, Adelaide—'

'I know. But I can't. . . think straight. . . with it.'

The nurse's face is flat with refusal.

'That's a Rechnov order,' says Adelaide.

When the nurse cuts off the supply she doesn't feel it at first. And then it hits her, and it's annihilating.

'We move on to the question of this city's disappearance,' Sosanya announces. 'I call upon the Osirian representation.'

Attention shifts to the two Osirians in the room, who so far have been silent, although Karis has observed them exchanging notes on a pad.

'Please confirm that you represent the two sides of your city, east and west.'

Linus Rechnov gets to his feet. Rechnov. Wasn't that the name mentioned by the officer on the ship?

'That is technically correct,' says Linus.

'But we're talking together today,' says the woman known as Dien. And Linus adds, 'The border has been removed.'

'Very well. Let's address the central issue at stake here. There has been no contact with this city for the past fifty years. What explanation do you have for this?'

Linus Rechnov speaks calmly.

'I'm afraid we have no explanation. Since the days of the Great Storm, no one has ever answered our distress call. We believed ourselves alone, the rest of the world lost. Most of us did. I have been somewhat notorious in our city for having views to the contrary, though I have never seen any evidence to confirm this belief. Until now.'

The Boreals wear open expressions of disbelief.

'It was I who encouraged the last expedition boat,' Linus continues. 'We had fallen into a trap of belief, taking our customs for granted. That is what I felt. Because all of our previous expeditions had failed, we lost hope. We decided the risks were too great; we couldn't afford to lose anyone else. But I believed it was necessary to try again, although others in my family did not. Our city, which we as Osirian citizens are so proud of, is in a state of stagnation. We've tried to preserve it – but we can no longer deny that without valuable resources, our society will collapse. It might not have happened immediately – perhaps not even within my lifetime – but the decline would have begun.'

Linus pauses, taking his time. Karis has a sense that he is walking a very fine line.

'Our call was answered, but not in the way I expected. I have to assume that the expedition boat which departed last October made it safely to land. No one has deemed it fit to inform us that this is the case.'

Nkem Sosanya confers with a colleague.

'I can confirm that the expedition boat did indeed reach land. There was one survivor. A man called Vikram Bai.'

Karis sits up. He knows that name. Fuck, he's even *seen* Vikram Bai, albeit in a holoma.

The revelation has a clear effect upon both of the Osirians. Dien sits bolt upright, her eyes wide with surprise. Her mouth opens, then she decides against whatever she was about to say. Linus has lost colour. For a moment, the Osirian politician is at a loss for words. He pulls himself together with apparent difficulty.

'And the rest?' he asks.

'Patagonian reports confirm the ship was wrecked on the coast. The other crew were lost at sea.'

The Alaskan Katu Ben gets to his feet.

'None of this goes any way to explaining fifty years of silence.'

Linus Rechnov turns to face the Boreal.

'We wouldn't mind an explanation from you, either. Why was our distress call ignored? Why did no one ever come to help, to find us?'

'We sent seventeen expeditions,' says Katu Ben. His face is the picture of charming bewilderment. 'None of them ever returned. We'd like to know why.'

Linus Rechnov wears an equally puzzled expression.

'Surely the explanation is entirely obvious? For the same reason we have never sent a successful expedition until now. They did not survive the journey.'

Nkem Sosanya gestures at the Boreal to sit down.

'Let me ask you once and for all, Linus Rechnov. Did you know about life outside of Osiris?'

The Osirian pauses for a moment, listening to the translation. Then his expression clears.

'No,' he says, without hesitation. 'But I suspected we were not alone.'

This man is a good liar, thinks Karis. And it occurs to him that the lies of Linus Rechnov may be the only thing standing between grace and destruction.

'And yourself?'

This time the question is directed at Dien, who listens, and laughs bitterly.

'You think I'd have stayed in this shitty city if I did? When I was a kid, almost every day of my life I asked the stars to send us a boat. Eventually I realized none was coming. I stopped asking. Kind of ironic that when you do show up, all you can talk about is who's going to take us over. But hey, I'm just a westerner. What do I know?'

The Boreals exchange irritated glances, clearly unhappy with the lack of resolution. Sosanya calls for attention.

'We move on to the technicalities of ownership. Records and treaties have been cross-referenced. Undisputed is the fact that the City of Osiris was built as a joint venture by the Boreal States of Alaska, Veerdeland and Sino-Siberia. Construction was begun in the year twenty-two eighty-six and not fully completed at the point of the Great Storm, leading to the subsequent division of the city into east and west.'

'It was built to spy on us!' shouts Aariak. In her rage she has reverted to her own language of the home and there is a moment's pause while the translation boxes compute. 'If their right is so legitimate, why did they come here in stealth, sneaking south in the night like thieves? Why did they meet with resistance from the rightful citizens of this city which we are endeavouring to liberate? Answer me that!'

'Silence, please! I will have silence. I will continue. As a joint venture, the city was an asset, the governance and value of which was divided between the three states. Each state had a representative on the Council of Osiris. Correct?'

The Boreals offer sullen acknowledgement.

'The city of Osiris declared independence in the year twenty-three forty-six. However, according to records this was never formally recognised by the Boreal States.'

Linus Rechnov gets wearily to his feet.

'It was agreed by the representatives on the Osiris Council at the time.'

'That agreement depends upon their authority to speak on behalf of the Boreal States,' answers Sosanya.

'Certainly independence was never ratified,' says Katu Ben, still in a tone of bemusement. Karis imagines this man stepping onto the Antarctican peninsula, with his murderer's smile and a submarine fleet at his back. He would revel in it.

'They were empowered as Councillors,' argues Linus Rechnov. 'The appointment gave them the legal right to make that decision. Their signatures validate the city's independence.'

The Solar Corporation delegates are pulling up texts of international law, their hands enshrined in the faint glow of the projection. They whisper in consultation, apparently shielded from the translation chamber. The wait stretches out. Karis fidgets.

'Unfortunately this is not the case.'

'We have been independent for over seventy years,' says Linus.

'And appear to have made some dubious decisions in that time,' says Sosanya, frowning.

Dien is standing, her hand jabbing at the air.

'You're talking about things so long ago none of us were even born. Hundreds of people died the night these people decided to stage their war inside our city. Why don't you talk about what that really is—' She glares around the Chambers. 'Like fucking murder?'

'We will come to the matter of human rights violation—'

'There is another testimony you need to hear,' says Linus. 'And I think now is the time. Adelaide Rechnov, the Silverfish. She was badly wounded the night the Antarcticans attacked.'

'Very well. Connect her.'

The wall behind the Africans flickers, resolving into an image of a young woman in a hospital bed. Her hair is very red. Her skin is very pale, almost translucent. There are tubes inserted into her nose and she is evidently having trouble breathing.

'Will you state your name, please?' says Sosanya.

The red-haired woman looks directly at the camera.

'My name is Adelaide Rechnov. Also known as. . . the Silverfish.'

'You have agreed to tell us about the night the Antarcticans arrived.'

'Yes. . .'

With difficulty, the young woman describes the night of the attack.

'There was no warning. We didn't know what was happening. My brother told me it was the Antarcticans – I didn't understand. First the Boreals, now this. What had we done to incite so much hostility?'

'I'm going to ask you the same question I asked your colleagues. Were you aware of a conspiracy to conceal the city of Osiris from the world?'

A look of bewilderment crosses the woman's face.

'No,' she says. 'When the Boreals came – I can't explain to you. . . how impossible that seemed. They might have been from another planet.'

Sosanya nods. 'Thank you for your testimony.'

'I want to say something.'

'Go on.'

Adelaide Rechnov's eyes close briefly. Karis can see the strain in her face. A membrane of moisture is forming on her skin with the effort of speaking.

'I don't know who is in that room. I don't know where you come from. But. . . hear me now: you know nothing of our way of life. We have a city, yes. But we're sea people. The sea is in our souls. We aren't like you. The places you come from – what do they mean to us, to an Osirian? Until a week ago, I didn't even believe. . . there was anything outside of. . . Osiris. All my life I've believed that. Believed a lie. You can never understand what it means to have your life turned upside-down – like that. So what gives you the right to make decisions about our fate? We have nothing to do. . . with your war.'

Magnified by the screen, those intense green eyes demand the attention of the room. Give me answers, say those eyes. Give me resolutions, give me an end. Listening, watching that face, Karis can see how this woman has commanded the hearts of both sides of the city. But however eloquently she makes her case, Adelaide and the Osirians do not stand a chance. The Boreals will never let go. It's a matter of principle; to acquiesce is weakness.

'The significance of your culture is noted, and regardless of the outcome, steps shall be taken to ensure its preservation,' says Sosanya. 'Unfortunately, we are all tied to the Nuuk Treaty. International law cannot grant independence where there is a prior claim.'

'Then grant Osiris independence now, and we can act as a mediating force,' Adelaide Rechnov argues. 'We can be a bridge. . . between north and south. That was the original. . . purpose of our city. Why not use this as an opportunity – to see it done properly?'

The two Osirians in the room are nodding their agreement. Karis can see the approval in Sosanya's face, but alongside it is caution. It's too late for pleas or promises. Perhaps the African has already come to this conclusion for herself; at any rate, she calls a recess. Adelaide Rechnov hovers for a moment, her face broadcasting passion and fury like an avenging angel in one of those old *Retribution* shows, before the link dissolves, leaving behind an empty marble wall.

Her eyes lock onto the nurse as he hooks up the morphine, the nurse's fingers, the crumple in the transparent plastic bag and the clear, precious solution within it. Her jaw is a clamp. Her lungs are drowning. Distantly she is aware that there are others in the room, doctors, surgeons, people talking in worried voices, hands adjusting medical equipment, but she can't think about anything but the pain, the impossible pain, and the infinitely slow trickle of morphine down the tube into the needle in her arm and into her blood.

'I lied,' she whispers. 'I said I wouldn't. . . any more. But I did know. About the white fly. . .'

'You did the right thing,' says Mikaela. 'Hush now. Don't tire yourself.'

'I'd like to take. . . the boat out.'

Ole nods. *Yes. Yes, we'll go. We'll go together. The three of us.*

Mikaela hushes.

They are frightened. They are trying not to show it. They can't hide it.

Delegates of the summit file from the Chambers. In the rush to talk to their own people and to find food and fresh air, Boreals and Antarcticans are pressed against one another. Karis finds himself directly in front of the cherubic-faced Katu Ben. The Boreal leans forwards slightly. Karis can smell his cologne, a sweetness to it, reminiscent of greenhouse flowers. He murmurs, softly enough that no one but Aariak and Karis can hear.

'We're going to torpedo the shit out of you.'

Karis feels Aariak stiffen, and his alarm deepens. For a moment he fears Aariak is going to punch the Boreal in the face, and Karis realizes with a slight shock that if she did he might be compelled to join her, and more, that he would relish the opportunity to bloody the Boreal's smiling countenance, but then the funnel clears and they are through the other side of the doors, and Katu Ben is with his people and they are with theirs. He glances back once and sees the two Osirians in intense discussion.

Without thinking, Karis makes a motion to return. His way is blocked by an African, who speaks stiffly in Boreal English.

'I'm sorry, we can't allow collaboration between parties.'

'You should come and see the view,' says Aariak tartly. Apparently she has taken it upon herself to take Karis under her wing.

Karis follows. Some of the delegates are peering down into the open core of the tower, or studying the aquarium columns. They pass Luciana Tan examining a cabinet labelled as Neon artefacts, apparently unable to contain her mirth. Now he thinks about it, Karis has no idea what he would have said to the two Osirians.

Aariak leads them out to one of the famous balconies. As soon as he steps outside, the wind pummels Karis with shocking force and the exit door slams shut behind him. Karis draws in gulps of fresh air.

He has to admit that the view is impressive. You can see the peaks of the towers, attired in pleasing tones of silver and green, stretching away in regimented lines like oceanic warriors. Further away, you can also see the damage inflicted by a fluke missile: rents torn into the side of a tower, the solar skin at the edges of the crater burned and blackened.

He looks down and instantly regrets doing so. He's never been good with heights.

He jerks back.

'How do they live here?'

Aariak shrugs. She's chewing on something, her jaw working furiously. Probably an energy-releasing gum. Karis wishes he had thought of that. She doesn't offer him a wad of the stimulant.

'What do you think?' she asks.

'About?'

Aariak waves an arm.

'How it's going.'

Karis hesitates, still undecided as to how honest it is in his interests to be. He decides he has nothing to lose.

'I think we're fucked. I think we should never have come here. I'm worried about the rest of the fleet. We know the ships aren't ready, we've already lost two.'

'I thought you might be. Don't worry. Qyn has a backup plan. That's what I wanted to say.'

'Backup?'

'You don't think she hasn't considered this possibility? Qyn wouldn't send us here knowing the Boreals had arrived if she didn't have a plan.'

Karis stares at her apprehensively.

'What kind of backup plan?'

She winks at him.

'Best if you don't know, Io. You're an analyst, not a defender. Leave the action to us.'

'Then what am I doing here?' he says, with sudden anger.

'We need analysts too. Keep a close eye on the Boreals. Watch their expressions. Their body language. Look, I understand. You've fallen into this. It wasn't how you expected to spend your summer. But you can be useful.' She gazes at him earnestly. She's what the Republic would call a true defender, Aariak. Reliable. Devoted. Qyn's protégée. 'You can do your duty to the Republic, Io, and you can do it well. I have faith in you.'

Her words prickle at him. He has a sudden, unpleasant memory of Shri Nayar sitting in his office while he issued the directive for her to do her civic duty.

'And what about the city?' he asks. He gestures towards the lines of towers. 'What about them?'

Aariak shrugs.

'This is war. Sacrifices are necessary. We all know that.'

She checks the time.

'Recess is almost up. I'll see you in there.'

She pulls the door open, battling for a moment against the wind, and ducks inside, leaving him alone on the balcony. Karis shivers. Once again, he forces himself to look down. He can see the streak of the waterway, very far below. The silvery wash is dotted with boats. A lot of boats.

Karis frowns. Even from this distance, there are definitely more boats than there were when they arrived. The Osirians, he thinks. They're gathering.

Again he is overwhelmed with a terrible sense of premonition. All these people in a room, weighing up benefit and cost, only the cost is in lives, his own included. It doesn't feel real. Karis wrenches open the door and hurries inside, not wanting to see the gathering boats below, or the majestic towers, orphans in what has so abruptly become a war zone.

He had never considered that open warfare might be possible within his lifetime. When he thought about life beyond Antarctica, which wasn't often, it had a hazy quality, like a scene in a popcorn visual. He remembers an immersive where all of the Boreals had metal skins, and along these skins ran pulsing wires like veins, and the Boreals did inadvisable things like attempting to communicate with aliens, Karis had quite enjoyed it actually, in the way you can enjoy something stupidly brash and meaningless. Maybe it was in that immersive or maybe it was another one where they succeeded in making contact, and of course one of the characters had sex with the alien, which resulted in the birth of some diabolical cross-species which consequently evolved into a monster who consumed the entire planet, leaving only a few survivors exiled in outer space, and it was all the fault of the silver-skinned Boreal who couldn't keep his bio-mechanical dick in his pants.

The afternoon is long and unsatisfactory for everyone and descends too quickly into the evening. By the time they leave the Chambers it is dark. The summit delegates are advised to leave the tower by one of the shuttle lines, instead of returning by waterway as they arrived. When Aariak asks why, they are told there is a protest outside. As Karis steps into the pod of the shuttle, twenty floors above the surface, he can see the glow of hundreds of boats gathered in the waterways below. The light is coming from flames. Torches, held aloft. The scene is disturbing; there's something primal about it that releases a deep-rooted inner fear. Anyone can become a barbarian. He looks away, focusing on the smooth, rounded interior of the tunnel in front of him, which quickly blurs into light as the shuttle pod whisks him from the Eye Tower.

They have been given accommodation in an opulent Osirian tower.

Karis and the other Antarctican delegates are each assigned a personal guard, something he finds more disconcerting than reassuring. Aariak invites him to join the defenders for dinner. She says they need to talk strategy.

The food is delivered by Solar Corporation officers who assure them it has been checked for contamination. Karis examines his plate: a classic Osirian dish, he is told, and overpoweringly salted. The food tastes as bad as it smells. The Antarctican delegation discuss the day with a vigour that exhausts him, patois punctuated with the occasional emphatic word of their individual languages of the home. Karis listens, having no desire to contribute, until Aariak asks, 'What were your impressions, Io?'

She looks at him, waiting, and he hears again her earnest voice on the balcony.

You can do your bit for the Republic, Io.

Karis does his best to replicate her tone.

'The Boreals are spoiling for a fight. They've as good as told us so. They don't believe the Osirian. The Africans don't believe the Osirian either but they have some sympathy for their situation.' He is surprised by how rational he sounds. Even as he speaks he can feel his words dulling the situation, reducing it to language, to something conceptual. 'They could have pushed them harder today but they didn't. Unfortunately they also consider themselves bound by the rule book. Nkem Sosanya's a stickler. She won't budge from that.'

Aariak nods approvingly. 'I agree we won't get any movement there. Which means we continue on the assumption that these talks will break down, tomorrow, perhaps the day after. In the meantime we retain our official line: we are here to liberate the city from its oppressors.'

'If we're here to liberate the Osirians, shouldn't we be speaking up for them?'

'Io, you just said it yourself. Sosanya won't be swayed by emotion. She's a cold-headed lawyer. There's no point in us wasting energy on hopeless intercessions.'

Murmurs of agreement from around the table.

'The Boreals are talking about demanding truth drugs,' says Aariak. 'We cannot let that happen. Linus Rechnov knows far more than he's letting on. It would be a debacle.'

'Can we get to him first?' asks another officer.

'We've scoped that possibility. They're all heavily guarded, just like us. But we've set up surveillance on all parties. If anything interesting happens outside these talks, we'll be the first to know.'

'Not to mention Io,' says the officer. They all look at him. Karis realizes with alarm that his role in Atrak has made him a liability.

'I can go back to the ship,' he says.

'No,' says Aariak at once. 'That will look suspicious. You need to stay where you are, with us. The important thing is we act before they can put Linus Rechnov on a drip. We need to move quickly now, before the Boreals do.'

'Do you want these talks to fail?' asks Karis.

Aariak looks offended.

'Of course I don't. I'm just being pragmatic.' She glances around the table. 'It may well come down to a simple question: do we want to get out of here alive, or do we want to be annihilated? Because I know what I'd choose. Maybe you don't, Io.'

Karis sits back, defeated. Aariak is right: he's not a defender, he never wanted to be one. He wonders what other discussions are going on at this very moment, in other rooms like this, with other delegates. He imagines the two Osirians, sat opposite one another with a small square table between them, ingesting a brine-heavy meal of the disagreeable Osirian diet, some kind of broth, he thinks, packed out with kelp, a forlorn quality apparent even in the food they are eating. Between them on the table is a glistening silver fish, its scales still wet from the ocean, its flat round eye upturned to the ceiling. The one from the east, Linus, with his smart, crumpled attire and handsome, weary face, the one from the west, Dien, whose disgust for humanity is evident in every contemptuous twirl of the spoon. Linus talking at first, a constant stream of patter as he tries to reassure himself and Dien, to pad out the silence, to push away the memory of words which fell in the Chambers like stones through water, all of which point to one outcome, but Dien's monosyllabic responses are a clearer, more accurate reflection of the situation, and in the end Linus gives up, his resources drained, the pressure of the day too great to maintain any illusion of buoyancy. Mid-sentence, he simply stops talking. Whatever he would have said, it doesn't matter. They sit in silence. The clink of the spoons against the bowls. The damp sounds of mastication. Dien pushes away her bowl, still half-full, then pulls it back, her disgust evidently extending to herself, and finishes the dish in a series of forced, unhappy mouthfuls. Then she pushes back her chair and stands up, looking at Linus but thinking about other people entirely, people who are important to her (who are they? Where are they? Are they with the people with the torches?), people she loves, deciding whether she should go to them, walk away from this farce – she has done what she can do.

And in a white-sheeted bed the red-haired woman, the Silverfish. Flitting in and out of consciousness, her heart and her breathing erratic, like a butterfly blown about in a forest of young pines.

And in another room the Boreals are lounging on sofas, relaxed, casual, their triumph already sealed. The one with the cherubic face crams something into his mouth, Boreal treats they brought with them in crate-loads, distrustful as they are of southern cuisine, and not without reason. Katu Ben's smiling lips work around the sweet. The group is concentrating, but only in jest. They are playing some manner of game, a digital construct that flickers between them, divulging in its glare their faces, hungry and impatient, or laughing as they flick in their bets – yes, it's a game of stakes, where everything may be risked on a single gamble – a game of winners and losers. Jokes fly between them, quick-witted and pitiless. In other circumstances, the competition might be more intense, but this is a mere dissipation of energy, a distraction before the storm, the clash of clouds before *we torpedo the shit out of you*.

And in another room the Africans, delegation of the Solar Corporation, with their scripts of law. Going over the day, feverish, working like bees, considering solutions. There must be solutions. He has an idea of Nkem Sosanya with a set of scales before her, that beautiful head tipped to one side, considering, infinite and wise like a mythical goddess, but the image resists him; it will not resolve, and instead he sees her sat on the toilet, hunched over, her face strained with the movement of her bowels after the unfortunate consumption of a plate of Osirian seafood.

The Antarcticans cradle glasses of another Osirian delicacy: coral tea. They are talking intently. The layout of the city, its strengths and stress points, the whereabouts of the Boreals, the likelihood of further, camouflaged submarines or submarines that have not yet surfaced, the movements of Antarctican underwater drones which even now are sweeping the city and its surrounding waters, penetrating the kelp forests and the darker depths of the ocean where the Atum Shelf falls away, searching, searching, searching.

Karis rises and excuses himself. He meets with no resistance. In a moment of paranoia he wonders if Aariak has decided his usefulness has expired, but then he remembers what she said: it would look more suspicious were he to disappear. The idea of disappearing depresses him.

Back in his room he paces up and down, running his fingertips along the strangely curving walls, marvelling at the architecture which has withstood the hyperstorms of the South Atlantic Ocean. The Boreals built this place, but it is beautiful. A conundrum. He examines everything in the room as though it might yield clues, to what he doesn't know, or even answers, to questions he can't bear to ask. He doesn't think he will sleep but when he stretches out on the bed, burying his face in the soft covers, his whole body seems to sink down and he finds he can't move and has no desire to.

When the singing starts, Ole goes to shut the window.

'Don't,' she says drowsily.

'It's too cold for you,' says Mikaela.

'I want to be. . . by the window. I want to see.'

The nurses comply. They would grant her any wish; in any case, it doesn't matter now. They sit her up in the bed. Together they watch the burning barges pass below.

'That will be me soon.'

'Will you stop being so defeatist?' A new voice, sharp and cross. Dien is here.

'Why not? It's true. Promise me you won't make a big thing of it. All that singing. All that. . . spectacle.'

'Demanding to the end, aren't you?'

'I mean it.'

She settles back with a sigh. The pain returns in vicious pangs and they increase the drug dosage again. It will take the pain away but it will take lucidity with it. These windows of consciousness are becoming rarer. She looks at Mikaela and Ole at her bedside and understands that this might be the last time she is able to communicate with them, and slow tears trickle down her cheeks. She tries to fight it but it gets harder every time. She is losing the battle. She has always been a realist. It was Vikram who was the romantic. Vikram, on the expedition boat, who made it to land.

She must be babbling, because Mikaela is placating her. Hush, hush. Save your strength. She wants to say things – *I love you. You saved me. I don't want to die, please don't let it happen* – but the morphine is doing its work. She tries to focus on those who are here. Linus, snatching an hour's sleep on the couch. Dien, alert, pacing. Ole, stroking her hand. Mikaela. But there are others now, who might be here, who cannot be here. There's the girl from the bridge, Liis. The girl who fell. There's Nils and Drake, their hair on fire, rifles in their arms. There's Jannike Ko in a seaweed dress. Her father, she thinks. Her mother. Vikram, waiting at the end of a pier, but despite everything that came after it's the first time she saw him that persists, that strange, angry young man who walked into a room full of roses one cold autumn night.

Then that image too evades her, and she's sinking, back to the seabed, the surface now an inkling of light, ephemeral and frail.

* * *

He wakes from a dream of a choir singing. He wakes muttering, or humming, words from songs he has long forgotten, songs his mother used to sing around the house, and for a few moments he lies there, thinking of her strong, forthright face, the bright eyeshadow she always wears, which used to embarrass him, and her voice as he heard it so many times on the weekends as a teenager, too lazy to get out of bed. He wonders if he will ever see her again. Or Bia, or his niece Grace. He wonders if Grace would miss him, and what Bia would say to the child about dead Uncle Karis, who told a lot of lies, some of them to Bia.

It's strange. The idea of his dying here is entirely possible, even, if the scales have tipped, probable – but he cannot consider it seriously. He cannot believe it could actually happen, that the world could continue without him in it. Perhaps, he thinks, because I have so little to leave behind. Perhaps he should make a promise.

If I live – if I live I'll—

He doesn't know.

He's humming again. He realizes the singing was not a part of his dream – or it might have been, but it is still resounding, the sound coming from outside, voices drifting up from the waterways.

Karis goes to the window-wall of his room and without turning on a light, switches the glass to clear. In the waterway below, a procession is passing. Hundreds of boats move slowly through the water. At the prow of each boat stands an Osirian woman, clad in white, hooded robes and holding aloft a torch. Others on accompanying boats hold images, or have their heads bowed in weeping. The larger boats are towing flat barges or rafts ablaze with fire. Through the flames, Karis glimpses the pale cloth of shrouds piled high upon the rafts, and he realizes that what he is witnessing is a mass funeral.

The Osirians are singing as they bear their dead through the city. Their voices rise, sometimes in unison, sometimes fractured by a lone note, projecting high or low through the throng. The singing makes Karis's hair stand on end. With each suspended note he feels as though the music is burrowing deeper into his head. Now he can hear his mother's voice, joining them, singing the funeral song of the Osirians. Why? he wants to ask her. But she just sings and smiles and sings. He wants to turn away and darken the glass, but he cannot. He watches, waiting for the boats to pass and the procession to end. But the boats keep coming.

PART EIGHT
NIRVANA

PATAGONIA

Mig wakes in a fit of coughing. His throat is raw and pulpy, like someone's mashed it with a fork, and when he opens his eyes they sting as if he's been rubbing lemon juice into the rims. He blinks. The sky shifts overhead, thick with congealing cloud. Branches of a tree, waving. Sky. Trees. He's outside. He's – where the fuck is he? He can't remember anything. His brain has turned to soup, dislocated images floating around in it, rising to the surface and sinking back before he can grab at them. He closes his sore eyes and tries to swallow back the coughing. The ground beneath him is earth.

The camp.

It's coming back. The Alaskan, on the cabin floor, her throat exposed beneath the rope – Vikram's face tight with rage at what Mig had done, had tried to do – camp members, scattering into the forest, screaming. Mig running, someone shouting his name, the sudden bulk of a Tarkie in front of him – and then the gas, and in the gas everything got mixed up again – the Alaskan, the gun against her head – the Alaskan, who he came so close to killing – the Alaskan—

'Mig. You're awake.'

He freezes. The voice is the Alaskan's. Very low, but unmistakably hers, coming from somewhere above his head.

345

'Don't move. Just tell me if you are awake.'

'I'm awake,' he whispers.

The light between the treetops is so horribly bright, even through the backs of his eyelids. The voice continues, like an ant crawling along his forehead. Or is there an ant? Yes, it's an actual ant.

'This is how things stand, Mig. I can, if I choose to, get us out of here with our bones and our fingernails intact. No, don't open your eyes – not yet. Don't let me know that you can hear me. Don't move. That's the first road you can take. I get us out and you stay with me, Mig. You help me. Then again, I can also get myself out of here alone and leave you to the mercy of the Antarcticans. You know a lot, Mig. More than anyone else here, perhaps. You know about our Osirian friend. I suggest the former. What's it to be?'

He squints his eyes half open, and takes a quick scan of the periphery of his vision. Sees people, close by. Sitting and standing. Sees guards, armed and foreign. Sees the tall heads of trees that border the clearing. Sees a tail of smoke. Sees the wheel of a chair, a pair of shoes, the toes angled towards one another. He stays where he is, curled up. He doesn't look at her face.

'I'll help you,' he mutters.

'Good. Then I will help you.'

He sees the chair turn and wheel one-handed through the mass of bodies, the chair pushing aside inert forms, the arm of the Alaskan reaching down to move a limb out of her way, ignoring the calls of the Tarkie guards to desist. At last one of them comes over to help clear a path, evidently realizing what Mig could have told them for a handful of peso: the Alaskan will not be deterred. Mig realizes that not all of the prisoners (for that is clearly what they are, him, the Alaskan, all of them) have regained consciousness. Typical of the Alaskan to recover first. Her lungs are probably immune to that poisonous shit.

Still feigning unconsciousness, Mig does a quick head count. Perhaps half of the camp are here, corralled together and ring-fenced by armed Tarkie guards. The Tarkies wear fatigues that blend in with the forest.

At times the cloth seems to ripple, making them difficult to see and giving Mig an unpleasant, dizzy sensation. Some of the bastards are taking advantage of the camp's stockpiles of food, enjoying a nice meal on the back of their attack. Mig imagines pissing on the food. He'd like to watch their faces contort as the ammonia hits their tongues.

There is no sign of the strange flying machines that gassed them in the middle of the night, but towards the perimeter of the clearing Mig notes the hump of bodies, covered over, but undeniably human-shaped. The sight turns him cold. Some of the camp members might have escaped. Some of them won't ever be leaving this place. After seeing those bodies he doesn't want to look at the rest of the prisoners, doesn't want to work out who's missing. It's like Cataveiro all over again.

A familiar sound, a door creaking open, alerts Mig. Slowly, furtively, he directs his attention to the cabin where Vikram used to sleep. A woman stumbles out. Her face is scrunched and tear-stained. Mig recognizes her at once. It's the doctor from Titicaca. It was Mig's job to bring her here when she first came looking for them. He brought most of them here, blindfolded and desperate, and after a time the desperation receded from their eyes and was replaced with something else. Something like acceptance. But now that, too, has been extinguished from the doctor's face. Mig can't tell if she has been hurt. In the doorway is a Tarkie in fatigues and boots with an angular, uncompromising face. The kind of face worn by guerrilla warriors during an impromptu raid of Cataveiro. A face that sees a prize and blinds itself to any distractions on the path to acquire it, including pain and death. It seems to Mig that there must be unscrupulous bastards everywhere in the world, but the southernmost continent seems to have a particularly high concentration.

The Tarkie officer's eyes follow the doctor as she is shepherded back to the group of prisoners, but are quickly diverted by the Alaskan, wheeling determinedly towards the cabin. Her presence seems to have paralysed the Tarkies. Perhaps the freak has cast a spell on them.

It is only then that Mig registers that Vikram is nowhere is sight.

What happened to the Osirian? Have the Antarcticans got him? Are they torturing him? Or did he get out before the gas? And if he did, what does that mean for Mig, stuck here with the woman he tried to kill?

He watches as the Alaskan wheels herself inside the cabin, dismissing an offer of assistance with one scornful hand. Her other wrist dangles uselessly. The flesh is bruised and unnaturally swollen. Mig's doing. He should feel good about the damage he has inflicted but he only feels sick. He's let down Vikram, again, not that it should matter or he should care.

With a lurch of dread, Mig realizes that his fate now rests with the nirvana. He doesn't doubt she can get them out, although – uneasily, he breathes in the odour of anxious, perspiring bodies – these people won't last five minutes under interrogation. They are idealists, not guerrillas, or even hardened street rats like Mig's old crew. One of them is bound to snitch to the Tarkies. All they have to say is that Mig knew Vikram well, he was close to the Osirian – and then Mig will be screwed.

It starts to rain. The prisoners who remained unconscious until now begin to revive, coughing and groaning, their red-rimmed eyes flickering open with the same disorientation Mig experienced earlier. They huddle together. He can hear the doctor relaying in broken murmurs the story of whatever happened inside the cabin to a group of other prisoners, until one of the Tarkie guards comes over and tells her in Portuguese to keep her mouth shut. Mig is suddenly certain that Vikram has escaped. Why else would the Tarkies still be here? They don't give a shit about Patagonians. They're only interested in the Osirian.

The thought doesn't bring him any comfort. He lies on one side, feeling the rain sinking into his clothes, wetting his feet in their sandals. At least it's some relief for his eyes. He has no desire to speak to any of the other camp members. Whatever it was that they made here, it's been crushed.

The ground beneath the prisoners is growing muddy. How long has the Alaskan been in there now? What if she can't protect him? And why would she, after what happened last night?

Mig feels a warm flood of shame when he thinks about those brief few moments. Last night it all seemed so clear. What he had to do. Like a mission. A destiny. And this morning, he's woken up to a different world, with different rules, and he doesn't know how to play the game.

Mig frowns. There's someone else who should be here, and isn't. What happened to that bitch Tarkie who betrayed them? He can't see the one she was travelling with, either. He knew they were trouble from the start. And he tried to warn Vikram, but Vikram wouldn't listen. . .

The door to the cabin opens. The prisoners tense nervously. Mig waits for the Alaskan to emerge, but she doesn't. Instead, a Tarkie guard is stepping through the prisoners, her eyes roving, moving from prisoner to prisoner until they alight upon Mig. Her hand reaches down towards his shoulder.

'Get off me!' Mig snaps.

The Tarkie straightens. She jerks her head towards the cabin. Her eyes are cold, indifferent. Mig thinks again: they don't give a shit about us, and fear envelops him. He gets to his feet before she can try and yank him up again.

Inside the cabin are the Alaskan, the Tarkie officer who seems to be in charge, and a second Tarkie officer, presumably subordinate to the first.

'This is the boy?' says the first officer, speaking in Portuguese. He is sitting at the table where Vikram used to sit. Vikram's map is still there, spread out across the tabletop, the paper marked with little dots which show the places the camp members came from. The dots reach as far north as Titicaca.

'This is him,' replies the Alaskan. Mig glares at her. Now she's turned him in?

'Sit down, Mig, I'm trying to help you,' she says. Mig detects a hint of impatience, quickly smoothed over. Resentfully, he sits. A quick look about the room tells him the map is not the only thing Vikram left behind. He was in a hurry.

'Tell the Antarctican what you know,' says the Alaskan. He gapes at her. Is she insane?

'Tell him how you met the Osirian, and how long you've been here, and how the Osirian got away.'

Mig checks again but the Alaskan isn't joking. She wants him to do this. Her black nirvana eyes focus on him and Mig reminds himself: the Alaskan is far from stupid. She must have her reasons. He hopes to hell she's got both their interests at stake.

He tells the tale as briefly as he can. The Tarkie asks a few questions, but for the most part allows him to continue uninterrupted. The other one is listening closely. At the end of it, the Tarkie in charge says,

'Where is he now?'

'How should I know? He was meant to meet the pirate.'

'This is El Tiburón?'

Mig nods. The two Tarkies say something in their own language and Mig looks at the Alaskan, trying to work out what's going on. The Alaskan appears unflustered. Mig gives up.

'And where was the meet point?'

Mig names the coordinates where they met El Tiburón.

'Your stories corroborate,' says the Tarkie officer. 'But I'm afraid we can't let the boy go.'

'The boy was part of the deal,' says the Alaskan sharply.

'He is also the closest party to the man we are seeking.'

Mig looks frantically to the Alaskan.

'You said you'd get me out!'

She gives him a silencing look but Mig is only aware of the two Tarkies, their faces as cold as their icy country, and he thinks of the stories of what they do to pirates caught in Antarctican waters, the way they are executed, the rumours of pirates suspended half underwater with bleeding feet to attract the fish, and the sharks.

'I've done nothing wrong! This is my country and you've attacked us! You're the ones who are in the wrong! You're murderers!'

'Mig—'

'You've killed people!' shouts Mig. 'I saw the bodies!'

There is a rap at the door and someone enters the cabin behind them. The first officer looks up, frowning at the interruption. A brief exchange fires over Mig's head. The Tarkies look first disappointed, then perturbed. The two officers move behind Mig and the Alaskan to convene with the newcomer at the door.

Mig looks to the Alaskan, agitated.

'What did they say?'

'They asked if the Osirian has been found. He has not,' she replies.

The Tarkie officer comes back to the table.

'You can go,' he says.

'Something's happened?' asks the Alaskan.

The Tarkie doesn't reply. He is distracted.

'Let me guess,' says the Alaskan, folding her arms. 'The Boreals have invaded the city of Osiris.'

The Tarkie stares at her. So does Mig, utterly confused. She's talking about the war again. He never used to believe it but with the position they're in right now, he has a nasty feeling she's been right all along.

'Who told you that?' says the Tarkie sharply.

The Alaskan shrugs.

'Just a hunch. And not a difficult one – it's been on the cards for the last month. So now you'll be heading that way yourselves, I assume?'

The Tarkie and the Alaskan face each other for what seems like an infinite amount of time. Mig squirms in his seat. He can sense the balance of power switching between them like a set of juggling balls. He wants desperately to run away, but to divert attention to himself in this moment would be cataclysmic.

At last the Tarkie speaks.

'You should be careful, old woman.'

'Take us to Fuego Town,' says the Alaskan.

There is a long, strained pause before the Tarkie nods.

Mig understands that a transaction has taken place but he doesn't understand what it is or how it has been achieved or, more importantly, what it means for him. On their way out of the cabin he snatches up Vikram's little box of salt which the Osirian always kept with him. The Tarkie officer frowns, but lets him take it. Outside it's still raining. The Tarkie soldiers are already on the move, pulling on their jackets, their packs and helmets. They melt away into the woods. The prisoners mill, surprised and suspicious at their abrupt release.

The officer barks orders to the remaining Tarkies. Mig and the Alaskan watch.

'Why did you tell them about El Tiburón?' asks Mig.

'Because they'll never find him,' says the Alaskan. 'Have you ever wondered, Mig, how El Tiburón has evaded capture for so long? That pirate has enough Boreal shit on his ship to ensure several lifetimes of executions. You might as well look for a ghost.'

They are not the only ones who have secured passage to Fuego Town. Mig spies the Tarkie woman, the one who betrayed them, sitting by the cabin windows, watching the islands slip by. Motionless. He positions himself nearby, though not too near, because there are enough Tarkie soldiers around eyeballing him with intent. It's only after he's been standing there a good five minutes that the Tarkie woman notices him. She starts.

'Fuck.' Recovering, she glares at him. 'What are you doing, creeping up like that?' she says in Portuguese. Mig bristles.

'You know, we were fine until you came along. Why did you have to fuck everything up?'

Shri Nayar ignores the question.

'How old are you, thirteen, fourteen?'

'I don't know,' says Mig. Which is the truth, and shouldn't matter, though somehow the question stings and he's annoyed with himself for answering.

'You must be a couple of years older than my daughter. Kadi. She's the eldest. A good kid.'

'Why do I care about her?'

She shrugs. 'It's an observation.'

'You didn't answer my question.'

'No,' she says. He waits, but there's nothing immediately forthcoming. Then she says, 'You were in Cataveiro, weren't you?'

'I live there.'

Which used to be true.

'What's it like?'

What's it like? That's an impossible question, a stupid question. But now she's the one waiting, apparently oblivious to the possibility that he might not answer, might not want to engage in casual chat with the person who betrayed the camp. Somehow he finds himself relating the story of the juggler, The Great Cataveiro, who played with air and gravity until the day he failed to catch something, which was his last day on this earth, thanks to a fool's bargain. There's a river, he tells her, where the jugglers work today. There's bicycles, there's trams, there's a station called Sabado where an angel lived, though he doesn't tell her that the angel had a name, and the name was Pilar. And there's music – but no, he can't be bothered getting into that. He'll be here all day.

She sucks it all up eagerly.

'Do you love it, the city? It sounds like you do.'

Another senseless question.

'I never lived anywhere else.'

'I used to be a patriot,' says Shri.

Mig realizes that the conversation he thought he was having is not the same as the one Shri Nayar is having, though what that is he couldn't say.

'What happened to your friend?' he asks.

'My friend?'

'The spy. Ivra.'

'He's dead.' Her voice is abrupt. Strained. 'It happened in the raid.'

Shri doesn't say whether it was a Tark or a camp member who killed him, but Mig can smell her guilt. Poor, hopeless Ivra. Mig could have predicted it.

'Are you going to Cataveiro?' he asks. She has one hand to her throat and there's a faraway look in her eyes, a yearning look, that makes him think she's about to say yes, she wants to go to Cataveiro, like a lunatic, to a city full of burning corpses, to search the ashen streets. They have something in common, though Mig doesn't care to admit it. Perhaps she's going to ask him to be her guide.

'No,' says Shri slowly, and this time there's a finality in her tone. 'I'm going home. To Nisha, and Sasha, and Kadi.'

Twenty-four hours later the Alaskan has a room in Fuego Town and a dozen second-hand radios and a strong inkling of déjà vu and a sensation of colossal momentum all at once, a sensation of speeding through time and space, galaxies unfolding around her, of moving at such velocity that it makes her lungs wheeze and her chest tight. Or maybe that is old age. Who can tell? The radios are saturated, dripping with news. It makes the Alaskan's heart skitter. Information. It doesn't matter what form it takes, as long as there's plenty of it. The Alaskan would thrive in the Blackout or she'd thrive as a brain fused into a metal carapace. Information. The oxygen she needs.

First there are broadcasts from the Boreals, claiming the city of Osiris. Then there are broadcasts from the Antarcticans, liberating the city of Osiris. Every now and then there is the sliver of a voice from the city itself, a feeble plea for help like a mouse caught between the jaws of a snake in the moment of dislocation, before the jaws snap closed, ensuring the mouse will never squeak again. The signals from Osiris are short-lived and quickly silenced – whether by the Boreals or the Antarcticans it is impossible to know.

The Alaskan listens. The Alaskan waits. All games must be played to the end, and the end is approaching fast. It's only a matter of who triumphs.

In the days after the Antarcticans drop them off at Fuego, Mig comes and goes and explores the town and prowls the harbour, listening for news of the pirate, of Vikram, but there is none.

The Alaskan enquires as to the health of Señorita Xiomara at the Fuego hospital. Xiomara lives. She has survived the course of medication and is being monitored closely. The Alaskan is not sure whether to be pleased or disappointed, but she cannot resist a visit. She retraces her path back to the hospital, down the long corridors with their antiseptic stench.

Xiomara's appearance is vastly improved; she has the luminous, martyr-like quality of one who has suffered and overcome. Irritatingly, it suits her.

'What are you doing here, Alaskan?'

Her tone is bullish, although she does not look as distressed as the Alaskan had hoped at the sight of her old nemesis. Fuego must be short of worthwhile antagonists.

'Passing through, passing through,' says the Alaskan. 'I trust you haven't been too bored without our little appointments?'

'Not at all.' Xiomara's girlish laugh ripples from behind a lace-edged mouth-and-nose mask. 'Things are changing, Alaskan. We have new people around here now, and I like that, I really, truly do. The Boreals.' She caresses the word. 'The Antarcticans. Such interesting people. There is. . . how shall I put it, how shall I. . .? A new order in play.'

'You'll be letting go some of the old baggage, then?' the Alaskan returns. 'Like the pilot?'

Xiomara's face darkens. Oh yes, she thinks gleefully. That still hurts.

'I will find the pilot,' says Xiomara. 'Eventually, even the teensiest of lizards must crawl out of its burrow. And when she does, I'll be here.' She gifts the Alaskan with a dazzling smile, or at least, it would be dazzling if the Alaskan could see her teeth. 'But do tell. What have *you* been up to?'

In the evenings, the Alaskan and Mig engage in stilted, wary conversations.

'Have you given any more thought to your future, Mig?'

'There's a war on,' says the boy flippantly.

'Oh, there's a war on? You believe me now, do you?'

'Maybe. Seems like it.'

'Seems like it.'

'I suppose.'

'Do you miss Cataveiro?' she asks.

Mig shrugs. He doesn't know. He doesn't know what he wants and so he cannot know what he misses, what he will never see, or never do or know. Too young for regrets, thinks the Alaskan. Yes, he will experience sorrow, but it will wash off him like water. That is the power of the young, to reinvent.

'Do you miss Alaska?' the boy asks boldly.

'What about it?'

'All that stuff you told me about. That robotics. Those. . . immersives.'

The boy utters the word with care. The Alaskan thinks of immersives. She remembers sinking through realities like falling backwards into the depths of a swimming pool, the realities folding over her like water closing over skin. She remembers the way they ripple through your brain, furrowing, burrowing, teasing out strands of experience and memory, shaping and restructuring, fitting the immersive around the way you view the world like slipping into a particularly well-made dress. She remembers the feeling of coming out of an immersive, like swimming from a great depth up towards the light, and the burst of disorientation as the surface breaks, followed by a light-headedness, a sense almost of transgression, the snap back to grey reality and almost at once the desire to repeat the experience. Many people in her country suffer from immersion addiction, especially with the onset of winter, but the Alaskan has never been one of them. The Alaskan can draw a box around pleasure the way she can draw a box around anything. Except perhaps love, if the Alaskan ever believed in love, which perhaps she did once but now the emotion seems both sordid and despicably innocent, a primitive gushing of oxytocin which the Alaskan should have put a box around the way she put a box around everything else. Where is the Scandinavian girl now? Old, decrepit, dead? The Alaskan imagines her body laid out on the forest floor, an oblong imprint on the peat, gradually covered in fallen pine needles until nothing can be seen but the tip of her patrician nose, the ends of her toes sticking up, toenails still growing, beetles in her hair. But that is probably not how it is at all. Probably she died in bed, in a luxurious retreat in the highlands of Veerdeland; the girl had ambitions for the law, although the Alaskan personally considered her too impulsive a character for such a calling. A cesspit of a country, Veerdeland. The Alaskan hates it, she hates Veerdeland and she hates Veerdelanders.

Mig is watching her, with that so-familiar combination expression of curiosity and wariness. She considers trying to explain immersion addiction and immigrants who steal your soul but discards the notion at once. The power of a word. The nothingness of a word. She thinks of lengths in a pool, a time when her legs worked, kicking through the water in smooth, streamlined motion. She thinks of redfleur manifestations and stricken towns exorcised from history. She thinks of a trip to Khabarovsk where she ate crab, a rare delicacy in these acid seas, and after the crab she delivered a presentation on a biomedical company's plans to regenerate the blood of pandas. Her eyes itched in the too-hot climate, she had to change her contact lenses, and in the bathroom someone saw her eyes and recoiled. There are mobs for nirvanas in Sino-Siberia. They crucify them.

And much, much further back: she hasn't thought of this for years, she remembers growing up on the Arctic Circle coast, long walks along the harbour front with a bracing wind at her back, or in her face, pushing back her hair; watching the shipping fleets coming in from across the Arctic Ocean, bringing goods from the Sino-Siberian Federation, bringing travellers, tourists, opportunists, informants. Watching the Boreal States play at trade and the seagulls spiral overhead, and it was the seagulls that interested the Alaskan, because they were always there but often overlooked, and in the moment of turning away, they acquired things.

In contrast, the Alaskan's darker-than-normal irises made people look at her twice. But just as kittens begin life with blue eyes, so the Alaskan's eyes were a shade lighter, a shade more innocuous, as a child. The nirvana gene came down the Alaskan's mother's side, not her father's; her father was in any case a feckless character, and her mother little better, although the mother had hyper-intelligence, like all nirvanas. You can take a lot away from a nirvana but you can't take that. She could have used it for almost anything but she chose to use it for gambling, and growing up the Alaskan was either very rich or very poor. She found both states interesting: preferred wealth, found her creative entrepreneurship flourished during poverty, but that wealth was needed to realize her ambition, so it was a vicious circle, one that ended in the Alaskan disowning both parents. They were a burden upon her and when they were gone she felt light.

She feels light now. Giddy. Almost manic.

'Do you?' Mig presses, tugging her back to the present. 'Miss it?'

The Alaskan reflects.

'No,' she says. 'It was a shithole.'

Shri collects the box from Ivra's house. Taeo's shoes. His shirts. A dead man's things in a dead man's home. There are some samples of dried grasses and seeds in jars which make no sense until she remembers he was meant to be posing as a botanist. That was his cover. For a mad moment she thinks about destroying everything, burning it or throwing the box into the sea, because what will she do with it all? When she puts these things next to the things back home, with his gloves and his skis, with their carnival masks from the day they met, that blazing day in Vosti celebrating First Light, will they be different? Will she shed more tears over these shoes, these shirts, because they came with him to Patagonia? Or will they just remind her every day of the might-have-beens, the things they could or should have done, the both of them?

But no. It wouldn't be fair to the children. They have to learn to live with grief, all of them, even Nisha, who will one day feel the loss for a father she was not old enough to remember, except perhaps as a feeling, an intuition of missing, a tale told by other people that she begins to believe is a memory. She told them she was going to find out what happened, and what happened is here, in this box, with its scraps of flora which if she looks closely enough includes the petals of a poppy, dark and curled.

Shri picks up the box. She says her thanks to the Antarctican who let her into Ivra's empty house (and who will mourn for Ivra? Does he have a partner, a family back home? She never asked) and makes her way down to the harbour. The town is on high alert, busy with soldiers and chattering civilians, a town on the brink of war, but she doesn't care about any of that. Her kids are waiting. They need her, and she misses them.

Ramona has never been so happy to see the silver lakes and sea channels of the archipelago come into view. Every part of her aches. Her knee and ankle joints are swollen and tender and her body is starting to rebel; she's going to pay for this expedition. But watching the mountainous islands peering through their misty crowns, she forgets her cramped muscles, forgets her smarting eyes, overwhelmingly conscious that a part of her expected never to see this landscape again. She said her goodbyes, way back in Panama, had thought herself resigned. Now the landscape appears to her with a new clarity, a place which possesses the uncommon beauty of water and prosperity, however small, however squeezed it might be between the ambitions of other, greater powers. The sight of it makes her heart sing.

Right now, though, she needs to worry about landing. Inés is chattering in her ear as she has been for the past hour, a pleasure and an irritation Ramona would not give up for the world, but one that is going to distract her at a time when she needs to focus.

'Ma, I have to concentrate now.'

'Yes, yes, all this asking and now she wants rid of me—'

'I've got to land this thing!'

'I'm going! Can she see I'm going?' Inés retreats into the passenger area, muttering to herself in a sulk which is either genuine or entirely fabricated, it's impossible to know.

Ramona tunes out her mother's grumbles, and puts her attention to the land below. She had been planning to take the plane directly to the Facility, but as they approach the harbour she sees an unusually large number of Antarctican ships lining the strait. She looks for Félix's ship, the *Aires*, but it isn't there. She notes the absence almost with relief; right now she just doesn't have the reserves to see him. In fact, there's barely a Patagonian vessel in sight. All at once she is wary of what might have happened in the time she has been away. It has been months. The journey south has not been kind.

Changing her mind, she banks and takes the plane away from Fuego, back over the mountains. She can make an aquatic landing in one of the lakes. Cautious of executing an unfamiliar procedure, she extends the landing gear well in advance. The plane seems to lose height very fast, and she needs all her remaining strength to control the landing. The lake rears up. It feels wrong, to land on water, she can't quite believe it will take the plane's weight, but she's put her faith in the foreign aircraft and it's got them this far. The nose of the plane hits the water with an awkward splash, then the belly crashes down. For an awful moment Ramona fears she has misjudged the landing. But the plane cruises forwards, rocking, then steadies. She taxies slowly over the water, bringing the plane as close to the shore as she can, and activates its exterior camouflage.

For a few minutes she sits in the cockpit, allowing herself to breathe, feeling the tears rising and doing nothing to stop them.

I thought I'd never see this place again.

She wipes her face and takes a long, shuddery breath. There are still things to be done.

Together, she and the passengers manage to get the bulky inflatable boat out of the plane and row themselves the short distance to shore. When she steps onto land, it feels unsteady. She supports her mother as she climbs out of the inflatable. Inés's breath is shallow, her first few steps are shaky. But she's alive, and standing on Patagonian soil, breathing in the warm archipelago air. Ramona feels the flood of emotion overtake her.

'Ma—'

'Yes, yes.'

The passengers hug one another, hug Ramona. For a while they are unable to let one another go. They are all weeping openly, and Ramona makes no attempt now to contain her own tears.

The Alaskan is dreaming. In the dream she is rattling along the rough track of a barren landscape on an old solar-cycle. There is no end to the track. It goes on, perhaps forever. There is a purpose to the journey but the Alaskan has forgotten what it is, only that she must keep going at all costs. The sky is red and apocalyptic and from time to time Jurassic birds flap across it in great flocks, and their calls sear the air like the calls of the last residents on earth. As she rounds an outcrop of rocks the Alaskan is confronted with a field of enormous solar panels, stretching away in front of her for as far as she can see. And she sees that the track stops where the solar panels begin. The only way across is to ride over the solar panels, which will result in burning, in the complete excoriation of her skin, in certain death. And while she is contemplating her next action, the Alaskan is dimly aware that she has been to this place before, that the solar fields of the Corporation are not unknown to her, and one by one the panels begin to turn towards her, swivelling on their stands with measured, robotic intelligence. When they all face in her direction the Alaskan knows what will happen next. They will collect the sunlight into a great lance and it will blind her.

Mig bursts into the Alaskan's room, upsetting one of the radios as he enters. The boy fumbles to pick it up but drops it again almost immediately in his excitement.

The Alaskan rubs at her eyes. The shadows of giant birds continue to march slowly across the backs of her eyelids. She feels groggy. Disorientated. This is what comes of wallowing in the past.

'Try and have a little care, won't you? What is it?'

Mig sets the radio straight. He is panting with exertion.

'The pilot. She's back.'

The Alaskan struggles upright in her chair.

'Good work, Mig. Very good work. You need to find her, right away.' She thinks but doesn't add: *before Xiomara hears the news.*

When the boy is gone she looks around the sparse rented room. At the radios. The information. It's done its purpose. Perhaps soon she'll be bidding farewell to this sequestered country after all.

Ramona accompanies her mother and the crew of survivors as far as Arturo's Place in the harbour town and leaves them there to decompress. They'll talk of course, but she isn't worried about that; it won't do any harm for them to tell the world their story – the faster and more widely it's broadcast, the more chance they have of action against the Boreals. She looks longingly at the interior of the bar, with its worn, comfortable seating, and offerings of wine and rum. A number of leisurely card games are in progress and Ramona is struck by the slowness of everything, the little hubbub that their entrance has generated. Nazca keep us but she could do with a drink herself.

Leaving Inés, she hesitates.

'You'll be all right here, Ma? I'll be as quick as I can.'

Inés gives her a look of what can only be described as outrage. Reassured, Ramona continues on her way.

Heading up through the harbour town to the Facility she notes the hurried, distracted appearance of those out on the streets. There are more soldiers visible than usual. Residents are staggering home under the weight of their purchases, or have children in tow, carrying extra bundles. Stockpiling, she thinks. Something's happening here. Or something's about to happen. But despite the tension in the air, everything looks disconcertingly as it was. The old road up the hill is quiet. Here are the soldiers' billets, here are the gates to the Facility, the checkpoint, and the face of the young soldier waving her through is familiar, unchanged. Here is the approach to the building that was once a centre for the architects of the forsaken sea city, Osiris, a pathway she has walked a thousand times. Could Osiris really be out there, as Félix suggested in Panama? She thinks again about those Antarctican ships and her misgivings double.

In the lobby, old Eduardo greets her like a woman risen from the dead, which she supposes she is, and certainly feels like, seeing his face. The reaction wrong-foots her. Eduardo tells her the government are in session.

'In session? Why?'

'It's a crisis meeting.' Eduardo is visibly teetering between the importance of the situation – whatever it is – and intense curiosity about where Ramona has been and why and how she has come back. But Ramona has no inclination for mind games.

'Dammit, Ed, this is urgent. I need to see them now. Is Lygia here?'

Ramona's boss appears almost as shocked as Eduardo to find her errant pilot standing in the lobby. Once again Ramona explains the urgency of the situation. Seeing Eduardo's expectant face she drags Lygia into the canteen, which is mercifully empty of customers. The clang of pots and pans filters through the kitchen shutters. She tells Lygia about the compound in the desert. About her mother. About the diaries. Lygia listens. When Ramona describes the experiments in their glass cubicles Lygia lifts a hand as though to push away the image, then drops it again. When Ramona has finished, Lygia sits in silence.

'Machines,' she says at last. She looks about the canteen, seeking concurrence from an audience who are not present. 'They're machines.'

'You see why I need to get in there?'

Lygia shakes her head slowly. Ramona can see her weighing things up as she struggles to make sense of this awful truth. She even looks empathetic. Ramona's hopes raise, only to crash again in the next moment.

'You can't interrupt them now, Ramona. They're in a crisis meeting. I don't suppose you've heard but the shit's hit the fan. The lost city?' Lygia drops her voice, then looks annoyed at herself for pandering to such absurd conventions. 'Osiris,' she says firmly. 'Osiris is out there. Talk about a revelation, eh? First the Boreals invaded, now the Antarcticans.' Lygia shakes her head. 'It's a clusterfuck.'

'Lygia, are you listening to me at all? I'm telling you the Boreals are kidnapping, *experimenting* on Patagonians and you're keeping me standing here? I need to tell people what's going on! They've got to do something!'

'Ramona, I hear you, and by the arse of the fucking whale it's horrendous, but there's a war breaking out in our back yard and we've got one side camped on our doorstep. This is an emergency! Whatever shit the Boreals are up to will have to wait. Come back in a few hours, they might be done by then. But until this crisis is over, we can't take any steps.'

'I can't believe this—'

Ramona's boss lifts a warning finger.

'And don't think you're getting away without an explanation. You've been missing for months. I want a full report.'

'Lygia please! Listen to me!'

Lygia stands. She is walking away as she makes her parting shot.

'A full report, Callejas!'

As she storms through the lobby, Ramona is aware of Eduardo goggling, his ears practically walking away from his head in his desperation to eavesdrop. Now her row with Lygia will be all over the archipelago within the hour.

Outside, she vents her rage upon the plant-choked walls of the Facility, kicking against the stonework until her sore, swollen feet shout with pain. On the walls beneath the foliage are the markings of the sea city. She feels like the place has been dogging her for months, riding on her back, that every time she turns her head it has ducked out of sight, unwilling to be seen. And now she can see clearly, and it's shitting all over Patagonia.

How can Lygia have heard what she has just said and tell her to wait? How could anyone?

She'll go back to Arturo's. She's in dire need of a finger of rum – or four. Striding back down the road, she lifts her head and howls her frustration to the wind.

'Fuck this! *Fuck this!*'

From the top of the hill she can see the Antarctican ships dominating the strait. She starts to count them and gives up. Looking at the ships she remembers Taeo, the Antarctican who broke her aeroplane. She should have sought him out while she was in the Facility and given him a piece of her mind. Later, she thinks. It will do her good to shout at someone.

As the coastal track levels out, weaving into the buildings of the town, houses and storefronts and drinking houses, all quieter than usual, she passes other residents of the island, and she cannot suppress the images of those stricken people in their glass cubicles – their coffins – in Tamaruq. They are still in there. She couldn't save them. She couldn't even give them a dignified death. She'll see them every day for the rest of her life. Each woman, man or child she passes in Fuego is a person at risk, a person who might be stolen away in the night. Davida Akycha Kvest is dead, but the raiders who took Inés and the others are still out there. Even now they might be targeting a village in the highlands.

Heading in the opposite direction towards her is a small, slight figure. There's something vaguely familiar about the walk, but not enough to make Ramona stop. She's not in the mood for pleasantries or remonstrations.

The pilot marches right past without even acknowledging him. Mig spins on his heel and runs after her.

'Hey! Hey, señora, remember me?'

She ignores him, striding along with her chin held high, deftly sidestepping anyone in her way. Mig hurries to keep up.

'Hey! I was in Cataveiro. Remember?'

He catches her wrist.

'I helped you with the salt woman.'

The pilot turns and snatches her arm away. Nothing about her face is approachable.

'What do you want?'

'I helped you with the salt woman,' Mig repeats. 'In Cataveiro.'

She looks at him properly then. Her face moves from anger to confusion to a dawning recognition. She looks different from what he remembers. Her hair. It's shorter. Ragged. Her face is tired.

'Cataveiro,' she says, approaching the word cautiously.

'Cataveiro,' says Mig.

'What do you want?' she says again.

'My employer has a proposition for you.'

The pilot keeps walking. Mig jogs along beside her.

'Who's your employer?'

'The Alaskan.'

'Why would I want to talk to her?' says the pilot. But she slows her pace.

'You'll want to,' Mig assures her. The pilot finally stops. She faces him. People carry on around them: a woman carrying a crate of fish, a man with headphones and a personal radio, adjusting the station, perhaps tuning into the same long-range channels that Mig and the Alaskan have been monitoring. Mig senses the pilot weighing up her options. It seems to take her a long time.

'All right,' she says at last. 'But this better be good.'

Ramona struggles to recall what she knows about the Alaskan. She has heard the name before, in Cataveiro, and outside of the city too, but never in any concrete way. The Alaskan's reputation is more spirit than human, someone that can slip through the noon of day without leaving a witness. She doesn't even know if the Alaskan is from Alaska, or if she's truly a Boreal – after all, a name is just a front, a door which can sometimes be opened and sometimes not, and many Patagonians whose work is of a dubious nature take names for themselves in this way, subsuming their identities until their real names are forgotten altogether. If Ramona knows one thing, she knows the Alaskan's work is dubious.

Mig takes her to a house close to the harbour front. She can hear the gulls screeching as they fight over scraps in the air, and she can smell the brine. There's a freshness to the sea air of the archipelago which is different to the hot haze of Panama or any other coast that Ramona has seen. Mig has a key. He lets them in, checking behind them, she notices, and instinctively she does too, although she sees nothing out of place.

The Alaskan is a frail woman in a wheelchair who appears to be listening to a dozen radio stations simultaneously. A woman who, in that first initial glance, reminds Ramona of her mother. The semblance dissipates in the next few seconds, when the Alaskan raises her head, redirecting all of her focus to Ramona, and Ramona undergoes the curious experience of being openly, unashamedly evaluated. This is a shrewd individual, used to control. The Alaskan's irises are so dark they are almost black. A memory – something that was said, though she cannot think where or when – flickers at the back of Ramona's mind, but she can't retrieve it.

Having finished her assessment, the Alaskan begins the deliberate process of switching off the radios, one by one.

'So you did come,' she says.

'Mig here says you have a proposition for me,' says Ramona. She glances about the sparse, functional room. Few furnishings; no belongings that she can see, except the radios. This is a transitory setup. 'I don't know what it is but I don't have much time.'

'You may want to make time,' says the Alaskan, silencing the final radio with a push of her index finger. Her other wrist, Ramona notes, has been recently broken, and doesn't appear to have had much attention since.

The Alaskan turns herself to face Ramona.

'Ramona Callejas, am I correct?'

'That's right.'

'You're the pilot.'

She thinks of *Colibrí*, abandoned, broken in the desert.

'I was.'

'Mig saw you return to the island.'

'So what, you want a ride?'

The Alaskan looks at her steadily.

'I'd make it *very* worth your while.'

Ramona feels an irrational sense of disappointment. No matter how exulted the customer, it always comes down to this. She's just a carrier.

'I have more important things to worry about than ferrying passengers.'

'You haven't asked where I want to go.'

'It doesn't matter. I won't be going anywhere any time soon.'

'And why is that?' asks the Alaskan coyly.

'Why would I tell you?'

'Why not? You're clearly preoccupied with something. You can't even keep still, or look at me while you're speaking. Sit down, share the load. Have a nougat.'

'A nougat?'

The Alaskan shrugs.

'I have other sweets.'

Ramona takes a perch on the edge of a chair. She's aware of the boy at the back of the room, fidgeting. He did help her. With Xiomara, when she believed Xiomara had medicine.

'What happened to your wrist?' she asks the Alaskan. A look passes between the woman and the boy, a look that Ramona does not understand.

'I had an accident.'

'Are you from Alaska?'

'I've been in Patagonia for over fifty years.'

'But you are from Alaska?'

'I was born there.' The Alaskan laughs. The sound sits deep in her throat, resulting in a spasm of coughing. 'Honestly, Callejas, do you think I'd be living in this country through choice? Think of me as whatever you want, but believe me when I say I have little left in common with a nation you so clearly despise.'

'They broke her spine,' says Mig.

'Enough!' The Alaskan cuts through sharply. 'Enough.'

Again, the lost memory flickers, but refuses to crystallize. Ramona considers the two of them; the boy and the old woman, bound by some strange and indefinable relationship which she cannot work out. A great weariness overcomes her. Why not tell these two? At least they are listening.

'I found out something,' she says. 'Something the Boreals are doing. Something. . . despicable.'

The Alaskan waits quietly. Mig has stopped fidgeting, and is listening intently. Ramona is unable to restrain herself any longer.

'They're kidnapping southerners. The Boreals. They're kidnapping them from their homes and taking them north of the belt and – and experimenting on them. With redfleur.' She spits the word.

A shudder runs through the young boy.

'It wasn't only redfleur either.' The words pour out of her; she knows she should hold back, should spare the boy, but having begun she can't stop. 'Before that, they were doing other experiments. Engineering people. Trying to change them. And not only up there. They had centres all over the place, in Sino-Siberia, and down here in the lost city—'

She stops abruptly, remembering the strange rumour told to her by Félix, back in Panama, a rumour that seemed too bizarre to be real, but has proved to be real, and then what Lygia said—

The Alaskan is staring at her, completely absorbed.

'The lost city, you say?'

'Yes.'

'You're behind the times,' says the Alaskan. 'The lost city – Osiris – has been invaded by the Boreals.'

'Lygia told me.' She slumps. 'So the government won't see me. They're in a crisis meeting. Apparently it's more important than this.'

'Well,' says the Alaskan. 'I hate to break it to you, but it's war. War has a tendency to redefine priorities.'

'Not like this,' whispers Ramona. 'Not like this.'

The Alaskan's mind is racing. Neurones surging towards one another, each pulse generating another connection of the greater, the overlying web. The lost city. The missing link. *Of course.*

The fact that the Boreals are experimenting on southerners is a revelation, but if she thinks far enough back. . . When the Alaskan was ascending the giddy heights of power, there were rumours of such centres. They were never spoken of. Only hints. Allusions. Conversations not quite concluded. Gaps in reports. No one asked, and so no one knew, and no one could reveal. That was before the emergence of redfleur, but it makes sense that the purpose of these centres would be diverted to such a wide-scale threat.

She looks at the pilot's tired, haunted face. It doesn't make sense to the pilot. There's a woman who's seen some things she won't forget. Such is this world. Not everyone can witness it and survive unchanged, or survive at all. Something about her – the impulsiveness, perhaps – reminds the Alaskan of the Scandinavian girl.

'The man Vikram Bai,' she says. 'He has immunity.'

The Alaskan is thinking aloud. The pilot looks confused.

'I don't know him.'

'He is Osirian. He was shipwrecked here, some months ago now. He is largely responsible for the rediscovery of Osiris. But he is of interest for other reasons. He has immunity to redfleur.'

'Immunity?' The pilot looks dazed at the idea. 'That's impossible.'

'Maybe not,' says the Alaskan. 'Think. Think what you have just this moment told me. The lost city was once an experimentation site. That is what you said.'

'Yes, an ancillary centre, that's what Kvest's diaries—'

'We know that the man who survived redfleur – the *only known survivor* – is from the lost city.'

The Alaskan waits, impatiently, for the moment of clarity to register. When it comes, elevating the pilot's features into an entirely different plane of cognizance, the Alaskan feels for a few blissful seconds nothing but the thrill, the volt of pleasure that comes of a covert knowledge shared.

The pilot takes a little more time to catch up in full.

'You think because of that he might – he might provide a cure?'

'It's possible,' the Alaskan muses. 'It is one possible explanation, anyway. And certainly the most tantalizing one, don't you think? But in any case, we can't ask him about his parentage because he's no longer here. No, Vikram Bai has gone to a war zone.'

The pilot jumps up from her seat and begins to stalk the tiny room.

'Then we need to get him back!'

'A ridiculous idea. The city is trapped between the Boreals and the Antarcticans. The long-range signals indicate a ceasefire, but that will never last. Neither side will concede.'

'Then we need to tell them. We need to get inside the city – find this Osirian – tell them what I know!'

The Alaskan casts a despairing glance in Mig's direction.

'Mig, you know what's happening here. Help me talk some sense into this madwoman.'

Mig regards her steadily. That secretive, cat-like expression that marks a door to the boy's other life.

'She's right,' he says. 'We have to find Vikram.'

'Mig—'

'We have to find him! You said he could provide a cure. That's what they all thought, at the camp. That's why they all came.' Mig swallows. 'That's why I went with him, after Cataveiro.'

'I said he might. Nothing is certain. How should I know, I'm not a scientist. I'm an old woman. What do I know?'

'He can end the experiments in the north,' says Ramona. She seizes Mig's hands. 'We'll find him.'

The Alaskan pops a nougat into her mouth and sucks it slowly. She observes the two of them, boy and woman, so suddenly alike in their evangelical fervour. She despairs of the human race. How can people be so imbecilic?

'Where did you find the site of the experiments, Callejas?'

'In the desert, north of the belt. A place called Tamaruq. Why does it matter where? When you hear what they were doing. . .' The pilot's eyes slide to Mig. She doesn't continue her sentence.

The Alaskan adjusts her weight in her chair and loads her next words with all the gravitas she can muster.

'In the desert. North of the belt. Deep into the uninhabitable zone. And how many other secret places do you think the Boreals might have in this world, for this, for other, as you would call them, atrocities? You may expose these crimes, but believe me, by the time that site has closed, another will have sprung up in its place. If not redfleur, something else. The world is too vast, Callejas. You cannot find out all of its criminals.'

The pilot shakes her head.

'I know what you're trying to do. But I don't care. This isn't an option. Don't you see? This isn't a choice. I've made up my mind. I made up my mind when I went into that lab and almost got my ma killed. I'm going to Osiris.'

'It's a suicide mission,' says the Alaskan.

'I'm going with her,' declares Mig.

'And you should come with us,' says the pilot. 'We'll need a navigator.'

'I've never been to the sea city. What makes you think I can direct you there?'

The pilot taps a radio pointedly.

'Don't tell me you don't know where it is.'

The Alaskan's eyes gleam. 'Sure you want an old nirvana with you on your little crusade?'

She notes the recognition spark in the pilot's eyes at the word *nirvana*.

Something has just clicked into place. But the pilot doesn't flinch. She's made of sterner stuff than that. The Alaskan respects that.

'We're going,' repeats the pilot. 'Mig here, and me, together. Are you with us?'

Getting the Alaskan to the plane is the problematic part. Ramona leaves Mig to stock up on provisions for the journey while she runs about town, trying to find one of the few drivers who can lend her a vehicle. The process is tedious and inevitably slowed by all the questions of people who want to know where she's been, questions that Ramona cannot begin to answer. At last she tracks down an old army contact who says she can loan his truck for an hour.

She runs back to Arturo's and finds Inés and her companions settled into a rhythm of steady drinking, surrounded by a rapt and growing audience. By the end of the day, each of the survivors will be famous across the archipelago. But the exhaustion on her mother's face is evident.

Ramona slips through the crowd of spectators.

'Ma, we need to get you a room.'

Inés shrugs her off.

'No, no, no—'

'You need to rest. I've spoken with Art. He's going to put you up for now, until you're strong enough to go home. Come on.'

She helps Inés climb the stairs, seeing with concern how slowly her mother moves, the extreme frailness of her body. In the relief of getting Inés to safety, she has almost forgotten that her mother is not safe at all; every day of the jinn is another day her immune system is defenceless. She tucks Inés into bed, wrapping the blankets securely around her, and places water and food at her bedside. There's a radio in the room, and Ramona moves that too within easy reach of the bed. She lifts her mother's wrist gently from the covers.

'This is the first patch.' She applies it carefully to her mother's inner wrist. Inés twitches but does not protest. 'Day one. It's not going to be easy. You have to be strong. Promise me you'll stay the course.'

Inés's voice is a murmur.

'Flying away, my little one?'

'There's something I have to do. I'll be back as soon as I can.'

'You have it from me,' says Inés.

'What's that?'

'The going. You have it from me.'

'Are you talking about the fugue?'

'I don't remember, Ramona. That is the thing.' Her forehead crinkles. 'I wake up in a place – oh, some places! and there is no memory. Where am I? How did I come to be here? Nothing. No places or people or things or. . . jaguars. Those journeys happened to a person who is not me. Sometimes I have a sense, in my stomach, a sense like my body has a memory that is not up here.' She taps her head. 'I have held this, I have done that. There are things I must have seen but. . . all I have is a fog.'

Ramona strokes her mother's hand.

'I'm so sorry, Ma. I didn't know.'

'No.'

'I wish you'd said, before. You should have said.'

'You ask me so many times. So I make up the stories. To have something. . . And now – now it's your turn. Give me a story before you go. Maybe it's my last.'

'It won't be your last. What story?'

'Oh, any, I don't care.'

'All right. Let's go with the parrot.' Her mother smiles. 'There was a parrot who lived in the jungle and rode on the back of the last jaguar,' begins Ramona. 'And as the years went by, the jungle grew smaller, and the animals grew fewer. But what most people don't realize is their voices did not vanish with them. When an animal disappeared, its voice flew up into the atmosphere, and the parrot, spying the voice, flew up to catch it in its beak. Some of the voices were hard and reedy and some were soft and hissing but it didn't matter to the parrot, it swallowed every single one. And when the jungle was gone the parrot had collected up all of the voices and had them safely in its stomach. But then a thing happened. The parrot. . .' Ramona founders. This story should run off her tongue by rote, but the end is evading her; her mind has gone blank. 'I'm sorry, Ma. I can't think.'

Inés's eyes are closed. For a terrible moment Ramona thinks she has slipped away while she was talking. Then she hears the soft hiss of an exhalation. Just sleeping. She presses her cheek to her mother's chest, embracing her as best she can without disturbing her.

'You're safe now,' she whispers. 'Get some sleep.'

As Mig is on his way back to the Alaskan's house a man steps directly in front of him, blocking his way. The man is heavy-set with a battered, pox-marked face and a tattoo at the edge of his eye. Mig, his arms full of bags, takes a step back.

'Where you going with those, kid?'

'Who wants to know?'

He darts to the side but the man moves and blocks him again.

'I said where you going with those?'

Mig eyes the man's frame warily, noting the way his jacket hangs. He is carrying a gun. Mig doesn't like the look of this, he doesn't like it at all.

'To my employer.'

'And who's that?'

'The Alaskan,' he says boldly. He has no idea if the Alaskan's name has the same effect here as it did in Cataveiro, but apparently she has made her mark in the few days they have been here, because the man hesitates.

'And the pilot?' he says.

'What about her?'

A gaggle of young kids stream past them with minders in tow, heading for the harbour. The kids are jabbering away and the minders are hassled, struggling to keep the kids together. Mig notices they all have luggage. The town is evacuating. He uses the diversion to slip away, feeling the stranger's eyes on his back as he hurries on.

He tells the Alaskan about the encounter.

'He asked about the pilot. I think he's looking for her.'

The Alaskan sighs.

'It's Xiomara. We have to be quick. Tell me, Mig, how is it that you always end up in the company of such dangerous people?'

None of them are as dangerous as you, thinks Mig, but now he looks at her again, something of the Alaskan's menace seems to have diluted. She can't force me to do what I don't want, thinks Mig. And she knows it. For a moment, he almost feels pity.

'She'll be here soon,' he says.

The pilot drives up in an old army truck. The Alaskan wheels herself outside, one-handed, sniffing the air. Mig helps the pilot lift her into the truck. The nirvana feels soft and floppy in their arms. It gives Mig a strange sensation, to touch her. Perhaps he expected her to be made of something other than flesh. He loads up the back seat with provisions and jumps in himself. The pilot lifts the chair into the back of the truck.

'Someone's looking for you,' the Alaskan tells the pilot.

'Who?'

'Xiomara. Did I mention she's in town? She hasn't forgiven you.'

The pilot doesn't say anything, but she puts her foot down on the pedal and the army truck rackets through the town's pedestrianized streets, the pilot driving fast and not speaking, the Alaskan hanging on to the door of the truck with her good hand. Mig is bounced about with the bags of food and water bottles. He doesn't mind. It's exhilarating, to be moving at such speed.

They drive out of the town, and the pilot takes them up the hill towards the mountains. Every few minutes she checks the mirror.

'Mig, is anyone following us?'

He looks back at the road behind them. It's empty.

'Not yet.'

She drives faster anyway, taking reckless turns, pushing the truck higher into the mountain, where the forestry closes in upon the road, and through the other side where the trees reduce to a few isolated pines, until the road peters out into a rough track of fallen stones. The wheels of the truck scrape along the uneven terrain. They have reached a ridgeway.

The pilot cuts the engine.

'We'll have to walk from here.'

She pulls on her pack and lifts the Alaskan from the truck.

'Mig, get our stuff. Rope it up – it'll be easier for you to drag it. Quick as you can.'

'Where are we going?'

'Down to the lake.'

The pilot goes first, carrying the Alaskan, the nirvana gripping with both arms around the pilot's neck. They struggle down the slick dirt track. Mig can see the lake glinting ahead, a broad silver sheen like a plate of glass, reflecting the sky and the rising hills which surround it. He scans for the aeroplane but can't see it. The bags are heavy. He stops for breath, panting, and glances back. Are Xiomara's people behind them? No one following can fail to spot the truck parked up there.

The pilot reaches the bottom of the track and sets the Alaskan down. The Alaskan's eyes dart about, taking in their surroundings. The lake is girdled with clumps of thick, lush reeds. An inflatable boat rests a few metres along the shore. She sees Mig puffing his way down the final few metres.

'Well done,' she tells the boy. Mig scowls, making it clear he doesn't care for her approval, but says nothing. The pilot clambers back up the track and lifts the Alaskan's chair from the truck.

'Leave it,' shouts the Alaskan. 'You won't get it in that boat.'

'We might,' the pilot shouts back. She manages to manoeuvre the chair awkwardly down the track.

This, thinks the Alaskan, is where things get interesting. Xiomara wants the pilot, but Xiomara is also beholden to the Alaskan, and the pilot and the Alaskan are now, to all external appearances, working together. A strike against the pilot is a strike against the Alaskan. Would Xiomara dare?

She keeps an eye on the track, the ridge, as Mig and the pilot help her into the inflatable boat, and the pilot pushes away from the shore, moving them further along the edges of the lake. The Alaskan can see the plane now. It's a Boreal passenger plane, one that uses camo-tech, but camo-tech is visible if you know how to look for it, if you look not for the thing itself but for the intrusions the thing makes on the space around it. So the Alaskan can see where the branches of overhanging trees are pushed upwards at unnatural angles; she can see the oblong of lake where the water looks like water but not like water.

She glances back. Her chair sits on the shore of the lake, awaiting the second trip. Nothing on the ridge. The inflatable bumps against the side of the plane. Mig gasps. The boy's never experienced anything like this before. The Alaskan used to be ferried by such airborne transports all across the northern hemisphere: planes and zeppelins, passage of the elite, the ultimate symbol of status. She hasn't been inside an aeroplane in over half a century.

The pilot switches off the camo-tech so Mig can see the aircraft properly and they pass up the bags, one by one, the Alaskan grunting with the effort, the little boat rocking.

And then they hear a shout.

She looks back. Figures, on the ridge. They've been spotted.

'Quick!' shouts the pilot.

A shot disrupts the still waters of the lake. Their pursuers are scrambling down the track. Mig pulls himself into the plane.

'Watch out!'

The Alaskan bends awkwardly forwards. A second shot hits the inflatable. She hears the hiss of escaping air. The boat begins to crumple around her. She can't swim, and the bastards shooting at them know it. A trickle of water licks at her shoes.

The pilot reaches down and grabs the Alaskan under the arms. The Alaskan can feel the strength in the pilot's shoulders, hears her gasping with the strain. Water is puddling inside the boat as the Alaskan is pulled inside the cockpit. She collapses against the interior, breathless with exertion and indignation. The pilot reaches past her and slams the hatch shut.

Xiomara's lackeys have reached the shore. The chair is kicked aside. One of them begins to wade into the lake, raising their rifle. The pilot powers up the plane's engines. Shot after shot glances off the cockpit windshield as the plane turns with painful slowness and begins to taxi over the water. The Alaskan feels the hum of the engines between her shoulder blades. She feels the base of power surge with the sudden resistance between plane and water, as the pilot prepares for take-off. She remembers a hundred take-offs, the specifics of each one presenting themselves to her with a pristine clarity – the weather and the mood she was experiencing and the greeting of the cabin assistant – these hundred take-offs lined up alongside one another, in preparation for a hundred destinations, a hundred goals which the Alaskan accomplished successfully, every time, because nirvanas, if they are not found out, inevitably are to be found operating at the highest levels of society, and that is where the Alaskan was, and she was good at it.

The plane lifts into the air. The pilot's concentration is absolute. Her mind and muscles and the plane are locked in a flawless symbiosis, the pilot an extension of the machine. Mig is crouched between the pilot seat and the co-pilot seat, his eyes wide with astonishment, his breath on hold, as the world drops away.

The Alaskan sees Xiomara's lackeys shrink to dots and vanish. As they gain height the archipelago separates into a patchwork, blue sea channels and dense green islands laced with cloud. Xiomara has defied her, outright. The Alaskan is reeling with the shock of it.

Her influence in Patagonia is waning.

The ocean to the east is as empty as the desert. The Alaskan gives Ramona co-ordinates for the sea city and the pilot obeys, locking the plane on a course which the Alaskan promises will take them directly there – to the war zone, as she says, with a reptilian glint in her black eyes which Ramona can't interpret, which could mean any number of things, none of which Ramona is keen to imagine.

The Alaskan shows her how to use some of the plane's robotic functions. She doesn't like it, but she lets the Alaskan fiddle with the controls. Even if she wanted to, she doesn't have the energy to resist. Mig watches suspiciously.

'What's that for?'

'I'm putting a coded call out to El Tiburón,' says the Alaskan.

'How are you doing that?'

'You wouldn't understand if I told you, boy.'

'I want to know.'

Ramona half-listens as the Alaskan explains her workings to Mig, the boy asking questions, the nirvana replying, their conversation a soothing circuitry as the sea passes by beneath them, dappled and wrinkled but unmarked by any other travellers. There is nothing but sea and sky, gunmetal grey and white and blue and the intermittent lance of the late afternoon sun. Cloud cover is altocumulus. Wind speed is moderate. Forget the war zone, it's the weather that concerns Ramona. If they hit a storm, there is no shortcut back to land. They could land on water, of course, but an ocean in a storm is no more comfort than a swamp in the uninhabitable zone. Ramona keeps one eye ahead and the other behind them, wary of building cumulus. She's afraid that her tiredness is going to affect her concentration.

As day folds into night, the plane glides on over the dark sea. Ramona checks the plane's charge and despite her exhaustion, decides to press on for another hour. Back in the passenger hold, Mig is stretched out, asleep, but beside Ramona the Alaskan is wide awake, a blanket spread over her legs, the fingers of her good hand supporting her damaged wrist. Other than the pinprick of stars, the only light comes from the console. The Alaskan's eyes are bright with it, a hard obsidian glitter, but the rest of her face is slack, and softened by the greenish glow. The plane is almost silent. Cocooned by the night sky, so far from anyone or anywhere, their aloneness feels infinite.

'I would offer to relieve you,' says the Alaskan. 'But I can't work the pedals.'

'You know how to fly?'

'I know the manual. That would suffice. If circumstances were different.'

'I'll set down soon. I have to sleep.'

'Then I'll keep a weather watch for you. I don't need to sleep tonight.'

Ramona believes her. The Alaskan's body might betray her age, but her face is perpetually alert. She wonders if it is even possible for the Alaskan to let her brain relax. Do nirvanas have dreams like other people do? Nightmares?

'I'll splint your wrist for you,' she says. 'When I've set down. You can't leave it like that.'

'Thank you.'

'Who were you?' Ramona asks. 'Before you came to my country, who were you?'

'I was a negotiator.'

'That shouldn't surprise me.'

'I was the best,' says the Alaskan simply.

'What did you negotiate?'

'Energy. Land. Contracts with the Solar Corporation.' The Alaskan's voice rasps like the strike of a match. 'They gave me the trickiest deals. They knew I could get results.'

'And in all these negotiations, you never heard anything about the experiments? The genetic engineering?'

'There were rumours.' The Alaskan turns her face to the dark glass of the windshield. 'The name you told me. Tamaruq. I remember hearing that word. Once, maybe twice. But it is easy for people to choose not to believe. How do you think I survived as long as I did?'

'I thought nirvanas were protected in the Boreal States.'

The Alaskan chuckles. 'If you mean there is a law, then yes, we are protected. But as you've seen for yourself, the law is an ethereal thing. Slippery. Very slippery. Malleable, one might say.' The Alaskan gazes out into the night sky. One part of her brain counts and names the southern constellations, an automatic process from which no conclusions are drawn. Just information. Gathered like dust. Dispersed like dust. 'This world is an ugly place, Callejas. Most people prefer to keep the demons at their back and forget they're wading through shit up to their ankles. True happiness, if such a state exists, can only be obtained through ignorance.'

'You believe that?'

'That is the truth.'

'Then you must be very unhappy.'

'I am what I am.'

'I never really believed in nirvanas,' says Ramona. 'I thought they were just a story. Something made up, to frighten children.'

'Everything's a story,' the Alaskan replies. 'A simple methodology to process chaos. You will tell yourself a story about what you have seen and done in the desert. You'll tell yourself you did what you could. That your choices were bound. That there was a certain – inevitability – to your actions.'

Ramona's anger flares. 'And you don't think I did? What I could?'

'It doesn't matter what I think. What matters is the story that is told. You will need yours, I think.'

Something flickers up ahead. For an alarming moment Ramona thinks it is lightning, but then she realizes the light is green, not white. As she watches, the sky to the south transforms into an amphitheatre of colour. Vaults of green and gold cavort across the sky, flickering in and out of being. Ramona has never seen anything so eerily beautiful. It feels as though a performance is being staged entirely for them. She leans back and nudges Mig awake.

'You should see this, kid.'

'Aurora australis,' says the Alaskan. 'The southern lights.'

'I'll use the light to land,' says Ramona. Exhaustion is crashing around her, taking out her senses one by one. She cannot resist it any longer. 'And I'll do your wrist.'

Late the next morning they reach their destination. The Alaskan, the pilot, and Mig watch as the city emerges from the horizon. For hours it has been a steady line, grey bleeding into blue bleeding into grey. Then something indistinguishable, a smudge or a blur interrupting the line, an emergent structure, mathematical edges gradually coalescing into form. They see the conical silver towers pointing skywards, woven together with fibres of shuttle lines and delicate bridges. Blips appear on the radar of the console as ships and submarines come into the aeroplane's range. The Alaskan fiddles with the console's settings, her head tipped to one side, listening, and the channel crackles with the static of conflicting signals. Mig crouches at the window. This is Vikram's city. This metallic fortress. All at once it fits, that sense of *special*, because to come from a place like this you'd have to be something different, something extraordinary.

'We need a landing point,' says Ramona. The Alaskan nods, and holds up her hand – wait a moment. They are approaching the city from the south-west. Ramona banks and takes the plane around its western flank, where the towers are less impressive; dull-faced, they don't reflect the sun. Some are derelict, cracked open to the sky, some bear the marks of recent attacks, and on the edges of the city, hundreds of small boats are packed tightly together. When they curve to the north, the city changes again, turning back to silver, although now they are closer Ramona can see that this part of the city has also suffered damage in the recent battle.

'Yes, this way,' says the Alaskan, still listening, and as Ramona banks once again, she says, 'We need to find El Tiburón.'

PART NINE
TO CATCH A GULL

OSIRIS

When Vikram was eight years old his friend Mikkeli showed him how to catch a gull. She had a knack with the net, and it wasn't long before they had snared their first target. As he watched the creature thrashing in the wire mesh, desperate to escape, Vikram saw the bird's eye turn upon him, an eye which it was said could hold the soul of a dead Osirian. He felt the bird's fear mirrored in the racing of his own heart. He wanted to tell Mikkeli to let the bird go, but to do so would be a betrayal of his friend. Then Mikkeli reached into the net, careful to avoid the scrabbling beak and talons, and snapped the gull's neck.

When the pírate El Tiburón asks him about the lost city, Vikram doesn't think of silver towers or Tarctic winds or even the sound of the sea at night. He thinks of the gull. He thinks of the feathers that were left in the net when they pulled the bird out, scraggly and damp from the sea and slightly oily to touch. In the months that followed that first capture, he became adept with the net, but it was always Mikkeli who committed the final act. This part, he does not admit to the pirate.

By the time Vikram comes up on deck they are already out in the open ocean. The coast of Patagonia has vanished, and a white frothing wake stretches out behind them, trailing back as far as he can see. The sun glints off the solar sails to the back of the ship, but it seems to be moving very fast, and Vikram cannot help wondering if there is some other, less visible source of power that is propelling them eastwards.

On the top deck, El Tiburón is stood in her tricorne hat, leathers, and tinted glasses. Vikram notes the pirate frowning at the wake as though she would like to erase it, but cannot, and does not quite comprehend how the ocean has failed to acquiesce to her demands. Vikram looks ahead, letting the wind batter his face, watching the empty horizon, wondering what he has done. He feels like a convalescent. His head is throbbing and the guilt is a weight of waterways on his back. Now he's away from Patagonia the fact is inescapable. He abandoned everyone. He left Mig behind. For all he knows, the boy is dead. And it's Vikram's fault. He let the boy come with him to the archipelago. He let him stay at the camp, knowing it was a risk. He left him there.

I should have stayed.

He cannot shift the thought. Whether he would have died there or not, he should have stayed. And then what? He'd never know the truth about himself: the truth about the redfleur, why he is immune, if there are others like him. But now the Boreals have invaded Osiris, there may be nothing left to find.

There are only bad choices, he thinks. And sometimes there is no choice at all. He has to live with that.

A shadow falls beside him. The pirate has come to stand at his side. For a moment they stand in silence, watching the waves.

'Why did you help me?' Vikram asks.

'I did not help you,' replies the pirate. 'I helped the Alaskan. We share. . . a commonality.'

'And that's why you helped us?'

El Tiburón adjusts the angle of her hat.

'The Alaskan has an eye for those who are useful,' she says. 'When the time comes for negotiations, you will count those who have aided you, I am sure. There are a number of death penalties on my head, Señor Bai. They are heavy. The time has come for these undesirables to, how shall I put it, to lift and fly away like young birds.'

'I'll do what I can, of course,' says Vikram. He thinks of the Boreals, who have invaded his city, a place where he never planned to return and now finds himself inextricably bound. 'If we get that far.'

The pirate's gloved hands curl and flex gently against the rail of the deck.

'I did consider your death,' she muses. 'Your eight pints of blood. One could make a nice presentation of those. I would say. But I decided you were of more value alive.'

'Should I say thank you?'

'It is advisable.'

'Then thank you.'

And fuck you, he thinks. Like everyone else, the pirate has placed a value on his head and calculated her moves accordingly.

'Do you know where we're going?' he asks.

'I have obtained the necessary co-ordinates.'

'How long will it take us?'

'Several days,' says the pirate. 'We will have to evade the Antarctican fleet, who will be heading in pursuit of the Boreals. I have no intention of engaging in unnecessary battle and risking my crew.'

Vikram looks down at the deck below. Once or twice he has caught a glimpse of a crew member, but for the most part, the ship seems to operate without assistance.

'This isn't a Patagonian ship, is it?' he asks.

'It was,' says the pirate. 'But I have made it something else.' Her fingers tap the deck rail lightly, playing an invisible spectrum of keys. 'Señor Bai. May I suggest you spend the next few days wisely, that is, out of sight. I will summon you when the city is in our sights. By all means listen to the radio broadcasts if you desire. I sense the Boreals are keen to share the news of their latest acquisition.'

* * *

Vikram does as the pirate advises and over the next few days he stays out of her way, confining himself to the cabin or the upper deck, listening to the broadcasts, eating the food the pirate's crew brings him without question or complaint. Sometimes he wonders if the pirate is telling the truth, or if she has some other plan, which will see him landed upon the shore of a Boreal coast, ready to be handed over for blood money. But when he is up on deck and watches the passage of the sun they appear to be headed in the direction the pirate says they are headed, and so he has no choice but to trust her. The broadcasts on the radio change and multiply. Now they come from the Antarcticans, now from the Solar Corporation. The world, which he had found to be vaster than he could have imagined, has contracted again to the tiny site that is Osiris. It doesn't feel real to him.

On the night of the fifth day the radio picks up an intermittent broadcast which Vikram thinks is o'dio Isis 100 and El Tiburón comes to find him in his cabin. The pirate cocks her head, listening a moment. Two journalists are discussing the ceasefire.

El Tiburón sweeps a hand across the table and a display of glowing dots appears, like constellations in the night sky, in a formation Vikram does not recognize but which feels nonetheless familiar. The pirate indicates.

'We have taken a wide berth south of Osiris and are now approaching from the south-east. This is your city, as my sensors have it. The Boreal fleet is located to the north. The Antarcticans have moved down to the south, but we passed them without detection. There are of course concealed vessels on both sides which are neither north nor south but somewhere in between, and in the case of the Boreals, underwater.'

The pirate looks at Vikram, her eyes dark and shadowy behind the tinted glasses.

'Do you have a plan? Who are you intending to contact?'

'There's a man called Linus Rechnov, if he's still alive.'

'Which side of the city will you find him?'

'East. But he could be anywhere. If so much has happened—'

'Is Linus Rechnov an Osirian like yourself?'

'Yes, of course.'

'You should consider taking your case to someone with authority. Your people no longer have authority here.'

'You think I should speak with the Boreals?'

'Personally I will not have dealings with the Boreals,' says El Tiburón. She looks at the representation of the city, a meditative expression on her face. 'They would have my body on a pike.'

That doesn't answer my question, he thinks. The journalists are now talking about the summit.

Little word from the inside – know there are Osirian reps. . .

'Wait—' says Vikram. 'I want to hear this.'

'If you wish to deal with the Boreals, you are on your own,' says El Tiburón.

Also know that Adelaide Rechnov's testimony was heard today by video link—

Vikram freezes.

'Did you hear that?'

'We are discussing the Boreals—'

'But they said—'

Spoke with her earlier today. . . advice for the city. . .

The pirate frowns.

'But I would very much suggest that you approach the Solar Corporation.'

I want to tell the Osirian people to remember our city's strength. It is a particular kind of power: the power of the ocean.

There's no mistaking it. He would know that voice anywhere. The voice emanating from the console, from a signal broadcast from the city of Osiris, belongs to Adelaide Rechnov. Vikram turns deliriously to El Tiburón.

'That's Adelaide Rechnov!'

The pirate reaches over to the console and cuts off the channel. The o'dio falls silent.

Vikram stares at the pirate in disbelief. El Tiburón ignores his gaze, either oblivious to or choosing to ignore the sudden turbulence in Vikram's head.

'It was her,' says Vikram. 'It was her speaking. It was Adelaide!'

'Adelaide Rechnov, yes, the Silverfish.' The pirate makes for the door. 'Are you coming? We are on the outskirts of Osiris. This is as far as I take you.'

Vikram stares at the console, numb with shock. The pirate's footsteps are receding. He runs after her.

'Will you listen to me? Adelaide Rechnov is dead. How can she be speaking?'

The pirate halts briefly.

'Did you know her?'

'Yes, I— she died, months ago. I was there!'

'Then she was resurrected,' says the pirate. 'But not for long, I fear. She was badly injured when the Boreals attacked and the border in your city fell, less than a week ago.'

She continues walking, climbing the stairs to the upper decks, ducking slightly to accommodate her hat as she passes through the hatch. Vikram stumbles after her.

'That can't be true. There must be some mistake—'

'I cannot tell you about the truth,' snaps the pirate, striding onto the deck. 'Whatever the truth is, I will leave you to discover it. This is as far as I go. These waters are infested with Boreals. I will not risk going any closer.'

'But I have to get into the city – we've come this far—'

'I can give you a boat,' says the pirate. 'But not a boat that may be detected, or any kind of motor that will be heard. One of my crew will row you there. The night should give you some cover.' She turns towards him, her eyes leaden behind their glasses. Her fingers flutter by the pistols at her hips with a soft, repetitive motion. 'Unless you wish to rescind on our bargain?'

Vikram remembers the scorpion in the envelope.

'Fine – yes, I agree. I don't care how I get there, as long as I can get inside the city.'

And find her.

'He will go with you.'

El Tiburón nods to a short, stocky man, who nods silently to Vikram.

'Does he have a name?'

'You can call him Juan. Are you ready?'

Vikram nods. His head is reeling.

'Then I bid you good hunting.'

She turns away. Vikram stares after her, still unable to comprehend what he has heard. Adelaide was in the tower. The tower collapsed. They hunted everywhere, Linus told him. Did Linus lie? If she survived, why wouldn't she come forwards?

As the small rowboat is lowered over the side of the ship, Vikram can see the ghostly green lights of the ring-net, stretching away on either side, and the faint shadow of the watchtowers. Is anyone manning them now? Beyond the net, the city glimmers, an invitation in the darkness. Cloud cover blocks the moon but between the clouds are patches of stars. The sea is a soft dark mass that folds around them as the boat settles into the water. The crewman he is to call Juan takes the oars and manoeuvres them away from the ship. There is no call goodbye from above, no face overlooking to watch them depart. Within a few strokes of the oars, El Tiburón's ship with its camo-tech skin is invisible to Vikram.

He looks ahead. They are approaching the ring-net. A large rent in the net is evidence of a ship's earlier passage into the city, whether Boreal or Antarctican Vikram does not know.

The lights of the ring-net worry him. Knowing how effectively El Tiburón's ship is shielded from sight he cannot help fearing there are other ships out here, ships on the watch, ships that might notice a boat slipping through, however small. He starts to say something to Juan but Juan shakes his head, indicating silence.

They approach the ring-net. He can hear the clanking of its chains, a sound that brings back instant, distracting memories. He thinks of Drake and Nils, driving out to the ice-field, the laser cutters dissecting the sheet into pieces. He thinks of Adelaide on a waterbike speeding towards the net, her hair streaming in the wind, her face intent and conflicted in a way he did not understand, and understands no better now. His chest is tight and the memories threaten to overwhelm him. She is alive. He cannot stop thinking that one thought, true or not. She is alive, and he didn't know.

The rent in the ring-net looms. Vikram realizes he is holding his breath. He forces himself to exhale slowly. This is the power of his city, though he has forgotten it; the power to suck you in, co-opting you to its slow agendas. He has to stay alert. Find Linus. Find the Solar Corporation. Get to the summit.

Find out what happened to Adelaide.

Juan lifts the oars and brings them together and the boat passes through the gap, the green lights of the ring-net washing over them, before they fall away again. Vikram waits for the shout, a warning shot to say they have been seen. But the sea remains quiet.

They are in Osiris waters now.

The clanking sound of the ring-net fades behind them. Now he can't hear anything except the soft lift and splash of the oars as Juan guides them through the waters, the beat of the oars never changing, alongside it the erratic rhythm of Vikram's own breathing, and his heart, faster than usual.

The structure of light that is Osiris begins to separate and solidify into individual towers. Vikram is struck by their height and power, a sight familiar but newly strange to him, like a scene from a dream.

Adelaide is alive.

They are coming into the south-east side of the City. Remembering not to speak, Vikram points to one of the towers which is less brightly lit and Juan adjusts the boat's course to head for it.

They are less than a hundred metres from the tower when Vikram feels something bump against the bottom of the boat.

His chest contracts.

'What was—'

Juan shakes his head, more vigorously than before. He lifts the oars and leans forwards, preparing for the backstroke. The oars dip again.

Juan stops his stroke. The boat drifts forwards a few more metres with the momentum and in the light from the tower Vikram can see the silhouette of Juan wrestling with the oar, pulling back at it with all his strength. Then he releases it. The oar clatters out of the oarlock. The boat rocks. Vikram stares at Juan. A terrible premonition creeps over him. Juan has frozen, both hands clutching the remaining oar.

'Row—'

Something bombards the boat from beneath. Vikram feels it topple, feels himself falling, the boat lurch beyond the point of no return. He grabs at the side of the boat and in the instant it capsizes he has time for one brief gasp of air before he hits the water.

Cold submerges him. He goes under.

He opens his eyes but he can't see anything. He kicks out but he can't feel anything. He can't tell where Juan has fallen. Something's in the water. Something's in the water with them—

Get to the boat!

Frantically, he kicks upwards. His head breaks the surface but still he can't see anything, he can breathe but he can't see. He flounders, hitting out, and realizes he's come up on the inside of the boat. His breath, short and petrified, is deafening within the confined space.

Something brushes against his foot.

He curls his legs upwards to his chest, his heart spasming in terror. *It's in the water. It's below you—*

The boat won't protect him. He has to get to the tower.

He takes a deep, shuddery breath, and ducks under the upturned gunnel of the boat. He comes to the surface. Intake of air. Cold. Sharp. The tower, fifty, maybe seventy metres away. In the water behind him, Vikram can hear something thrashing.

He strikes out, moving as fast as he can with his numb, cold-shocked limbs. The tower decking is in sight. Forty metres away. Thirty—

He hears a single scream. A scream that goes on for a long time, echoing around the arena of the ocean.

Still he can hear the sound of limbs thrashing, limbs in desperate throes – he can imagine what is happening – twenty metres from the tower, ten—

The scream cuts off. The water has gone quiet. He forces himself to keep moving. The sea is buffeting him. His arms and legs feel as though he's swum a hundred times the distance, heavy and throbbing – his heart is a spike of pain in his chest—

His hand touches the platform. He hauls himself up and rolls away from the edge. He is shuddering uncontrollably. He thinks he sees something, pale and upright, moving at speed, moving towards the tower. He rolls again, forcing himself further away from the water. He feels a bump against the decking and then it's gone.

When he looks back, all he can see is the outline of the boat, upturned in the water, and the faint glimmer of the stars.

He's on his own.

He enters the tower, soaked and shaken to the core. It's a City tower, residential, and at this time of night he doesn't expect anyone to be about. But when he takes the lift and steps out at the level of the first bridge, he finds a group of Citizens gathered in the lobby area nearby, drinking and talking animatedly. They are dressed in a way he hasn't seen since one of Adelaide's notorious parties, draped in jewel-coloured velvet and silks, the women wearing extravagant headdresses and corsages at their wrists, teetering on elevated heels.

As Vikram approaches, dripping seawater with every step, they look at him in surprise.

'What happened to you?'

'Shark,' he says. 'My friend—'

He can't manage anything more: the horror is still too near. Their faces turn to aghast. They crowd around him, touching and stroking him, an air of wonderment about their gestures. Vikram gets a whiff of alcohol and realizes they are all very drunk.

'The Boreals let it in,' says one of the party. 'It's something old, you know. All this time it's been out there, waiting. . .'

'It's just a large white. A fucking enormous one, I'll give you that—'

And, 'That's the fifteenth attack.'

'I heard it was more like twenty—'

'Twenty-*five*.'

'It doesn't matter anyway—'

'We'll all be dead soon—'

'It can have its pick.'

And they laugh, collectively, hysterically, for a long time.

'What do you mean?' Vikram says.

The first speaker, a woman, shrugs. 'The talks won't last another day. That's what they're saying, isn't it? Tomorrow it's war!'

One of the men begins to caper, dancing around the younger, shorter woman and pulling faces until she bends double with laughter. He grasps her hands and whirls her about.

'Oh stop, stop,' she says, gasping and laughing at once, but the man won't take no for an answer. She kicks off her shoes and they gallop away down the corridor, both shrieking. The first woman watches them go. Her eyes are bright and her make-up is smudged.

'It's only a matter of who strikes first,' she says. 'Either way, we'll be dead by tomorrow night. Perhaps your friend was lucky.' Vikram thinks of the scream and cannot suppress a shiver. She squeezes his arm kindly. 'Here, have a drink.'

She passes him a bottle of voqua.

Vikram takes a glug. That sharp tang. That red-haired girl.

'Adelaide Rechnov,' he says.

'The Silverfish?'

'I don't know – the Rechnov girl, the Architect's granddaughter – is she alive?'

'She was this morning—'

'But they say there's no hope—'

'That family is cursed.'

Each utterance feels like another kick slamming into his chest.

'But where is she? Which hospital?'

They don't know. Vikram struggles to gather his wits.

'What about the Solar Corporation? Linus – Linus Rechnov, the Councillor – is he alive? I need to find them. I have something that can stop this.'

They look at him pitiably and he can tell they don't believe him. But one of them says, 'They're all lodged in the area around the Eye Tower, on the Crocodile line. The Africans are in S-twenty-three-east.'

'No, that's the Antarcticans. S-twenty-four-east.'

'Are you sure?'

'Well, I thought—'

The gallopers are on their way back, their faces flushed and sweaty. They grab the voqua bottle and take long, greedy gulps. The girl hiccups.

'And Linus?'

'Have you been hitting the manta a bit too hard? He's in the talks.'

'I'll go that way,' says Vikram. Linus will know where he can find Adelaide. 'Thanks.'

He heads for the bridge.

'You sure you don't want to stay?' calls the first woman. One of the others drapes his arm about her shoulders and adds, 'Yes do, do stay.' Their expressions are at once forlorn and inviting.

Vikram shakes his head. He has no time to waste now. They shrug – a joint, philosophical kind of shrug – and turn back to their party.

He crosses the bridge quickly. These City towers are heated but his clothes are damp and his shoes squelch and he can't shake the feeling of cold. As he makes his way through the eastern quarter, wending up and down the towers and over the closed, slender tunnel bridges, he comes across many parties like the one in the first tower. Citizens, out of their apartments, gathered in groups and talking at speed, aware there may be only hours left to expel all the thoughts they have left unspoken for years. People kissing. People crying. People confessing secret, never-disclosed passions. People embracing lifelong enemies. And not only Citizens. He sees people who are unmistakable as westerners, in the same towers, in the same groups, together. All with the same, frantic intensity. He passes a couple, fucking against the wall, oblivious to him or to anyone else in the vicinity. He passes a man slumped against a door, a knife sticking out of his chest, his palms open at his sides. He sees fireworks to the left of a bridge, clusters of gold and silver and purple and green, one burst after another, spheres exploding within spheres. He hears shouts and cheers from a roof terrace. He sees a figure plummet from a balcony. He sees a glider angling between two towers, the athlete suspended like the body of a moth beneath the wings, and people gathered at windows and on balconies, watching, pointing. Some of the towers have been bombed. Some have craters etched into their walls. In some of the craters are people, dancing to torchlight, their shadows dancing behind them. He hears strains of music. Jazz. Piano. The shudder of bass.

At each tower he asks the same question. Where are the Africans? Where is the Solar Corporation? The answers vary. S-twenty-five-east. No, S-twenty-four. It's definitely S-twenty-four. What floor? The fiftieth. The fifteenth. The fiftieth, it's the fiftieth, I've seen them with my own eyes, I've seen them. He passes a convention of Tellers, sat in a circle, their eyes closed and their voices incanting in dual tones and their bodies swaying in harmony. He hears the story of the last balloon flight narrated in quiet voices, only now there is a new ending, the balloon will arrive, it will take them far from the city, it will bring rescue. He hears stories of the shark: it's rabid, it's prehistoric, it's sentient, it's come to enact justice. He sees a symbol painted on doors, a silver fish in the act of leaping. After what feels like hours of walking he reaches the district of the Crocodile line. Hands tug at him as he passes through the towers. Join us! Join us! Tomorrow we'll be dead. Tomorrow we'll drink with the ghosts. He half-expects to see a familiar face, a Shadiyah or a Jannike Ko or a Linus Rechnov. He half-expects to see Adelaide, the woman he thought was dead and is not, so why shouldn't she cheat death a second time? But no one recognizes him. No one calls his name. And as he nears the Eye Tower, which stands in the ocean alone and magnificent, the towers begin to quieten.

He doesn't hear music now. He doesn't see people. The doors are shut and the stairwells are empty again.

He checks his bearings. S-twenty-four-east is the next tower.

He takes the lift to the fortieth floor and walks slowly across the bridge. He wishes now that there were people here. That he didn't have to do this alone. He feels the weight of it on his shoulders and he longs more than anything to be able to return to that first group, share their voqua, dance like a demon around the window-walls and drink to death and destruction.

He enters S-twenty-four-east and looks about. Everything is quiet. It's an opulent, residential Osirian tower. Vikram can imagine the kind of people who would live here. People like Adelaide Rechnov.

People like Adelaide Rechnov used to be.

It could be any floor. They said the fiftieth – many of them said the fiftieth. So he'll start there. He'll look all night if he has to. Knock on every door. Tell them what he knows and find out where she is. He climbs the stairs. It's so quiet. As if they've already evacuated. He finds himself thinking about the time they broke into her dead twin's apartment, Adelaide and he, the strange conversation that followed in the tea house. A softening between them, although he hated her, at the same time. A beginning.

Someone will listen to him. They have to.

He exits the stairwell.

The assailants step out from both sides. Before he can react, hands seize him, a blindfold comes over his eyes and he feels something stick into his stomach. For a few, futile seconds he tries to move. But his body is failing to respond.

He falls limp.

In the minutes that follow he feels himself being carried, although his eyes refuse to open and he cannot sense his hands or feet. He hears voices.

'Careful—'

'Get the door!'

'Here, lift his feet – that's it.'

'No one saw you—'

'Of course not—'

A pause.

'Is that – is that Vikram Bai?'

'Shut up, Io—'

'But what—'

And then blackness.

They find El Tiburón on the side of the city furthest from the Boreals, outside of the ring-net. Ramona listens to the pirate's voice over the radio channel, distant and faintly distorted. 'He was here, but he is gone.'

'What do you mean, gone?'

She scans the waves below but can see no evidence of El Tiburón's ship. Not that she expected to do so. She maintains the plane on a wide curving course around the outskirts of the city.

'He went into the city last night. My man went with him. Neither of them has returned.'

'And you've heard nothing?'

'I did not expect to hear,' replies the pirate. 'But I expected my man to have returned by now.'

Ramona and the Alaskan exchange glances.

'Where was he headed?'

'He intended to find the Solar Corporation. The international police.'

'Maybe he found them,' says Ramona. 'Maybe he's in the summit now.'

The Alaskan shakes her head.

'There would be talk of it. We've heard nothing, only that the talks are in progress. There's been no mention of his name.'

'Then we need to get inside ourselves—'

'If you find my man, tell him to come back,' says the pirate. 'There is a code. He would not have left without incident. And don't forget the deal. I'll be here. Waiting.'

The channel closes abruptly.

'What's happened? Where's Vikram?' demands Mig.

'We don't know,' says the Alaskan.

'What are you going to do?'

'Find him.' She looks to the pilot. 'Callejas, you can navigate through the city?'

'Yes, if I'm careful. But we don't know where we're going.'

'We're going to the Eye Tower. Look for the tallest building. It will be in the heart of the city. Mig, you keep a look-out for Callejas. She needs both our eyes.'

The boy nods. Ramona's shoulders are rigid as she takes the plane in over the city, slowing as much as she dares. There is too much at stake now, thinks the Alaskan. Vikram's disappearance is a blow, but they can't go back now even if they wanted to. She peers down. The city glints back at her. With the sky so clear, it is impossible to see anything other than the sun refracting off the solar skins and the sea sparkling between them.

'Take us lower,' she instructs.

'That's not a good idea—'

'There's space, you can manage it,' says the Alaskan.

Ramona drops the plane into a corridor weaving between the conical towers. The radio crackles.

'People are trying to hail us,' says the Alaskan. 'Ignore them.'

The pilot doesn't respond. All her attention is focused upon navigating the perilous pathway between the towers, a pathway obstructed with slender bridges and sinuous transportation lines. The Alaskan and Mig hold on tightly as the plane jerks in a series of abrupt manoeuvres.

'There!' shouts Mig, pointing. 'That one.'

It has to be the one. He's never seen anything so magnificent. It makes his heart pound just looking at it; a place like this must have been built by giants.

Ramona risks a quick look. Mig is right. This is the tallest tower they have seen, rising several metres above the closest peak.

'Down?' she asks.

The Alaskan nods.

Ramona grips the yoke tightly. The aeroplane barrels out of the sky at speed. Ramona's jaw is clenched as she lifts the nose of the plane over a bridge, then dives back down towards the waterway. The plane touches down heavily and sloughs a path through the water, its wings narrowly missing several small boats which slide sideways in the swell. Ramona powers down the engines and nudges the aircraft into a slow turn towards a star-shaped decking skirting the base of the Eye Tower. She can see people on the decking standing and pointing, their mouths agape. Like most Patagonians, they will never have seen an aeroplane before.

The plane comes to a stop. For a few moments there is silence.

'I'll guard the plane,' says the Alaskan. Ramona turns in her seat.

'Mig, you coming with me?'

'Yes!'

He's not going to miss this. Not for anything.

'It's going to be a short swim. Can you swim?'

'No,' says the boy.

'Then hang on to me. And keep my rifle out the water.'

'Get into the summit,' says the Alaskan. 'Find the Africans. Tell them Vikram Bai is in the city. Tell them everything you know. Don't worry about the language, they'll have a translation chamber. Don't speak to anyone else. You can't trust the Boreals or the Antarcticans.'

Ramona nods. She opens the hatch.

'Remember the words I told you,' calls the Alaskan.

'Yes. *Redfleur*. *Cure*. I remember.'

She drops down into the water.

'Come on,' she shouts to Mig. The boy hesitates only a moment, staring at the turbulence of the waves, then jumps after her with a yell.

The Alaskan closes the hatch. She watches as Ramona swims the short distance to the tower decking, the boy clinging to her shoulders. For the first time in years she feels a spark of anger towards her inert legs. Someone gives the woman and the boy a hand out of the water. She sees Ramona exchanging a few quick words, then she strides into the tower, the rifle on her back, Mig scurrying after her. The attention of those on the decking turns to the Alaskan, trapped in the cockpit of the plane like an artwork on display. They wave at her. She gives them the finger. They look taken aback.

'Heathens,' mutters the Alaskan.

Karis Io sits in silent incredulity as the Chambers descend into chaos. The Solar Corporation leader is not even bothering to ask for quiet; she sits back with her chin resting on her knuckles while the delegates shout over and above one another. Evie Aariak is on her feet, shouting and pointing. The second officer twitches beside her. He's only waiting to get back to the trigger.

He looks to the Solar Corporation convenor, issuing a silent plea. Surely there are persuasions she can use, some trick or slip of the law, or just the might of the Solar Corporation to force a resolution. Perhaps there are, and perhaps she has used them, or perhaps she has already decided that the situation is not worth what's left in her arsenal. Her face is tired, and as the minutes tick by it alters further, a resignation identifiable that was not there in the previous day. Karis can imagine the second narrative that is running through her mind; she has the Corporation's welfare to consider, and if the talks fail and hostilities resume, her responsibility is with the Corporation ship, now waiting alone and vulnerable to the east of the city. How fast can it get out of range? How fast can she get her people safe? She's done what she can. She's exercised her duty and if these people cannot reason or will not adhere, well, then she won't compromise African lives. That's not a part of the Nuuk Treaty.

Tuning out the noise of the summit, Karis becomes aware of some other kind of disturbance at the doors. Raised voices carry from outside. Nkem Sosanya has noticed too. She beckons one of the Corporation guards and gives him an instruction. He goes outside.

Aariak leans back.

'Io.'

'What?'

She doesn't speak but jerks her head in the direction of the door. Karis gets the picture. She wants him to check it out. He resents the order, but then he thinks, why the hell not? He's had enough of his seat in these chambers for one lifetime.

He slips from the tiered seats and makes his way around the back of the delegates. In the corridor outside, he finds the security guards and Sosanya's man trying to pacify a fierce-looking woman with a rifle and an adolescent boy who darts at the door when Karis steps out, only to be caught and yanked away by one of the guards. Karis stops, taken aback. The woman is shouting in a language that sounds like Portuguese but isn't. Spanish. Is she Patagonian? How the hell has she got here?

The situation is escalating. The woman grasps her rifle and speaks threateningly. The guards' hands go to their guns. Now the boy is shouting too, jumping up and down. The woman turns in despair to Karis and tries again with him. He spreads his hands.

'I'm sorry, I don't know what you're saying.'

She raises her eyes to the ceiling and shouts something in her own language that Karis takes as a curse, directed at him, or some higher entity. Then she addresses him again.

'Vikram Bai,' she says. 'Vikram Bai. Is. Here.'

The name goes through him like an electric shock. How the fuck does she know about Vikram?

He glances back at the doors. Has anyone else heard the commotion? Where have these two come from? He should go back in. Tell Aariak. Tell her they've been rumbled.

The woman's eyes are fixed on his, the boy's as well, the boy is looking at him like he's a murderer. They can tell something is up. Move, he tells himself, but everyone is staring at him now and his feet refuse to obey.

The woman gestures; she wants something to write with.

Karis pulls the smartcloth they've been using to communicate while in session from his pocket and unfolds it. He offers it to the woman. She stares at it warily, then takes it with her fingertips. She taps out three words in Boreal English. She hands the cloth back to Karis.

Vikram.

Redfleur.

Cure.

He stares at her. She stares back at him, the desperation in her eyes clear as she tries to convey whatever it is that she needs to communicate.

Karis thinks of Vikram Bai, the Osirian man who the Antarcticans found through their spy cameras walking into the African tower last night. Vikram Bai, who Karis knows is their one remaining bargaining chip, a last chance to keep foreign feet from landing on the peninsula. Vikram Bai, who is rumoured to have a cure for redfleur, as this woman clearly knows.

He knows what Evie Aariak would do. She'd take this pair away and she'd shoot them in a deserted waterway.

If he lets Vikram go, he could be exiled for treason. Aariak will make it her mission to end him. She's a true defender. He looks at the woman and the boy who are suddenly at his mercy. Everything he has heard within the Chambers and outside of it is tangled up with these two skinny Patagonians. The singing at the funeral, his mother's singing, Shri Nayar, standing in his office: *you should be ashamed*. And it occurs to him that all his life he has done things without thinking about whether they matter.

'Come with me,' he says. He holds out his hand. 'Come.'

The Patagonian woman looks at him suspiciously.

'Antarctican?'

'Yes,' he says. 'You have to trust me.'

She might not understand the words but she takes his meaning. He can see the consternation in her face as she makes her decision. She looks to the doors of the Chambers. They can both hear the shouting on the other side. He senses there isn't much time left. Then she nods.

'Yes.'

The noise. Cutting through Vikram's head like a laser bisecting ice. He doesn't know where the commotion is coming from or what is making it but it hurts and he wishes it would stop. It doesn't stop. It grows louder.

He hears the distinct sound of a shot.

His eyes open. His vision is blurred and he panics momentarily, thinking he's been blinded but then it clears, leaving a bright keening pain behind his eyes. He finds himself lying in an empty bathtub, bound at the ankles and the wrists, in a bathroom he's never seen before. Fragments of memory return one by one – last night, the shark – walking through the city – the silent towers – the assailants coming at him from either side—

He can hear the creak of footsteps making their way through what must be another part of an apartment. He wriggles backwards. Manages to get to a sitting position. Somehow it's important to be sitting when he dies.

The footsteps grow closer. They'll find him, any minute now. There's a certain irony, he thinks, in having made it this far. Right to the heart of Osiris. One regret burns at him. Adelaide. He didn't find her. She was here and he didn't find her.

The door handle turns. Vikram keeps his eyes steady. Whoever it is, he'll meet them face on.

A slight, furtive figure steps through the doorway.

'Hello,' says Mig. He is grinning.

Vikram looks at him and begins to laugh. He can feel the relief crashing off him in waves. The boy's alive.

Mig explains as they untie him. They've all come. Him. The pilot. The Alaskan, though she's in the aeroplane. This one – he jerks a thumb behind him, and Vikram sees an unfamiliar man hovering in the apartment behind – is a Tarkie. But he brought us to you.

'What time is it?' Vikram asks. 'Are the talks still going?'

The pilot nods.

'But I don't think there's much time.'

'What about Adelaide? Adelaide Rechnov?'

The pilot looks blank, but the Antarctican obviously recognizes the name. He switches to Boreal English, resisting the urge to seize the man's shoulders and shake the information out of him.

'Do you know if she's alive?'

'I don't know. They didn't expect—' He stops, seeing Vikram's face.

'I have to see her,' he says urgently.

'If you don't go into the talks right now, this place will be bombed before you can. There's no time for anything else. We have to get in there.'

'Come on,' says the pilot impatiently. 'Why are we waiting?'

Vikram looks from face to face, divided. Mig. Ramona. Karis. Their expectation is perfectly clear. They've come for him. Why is he waiting? What could be more important than this? He knows they are right, but it doesn't reduce the compulsion to run, run away, run to her, to rush into a room and say: *how is this possible that we are both here in this place, not dead?*

But the three of them are standing there, waiting for him.

Mig puts a tentative hand on his elbow. He starts to steer.

'This way.'

As they help him out of the apartment, Vikram sees the uniformed body of an Antarctican sprawled in the doorway. The pilot steps over it. Her face is grim. She still has her hand on the rifle. As they hurry back towards the Eye Tower, Mig begins to tell him their tale.

'You can't go in there, the summit's still in session—'

'And it's about to break down,' says Karis. 'Unless I can get this man in front of Sosanya. So let us through or—'

The pilot raises her rifle and points it resignedly at the head of the guard.

'I can vouch for them,' says Karis. 'They're here to help.'

As the doors inch ajar Vikram can already hear the conflicting voices welling from inside. Numbly, he remembers there was a time when he was here before, when it was he and Adelaide against the world. Now the world is larger and darker and she's gravely injured in a hospital room and he's on his own.

He steps inside the Chambers. The other three move defensively to surround him. He sees the faces of those in the room, bright with anger, no one he recognizes, no one he knows except – he sees Linus Rechnov, the man turning pale with shock – people are turning towards the speaker's platform where a woman with a shaved head rises, protesting over the intrusion, and the man called Karis runs up to the speaker's platform and whispers in the woman's ear.

She sits upright, startled. Her gaze settles upon Vikram. He is intensely aware of her scrutiny, of the others at his side, Mig bristling with pre-emptive outrage, the pilot warily resting one hand on her rifle; of the Antarcticans staring at him in trepidation, and one woman in particular at Karis with hatred.

Quiet falls through the room.

The Solar Corporation leader stands.

'Lock down this room. No one leaves until I say.' She beckons to

Vikram's party. 'Come with me.' She glances across to Linus and another woman who Vikram recognizes instantly as a westerner. 'You two as well.'

There is one more person they need, the pilot tells him. The Alaskan. They sit around the table, Sosanya insisting upon silence until she arrives, escorted by Solar Corporation guards. The Alaskan settles into her chair with a grunt. She looks happier than anyone else in the room.

The African, Nkem Sosanya, folds her hands. She looks directly at Vikram and speaks in Boreal English, causing Karis to start with surprise; she's been concealing her knowledge of the language all along.

'Karis Io says you have an immunity to redfleur.'

Now that he is here, the focus of the room and of this quietly commanding woman, the words seem strange and difficult.

'I survived it once. I don't know what that means. I believe the answer lies with this city.'

'Yes. I can see the scars on your face. We have been fortunate to keep redfleur outside of the Corporation's zones, but our citizens abroad have not been so lucky. If you really have immunity, you have the potential to save millions of lives.' She glances to the door. 'There is not much time. The Boreals and the Antarcticans are on the brink of open warfare. I will have to make an announcement.'

The pilot says something urgently to the Alaskan, who clears her throat.

'I'm afraid it's not just the matter of Vikram Bai and his immunity. Or rather it is, but it goes deeper than that. Ramona Callejas has uncovered a Boreal experimentation site north of the belt. The experiments are kidnapped southerners. We have the diaries of the head scientist which suggest that this city was once used as an ancillary centre for genetic experimentation.'

The Alaskan nods towards Vikram.

'It's possible that this is linked to this man's immunity.'

'Or it's something to do with Osiris itself,' says Vikram. 'Like the tea. I always wondered about the coral tea.'

Sosanya takes the news with more equanimity than might have been expected. Vikram wonders if anything would faze her.

'We'll need verification for what you are saying.'

The pilot leans forwards, tapping the table. 'You can hear the diaries for yourself.' The Alaskan translates. Sosanya nods.

'An experimentation site?' Her face wrinkles with disgust. 'This will take days to unravel. For now, I need to make an announcement.'

The Alaskan coughs and Vikram says, 'There are some conditions attached.'

'You'd better state them quickly.'

'The Alaskan requests Antarctican citizenship. El Tiburón,' Vikram sees Sosanya's eyebrows raise at the name but she says nothing, 'requires international immunity. And you must promise to make a formal investigation into Tamaruq, the centre in the north.'

'I can make this happen.'

The pilot speaks to him quickly, gesturing to Sosanya.

'Ramona wants your personal guarantee that you will not let Tamaruq go. She wants to know that you will give your last breath if necessary to shut it down.'

Sosanya turns to the pilot.

'I give you my word, Ramona Callejas.'

Ramona nods, apparently satisfied, and continues to watch the exchange closely.

'Osiris gets independence,' says Vikram. He glances at Linus and the western woman. 'As a unified city.'

'Agreed.'

Vikram looks around the table. His mouth feels dry.

'Have I missed anything?'

No one speaks.

'And you.' Sosanya looks at him straight on. 'Have you considered what this means? Your life will no longer belong to you.'

'I won't go with anyone,' he says. 'They can take my blood, samples, whatever they need, but I won't be put in a laboratory.'

'That is not what I meant. Yes, I can make this a condition, but what I meant is your life is not your own, at least for the immediate future, until your immunity is established and can be formulated into something usable. You will need to be protected. You will have no privacy. People will come here from all over the world, scientists, the curious. It is my duty as the leader of the Nuuk Alliance to act in the interests of global health but it is my duty under the same act to advise you as a citizen. Do you understand me?'

'I understand.'

'We will have to test others, of course. Regardless of the cause of your immunity, it seems clear to me that it's related to the city. The more people we can find like you, the better our chances of brokering peace. For now, please stay here. None of you go anywhere. You're under the protection of the Solar Corporation.' She stands. 'And now I have to avert a war between two hemispheres.'

'There's someone I need to see—'

Linus is also on his feet. 'My sister—'

'I will find out her status.'

When Sosanya has left the room there is a moment when nobody says anything and then they all start talking at once. Vikram's attention turns to Linus Rechnov. He speaks quietly.

'Can't you find out? About Adelaide?'

'Our comms are blocked during the summit.'

'But she's alive? Won't someone just tell me that?'

'She was this morning,' says Linus.

Vikram struggles to keep the accusation out of his voice.

'Did you know she got out the tower?'

'No! Stars, no. I thought she was dead. When we got you out we looked for her, everywhere, like I told you. I wouldn't have kept that from you.' His voice is earnest. 'My people died inside looking for her.'

'He's telling the truth,' says the western woman, Dien. 'I was there when he found out. She was picked up by two of us. Two westerners, they're with her now. Then she worked with us. She had a pseudonym. The Silverfish.'

'Dien was with her,' says Linus. 'When it happened.' He looks tiredly at Vikram. 'I don't understand what just happened. I don't understand what you are, what this immunity is, what you're talking about with this redfleur. But if it makes these people leave us alone then I'm eternally in your debt.'

'I don't know what I am either,' says Vikram slowly. 'But I know it's something to do with Osiris. Maybe it's related to what Ramona found. Maybe it's something else. I might never know.'

'Sometimes it's best not to ask,' says Dien abruptly.

Vikram wants to ask Dien if Adelaide has talked about him, about their time together, or how she felt about him, or the day she thought he died. He wants to ask all these things and more about the woman he doesn't know. This other Adelaide. The Silverfish. What she's done. Why she has become an emissary for the west. But looking at Dien's exhausted face he knows she won't have the strength to lie, and he's not sure he is ready for the truth.

After that they sit and wait for Nkem Sosanya to return, no one having any more energy or desire for conversation. The sun through the window-wall casts a soporific warmth across the table. The room is one Linus Rechnov has sat in many times, for sub-committees and private meetings, meetings designed to flatter and persuade, meetings from which Linus usually emerged with a card in hand, but he doesn't recognize it today, or the people in it, or the city outside. Even Vikram is a stranger now, not that Linus ever knew the man, or rather he knew him in order to use him, more than once, though not without honourable intentions. Honour is a foolish concept anyway, an ideal admirable in theory but in practice deeply problematic, almost impossible to uphold, and yet he's going to need it now, if Osiris is to have a future. And somehow Vikram's return has made that a possibility, when for months it has felt like there were none, only the abyss of his family's legacy, a legacy that Adelaide, with the impossibility that is so fucking typical of his sister, has managed to subvert. By reincarnating only to get herself shot.

Across the table, Dien puts her head in her arms and sleeps, or seems to sleep. In her dream, or daydream, there is a line of trees. She grasps the branches of the first and levers herself up into the canopy, and then she swings to the next branch, and keeps on swinging, because the trees don't stop, they continue, perhaps forever, and beneath them is a field of flowers. The blooms reach towards her feet, petals caressing her soles. She hears a cry. Let go, she tells herself. You have to let go. And she waits for the moment where her fingers will straighten.

Unnerved by the quietness of his companions, Mig goes to stand by a wall which is made entirely of window and taps the glass experimentally. It sounds like glass, tough and satisfying, and through it he marvels at the view. There are towers like nothing he has ever imagined, conical towers draped in greenery with shimmering tubes winding in and out of the towers like coral snakes, and when he looks down he can't see the sea, or he sees something but it makes him dizzy just to look, never mind focus. When he looks up again he catches a glance of something perched like a statue on the tower opposite, something that might be Pilar's spirit, there for a second then invisible again to the eye. Mig flattens his hand against the glass and puts his forehead against it too, staring at the tower's peak, acknowledging that he's seen her; he knows she's here, looking out for him. Then he lets his gaze wander again and he sees a boat moving in the water, a long way down but fast, pleasingly fast, and Mig imagines himself on the boat with the wind in his face and everything that passes a blur. He likes the idea. He likes it a lot.

The Alaskan observes the boy goggling. It's lucky for his sake she prepared him; if it weren't for her telling him something about the world beyond Cataveiro his poor brain would have overloaded by now, he'd be catatonic with information. The rest of the party is certainly feeling the strain. The Alaskan assesses them critically and considers her options. Antarctican citizenship: yes, she'll take it, if only as a safeguard, but Antarctica is almost too easy, too safe an option. The Alaskan can imagine life there. It will be comfortable, very comfortable, and she will have asylum, better protection than her own country ever offered, but she'll always be a Boreal to them. Whereas here. . . Here it's messy. There's feuds and factions; it's a city that does not yet know what it is or what it could become. Yes, the Alaskan can see that her particular set of skills could be put to use in Osiris. It's only a shame she'll never persuade the pilot to stay. It would have been nice, she muses, to have a private aircraft again.

Callejas herself is deep in thought. Troubled, thinks the Alaskan. She'll always be troubled now, although in fact Ramona's thoughts are with her mother, as she counts the hours in her head since Inés took the first patch. It's only the second day of the course. It feels like she has been away for weeks. She cannot bear to think of her mother alone for a moment longer, or of the dreadful possibility that Inés might not be strong enough to endure the next twenty-eight days. As soon as the Solar Corporation leader has tied up the mess here, and she knows that Tamaruq is in someone else's hands, she'll be out of this strange city, and at Inés's side, and she won't leave her until the course is done. Whatever happens.

You just have to wait for me, Ma. I won't be long now. I promise.

And then, my lucky one?

I don't know, Ma. I don't know. I don't have a plan. I never did. Does anyone, really? Do these people in here? Do you?

But something tugs at her. *Colibrí*, in the Amazon Desert, the sun scorching on the broken fuselage, the soft piling dunes. She restored the plane once.

The sun moves and a stripe of morning light falls across Karis's face, making him squint. When he glances across to the window-wall, where the boy is drawing shapes on the bufferglass, he sees the unmistakable shape of a fin to the east, slicing through the waterways, a severe and unflinching line as the shark heads towards the edge of the city, as though it wants to be witnessed leaving. Karis thinks of the Bokolu. He realizes with a jolt of regret that he will never finish that game. Even if he makes it back home, he can't go back to Tua'pala. This, and other aspects of his life, will have changed too greatly. A part of him will always be left with the elusive Bokolu just in his sights, knowing the creature has met his eye, knowing they have seen one another, acknowledged one another, but unable either to advance or retreat.

When he looks back at the ocean, he can no longer make out the fin, and wonders if he imagined it after all. The shark is far away now; it passes the easternmost structure and dives. Building speed, it continues, out towards the ring-net, where the Atum Shelf drops away and the open waters beckon, deep and impenetrable. There is a still a gap. The shark slips through. Now there is a voice, an irresistible voice that sings of sleep and dreams to come, and with a flick of its tail, the shark is gone.

Sosanya returns. The mood in the room sharpens, immediately alert.

'We have a ceasefire,' she says. 'Testings for immunity will commence as soon as the conditions are suitable.' She looks around the table, acknowledging each of them. 'This is a good outcome. We've made progress today.'

'And Adelaide?' asks Dien.

Vikram looks to Sosanya and her face gives him his answer before she speaks.

'I'm sorry,' she says. 'Adelaide Rechnov died thirty minutes ago. The surgeons did everything they could. She wasn't in pain.'

He turns away, from her, from the sudden, unbearable sympathy in the room, from Linus's agonized face. His throat is strangled. There's a wail of anguish inside him but it won't come out; something is blocking it.

He's too late.

* * *

In the central part of the city, the border is gone. The posts which supported it protrude starkly at intervals along the waterway, stripped of the netting which for so many years has obscured one side of the city from the other. Some of them bear banners which lift and flutter in the wind, the slogans now faded but the banners clinging tenuously on.

It is not difficult to find the site. The flowers have mostly faded, and some are beginning to rot, but the salt tins tied to the post make it impossible to miss; salt tins in their hundreds, tier upon tier of them, cheap and precious, worn and new. A temporary raft rack has been built out to the memorial. Two other visitors are ahead of Vikram, and he cuts the motor, holding back. A man and a woman stand quietly. The woman has a salt tin and while Vikram waits the woman opens the tin and throws the salt over her shoulder, and hands it to the man to do the same. Then the man closes the tin and the woman attaches it carefully to the border post. They walk back along the raft rack to an old blue and white striped boat.

Untying the boat they nod, briefly, to Vikram.

He approaches the memorial, aware of his Solar Corporation escort, who is never more than a few metres away. He looks about, trying to imagine the scene. Dien has told him about that night. The two crowds. The lights in the sky, the shouts and the banners and the lasers and axes tearing down the border, the jubilation in the air. Adelaide, standing upright, shouting with the westerners. He tries to imagine it, but the sky is misted, the sea is sullen and there's nothing here but a post with some tins attached.

We don't know who it was, said Dien. A skad, or a Boreal. Maybe even one of our own.

Vikram looks up. A boy in a boat is watching him. It's Mig. The boat is a neat little craft, sleek and motored. Mig looks pleased with himself. Behind Mig, clinging to the gunnel with both hands, is the Alaskan. She is drenched, and does not look pleased at all. Vikram has the unfortunate suspicion that the boy's driving prowess is not as advanced as he hopes or believes it to be.

'Where did you get that?' he asks.

The boy shrugs.

'It doesn't belong to you, does it?'

Mig grins. Then his face turns serious.

'Is this the place?'

'Yes. This is it.'

'I brought something. You left it in Patagonia.' The boy holds aloft a small salt tin. 'I thought you might need it.'

The Alaskan is studying the memorial.

'Who was she?'

Who was she? He thinks of a red-haired woman with green eyes and a bold stare. Of roses, and a piano, and drowsy limbs on silk sheets. He thinks of a room in a derelict tower, Adelaide curling against him, her arms fragile like petals, as if she were already disintegrating, Adelaide whispering, *hold me*. He thinks of his last glimpse of her, through the dust and debris of an explosion, her eyes wide with shock and terror, stumbling to her feet. He thinks of the interview on the o'dio which Dien played for him, the voice so calm and steady and certain. Familiar and unfamiliar. These are the words left for him, words she spoke to other people, in another life. *I'm doing this for Vikram Bai.*

He speaks without looking at the Alaskan.

'She was someone I knew.'

'Do you want the box?' Mig asks. 'I put more salt in it.'

He shakes his head. 'You keep it. Go on, I'll catch you up.'

Silently, he says goodbye to Adelaide, the woman he loved, to the Silverfish, who he did not know. The woman who died a second death. Across the waterway he can see Mig driving away, the boat jerking in haphazard motion, throwing up spray, the Alaskan shouting in protest. He wonders what they make of his city, a place of possibility, or a place that has run its course, or something else that Vikram cannot envision at all. Overhead he hears the flap of wings. A gull lands on the post of the memorial. Its wings lift and settle. It cocks its head, considering him, and for a moment he thinks of the old saying, that the souls of dead Osirians come to rest in the hearts of birds. And then he remembers that Adelaide never liked birds. A few towers along, Mig and the Alaskan have stopped. They're waiting for him. He pauses, watching for the gull to fly off, but it remains stubbornly where it landed, one dark eye locked to his, and he finds he can't look away.

ACKNOWLEDGEMENTS

My sincere thanks to the many friends who have supported me from the beginning to the end of The Osiris Project. In particular, I want to thank my agent, John Berlyne; my fantastic editors: Michael Rowley, Emily Yau, and Rob Clark; Clare Stacey, for her beautiful, evocative cover designs, and all the supporting team at Del Rey UK who do so much behind the scenes. Thank you to M-P, who was there at the very start of it, and with whom I've mulled over many an idea; to book friends Clare Bullock, Alexa Brown, Camilla Corr, Bridie France, who continue to inspire and encourage me; to my wonderful family; and to James, who picks me up when I'm down, and reminds me that sharks make everything better.

Also in the Osiris Project series:

OSIRIS

Nobody leaves Osiris.

Adelaide Rechnov
Wealthy socialite and granddaughter of the Architect,
she spends her time in pointless luxury, rebelling against
her family in a series of jaded social extravagances and scandals
until her twin brother disappears in mysterious circumstances.

Vikram Bai
He lives in the Western Quarter, home to the poor
descendants of storm refugees and effectively quarantined
from the wealthy elite. His people live with cold and starvation,
but the coming brutal winter promises civil unrest, and a
return to the riots of previous years.

**As tensions rise in the city, can Adelaide and Vikram bridge
the divide at the heart of Osiris before conspiracies bring
them to the edge of disaster?**

DEL REY

Also in the Osiris Project series:

CATAVEIRO

A shipwreck. And one lone survivor.

For political exile Taeo Ybanez, this could be his ticket home.
Relations between the Antarcticans and the Patagonians
are worse than ever, and to be caught on the wrong side
could prove deadly.

For pilot and cartographer Ramona Callejas, the presence of the
mysterious stranger is one more thing in the way of her saving
her mother from a deadly disease.

All roads lead to Cataveiro, the city of fate and fortune,
where their destinies will become intertwined and their
futures cemented for ever . . .

DEL REY

DEL REY

DEL REY

The home for the best science fiction and fantasy books.

www.delreyuk.com

The Del Rey website is your SFF hub. Here you can find out about our books, our authors and the mechanics behind the worlds they have created.

Expect the unexpected: exclusive content, author interviews, news from Del Rey HQ at Penguin Random House, musings on SFF in popular culture and much much more!

You can also follow us on twitter:
@delreyuk

. . . and facebook:
Del-Rey-UK

So, come join the conversation, and be the first to hear about the exciting things happening at Del Rey!